Indian Sound Cultures, Indian Sound Citizenship

I0892883

Indian Sound Cultures, Indian Sound Citizenship

Laura Brueck, Jacob Smith, and Neil Verma, editors

University of Michigan Press • Ann Arbor

Copyright © 2020 by Laura Brueck, Jacob Smith, and Neil Verma
All rights reserved

For questions or permissions, please contact um.press.perms@umich.edu

Published in the United States of America by
the University of Michigan Press
Manufactured in the United States of America
Printed on acid-free paper

First published April 2020

A CIP catalog record for this book is available from the British Library.

ISBN 978-0-472-07434-1 (hardcover : alk. paper)
ISBN 978-0-472-05434-3 (paper : alk. paper)
ISBN 978-0-472-12623-1 (ebook)

Contents

Digital materials related to this title can be found on the Fulcrum platform via the following citable URL: https://doi.org/10.3998/mpub.11374040

Acknowledgments

The chapters in this collection grew out of a series of lectures and workshops at Northwestern University from 2016 to 2018. For their generous support of these events the editors would like to thank the Center for Global Culture and Communication and the Northwestern Buffett Institute for Global Affairs. For additional support we would also like to thank Northwestern University's School of Communication, Department of Asian Languages and Cultures, Asian Studies Graduate Cluster, Asian Studies Program, Screen Cultures Program, Department of Radio-TV-Film, and Department of Communication Studies.

INTRODUCTION

Out of the West, Out of the Text

LAURA BRUECK, JACOB SMITH, AND NEIL VERMA

What might it mean to situate the field of sound studies in a South Asian context, away from the Western settings, questions and formations that have given the field its language and canonical objects of study? What might it mean to consider the ramifications of a "sonic turn" in South Asian studies, drawing it from the textual and visual foci that have long dominated the field? This collection makes the case for cultivating a research program around these questions. With this book, we make two interventions at once, integrating interdisciplinary scholarship that exists at the nexus of sound studies and South Asian studies, thereby expanding and challenging concepts and terminologies in sound while also hearing aspects of South Asian culture and society with fresh ears. Our hope is to help set an agenda for specialists in both fields. In this way, *Indian Sound Cultures, Indian Sound Citizenship* follows a path laid out twenty years ago by Dipesh Chakrabarty with his famous gambit to "provincialize" Europe, a task of disciplinary renewal in part rooted in coming to terms with the way European thought is at once "indispensable" to and "inadequate" for thinking through historical consciousness and political modernity in non-European contexts.[1] What goes for modern thought goes for modern sound, too, and in the pages that follow we highlight a double indispensability—of South Asia to sound studies and sound studies to South Asia—and at the same time seek places of inadequacy and mismatch that could be developed into sites of growth and renewal. What we hope to develop is one version of how to "do" sound studies beyond its current Western/Euro-American center, one in which the East is not just an acoustic mirror of things already resonating in the West (as the "bearer" of signals and the means to decode them) but is instead itself a blaring loudspeaker.

In this book our authors make a start at that endeavor by focusing on multifaceted aspects of sound in Indian cultures and media across particular sites in the last hundred years or so in hopes of opening up fresh territory and challenging peers to find new ways to pursue familiar objects of study. What if, for example, recent studies of pop sound and bodily gender expression from Robin James's work on black femme pop music to Allison McCracken's work on Rudy Vallee's crooning could be read alongside studies of the visceral vocal performances of the Indian pop and jazz singer Usha Uthup?[2] What if studies of the intimate radio publics captured by Franklin Roosevelt's *Fireside Chats* and J. B. Priestly's *Postscripts* could be contrasted with the approach of contemporaneous Indian writer and broadcaster Mulk Raj Anand's *New Weapons of War* series?[3] And how might today's Indian sound art scene reorganize and rethink the divide between the emplaced approach to audio embodied in the work of R. Murray Schafer and the more abstract approach to sound art linked to Pierre Shaeffer?[4] The chapters that follow are designed to make rich questions like this possible, in many cases for the first time.

The essays in this collection grew out of a two-year-long set of lectures and workshops at Northwestern University dedicated to getting sound studies "out of the West" and South Asian studies "out of the text." In the course of running this project, we found significant overlap between the questions our presenters were asking in their research. Broadly speaking, our authors shared a common interest in the ways in which sound is bound up in issues of citizenship, identity, and belonging in India; they also shared a fascination with sound cultures that formed around that process. The entwining of these two themes is apparent in many of the chapters that follow. Aswin Punathembekar and Sriram Mohan's work, for instance, focuses on how what they call "sound bridges" enable a conversation about "sonic citizenship" based on encounters between citizens, journalists, and politicians in the online space, where the nature of political participation is increasingly negotiated in everyday conversations. Kathryn C. Hardy and Samhita Sunya, meanwhile, focus on the ways in which other particular sonic figures—Bhojpuri devotional songs in Mumbai and noise pollution regulations as reflected in cinema, respectively—produce and test discourses of "acceptable" political expression, as well as attitudes toward modernity and economic change.

Our notion of citizenship in these pages is particularly cultural in nature, just as our notion of culture is bound up in politics. As Chakrabarty noted, the political is also the performed, and nowhere is that more apparent than in India's many multicultural expressions of noise, slogan, and song.[5] What's more, many of the subjects in this book are perfectly aware of this fact, not least of whom is Prime Minister Narendra Modi, whose *Mann Ki Baat* broadcasts are brilliantly deconstructed by Praseeda Gopinath.

Over time the work we cultivated in the lectures and workshops at Northwestern coalesced into three thematic areas, which have given us the structure of this book. First, a number of our authors were concerned with the spatial and circulatory ways in which sound "happens" in and around Indian sound cultures (including diasporic cultures), essays we group here under the theme "Scapes, Sites, and Circulations." Second, a group of our chapters put the emphasis on voices that seemed to embody a variety of struggles and ambiguities, particularly around gender and performance, which gave us our second section, "Voice." Finally, a number of our authors made specific arguments about film sound in the Indian context, from the earliest days of talkie technology to contemporary Hindi films and experimental art installations, a set of chapters we group under "Cinema Sound." Together the contributions to this volume have a common emphasis in their exploration of the diverse ways in which sound has been and continues to be crucial to the ideological construction of a unifying postcolonial Indian nation-state, as well as insistent articulations of communal difference and specificity from multiple publics. How is that sense of individual and group belonging—or unbelonging—mediated by the sounds of India, in India, and representing India—from the street to the festival ground to the cinema hall to the mobile phone? How do Indians generate, inhabit, and interact with the multiplicity of soundscapes through which they move? What are the aesthetic, pragmatic, and political choices that artists make when sonically representing Indian culture(s) and national identit(ies) through media—on the radio, in an audiobook, in social media, or in a sound art festival? These are the kinds of questions to which *Indian Sound Cultures, Indian Sound Citizenship* offers fresh and sophisticated approaches.

Disciplinary Foundations

One of the disciplinary foundations of our collection is sound studies, a field that can still claim to be relatively young and is also changing rapidly.

A number of key texts were published around the turn of the twenty-first century that heralded the emergence of this area as a vital field in the humanities. Michele Hilmes's *Radio Voices* (1997); Lisa Gitelman's *Scripts, Grooves, and Writing Machines* (1999); Emily Thompson's *Soundscape of Modernity* (2002); Jonathan Sterne's *Audible Past* (2003); Rick Altman's *Silent Film Sound* (2004), these and other books have been associated with what Sterne calls an "interdisciplinary ferment in the human sciences."[6] Taken as a whole, these books showed that the field was open in terms of disciplinary boundaries, incorporating history, gender, and sexuality studies, literary studies, cultural studies, and media archaeology. At the same time, however, work could come across as narrow in national and linguistic scope. The works noted above, and many other prominent ones (including some by two of the coeditors), were largely based on Western arts, histories, theories, and technological cultures. As sound studies gains traction, manifesting in a surge of academic publications, journals, professional organizations, course syllabi, and curricula, it is important to address the relative lack of global engagement in the field and to ask how the incorporation of a more robust international and diasporic perspective might prompt a modification of scholarly terminologies, targets of study, and sensibilities. In this sense, this volume heeds the call of a number of writers who have argued for an emerging new wave of work that would bring to sound studies an increased emphasis on race and other forms of social difference, including in post- and anticolonial contexts; we are particularly indebted to the work of writers such as Jennifer Stoever, Vincent Andrisani and others who consider how sound constructs identity through forms of often racialized "sonic citizenship."[7] The case of sonic citizenship in India holds much promise for this endeavor because of the sonic richness of sound traditions on the subcontinent and because of the manifest ways in which sound is increasingly a political matter in Indian media culture. Signs of the possibilities of work in this area have emerged in recent years. In *Remapping Sound Studies*, for example, Gavin Steingo and Jim Sykes chart a similar approach, attending to sound cultures from Africa to Micronesia while noting that theories of the South and sound are "conjoined concepts lying at the heart of modernity" and asking how to come to terms with that fact by thinking of sound "not *as* the South (or as analogous *with* the South) but, rather, *in* and *from* the South."[8] In Praseeda Gopinath and Monika Mehta's groundbreaking 2017 *Sounding Out* forum on gender and sound in India, meanwhile, authors sought not only to "expand the terrain of what constitutes sound and voice in India" but also to "offer new modes of listening" that help articulate, among other things, the way sound is gendered along public and private lines.[9]

Gopinath and Mehta's work seems so fresh because, for its part, South Asian studies has tended to privilege visual and textual methodologies and sources. Sonic phenomena are rarely considered in the theoretically and methodologically situated way that a sound studies approach presumes.[10] In an oft-cited special issue of the journal *South Asia*, published in 2014, Sandria Freitag, a historian of Indian visual culture, described a "visual turn" in South Asian studies and expressed enthusiasm for how it might cut across traditional disciplinary boundaries to focus on transregional and transperiod questions related to the ways in which people engage with visual artifacts.[11] The chapters in this collection suggest that a "sonic turn" in South Asian studies could create a similarly interdisciplinary and innovative network of scholarship, extending Sterne's "interdisciplinary ferment" into new and vibrant transnational and multilingual contexts.

Indeed, there is ground prepared for a sonic turn in South Asian scholarship. Our task here is more a question of effective articulation than invention. Sound studies already exists in the field, in a diffuse way, across academic domains such as religious studies, ethnomusicology, and film studies, where we find sporadic considerations of "what sound does in the human world and what humans do in the sonic world" in a variety of Indian contexts.[12] Sound studies and South Asian studies share the disciplinary neighbor of ethnomusicology, for example. Ethnomusicology has been an important interlocutor for sound studies in part because it has tended to be more open to studying material cultures and technologies of sound, as well as popular forms that have fallen outside of the purview of classical musicology.

As a discipline, ethnomusicology has roots deeply embedded in the colonial imaginary. Like the colonial fascination with Indian languages, caste structures, and religions, "Indian music" and its exotic instrumentation and system of scales fascinated early travelers to and scholars of the subcontinent and gave way by the early twentieth century to a late colonial and early Indian nationalist emphasis on the collection and preservation of "classical" Indian music. Joep Bor, in his essay "The Rise of Ethnomusicology: Sources on Indian Music c. 1780–c.1890," explains the centrality for colonial era ethnomusicologists of the Tagore family's English-language publications on the "Hindu" musical traditions of India.[13] Much of this early ethnomusicology, and the political uses to which it was later put by nationalist reformers, worked to define a classical "Indian" heritage in the wake of hundreds of years of first Mughal and later British imperial formations. Nonetheless, in recent years ethnomusicologists have turned their attention to the transnational flows of popular music.[14] That global perspective, along with an openness to sound understood broadly, makes it an important point of reference for some of the essays in this collection. As indicated by the example of ethnomusicology, there are research trajectories in sound studies that align with trends in South Asian studies, and that alignment is reflected in the three sections into which the chapters in this book have been placed, each of which has a voluminous sound studies literature echoing through it.

Scapes, Sites, and Circulations

The series of events at Northwestern that inspired this volume were meant to address the theme of the "Sounds of South Asia." What emerged from these lectures and workshops however, was the notion that the circulation, technologies, and ideologies of sound are inseparable from specifically *national* political and aesthetic imaginaries, as well as opportunities for modeling citizenship. Thus, the complex realities of *Indian* sound cultures, and *Indian* sound citizenship, came to the fore and provided a focus for the principal themes of the volume. As one of the most potent sites and sources of postcolonial studies in the twentieth century, questions of nation, citizenship, and publics have long been themes in scholarship on India in a wide range of fields, including historical, literary, and visual studies. The "nation" and various ways of performing citizenship have been absolutely paramount in the Indian political and aesthetic imagination in the wake of British colonialism and the brutal partition of India and Pakistan in 1947. Understanding the formation of different publics based on regional, linguistic, religious, caste, or class affiliations, and the ways in which they inhabit both physical and imaginary space within the nation, has been a central concern in cultural studies broadly and literary studies in particular, which has sought to delineate reading publics and their political engagements in the colonial and postcolonial states.[15] Critical to this differentiation is an engagement with the category of the "vernacular," a term that resonates on multiple levels in a country with more than two dozen official languages (spoken as a native language by one million people or more) and a long political and religious history of exclusive and exclusionary languages of the ruling classes: Sanskrit, Persian, and English. According to Taberez Ahmed Niyazi,

Akio Tanabe, and Shinya Ishizaka, "the vernacular public arena is the expanding space of socio-political negotiation and interaction in which diverse groups and individuals raise their vernacular voices to reassemble and redefine the public."[16] The idea of "voice" becomes significant here; if, as Francesca Orsini says, "print-languages create boundaries," spoken (or sung or chanted) languages and other sonic objects have the capacity to transcend them.[17] Multiple sound cultures therefore subvert singular ideas of "nation" and "citizenship," opening ways to consider both as in a permanent state of fluctuation and negotiation.

The centrality of work on nation, publics, and citizenship in South Asian studies intersects with sound studies scholarship that examines "listening publics" and the sonic dimension of a sense of space and place. Kate Lacey is among scholars who emphasize the social and political aspects of listening. Lacey stresses that listening is an active endeavor that is shaped by culture.[18] She makes a distinction between "listening in" to a specific media text and a "listening out," which involves an openness to others in the act of listening that is a precondition for political action. The latter kind of listening "constitutes a kind of *attention* to others (and otherness) . . . that is the prerequisite both of citizenship . . . and of communicative action."[19] Other scholars have brought the paradigm of listening to the analysis of online publics and examined the role of radio listening in creating a sense of nation.[20] Sound studies work on listening publics provides a theoretical framework for analyses of sonic citizenship in this collection.

The concern with place and nation in South Asian studies also resonates with sound studies approaches that descend from Schafer's notion of "soundscape," which Emily Thompson has defined as "an aural landscape that is both a physical environment and a way of perceiving that environment; including not only sounds, but the material culture of sound, ways of listening, and the listener's relationship to that environment."[21] Schafer's work provided a vocabulary for describing the sounds of the lived environment and has influenced not only scholars but a genre of sound art based on field recordings (see Alexis Bhagat and Lauren Rosati's contribution to this collection). Schafer is not without his critics, who have pointed out his nostalgia and antiurban bias; more recent writers have used this framework to raise questions about the hidden politics of soundscape studies and sound ecology, questions that authors in this volume seek to sharpen in the Indian context.[22] The investigation of sonic environments would benefit from a deeper engagement with non-Western case studies, and Indian discourses of place and space make for a particularly rich and compelling terrain for that project.

With these questions in mind, the section "Scapes, Sites, Circulations" explores some of India's resonant spaces and listening publics. In chapter 1, Aswin Punathambekar and Sriram Mohan provide a conceptual cornerstone for the volume through a careful consideration of the place of sound and listening in the mediation of citizenship in Indian public culture. In the course of tracking the cultural life of a Tamil film song, Punathambekar and Mohan reimagine the term *sound bridge* to extend its use beyond film sound aesthetics and establish a conceptual framework for understanding how a sonic cue moves across diverse publics, digital platforms, and cultural and political domains. Their discussion of this expanded notion of the sound bridge places modes of listening and sonic expression at the heart of citizenship in a digital era. Kathryn C. Hardy, in chapter 2, examines the sonic practices of religious stage shows in Mumbai, where soundscapes become politicized, calling forth debates about migration, amplification, citizenship, and devotion. Peter Kvetko, in chapter 3, hears new modes of intimacy, domesticity, embodiment, and citizenship being sounded in the Indipop musical genre of the 1990s and shows how the genre developed both orientalist fantasies for foreign consumers and nationalist messages for Indian consumers at home and abroad. In chapter 4, Samhita Sunya tacks between an analysis of public discourse about noise in India and three films that are structured around the motif of noise. Her insightful reading of these films reveals discourses of noise to be tied to gendered violence, attempts to maintain patriarchal control of urban spaces, and tensions between sound amplification and the private spaces of upper-middle-class urban apartment living. From digital platforms to film soundtracks, music videos, and religious bhajans, citizenship across these essays is bound intrinsically to sonic identities and cultural phenomena.

Voice

As the earlier reference to "vernacular voices" indicates, another opportunity for cross-disciplinary dialogue centers around questions of the voice. In the context of South Asian studies, one place where work on the voice can be found is in discussions of sacred sound in Sanskrit linguistics and Hindu ritual practice. According to Guy Beck, "the Hindu experience of the divine" is "fundamentally sonic, or oral/aural, [and] the theological position of sacred sound constitutes a kind of *mysterium magnum* of Hinduism."[23] In his 2012 *Sonic Liturgy: Ritual and Music in Hindu Tradition*, Beck argues, "The Hindu tradition provides perhaps the most consistent and enduring exemplification of sonic liturgy—the ritual order or pattern of specific events that include sound and music on a variety of levels."[24] Not least among the origins of the centrality of sonic experience in Hindu ritual traditions is the understanding of the "sacred syllable" *om* as the primeval sound, among whose reverberating sound waves the universe itself was created.

Beck's work on the sonic dimensions of Sanskrit and Hindu religious practice stands apart from the majority of scholarship on Sanskrit and classical Hindu traditions, which tend to focus on texts and images, even if these forms of expression often seek to harness and represent the fundamentally sonic character of Hinduism. The interest in voice in relation to "sonic liturgy" has led to comparisons of oral and written practices. Sheldon Pollock explains, "Written literature in pre-modern South Asia, as in Western Europe, undoubtedly preserved features realized only in oral performance, and listening to rather than reading literature long remained the principal mode of experiencing it."[25] Thus, sonic dimensions of religious practice from premodern to modern South Asia offer an entry point for thinking about cultures of the voice in the South Asian context despite the fact that they remain enduringly elusive to religious studies scholars, who continue to privilege textual sources.

There is a parallel to be made with sound studies, where one disciplinary trajectory leads from the study of "oral poetry" by folklorists and anthropologists. Scholars such as Albert Lord and Milman Parry developed an argument about poetic composition in cultures that made relatively little use of writing. The impulse to demarcate "oral" and "literate" modes of expression was later applied to relationships among media cultures and sensory experience, as in the work of Marshall McLuhan, who wrote about the differences between visual and acoustic space.[26] McLuhan's student, Walter Ong, continued this line of argument, making observations about the nature of sound, the "psychodynamics of orality," and the "secondary orality" brought about by audiovisual media.[27]

The work of McLuhan and Ong helped to galvanize an interest in the comparative study of media and the theorization of sound, but it is problematic to the extent that it is marked by technological determinism, creates a "great divide" between oral and literate cultures, and reinforces what Sterne has called an "audiovisual litany" that posits essential differences between hearing and vision.[28] Sterne's critique did much to clear the ground for more nuanced work on auditory culture in sound studies, but the center of gravity for that work has tended to remain within a McLuhanesque domain of Western media technologies, making the case studies in this book valuable as another way forward for the field.

One way in which sound studies scholars have moved beyond McLuhan and Ong is to pursue more ethnographic or sociolinguistic methods. Here we find research on what anthropologist Steven Feld calls "acoustemology": the ways in which sound is "a modality for knowing and being in the world." The influence of Feld's ethnographic approach to the cultural specificity of sonic practices can be felt in work by Stefan Helmreich, Nina Sun Eidsheim, Charles Hirschkind, and Patrick Eisenlohr.[29] This is the strain of sound studies that has been most concerned with cultural exchange and a global perspective and is what this collection seeks to amplify. Sound studies has also drawn inspiration from the sociolinguistics of Erving Goffman, who wrote a long essay on "radio talk," as well as the "trans-linguistics" of M. M. Bakhtin, who had a predilection for sonic metaphors such as voice, dialogue, accent, and polyphony.[30] Drawing on these and other influences, there is now a rich and growing scholarship on the voice in sound studies.[31]

Bakhtin famously described the literary author as a voice among others. He wrote that prose writers were concerned with the "heteroglot voices" among which their own voice must sound.[32] In literature, education, and other forms of public culture, India's extreme multilingualism pushes the category of "voice" even more to the fore, as does the linguistic legacy of British colonialism and both its marginalization of vernacular languages and cultures and its contributions to India's culture of translation. Tejaswini Niranjana, in *Siting Translation*, quotes the British administrative official Charles Trevelyan's 1838 treatise *On the Education of the People of India*: "Non-western peoples attain maturity and subjecthood only after a period of apprenticeship in which they learn European languages and thereby gain 'a voice.'"[33] And who can deny that the postcolonial condition of the vernacular voice—in the context of postcolonial reconstructions of peasant resistance to the colonial state—was never so succinctly evoked as in Gayatri Spivak's provocative question, "Can the subaltern speak?"[34]

The essays in the second section of the collection move across these various meanings of voice and its relationship to the physical bodies from which voices emanate, and across various forms of sound media, showing how particular voices interact with media to produce or modify what it means for a voice to "sound Indian." In chapter 5, Pavitra Sundar describes the cultural specificity of Usha Uthup's singing voice both in and beyond the cinema, suggesting that her "husky, heavy" voice, physically embodied in the figure of a sari-clad Indian matriarch, allowed her to transcend normative cultural codifications, suspended as she was in the tension of an aural and visual mismatch. In chapter 6, Praseeda Gopinath considers the vocal performances, and their reenactments by imitators, of Prime Minister Narendra Modi across the sonic platforms of the campaign speech, the folksy radio address, and the promotion of national policy propaganda, teasing out the ways in which his vocal modulations and embodied gestural accompaniments create specific ideas about performing national citizenship. She demonstrates how listening carefully to Modi's weekly radio address allows us to hear the way he "vocalizes into being a supposedly vast national, enlightened, and enthusiastic citizenry." Roanne L. Kantor in chapter 7, explores questions of performing an "Indian" voice in the audiobook industry in pursuit of an "authentic" reality affect, ultimately demonstrating the complex ethics involved in the mediation of minoritized voices. Finally, in chapter 8, Sejal Sutaria examines Mulk Raj Anand as both an author and a radio personality, exploring in particular the way in which the "sonic resistance and aesthetic interruption" exemplified in his understudied radio appearances navigate the gulf between metropole and colony in pre-Independence Britain and India.

Cinema Sound

An important early body of work in sound studies was produced by film scholars who explored the sonic dynamics of film exhibition, as well as the aesthetics of music and sound design in the cinematic soundtrack.[35] Many scholars became interested in sound in the first place as a direct result of special journal issues on this subject, such as a landmark 1980 issue of *Yale French Studies* edited by Rick Altman, which brought together a key set of authors and topics around a bibliography compiled by Claudia Gorbman. Language circumscribed the ambit of that issue, however—while there is interesting work to be found on Marguerite Duras's 1975 film *India Song*, there is little on Indian song in film.[36] Today, however, scholarship on modern and contemporary South Asia frequently crosses into the fields of film and media studies. Music has often been put forward as a defining component of a distinctly Indian popular cinema, and anthologies about popular Indian cinema typically include a chapter on music. Nevertheless, film studies in India, not long ago a nascent field longing to move beyond the shadow of Satyajit Ray and bent on justifying its value at a time when cinéphiles around the world looked askance at the pleasures of "Bollywood" cinema, has tended to privilege both the visual and the narrative elements of films.[37]

Despite the acknowledgment of the centrality of music in Bollywood cinema, the meaning and technology of sound in cinema has long been subservient to visual spectacle. When scholars and critics do discuss sound in Indian popular films, it has often been in the service of the "picturization" of a song sequence and its place in the narrative momentum of a film rather than as part of a larger consideration of the soundtrack itself. One of the important contributions of sound studies to the domain of cinema has been to expand the scope of study beyond music. Work at the intersection of sound studies and South Asian studies can expand an appreciation of the aural experience of cinema and even move beyond the cinema hall to explore diverse, mobile, and emergent sound media practices and publics.[38] This is not to say that music is off the agenda but that it is considered in a new context, one in which musical sounding is just one of several culturally informed sound practices linked to cinematic representation and experience.

The third section of the collection, "Cinema Sound," builds on scholarship that combines the study of Indian film, music, and sound. In chapter 9, Neepa Majumdar, whose pathbreaking work on Indian playback singers was a crucial inspiration for this collection, offers a new way to think about song sequences through an analysis of several films that feature Shanta Apte, a major star at the Prabhat studio in the 1930s. By comparing Apte's song sequences to her "rage sequences," Majumdar shows how tensions having to do with female resistance and modesty were mapped onto a range of sound/image dynamics during this era. In chapter 10, Jayson Beaster-Jones, one of several recent scholars who have brought a new rigor to the study of Indian film music, examines the practices of musical scoring in popular Hindi film through the case of *Dilwale Dulhaniya Le Jayenge.* Beaster-Jones situates the film's score in the history of Indian cinema, the labor of composition, and the cultural resonance of the mandolin, and in the process demonstrates how film scores take part in an intertextual network at the same time that they serve as portable aural references that can be mobilized in everyday experience. Madhuja Mukherjee, in chapter 11, examines the transition to sync sound technology in Bengali cinema during the 1930s. Mukherjee charts a fascinating history, one in which short-lived technologies and unsuccessful films—such as the Csystophone Sono-system used for the futurist-comedy *Bengal 1983* (1932)—are presented through a wide range of primary sources and reveal the ways in which sound technologies were inflected by discourses of the nation. In chapter 12, Alexis Bhagat and Lauren Rosati explore the intersection of sound art and cinema by documenting their own experience utilizing cinema theaters as a site of exhibition for multichannel works by sound artists. Their program, *Listen My Heart*, demonstrated the promise and challenge of presenting sound art in cinemas and rediscovered an underappreciated classic of Indian sound design: Kamal Swaroop's *Om-Dar-b-Dar* (1988).

A Sonic Turn

Across these three sections, the essays in this volume enact a sonic turn in South Asian studies by understanding sound in its own social and cultural contexts. These are essays on sonic objects that could be housed in collections on Indian religion, politics, or media but taken together crystallize a sound studies approach that thinks "across sounds, to consider sonic phenomena in relation to one another."[39] Conversely, sound studies is given a chance to broaden its geographic, linguistic, and cultural horizons and thereby confront the Western bias of its short institutional history. In the process, the glossary of terms in sound studies is reconsidered and expanded. In the afterword to *Sound Theory, Sound Practice*, a book published in 1992, Rick Altman wrote that the contributors to the volume had renewed the study of film sound by utilizing "a new vocabulary," one that was more attuned to the way in which sound "makes, rather than merely possesses, meaning."[40] Now, twenty-five years later, much of the terminology that was new then has become standardized and is in danger of becoming ossified if restricted to an Anglophone context. By taking up a new position in contemporary India, and thereby turning those terms from clarion calls to distant echoes, perhaps we can "renew" the study of sound again and in the process open the ears of South Asian studies.

Notes

1. Dipesh Chakrabarty, *Provincializing Europe: Postcolonial Thought and Historical Difference*, 2nd ed. (Princeton, NJ: Princeton University Press, 2007), 6.

2. See Robin James, "Listening to Sounds in Post-feminist Pop Music," February 15, 2016, *Sounding Out! The Sound Studies Blog*, accessed January 28, 2019, https://soundstudiesblog.com/2016/02/15/listening-to-sounds-in-post-feminist-pop-music/; Allison McCracken, *Real Men Don't Sing: Crooning in American Culture* (Durham, NC: Duke University Press, 2015).

3. See Jason Loviglio, *Radio's Intimate Public Network Broadcasting and Mass-Mediated Democracy* (Minneapolis: University of Minnesota Press, 2005); Ian Whittington, *Writing the Radio War: Literature, Politics, and the BBC, 1939–1945* (Edinburgh: Edinburgh University Press, 2008).

4. Brandon LaBelle, *Background Noise: Perspectives on Sonic Art* (New York: Continuum, 2006), 204–5.

5. Chakrabarty, *Provincializing Europe,* 10.

6. Jonathan Sterne, "Sonic Imaginations," in *The Sound Studies Reader,* ed. Jonathan Sterne (London: Routledge, 2012), 2.

7. Jennifer Stoever, *The Sonic Color Line: Race and the Cultural Politics of Listening* (New York: NYU Press, 2016). See also: Vincent Andrisani "The Sweet Sounds of Havana: Space, Listening, and the Making of Sonic Citizenship" Sept. 17, 2015, Sounding Out! The Sound Studies Blog, accessed Oct. 30 2019, https://soundstudiesblog.com/2015/09/17/the-sweet-sounds-of-havana-space-listening-and-the-making-of-sonic-citizenship/; Milena Droumeva, "Review: *The Sound of Culture: Diaspora and Black Technopoetics,*" *Cultural Sociology* 11, no. 4 (2017): 545–47; Gus Stadler, "On Whiteness and Sound Studies," July 6, 2015, *Sounding Out! The Sound Studies Blog,* accessed April 15, 2019, https://soundstudiesblog.com/2015/07/06/on-whiteness-and-sound-studies/

8. Gavin Steingo and Jim Sykes, eds., *Remapping Sound Studies* (Durham, NC: Duke University Press, 2019), 8.

9. Praseeda Gopinath and Monika Mehta, "Gendered Soundscapes of India: An Introduction to the Forum," Oct 16, 2017, *Sounding Out! The Sound Studies Blog,* accessed June 22, 2018, https://soundstudiesblog.com/2017/10/16/introduction-gendered-soundscapes-of-india-2/

10. Sterne described this as a combination of *both* object and approach with an essential critical element ("Sonic Imaginations," 4–5).

11. Sandria B. Freitag,, "The Visual Turn: Approaching South Asia across the Disciplines," *South Asia* 37, no. 3 (2014): 398–409.

12. Sterne, "Sonic Imaginations," 2.

13. Joep Bor, "The Rise of Ethnomusicology: Sources on Indian Music C.1780 - C.1890." Yearbook for Traditional Music, vol. 20, 1988, pp. 51–73 www.jstor.org/stable/768166. See also Rabindranath Tagore, *Treasury of the Musical Instruments of Ancient and of Modern India and of Various Other Countries* (Calcutta: 1875) and S. M. Tagore's *The Musical Scales of the Hindus* (Calcutta: 1884).

14. See, for example, Anandam P. Kavoori and Aswin Punathambekar, eds., *Global Bollywood* (New York: New York University Press, 2008). This book includes essays on film texts and audiences and both the star and fan "cultures" of Bollywood film, as well as an essay by Natalie Sarazzin titled "Songs from the Heart: Musical Coding, Emotional Sentiment, and Transnational Sonic Identity in India's Popular Film Music" (203–22). See also another book with the same title, Sangita Gopal and Sujata Moorti, eds., *Global Bollywood: Travels of Hindi Song and Dance* (Minneapolis: University of Minnesota Press, 2008).

15. See, for example, Francesca Orsini, *The Hindi Public Sphere, 1920–1940* (Oxford: Oxford University Press, 2002); Ulrike Stark, *An Empire of Books* (Delhi: Permanent Black, 2008); Carol Breckenridge, ed., *Consuming Modernity: Public Culture in a South Asian World (Minneapolis: University of Minnesota Press, 1995);* Veena Naregal, *Language Politics, Elites, and the Public Sphere* (Delhi: Permanent Black, 2001).

16. Taberez Ahmed Niyazi, Akio Tanabe, and Shinya Ishizaka, *Democratic Transformation and the Vernacular Public Arena in India* (New York: Routledge, 2014), 1.

17. Orsini, *Hindi Public Sphere*, 1.

18. Ibid., 22.

19. Kate Lacey, *Listening Publics: The Politics and Experience of Listening in the Media Age* (Cambridge: Polity Press, 2013), 165.

20. See Kate Crawford, "Listening as Participation: Social Media and Metaphors of Hearing Online"; Michele Hilmes, *Radio Voices: American Broadcasting, 1922–52* (Minneapolis: University of Minnesota Press, 1997); Carolyn Birdsall, *Nazi Soundscapes: Sound, Technology, and Urban Space in Germany, 1933–1945* (Amsterdam: Amsterdam University Press, 2012).

21. Emily Thompson, *The Soundscape of Modernity: Architectural Acoustics and the Culture of Listening in America, 1900–1933* (Cambridge, MA: MIT Press, 2002).

22. Ari Y. Kelman, "Rethinking the Soundscape," *Senses and Society* 5, no. 2 (2010): 212–34.

23. Guy Beck, *Sonic Theology: Hinduism and Sacred Sound* (Columbia, SC: University of South Carolina Press, 2009), 3.

24. Guy Beck, *Sonic Liturgy: Ritual and Music in Hindu Tradition* (Columbia: University of South Carolina Press, 2012), 2.

25. Sheldon Pollock, *The Language of the Gods in the World of Men: Sanskrit, Culture, and Power in Premodern India* (Berkeley: University of California Press, 2006), 4.

26. See discussion of McLuhan in Lacey, *Listening Publics*, 5–6.

27. Walter Ong, *Orality and Literacy* (New York: Routledge, 1982), 32, 71.

28. Jonathan Sterne, *The Audible Past* (Durham, NC: Duke University Press, 2003), 18. See also Ruth Finnegan, *Literacy and Orality* (Oxford: Oxford University Press, 1988).

29. See Stefan Helmreich, *Sounding the Limits of Life* (Princeton University Press, 2015); Lucas Bessire and Daniel Fisher, eds., *Radio Fields: Anthropology and Wireless Sound in the 21st Century* (New York: New York University Press, 2012); Nina Eidsheim, *Sensing Sound: Singing and Listening as Vibrational Practice* (Durham, NC: Duke University Press, 2015); Charles Hirschkind, *The Ethical Soundscape* (New York: Columbia University Press, 2009); Patrick Eisenlohr, *Sounding Islam* (Berkeley: University of California Press, 2018).

30. See, for example, M. M. Bakhtin, *The Dialogic Imagination* (Austin: University of Texas Press, 1981). See also the discussion in Robert Stam, *Subversive Pleasures* (Baltimore: Johns Hopkins University Press, 1989).

31. See, for example, Nina Sun Eidsheim, *The Race of Sound* (Durham, NC: Duke University Press, 2018); Jennifer Fleeger, *Mismatched Women* (Oxford: Oxford University Press, 2014); Jean Ma, *Sounding the Modern Woman* (Durham, NC: Duke University Press, 2015); Amanda Weidman, *Singing the Classical, Voicing the Modern* (Durham, NC: Duke University Press, 2006); Jacob Smith, *Vocal Tracks* (Berkeley: University of California Press, 2008); Mladen Dolar, *A Voice and Nothing More* (Cambridge, MA: MIT Press, 2006); Allison McCracken, *Real Men Don't Sing: Crooning in American Culture* (Durham: Duke University Press, 2015).

32. M. M. Bakhtin, *The Dialogic Imagination* (Austin: University of Texas Press, 1981).

33. Tejaswini Niranjana, *Siting Translation: History: Post-structuralism, and the Colonial Context* (Berkeley: University of California Press, 1992) 164.

34. Gayatri Spivak, "Can the Subaltern Speak?," in *Marxism and the Interpretation*

of Culture, ed. Carey Nelson and Lawrence Grossberg (Champaign: University of Illinois Press, 1988), 271–316.

35. See, for example, Rick Altman, ed., *Sound Theory/Sound Practice* (New York: Routledge, 1992); Michel Chion, *Film, a Sound Art* (New York: Columbia University Press, 2009); James Lastra, *Sound Technology and the American Cinema: Perception, Representation, Modernity* (New York: Columbia University Press, 2000); Elisabeth Weis and John Belton, eds., *Film Sound: Theory and Practice* (New York: Columbia University Press, 1985).

36. Rick Altman, ed., "Cinema/Sound," *Yale French Studies* 60 (1980).

37. For example, in one of the key books that ushered in the age of scholarly attentiveness to Indian popular cinema (Bollywood), Vijay Mishra's *Bollywood Cinema: Temples of Desire* (New York: Routledge, 2002), Mishra casts the film narrative, and even the actors' intermedial self-referentiality, as "texts," a critical framework that has proven influential in twenty-first-century Indian cinema studies. Scholarly "guides" to popular Indian cinema such as Tejaswini Ganti's *Bollywood: A Guidebook to Popular Hindi Cinema* (New York: Routledge, 2004) and Rachel Dwyer's *Bollywood's India: Hindi Cinema as a Guide to Contemporary India* (London: Reaktion Books, 2014), privilege sociological readings of film narratives and visual signifiers over the sonic dimensions of film.

38. Lacey, *Listening Publics*, 165.

39. Sterne, 3.

40. Rick Altman, "A Baker's Dozen Terms for Sound Analysis," in *Sound Theory, Sound Practice*, ed. Rick Altman (New York: Routledge, 1992), 249.

SECTION ONE

Scapes, Sites, and Circulations

ONE | Sound Clouds

Listening and Citizenship in Indian Public Culture

ASWIN PUNATHAMBEKAR AND SRIRAM MOHAN

A young man in a blue shirt, jeans, and sneakers walks around onstage clutching a microphone.[1] In Tamil he warns the audience that if you sing about society, like he does, you will be branded a *camūka virōti* (an anti-social element). He pauses and points the microphone at the audience as he asks them how this is usually said in English. The crowd responds almost instantly, screaming "anti-Indian!" Even as the ominous sound of marching boots fills the air, he smirks and declares that he is proud to be considered an anti-Indian.

On the screen behind the young man is a collage of portraits: B. R. Ambedkar, Malcolm X, Martin Luther King, and other revolutionaries on one side and artists such as Bob Marley, Michael Jackson, Kanye West, and Childish Gambino on the other. The young man is now front and center on the stage as he starts rapping the Tamil lines *E<u>n</u><u>n</u>a? Nā u<u>n</u><u>n</u>akku ā<u>n</u>ṭi-intiya<u>n</u>-ā? Enna? Vōṭṭai pōṭṭa paccai tami<u>l</u>a<u>n</u> nā!* (What? Am I an anti-Indian to you? What? I am a Tamil who votes!). Another rapper joins him, as their names—Arivu and ofRO—flash on the screen and their angry voices reverberate over the beat. A few powerful verses later, the song samples a snippet of a local Hindu nationalist politician who gained notoriety by routinely dismissing all dissenters and critics as anti-Indians.

Authors' note: This is a significantly expanded and revised version of, "A Sound Bridge: Listening for the Political in a Digital Era," *International Journal of Communication* 11 (2017): 4610–29.

The beat stops for this voice clip and the words "I am not prepared to answer you, you're an anti-Indian" in the politician's inimitable tinny voice rung clear. The beat starts again, the rappers encourage the audience to join in, and they continue to register their protest by persisting with their questions in verses.

Taking place at an arts festival designed to open up conversations about social issues such as caste and gender discrimination, this performance rests almost entirely on the inversion of the sonic cue that is the term *anti-Indian.* A dangerous mnemonic aiding the criminalization of dissent, its use here is animated by anger and anxiety as much as it is by derision and disbelief. A sense of threat accompanies it, and it is this threat that polices its circulation and renders the act of declaring oneself an anti-Indian subversive and edgy. Indian sound cultures in the digital realm, meanwhile, are also animated by other sonic cues—a popular song, a catchy phrase, or a resonant voice—ones that allow for political participation with much less risk. Some even endure as communicative structures capable of recording a range of discontent, offering other pathways to reimagining citizenship in the Indian context.

This chapter examines the centrality of sound and listening practices in the mediation of politics and citizenship in Indian public culture and develops some theoretical and conceptual resources that might better enable us to understand these processes. Drawing attention to the auditory dimensions of mediated political cultures, we examine how sonic cues can be transformed into hybrid communicative structures that, in turn, enable new ways of listening and new modes of participation—expressions of sonic citizenship—in a digital era. Tracking the movement of a particular sonic cue—a phrase from a Tamil film song—across digital and mobile platforms enabled by media infrastructures and propelled by creative user practices, we argue that sound technologies and practices constitute a vital cultural and material infrastructure on which a bridge between the popular and the political can be built. In doing so, we also hope to join ongoing efforts to place sound at the center of debates on global digital cultures (Lacey 2013; Crawford 2012) and in particular the South Asian context.

Given the dominance of textual and visual approaches to understanding media cultures, it is hardly surprising that the sonic dimensions of the digital turn have also received comparatively less attention. To make the connection, we take our cue from Peters's (2015) efforts to ponder the material and infrastructural links between sound and media infrastructures, including, crucially, cloud computing. Clouds have come to shape our digital lives and afterlives, and we now have a growing body of scholarship on the infrastructural dimensions of clouds, the "nebulous conflation of information, capital, and geography" (Mattern 2016) that shapes digital cultures across the world. But scholarly attempts to discern the presence of clouds and understand how they are made real treat clouds as largely silent infrastructures. For instance, in *A Prehistory of the Cloud*, Tung-Hui Hu (2016) has argued that the cloud is silent, in the background, and almost unnoticeable. Because it is pervasive and for the most part stable, he writes, "The cloud is a particularly mute piece of infrastructure. It is just there, atmospheric and part of the environment" (ix). We disagree. Understanding our digital and global present and future requires opening up a channel for thinking about sounds and clouds and, more to the point, listening practices.

In rich accounts of how sounds and clouds are intertwined in complex ways today, both Hussain (2013) and Mattern (2016) draw our attention to the deeply troubling world of drone warfare and drone strike footage, which attract millions of viewers around the world. Hussain points out that for both the drone operators and the millions of people watching the videos released online the world below is visible but silent. The people on the ground, however, experience the opposite. For those who are gazing up at the clouds, it is all about the sound, "a low-grade perpetual buzzing, and a signal that a strike could occur at any time" (Hussain 2013). The sound emanating from the clouds above can be suffocating. While certainly a disturbing example, it encourages us to be more attentive to the many ways in which cloud infrastructures do in fact hold, store, transmit, and enable us to manipulate and circulate sounds. If the cloud as an idea has, in Hu's account, "exceeded its technological platform and become a potent metaphor for the way contemporary societies are organized" (2016, xiii), we would argue that cloud infrastructures, coupled with digital platforms, including SoundCloud, Twitter, YouTube, and WhatsApp, have become central to the mediation of politics and citizenship. From the routine practices of voice-enabled artificial intelligence platforms (e.g., Amazon's Alexa, which "lives in the cloud") or sharing music to the more politically potent practices of doctoring sounds, it is clear that contemporary political cultures are articulated in sound as much as through other sensory registers.[2] The question, then, is how to listen for political participation and evaluate claims about citizenship that are increasingly made through creative sound work as much as through textual and visual practices. Our site for this analysis is one particular sound that, amid numerous others that came and went, endured, circulated, and resonated in a dense and crowded audiovisual sphere.

A Sonic Cue: #Kolaveri

Why This Kolaveri Di (henceforth *Kolaveri*) was released on YouTube in November 2011 as part of the marketing strategy for a Tamil-language film titled *3*. Shot and edited in a "making-of" style and featuring the film's lead actors, director, and music director, the song became popular within a few hours of its online release. The quirky Tanglish (a portmanteau of the Tamil and English languages) lyrics appeared on the screen as hard-coded subtitles, thus making it easy to follow and sing along with, which contributed to the song's popularity among non-Tamil-speaking audiences in India and across the world. Over a span of two or three months in late 2011 and early 2012, individuals in different parts of the world uploaded cover versions and remixes. And, not unlike the circulation of other global pop hits such as *Gangnam Style, Kolaveri* also inspired flash mobs in different cities. What was different in this case, however, was the way the song—the catchy opening line and the word *kolaveri* (murderous rage) in particular—was redeployed and drawn into a broader and explicitly political arena to make sense of the scale and complexity of corruption and governance. Here is one of many tweets that used the refrain of the song to connect *Kolaveri* to ongoing political conversations.

> Petrol price, Inflation, Corruption, Infrastructure, Politics and many such specials make you go. . . . .Why this..Why This. . . . #Kolaveri Di . . . .
>
> (November 23, 2011)

The song struck a chord with a wide swathe of urban and semiurban middle classes across the country whose political imaginations had been stoked by a series of investigative "sting operations"—exposés carried out by various news organizations—that revealed links among political figures, business leaders, and, in one particularly damning instance, prominent journalists (#Radiagate) (2012). It was not entirely surprising that *Kolaveri* resonated with the anticorruption protests launched by Anna Hazare in April 2011, which gained immense political traction under the guidance of Arvind Kejriwal, the political and public relations face of the anticorruption movement, who has since gone on to launch the mercurial AAP or Aam Aadmi Party (Common Man Party).[3] Moreover, the fact that #Kolaveri is going strong to this day, more than five years after it first captured attention, seems all the more remarkable in a media and political culture marked by networked and mobile publics that shift shape as events unfold (Papacharissi 2015; Kraidy 2016; Punathambekar 2010).

This is, in some respects, a familiar story. We now have a growing body of scholarship on the surprising ways in which symbols and icons from popular culture are deployed at times with great effect in the political sphere (Jenkins et al. 2016; Kumar 2015; Yang 2009). In the Indian context, too, the phenomenal expansion of mobile and digital media infrastructures and platforms since the early 2000s has transformed the ways in which popular culture mediates the political, recasting the ways in which political talk and engagement are woven into the rhythms of everyday life. However, scholars have tended to pay attention to the proliferation of screens and the visual dimensions of public political discourse while ignoring the accompanying changes in the soundscape. In fact, even when we consider the auditory experience of politics, our language remains in thrall to visual metaphors (Ihde 2007). Drawing on recent work in sound and digital media studies (Kheshti 2015; Lacey 2013; Manoukian 2010; Stoever 2016), we trace the way #Kolaveri was taken up in remix videos, news parodies, political campaigns, and Facebook pages and redeployed on Twitter to make sense of corporate and political corruption over a four-to-five-year span.[4] Exploring the sonic dimensions and aural imaginaries at play, we argue that #Kolaveri functioned as a sound bridge that enabled a range of potent encounters among journalists, politicians, and citizens embroiled in long-standing and heated debates about citizenship and political participation.

A sound bridge is a familiar media unit and editing technique that is used to aid smooth transitions between scenes in a film, particularly when setting up expectations that are immediately confirmed (Bordwell and Thompson 2004). It is, in many respects, the aural equivalent of the cross-fade. However, a sound bridge can also surprise and disorient viewers. As Murch suggests, unexpected combinations of visuals and sounds can be deployed such that the audience is unable to "relate the sound to the visual except perhaps metaphorically," thereby inviting them to make deeper and more meaningful connections between sound and visuals than they would otherwise (2004, xiii). Creative uses of sound bridges can produce, in other words, a "greater dimensionality of experience" (xiii). Murch also points out that an untethered sound is particularly potent, seemingly everywhere (xiv) and nowhere, in part because audiences cannot place its source. Once it is unmoored from its filmic origins, a catchy sound like *Kolaveri* has the capacity to connect to diverse contexts. This sense of a sound bridge being connective also encourages us to think about sound in relation to urban spaces and infrastructures. A wealth of recent scholarship in geography and other disciplines has alerted us to the manifold links between sound and space, showing how sounds have the capacity to "mark out territories," produce "acoustic arenas," and more generally contribute to the "production of space" (Gallagher, Kanngieser, and Prior 2016; Revill 2016). Taking a spatial approach also encourages us to consider the fact that bridges are designed, in the first instance, to overcome division(s) in the world. Even though bridges can and do collapse and are often actively destroyed in times of conflict, they are sites of chance and at times charged encounters, and they enable and constrain linkages between individual practices, collective rituals, and the built environment (Sabry 2010). Thus, examining the difference that catchy sounds might make in densely mediated political cultures involves following the links and associations that a sound like *Kolaveri* makes across different private and public spaces and considering the relations among media infrastructures, platforms and their affordances, and a range of user practices.

Adopting this expansive perspective, we show how #Kolaveri functioned as a sound bridge that was separated from the filmic context and used in a range of metaphorical and connective ways by journalists, politicians, and citizens coming to terms with a thoroughly mediated anticorruption movement and, more generally, a political culture shaped by new media logics. Far from being a "viral" expression of senseless, irrational, and fleeting antipolitical rage by angry citizens, sound bridges like #Kolaveri can be understood as mobile communicative structures that enable political participation—in this case, a deeply felt sentiment of outrage—in the face of technological, political-economic, and sociocultural constraints and transformations. In making room for and gathering all manner of sentiments, expressions, aspirations, and identities, #Kolaveri discloses new ways and locales in which we might listen for the political and discern new modes of participation—the expression of sonic citizenship—in a digital era.

Sounding Out (South Asian) Media Studies

The sonic turn in the humanities, particularly in film and media studies, has been long overdue. In the South Asian context, as elsewhere, scholarship on media and public culture has been dominated by a focus on visual practices. While the study of media gradually became a more transnational affair during the 1990s, tracking closely the globalization of media across Asia, Africa, and Latin America, scholarly attention has remained attuned to screen cultures. With "public culture" emerging as an analytic framework for understanding media, consumption, and culture in the postcolonial world in an era of economic and cultural globalization, visual forms (film, television, and advertising in particular) and a focus on viewers, spectators, and interocular fields came to structure studies of media and mediation throughout the 1990s and early 2000s (Appadurai and Breckenridge 1995; Bhatti and Pinney 2011; Kumar 2006; Mankekar 1999; Mazzarella 2003; Pinney 2001). That we have approached the link between media and the political from a visual perspective becomes all the more apparent when we consider the very direct connections between cinema and politics in South India where former film stars have mobilized their star image and fan base to run for political office (Pandian 1992; Srinivas 2013). Even in the detailed and richly theorized accounts of the performative dimensions of politics in South India, the focus remains on visual symbols and logics. The circulation and impact of songs, dialogues, and the varied listening practices that shaped these actors' star images and the fan cultures and associations that were crucial for electoral mobilization remain understudied. The title of Pandian's seminal book on cine-politics, *The Image Trap* (1992), signals a broader theoretical trap that media scholars have only recently begun to undo.

To be sure, there were notable exceptions, including key studies of oratory and language (Bate 2009), cassette culture in India and Iran (Manuel 1993; Sreberny-Mohammadi and Mohammadi 1994), and some focus on music and music videos on satellite television (Kumar and Curtin 2002; Kvetko 2004). With the consolidation and gradual institutionalization of film studies in the South Asian context beginning in the 2000s, there has been a surge of interest not just in film music (Booth 2008; Majumdar 2001; Sundar 2014) but also in other sites and forms of sound work, voice, and the formation of listener communities. For instance, Jhingan's (2016) work on the ways in which specific media technologies and formats transformed the circulation of music, music industry logics, and listening practices has been key to an emergent body of scholarship that is moving away from a strict focus on cinema.

Furthermore, the link between media and the political has been framed largely in relation to news and the rapid expansion of television infrastructures and the phenomenal growth of 24/7 news channels beginning in the mid-1990s. The impact of television news on the political public sphere has been analyzed predominantly through visual logics, with witnessing, displaying, and making visible being key to the democratizing possibilities of media infrastructures (Peters 2001). Also, given the linguistic and regional politics in the Indian context, scholars have drawn attention to the democratizing potential of bringing "small-town, non-metropolitan, or provincial actors" (Roy 2011, 761) into a broader visual field. The impact of television news, moreover, is gauged in relation to the genre of talk TV and debate TV, which networks, including NDTV, CNN-IBN, and Times Now among others, invested in extensively. Programs such as *We the People* (NDTV), *Face the Nation* (IBN), and *News Hour* (Times Now) allowed news networks to make claims about their centrality to the formation of an informed and deliberative public in India. Drawing on global formats, these programs have thrived on a mix of breaking news segments and panel debates involving business, bureaucratic, and political experts to frame issues as pertaining to the national interest and citizenship, which then spill over and continue across other media platforms, including online social networks.

With crowded ticker tapes, flashy graphics, hectoring anchors, and multiple talking heads shouting over each other, the genre of debate TV has come under intense criticism for both its sensationalist impulses and its shrillness. The critique that the visual dimensions of mediated politics has detracted from the act of listening was recently furthered by television news anchor Ravish Kumar as well in a remarkable telecast produced in February 2016 following agitation at Jawaharlal Nehru University in New Delhi and threats leveled against journalists who sought to clarify claims about antinational slogans raised during student protests. In this special broadcast, modeled as an impassioned plea for genuine deliberation, Kumar frames the dream of television news leading to an informed and engaged citizenry as having turned into a nightmare. What is of importance for us here, however, is the darkening of the television screen (or shutting off the visual) as a narrative device to denote India's plunge into darkness. As Kumar spells out the "pressures" of the debate TV format and its implications for the tenor of discussions about nationhood and citizenship, the screen fades into black rapidly, with his voiceover urging a return to deliberation based on careful listening. This strand of critique extends to the realm of digital and social media as well, with a number of scholars pointing out that the democratic potential of networked and peer-to-peer communication remains bedeviled by many of the same problems associated with other media forms. Kumar's criticism is also centered on the familiar tropes of the tabloidization of news and the decline of civil discourse (Gripsrud 2000; Turner 1999), updated to allow for the polarized and abusive nature of online conversations (Udupa 2015). Listening, as it is used here, is about watching and paying attention, being informed, and thus being an engaged citizen. What isn't taken into account by critics like Kumar is the vastly reconfigured soundscape that audiences are immersed in on a daily basis, which has transformed ways of listening in private and public life.

Following Lacey, we situate the #Kolaveri phenomenon as part of a much broader "re-sounding of the public sphere" (Lacey 2013, 11) that accompanied the expansion of media infrastructures, platforms, and practices beginning in the mid- to late 1980s in a number of postcolonial nations that were making the transition to neoliberal market economics. In the Indian context, one key milestone in the aural resignification of the public sphere during the 1980s would be the use of cassette tapes during the 1989 elections, which, as Manuel (1993, XV) argues, "provided many of the basic prerequisites for . . . a democratic restructuring of media content and control." While Manuel's emphasis on the grassroots and participatory dimensions of cassette culture is questionable given the organization of the music industry in India and the uneven spread of the technology, we can recognize the advent of cassette technology as having put in place new logics of circulation and uses of sound. As Shikha Jhingan's work shows so well, cassette culture not only remade the political domain during, say, campaign season but also quickly became an unobtrusive and taken-for-granted part of public and private spaces across the subcontinent. The take-up and diffusion of cassette technology also transformed a public culture that was, until the mid-1980s, largely tuned in to film music. Within a matter of years, India's soundscape went from being dominated by state-run broadcasting to a varied musical culture that included various regional, religious, devotional, folk, and pop songs and sounds.

The shift away from a statist media system that cassette culture, among other media technologies and forms, including the VCR, inaugurated during the 1980s can now be seen as having set the stage for a series of policy, technology, and media transitions throughout the 1990s and 2000s involving FM radio, cable and satellite television, and mobile and digital platforms (Pavarala and Malik 2007; Sen 2014). These transitions, moreover, are marked by audience/user practices such as the routinization of calling in and interacting with radio jockeys and other listeners on FM radio networks, creative uses of caller tunes and ringtones (Gopinath 2005), the circulation and sharing of music and other sounds via inexpensive SD cards (Mukherjee 2016), and the emergence of a vibrant new sphere of remixing, fusion, and other kinds of sound performances on platforms such as SoundCloud and YouTube. Quotidian and popular media uses that have proliferated over the past two decades suggest that substantive sound work has been happening alongside Photoshop, remix, and mashup practices that mark participatory culture(s) across the world. To be sure, #Kolaveri can be situated within a broader history of sounds and protest cultures. There is a rich archive of religious hymns, marching songs, and catchy slogans in South Asia that scholars are only now beginning to mine from a sound studies standpoint. While rooted in ethnomusicology, Sherinian's account of Tamil folk music, in which she traces the way the work of Dalit composer/theologian Rev. Dr. James Theophilus Appavoo "brought about a consciousness of oppression," marks an important start (2014, 242). Tracking the production, circulation, and reception of songs, Sherinian shows how "shared musical relationships . . . can become a way for people to create a context for liberation" (4). Damodaran's (2017) account of the musical repertoire of the left-wing Indian People's Theatre Association also adds to our understanding of sounds and social movements, particularly in showing how music served as a bridge between various artistic forms, including dance and theater. If the history of progressive social movements is one space in which to explore the politics of sound, another point of entry would be the fierce debates around what constitutes "noise," noise control, and abatement policies in different cities around the world (Cardoso 2012) and the ways in which varied sounds and accompanying listening practices have come to mark religious, racial, and ethnic identities (Stoever 2016). As Zuberi (2017) points out in a trenchant essay on music, race, and religion, listening to music enables negotiations of Muslim identity even as "speaking as Muslim" has become a fraught affair in a post-9/11 context.

Needless to say, this thumbnail sketch of complex transformations of soundscapes needs careful elaboration and is beyond the scope of this chapter. It is possible, however, to discern the emergence of varied listening publics and ensure that we situate links among sound, politics, and citizenship in a transnational context, as well as a longer historical trajectory. To be clear, we do not privilege the aural as a corrective to the visual. Indeed, our analysis pays close attention to a wide range of media forms and practices. Rather, our emphasis on the sonic dimensions of #Kolaveri and the movement of this sonic cue across media platforms calls attention to and takes seriously the intersensorial nature of mediated public cultures (Connor 2004). We amplify the soundscape to suggest that sound technologies and practices constitute a vital cultural and material infrastructure on which a bridge between the popular and the political can be built and, in rare instances, maintained over time. #Kolaveri was one such rare and resonant sound bridge. In what follows, we build on scholarship on mediated activism and the work that cultural symbols do to argue that a sonic cue must be *available, performative,* and *resonant* to become a sound bridge and facilitate connections across cultural and political domains.

#Kolaveri: The Making of a Sound Bridge

Available

Kolaveri was released on YouTube on November 17, 2011, and made available on a range of media platforms, including FM radio programs, television channels, as a caller tune for mobile phones, and as a digital file for download and circulation. As the most-searched-for song on YouTube during that week, featured on MTV that weekend (November 19–20), widely publicized on CNN as the most watched YouTube video of 2011, and global news coverage of a surprising "viral" hit from South India, *Kolaveri* was clearly available as a digital artifact. Not surprisingly, in popular commentary about the song, the focus was predominantly on the question of *how* this song from a South Indian film could possibly go viral on a global scale. Of the efforts to determine the causes of this viral success, some themes found more circulation than others: the use of Tanglish in the song; the simple rhythmic pattern, which allowed the song to serve as a format on which everything from Chipmunks to politics could be transposed; and the clever marketing strategy of releasing a making-of video, which decoupled the song from its filmic origins.[5] However, this marketing-oriented discourse—one that is rehearsed with every instance of a purportedly viral proliferation (*Gangnam Style,* for instance)—repeatedly fails to account for why this particular song and not another captured people's imaginations. We would point instead to the affective dimensions of *Kolaveri*—its rootedness in a very specific caste- and class-based experience of masculinity, romance, and tragedy and its cathartic framing of the quotidian experience of young men coming to terms with the impossibility of some of their desires.

In many ways, *Kolaveri* was the breakout example of a Tamil film song featuring a male protagonist singing a song that involves him ruing the act of falling in love and castigating the woman he fell in love with or, as is usually the case, women in general. His angst invariably forms the kernel of such songs, which have then been articulated in various ways over the years. Part lament and part outburst, these songs of failed love condemn the notion of romantic love itself and frequently celebrate male bonding and friendship as the antidote to the ill effects of falling in love with a woman. The male protagonists in these songs see romantic love as an affliction and subsequently cast themselves as suffering subjects. Songs about impossible love are a staple of Tamil cinema and have acquired a particular affective charge as caste and class politics have been transformed under the impact of economic and cultural globalization since the late 1980s. Consider, for instance, the song *Take it Easy, Urvasi* from the 1994 film *Kadhalan* (Lover), a song seen as a celebration of the "euphoria of consumption" (Dhareshwar and Niranjana 2000, 199–200). However, even as the song celebrates commodity culture and youth culture's centrality to global signs and symbols, the song (and the hook, "take it easy policy") also tried to address anxieties about the benefits of economic reforms that would, in the fullness of time, reach them. In one sense, the call to "take it easy" can be seen as the precursor to the rage indexed by #Kolaveri, a rage about corruption and dispossession that animates urban middle-class citizens' concerns and is channeled through a range of social networking platforms. In other words, the distance traversed from *Take It Easy, Urvasi* (1994) to *Why This Kolaveri Di* (2012) is a mark of the deep sense of disappointment that the promises of economic and cultural globalization were never kept.

As Kohli (2012) and other scholars have pointed out in recent analyses of reforms and their impact on poverty, "Three decades of economic growth have been accompanied by growing inequality" (2). It is crucial, moreover, to grasp that the frustration with the state of democratic politics that the anticorruption movement mobilized in 2011 had been brewing over a long period of time. Recent expressions of what Roy calls a "distinctive public form of civic anger" (2015, 362) can be located in relation to the profoundly uneven impact of economic reforms throughout the 1990s and 2000s and, even farther back, in key political economic realignments during the late 1970s and early 1980s. It is hardly a surprise, then, that the lighthearted suggestion that a newly emergent youth culture should "take it easy" and wait for the benefits of globalization to reach it could not be sustained or reinvoked two decades later.

We situate *Kolaveri* within this longer trajectory of cultural politics in order to move away from both marketing and academic discourse about virality and to argue that the tragicomic register on which the song works, coupled with the indeterminacy of *veṟi* (rage), made the song radically available for appropriation, remixing, and recirculation by a range of actors. It is worth noting again the availability of the song's lyrics in the original video as hard-coded subtitles that enabled users to rework it, thus adding to the song's ambivalent affective appeals (let us not forget that the performance in the original video did not signal rage or anger). As Papacharissi (2015) has argued, the "affective attunement" at work in music also shapes interactions on social media platforms. And where "Kolaveri" is concerned, in less than a week of the song's release we began to see numerous "affective gestures" being made across platforms (YouTube-Twitter-TV news), which in turn called "networked publics into being" (24; Yang 2009). For instance, on November 24, 2011, a week after the release of "Kolaveri," minister, cricket administrator, and veteran politician Sharad Pawar was slapped by a young man in New Delhi. Within a matter of hours, a number of citizens began using #Kolaveri (and less frequently #KolaveriDi) and the phrase "Why This Kolaveri" to discuss this expression of rage against a corrupt politician. Some users even uploaded mashup videos using television footage of the politician being slapped, with their own "take" featuring the "Kolaveri" song as background music. Set to the tune of the song, but with lyrics rewritten to address political corruption, and layered with images of Pawar and other politicians' implication in various scandals, these videos were an early indication of how #Kolaveri became available as a potent sonic cue in a public sphere already structured by deeply felt sentiments of rage and frustration.

Performative

If *Kolaveri's* availability as a digital artifact and a deeply meaningful sociocultural referent is one dimension of its becoming a sound bridge, the remarkable range of the uses to which it was put rested on the song's *performativity* and in particular the refrain it offered. Within days of the song's release and #Kolaveri emerging across social media platforms, a range of remixes and mashups that were familiar in terms of popular music and memetic culture made their way onto YouTube, Twitter, and Facebook.[6] However, performativity here is about more than being able to sing, dance, and orchestrate a flash mob. It is first about numerous users—from journalists and politicians to everyday citizens—employing the opening line of the song ("Why This Kolaveri"), as is, to express a sense of bewilderment regarding the scale of political corruption. The repetition of this line across media platforms as an insistent question led to #Kolaveri becoming an instantly recognizable sonic cue in a political culture anchored predominantly in visual cues. Consider, for instance, the following set of tweets about the 2G spectrum scandal and the Bharatiya Janata Party's (BJP) position on foreign direct investment (FDI).

> "Why this #kolaveri kolaveri kolaveri di?"—P Chidambaram to BJP parliamentarians
>
> (November 22, 2011)
>
> Apt for Why this kolaveri RT @ibnlive: 2G: No bail for Kanimozhi, hearing on Monday
>
> (November 25, 2011)
>
> Why this kolaveri kolaveri kolaveri di? RT @ndtv: BJP leader Arun Jaitley: FDI will hurt Indian economy
>
> (November 27, 2011)
>
> So will the speaker today sing in the parliament: "Why this Kolaveri Kolaveri Kolaveri di?" #BJP #India
>
> (November 27, 2011)
>
> Has some one asked BJP "Why this kolaveri di"They need to come up with better answers for opposing FDI in retail than what they are doing now
>
> (November 28, 2011)

These tweets—performative statements that linked #Kolaveri to a range of political concerns from foreign direct investment in retail to corruption in spectrum allocation for mobile telephony—call attention to the ways in which a shared and recognizable sonic cue can weave political matters into the rhythms of daily conversations on Twitter and other platforms already marked by frenetic news media coverage. The continual use of #Kolaveri alongside other hashtags that invoke or name political parties (BJP, Congress, AAP, etc.), key politicians, and events and scandals places the sound within a vibrant and networked intertextual field that includes jokes, memes, and videos circulated via Facebook, WhatsApp, and so on, which, on the whole, reveal that citizenship is constituted as much by play and performance as it is by normative understandings of deliberation and participation (Bayat 2009; Jones 2013).

Repetition, a crucial dimension of such performances, was thus the first signal of the aural register at which hybrid platforms like Twitter can operate. For a hashtag is not only a "performative statement," as Bruns and Burgess (2011) have argued, but can also be, as Lacey (2013) has pointed out, an invitation to listen rather than read. For what the song offered, beyond a catchy opening line, was a refrain and rhyme scheme that users could appropriate, rework, and sound out. The key linguistic device employed in the song is the epenthetic *-u* inserted to ensure the flow of the rhyme scheme, signaling both emphasis and a break that allows the song to proceed. This formal element of the song facilitated creatives uses of the refrain that in turn gave #Kolaveri a promiscuous and catalytic charge.[7] For instance, here is a tweet that cannot be read but in fact has to be sung or sounded out.

> Handle Suitcase, 2G scam-u, Suitcase full ah Currency. Now she gets Bail-u. Why this Kolaveri Kolaveri Kolaveri Di? #Kanimozhi
> (November 28, 2011)

In this tweet, it is the refrain premised on the epenthetic *-u* that links different elements of a political scandal: suitcases used to carry cash for bribes, the 2G spectrum allocation scandal, and judicial decisions involving Kanimozhi, a major political figure. Yoking the popular song to an ongoing political issue, #Kolaveri thus works as a powerful refrain—an element in a song that marks a "break" but also has the potential to "break up and break open" ("Online Etymology Dictionary" n.d.). In other words, #Kolaveri moves away from the song's filmic and seemingly apolitical origin to become a shared cue for conversations in an otherwise fractious political sphere.

This kind of redeployment of a sonic cue is, to be sure, not limited to the Indian context and can be predicated on public performances at the intersection of, say, religion and politics as well. Consider Roshanak Kheshti's analysis (2015) of the aural dimensions of postelection protests in Iran in 2009. In her account of Iranians expressing dissent against the state, Kheshti draws attention to a video entitled *Inja Kojast* (Where is this place?). The video is powerful not because of its visuals but rather due to the nightly rooftop chanting that makes up the soundtrack: "All-Ahu-Akbar . . . Inja Kojast?"—which was taken up in numerous other anonymous videos circulated via YouTube. Kheshti's emphasis on the "sonic performative" also draws attention to a refrain. Where #Kolaveri is concerned, if the refrain marked an acoustic territory that could attract a range of voices, expressions, political statements, and conversations, it was the performance of the refrain that produced a space—a multilane sound bridge—where the popular and the political converged in unpredictable ways. Performativity, more broadly, is what gave a popular and semiotically open sound like that of "Kolaveri" a political charge.

Resonant

The power that this refrain accrued, however, cannot be understood solely in relation to social media platforms. The territory that #Kolaveri marked out as a site for political performance must account for not just interactions between users but also processes of media convergence (Jenkins 2006; Kraidy and Mourad 2010) that shape the way a particular sound moves across media platforms, becomes resonant, and gathers publics over time. In our understanding of how cultural symbols or representations gather force and significance in a given cultural context, we often turn to resonance and relevance. Schudson is right to point out that the resonance of a given symbol or cultural artifact has to do in part with how well it speaks to audiences and how "a public and cultural relation among object, tradition, and audience" emerges (1989, 170). This emphasis on relevance and significance becomes even more acute in a context in which a vast majority of digital artifacts that engage the political on a daily and routine basis find limited circulation. To be sure, this is not to reduce participatory culture to a narrow question of short-term effects. However, in a country where a small percentage of the total population actively participates on platforms like Twitter and YouTube, the question of resonance hinges on whether a given digital artifact and its uses—the various remixes and political deployments of "Kolaveri" in this case—are widely recirculated and discussed in other media channels. In the Indian context, we would point to television's role, particularly television news, in resounding a sonic cue that was first produced and heard on social networking sites.

Among the many news programs that devoted attention to #Kolaveri, one show stands out for the manner in which the sonic cue was deployed: *GustakhiMaaf* (Pardon the Transgression), a daily satirical puppet show broadcast on the Hindi-language channel of NDTV.[8] Launched in 2003 as an official adaptation of the successful French puppet show *Les Guignols de l'info* (News Puppets), *GustakhiMaaf* features a host who introduces short skits that offer comedic interpretations of news and current affairs. Producers have successfully localized the program, as Kumar

(2012) outlines, by using popular film songs (from Hindi-language Bollywood films) "to amplify themes of love, betrayal, and loyalty to describe shifts in political coalitions and changes in personal fortunes in Indian politics" (85). Given the long-standing practice of rewriting song lyrics to fit a particular skit, it is not surprising that *Kolaveri* was also taken up on this program. In one segment, broadcast on November 28, 2011 (less than ten days after *Kolaveri* was released on YouTube), *GustakhiMaaf* featured a cast of puppets of major politicians who were all implicated in the 2G spectrum corruption scam as well as the anticorruption movement. Echoing tweets that framed South Indian politicians in the scam in relation to broader discontent involving other corporate and political figures, these skits featured puppets of the sitting prime minister (Manmohan Singh), Sonia Gandhi (president of the Congress Party), Anna Hazare and Arvind Kejriwal (the figurehead and architect of the anticorruption movement), and others singing, to the tune of *Why This Kolaveri*, about their political misfortunes: "Why is Lokpal very, very weak / Government full of goon-u Goon-u / Wearing khadi white-u / For public all is night-u, public future black-u." Again it is worth noting here the use of the refrain, the rhyme scheme, and the play with words to refer specifically to the demand for a Jan Lokpal, an independent investigative body, to handle cases of political and bureaucratic corruption.

It goes without saying that these skits had tremendous rhetorical force given the influence that NDTV wields in the Indian political landscape and the fact that television news had focused intensely on the anticorruption movement since April 2011. Moreover, this program had built its reputation to the extent that politicians were eager to be featured as puppets, with some skits even staging conversations between a politician and his or her puppet.[9] Beyond the issue of news parody, this is a program that reveals how puppetry as a creative form reconfigures, as Kraidy argues, "the scale between the human body and the body politic" (2016, 145). By bringing the issue of corruption into a "humanly portable arena" and using a sonic cue that had already drawn connections between various actors, *Gustakhi Maaf* allowed audiences to grasp the political in its entirety and, in the process, served to consolidate #Kolaveri as a sound bridge on which a televisual public could gather.

Another dimension of the resonance of *Kolaveri* across media spaces is illustrated by its use in support of the anticorruption movement by Dr. Parag Jhaveri, a local politician in Mumbai. Within three weeks of the release of the original track, Jhaveri had capitalized on the song's availability and performativity (through the refrain and rhyme scheme) to produce a remixed version, what he called a "political song," to proffer support to the anticorruption protests headed by Anna Hazare in New Delhi. English and Hindi television news channels amplified the reach of Jhaveri's song by cutting to performances of the remixed version by the politician and his supporters in between their coverage of the protests in the nation's capital. The voiceovers employed in these news segments are as instructive as the act of the remix itself, with the commentary typically focused on the original on everyone's tongues. In narrativizing the song's success using such metaphors, the news reports linked the song's resonance to both corporeal dimensions (its affect of rage and dispossession) and the linguistic openness enabled by its inventive incorporation of English words with the Tamil epenthetic *-u*. But in building the remixed "political song" into their coverage of the anticorruption movement, television news outlets also participated in furthering its resonance across a media and political system deeply fractured by longstanding regional and linguistic divisions. The networks of circulation for the remixed song also folded back into social media, with regional chapters of India Against Corruption (IAC) then discussing on Twitter the possibilities of producing more versions of the song to reiterate their key political demand, that is, the formation of a Jan Lokpal.

> Follow us on Twitter (@IACCoimbatore) as well for more and more dynamic updates
> (December 4, 2011)
>
> @IACCoimbatore great job iac coimbatore.make why this kolaveri song for lokpal movement? @janlokpal
> (December 4, 2011)

By moving across media platforms and forging links among audiences constituted along linguistic and regional lines, #Kolaveri thus served as a sound bridge between the popular and the political. To be sure, *Kolaveri* was not the only sonic cue available in Indian public culture that could have been mobilized during the anticorruption movement. It became a sound bridge because of the half-fortuitous combination of its being available, performative, and resonant. We say half-fortuitous to signal the political, socio cultural, and technological constraints at work and to acknowledge other sonic cues that are not amplified and are often dampened, muffled, doctored, or silenced. It is also worth noting that there is nothing sacrosanct about *Kolaveri*; the fact that people could be playful and use the song in any way they deemed fit is central to its influence.[10] In sharp contrast to other powerful cues such as "Azaadi" (Freedom) and other slogans deployed in protests, the playfulness and attendant wistfulness of *Kolaveri* ensured its circulation. By virtue of not being weighed down by explicit political connotations, #Kolaveri became a sound bridge on which ordinary citizens seething with rage, as well as journalists, politicians, and other elites, could gather and pose the same question: Why this murderous rage?

Conclusion: Sound, Listening, and Sonic Citizenship

Suggesting that sound technologies and practices constitute a vital cultural and material infrastructure on which a bridge between the popular and the political can be built, we have traced the way a sonic cue (*Kolaveri*) can initiate the making of a sound bridge (#Kolaveri) in a given social and political context. By sound bridge, we do mean a particular sound that connects two distinct settings, scenes, or contexts but also "sound," as in sensible, reasonable, grounded, and carefully designed. Moving beyond established notions of sound bridges in film studies, we suggest that sound bridges disclose to us new ways of listening for the political and new modes of participation—the expression of sonic citizenship—in a digital era. In doing so, we have privileged sonic and aural dimensions while accounting for a range of media forms that were crucial to #Kolaveri being available, performative, and resonant. This is not to ignore or downplay the visual. After all, the affective appeals, resonance, and circulation of the sonic cue we have analyzed here did rest on a rich set of visual cues, including a "making of" video with subtitles, television news segments, and, crucially, puppets resembling politicians. However, as Sterne (2003) and other scholars have pointed out, "sonocentrism" is a strategy for analyzing an event, phenomenon, or cultural artifact that takes the sonic as a starting point. Such a move becomes even more crucial, as we have detailed, in global media and communication studies, where scholarship has tended to privilege the visual. Put simply, we want to reflect on what forms of political life are being imagined and brought into being through new forms of sound work and modes of listening that digital media render possible. If #Kolaveri captured our attention and nudged us to engage with the political in a playful vein, Arivu and ofRO's performance of an insurrectionary "anti-Indianness" pushes us to consider not only the work of building (sound) bridges but also interruptions that demand listening.

With our emphasis on sound and listening practices, we also hope to join a broader conversation about the ways in which digital infrastructures, platforms, and practices have transformed political cultures worldwide. In an era marked by the relentless corporate makeover of news media and a concomitant decline in public trust in journalism, the routine creation and circulation of a range of content via mobile and digital networks does offer a strikingly different and immensely popular mode of engagement with the political. However, our understanding of emergent logics of digital remediation will always have an "analytical deficit," as Chakravartty and Roy (2015, 313) argue, if we continue to emphasize "numerical salience" and focus solely on electoral politics. Framing the link between the popular and the political in terms of effects will only ensure that "the varied institutional shifts and practices of interpretation, interaction, and contestation that generate political agency and social life remain hidden from view" (313). We cannot grasp the significance of #Kolaveri either in the power of participatory culture or its failure to reshape electoral outcomes. Rather, it affords us a glimpse into the shifting cultural foundations of democratic politics. Moving away from thinking about how popular culture can serve as a terrain for learning and practicing skills that can then be applied, in some stagist fashion, to the political, we have tried to capture here the complex interplay between established media institutions (TV news, film industries), digital platforms (Twitter, YouTube, etc.), and user/audience imaginaries and practices. And within this emergent media landscape apprehending political shifts and transformations involves listening as much as looking and seeing.

Notes

1. See the "Anti-Indian" song performed by Arivu and ofRO at the Vaanam Arts Festival in December 2018, YouTube, https://youtu.be/bx3gAvU-VIs?t=507. Arivu is one of the members of the Casteless Collective, an independent music group making "music to fight oppression" (Mohandas 2019).

2. Sound is also often central to subverting state censorship in the digital age, with activists in China routinely using homophones of censored keywords to bypass keyword-matching algorithms. Hiruncharoenvate, Lin, and Gilbert (2015), for instance, have devised a homophone-generating algorithm to create false positives for Chinese censors in order to complicate the detection of online conversations around banned topics and themes.

3. For an account of the anticorruption movement, the formation of the Aam Aadmi Party, and shifts in political power in India, see Roy 2014; Sitapati

2011; and the series of essays published on the influential collaborative blog *Kafila,* https://kafila.online/tag/anna-hazare

4. *Kolaveri* also proved effective in bringing up a range of other issues, including caste injustice, sporting scandals, and gender and sexual violence, during this time period. But we have chosen to limit our focus to the issue of political corruption.

5. For a marketing perspective on why *Kolaveri* went "viral," see Jack In The Box Worldwide 2011.

6. There are a number of such instances, from *Gangnam Style* to the use of music in election campaigns and protest cultures in various African contexts (Gunner 2009; Nyairo and Ogude, 2005).

7. For another instance of a formal or structural element in a song that enables creative expression, see Nyairo (2005) in the Kenyan context.

8. *Les Guignols de l'info/* has run for more than twenty-five years on French television. For more on this program's adaptation for an Indian audience, see Kumar 2012.

9. Prannoy Roy, the founder and CEO of NDTV, recalled in an interview that one politician demanded to know why *GustakhiMaaf* had not yet made a puppet in his image and even offered do his own voiceover if necessary. See Kaushik 2015.

10. The song also sparked discussions about misogyny in Tamil film music. See Kumar 2011.

References

Andrisani, V. 2015. "The Sweet Sounds of Havana: Space, Listening, and the Making of Sonic Citizenship." *Sound Studies* (blog), September 17. https://soundstudiesblog.com/2015/09/17/the-sweet-sounds-of-havana-space-listening-and-the-making-of-sonic-citizenship/

Appadurai, A., and C. A. Breckenridge. 1995. "Public Modernity in India." In *Consuming Modernity: Public Culture in a South Asian World,* edited by C. A. Breckenridge, 1–20. Minneapolis: University of Minnesota Press.

Bate, B. 2009. *Tamil Oratory and the Dravidian Aesthetic: Democratic Practice in South India.* New York: Columbia University Press.

Bayat, A. 2009. *Life as Politics: How Ordinary People Change the Middle East.* Stanford, CA: Stanford University Press.

Bhatti, S., and Pinney, C. 2011. "Optic Clash: Modes of Visuality in India." In *A Companion to the Anthropology of India,* edited by Isabelle Clark-Decès, 223–240. West Sussex: Wiley-Blackwell Publishing.

Booth, G. D. 2008. *Behind the Curtain: Making Music in Mumbai's Film Studios.* New York: Oxford University Press.

Bordwell, D., and K. Thompson. 2004. *Film Art: An Introduction.* Boston: McGraw-Hill.

Bruns, A., and J. E. Burgess. 2011. "The Use of Twitter Hashtags in the Formation of Ad Hoc Publics." In *Proceedings of the 6th European Consortium for Political Research (ECPR) General Conference, 2011.* Reykjavik: University of Iceland. http://www.ecprnet.eu/conferences/general_conference/reykjavik/

Cardoso, L. 2012. "Sound Politics in Sao Paolo, Brazil." *Sound Studies* (blog), October 15. https://soundstudiesblog.com/author/cardosoleo/

Chadha, K. 2012. "Twitter as Media Watch-Dog? Lessons from India's Radia Tapes Scandal." *Global Media and Communication* 8, no. 2: 171–76.

Chakravartty, P., and S. Roy. 2015. "Mr. Modi Goes to Delhi: Mediated Populism and the 2014 Indian Elections." *Television and New Media* 16, no. 4: 311–22.

Connor, S. 2004. "Edison's Teeth: Touching Hearing." In *Hearing Cultures: Essays on Sound, Listening, and Modernity*. New York: Bloomsbury Academic.

Crawford, K. 2012. "Following You: Disciplines of Listening in Social Media," in *The Sound Studies Reader*, ed. Jonathan Sterne. Routledge: New York, pp 79–88.

Damodaran, S. 2017. *The Radical Impulse: Music in the Tradition of the Indian People's Theatre Association*. New Delhi: Tulika Books.

Dhareshwar, V., and T. Niranjana. 2000. "*Kaadalan* and the Politics of Resignification: Fashion, Violence, and the Body." In *Making Meaning in Indian Cinema*, edited by R. S. Vasudevan, 191–214. Delhi: Oxford University Press.

Gallagher, M., A. Kanngieser, and J. Prior. 2016. "Listening Geographies: Landscape, Affect, and Geotechnologies." *Progress in Human Geography*, August 10, 2016. DOI: https://doi-org.proxy.lib.umich.edu/10.1177/0309132516652952

Gopinath, S. 2005. "Ringtones, or the Auditory Logic of Globalization." *First Monday*, 10, no. 12.

Gripsrud, J. 2000. "Tabloidization, Popular Journalism, and Democracy." In *Tabloid Tales: Global Debates over Media Standards*, edited by Colin Sparks and John Tulloch, 285-300. Lanham, MD, Boulder, CO, New York and Oxford: Rowman and Littlefield.

Gunner, L. 2009. "Jacob Zuma, the Social Body, and the Unruly Power of Song." *African Affairs* 108, no. 430: 27–48.

Gürsel, Z. D. 2013. "#potsandpans: Rethinking Social Media in Istanbul during Occupy Gezi." *Anthropology Now* 5, no. 3: 67–73.

Hiruncharoenvate, C., Z. Lin, and E. Gilbert. 2015. "Algorithmically Bypassing Censorship on Sina Weibo with Nondeterministic Homophone Substitutions." Paper presented at the international conference Web and Social Media, AAAI, Oxford, United Kingdom.

Hu, Tung-Hui. 2016. *A Prehistory of the Cloud*. Cambridge, MA: MIT Press.

Hussain, N. 2013. "The Sound of Terror: The Phenomenology of a Drone Strike." *Boston Review*, October 16, 2013. http://bostonreview.net/world/hussain-drone-phenomenology

Ihde, D. 2007. *Listening and Voice: Phenomenologies of Sound*. 2nd ed. Albany: State University of New York Press.

Jack In The Box Worldwide. 2011. "Kolaveri Di: Official Case Study," December. http://www.slideshare.net/jackintheboxww/kolaveri-di-official-case-study

Jenkins, H. 2006. *Convergence Culture: Where Old and New Media Collide*. New York: New York University Press.

Jenkins, H., S. Shresthova, L. Gamber-Thompson, N. Kligler-Vilenchik, and A. Zimmerman. 2016. *By Any Media Necessary: The New Youth Activism*. New York: New York University Press.

Jhingan, S. 2016. "Sonic Ruptures: Music, Mobility, and the Media." In *Media and*

Utopia: History, Imagination, and Technology, edited by A. Rajagopaland A. Rao, 209–34. New York: Routledge.

Jones, J. P. 2013. "Parody, Performativity, and Play." In *A Companion to New Media Dynamics,* edited by J. H. AM, J. Burgess, and A. Bruns, 396–406. Wiley-Blackwell.

Kaushik, K. 2015. "The Tempest." *Caravan,* December 1. http://www.caravanmagazine.in/reportage/the-tempest-prannoy-radhika-roy-ndtv

Kawade, A. 2016. "The Meaning of JNU's Presence." *Kafila* (blog), November 11. https://kafila.online/2016/11/11/the-meaning-of-jnus-presence-ankit-kawade/

Kheshti, R. 2015. "On the Threshold of the Political: The Sonic Performativity of Rooftop Chanting in Iran." *Radical History Review* 2015, no. 121: 51–70.

Kohli, A. 2012. *Poverty Amid Plenty in the New India.* Cambridge: Cambridge University Press.

Kraidy, M. M. 2016. *The Naked Blogger of Cairo Creative Insurgency in the Arab World.* Cambridge, MA: Harvard University Press.

Kraidy, M. M., and S. Mourad. 2010. "Hypermedia Space and Global Communication Studies Lessons from the Middle East." *Global Media Journal* 8, no. 16.

Kumar, S. 2006. *Gandhi Meets Primetime: Globalization and Nationalism in Indian Television.* Champaign: University of Illinois Press.

Kumar, S. 2011. "Why This Kavala-Worry Kavala-Worry Di?," *Kafila* (blog), December 5. https://kafila.online/2011/12/05/why-this-kavala-worry-kavala-worry-di/

Kumar, S. 2012. "Transgressing Boundaries as the Hybrid Global: Parody and Postcoloniality on Indian Television." *Popular Communication,* 10, nos. 1–2: 80–93.

Kumar, S. 2015. "Contagious Memes, Viral Videos, and Subversive Parody: The Grammar of Contention on the Indian Web." *International Communication Gazette* 77, no. 3: 232–47.

Kumar, S., and M. Curtin. 2002. "Made in India." In *Between Music Television and Patriarchy. Television and New Media* 3, no. 4: 345–66.

Kvetko, P. 2004. "Can the Indian Tune Go Global?" *TDR: The Drama Review* 48, no. 4: 183–91.

Lacey, K. 2013. "Listening in the Digital Age." In *Radio's New Wave: Global Sound in the Digital Era,* 9–23. New York: Routledge.

Majumdar, N. 2001. "The Embodied Voice: Song Sequences and Stardom in Popular Hindi Cinema." In *Soundtrack Available: Essays on Film and Popular Music,* edited by P. R. Wojcik and A. Knight. Durham, NC: Duke University Press.

Mankekar, P. 1999. *Screening Culture, Viewing Politics: An Ethnography of Television, Womanhood, and Nation in Postcolonial India.* Durham, NC: Duke University Press.

Manoukian, S. 2010. "Where Is This Place? Crowds, Audio-Vision, and Poetry in Postelection Iran." *Public Culture* 22, no. 2: 237–63.

Manuel, P. 1993. *Cassette Culture: Popular Music and Technology in North India.* Chicago: University of Chicago Press.

Mattern, S. 2016. "Cloud and Field." *Places Journal,* August 2016. Accessed 10 October 2019. https://doi.org/10.22269/160802

Mazzarella, W. 2003. *Shoveling Smoke: Advertising and Globalization in Contemporary India.* Durham, NC: Duke University Press.

Mohandas, V. 2019. "Voice of the Voiceless." *Deccan Chronicle,* January 4. https://www.deccanchronicle.com/lifestyle/viral-and-trending/040119/voice-of-the-voiceless-1.html

Mukherjee, R. 2016. "Reconfiguring Mobile Media Assemblages: Translocal Flows of Affective Platforms." Paper presented at the conference The Internet, Policy, and Politics, Oxford Internet Institute, University of Oxford. http://ipp.oii.ox.ac.uk/2016/programme-2016/track-c-markets-and-labour/regional-platforms-asian-mediations/rahul-mukherjee-reconfiguring-mobile

Murch, W. 2004. "Foreword: Collaborating with Coppola." In *Godfather: The Intimate Francis Ford Coppola,* edited by G. D. Phillips. Lexington: University Press of Kentucky.

Nyairo, J. 2005. "'Zilizopendwa': Kayamba Afrika's Use of Cover Versions, Remix, and Sampling in the (Re)membering of Kenya." *African Studies* 64, no. 1: 29–54.

Nyairo, J., and J. Ogude. 2005. "Popular Music, Popular Politics: Unbwogable and the Idioms of Freedom in Kenyan Popular Music." *African Affairs* 104, no. 415: 225–49.

Online Etymology Dictionary. N.d. Accessed February 4, 2017. http://www.etymonline.com/index.php?allowed_in_frame=0&search=resonance

Pandian, M. S. S. 1992. *The Image Trap: M. G. Ramachandran in Film and Politics.* New Delhi: Sage Publications.

Papacharissi, Z. 2015. *Affective Publics: Sentiment, Technology, and Politics.* Oxford: Oxford University Press.

Pavarala, V., and K. K. Malik. 2007. *Other Voices: The Struggle for Community Radio in India.* Thousand Oaks, CA: Sage Publications.

Peters, J. D. 2001. "Witnessing." *Media, Culture, and Society* 23, no. 6: 707–23.

Peters, J. D. 2015. *The Marvelous Clouds: Toward a Philosophy of Elemental Media.* Chicago: University of Chicago Press.

Pinney, C. 2001. "Public, Popular, and other Cultures." In *Pleasure and the Nation: The History, Politics, and Consumption of Public Culture in India,* edited by Rachel Dwyer and Christopher Pinney, 1-34. New Delhi: Oxford University Press.

Punathambekar, A. 2010. "Reality TV and Participatory Culture in India." *Popular Communication,* 8, no. 4: 241–55.

Qiu, J. L. 2015. "Go Baobao! Image-Driven Nationalism, Generation Post-1980s, and Mainland Students in Hong Kong." *positions* 23, no. 1: 145–65.

Rajagopal, A. 2001. *Politics after Television: Hindu Nationalism and the Reshaping of the Public in India.* Cambridge: Cambridge University Press.

Revill, G. 2016. "How is Space Made in Sound? Spatial Mediation, Critical Phenomenology, and the Political Agency of Sound." *Progress in Human Geography,* 40, no. 2: 240–56.

Roy, S. 2011. Television News and Democratic Change in India." *Media, Culture, and Society* 33, no. 5: 761–77.

Roy, S. 2014. "Being the Change: The Aam Aadmi Party and the Politics of the Extraordinary in Indian Democracy." *Economic and Political Weekly* 49, no. 15: 45–54.

Roy, S. 2015. "Angry Citizens: Civic Anger and the Politics of Curative Democracy in India." *Identities: Global Studies in Culture and Power*, 23, no. 3: 362–77.

Sabry, T. 2010. *Cultural Encounters in the Arab World: On Media, the Modern, and the Everyday*. London: I. B. Tauris.

Schudson, M. 1989. "How Culture Works: Perspectives from Media Studies on the Efficacy of Symbols." *Theory and Society* 18, no. 2: 153–80.

Sen, B. 2014. "A New Kind of Radio: FM Broadcasting in India." *Media, Culture, and Society* 36, no. 8: 1084–99.

Sherinian, Z. 2014. *Tamil Folk Music as Dalit Liberation Theology*. Bloomington: Indiana University Press.

Sitapati, V. 2011. "What Anna Hazare's Movement and India's New Middle Classes Say about Each Other." *Economic and Political Weekly* 46, no. 30: 39–44.

Sreberny-Mohammadi, A., and A. Mohammadi. 1994. *Small Media, Big Revolution: Communication, Culture, and the Iranian Revolution*. Minneapolis: University of Minnesota Press.

Srinivas, S. V. 2013. *Politics as Performance: A Social History of the Telugu Cinema*. Ranikhet: Permanent Black.

Sterne, J. 2003. *The Audible Past: Cultural Origins of Sound Reproduction*. Durham, NC: Duke University Press.

Stoever, J. L. 2016. *The Sonic Color Line: Race and the Cultural Politics of Listening*. New York: New York University Press.

Sundar, P. 2014. "Of Radio, Remix, and 'Rang De Basanti': Rethinking History through Film Sound." *Jump Cut: A Review of Contemporary Media* 56. https://www.ejumpcut.org/archive/jc56.2014–2015/RangDeBasanti/

Turner, G. 1999. "Tabloidization, Journalism, and the Possibility of Critique." *International Journal of Cultural Studies* 2, no. 1: 59–76.

Udupa, S. 2015. "Abusive Exchange on Social Media: The Politics of Online Gaalicultures in India." June 11. http://www.mediaanthropology.net/file/udupa_abusive_exchange_final2.pdf

Yang, G. 2009. *The Power of the Internet in China: Citizen Activism Online*. New York: Columbia University Press.

Zuberi, N. 2017. "Listening while Muslim." *Popular Music* 36, no. 1: 33–42.

TWO | Sounding Out the Crowd

Sonic Political Futures in Migrant Mumbai

KATHRYN C. HARDY

Introduction: Migrant Belonging on Juhu Beach[1]

Juhu Beach unwinds along the western edge of suburban Mumbai, six kilometers of sand marked for recreation and public use between increasingly squeezed fishing settlements to the south and rockier beaches to the north. It is used by thousands of people daily who come from all over: people on holiday from elsewhere in India and abroad, Mumbaikers having a snack and a stroll after work, and nearby locals who make the beach their daily meeting point for gossiping with friends. Juhu Beach does not usually have an overt regional, religious, or class identity. Iconic of Mumbai, it usually seems cosmopolitan in the literal sense, a microcosm of the city, an open, public space that anyone can wander into, less policed than the mall, more expansive than any park, and actually free to access. But occasionally the beach is claimed as a space of regional solidarity, where specific communities stage linguistically and geographically specific politics. The largely Bihari festival of Chhath Puja is such an occasion.

Six days after the mainstream Diwali holiday—*chhath* means "sixth"—Juhu Beach thrums with activity that is palpable from kilometers away, visibly and audibly irrupting as a space of joyous migrant festivity and belonging. Traffic jams begin early in the day, as autorickshaws, vans, and rented commercial trucks filled with people all slowly snake toward the seaside. Long, green, telltale sugarcanes poke out the back of vehicles coming from suburbs as far as Navi Mumbai, marking the cars and trucks as celebrators of Chhath Puja, and therefore as migrants, not native Mumbaikars or Maharashtrians. Migrants to Mumbai from Bihar and the adjoining districts of Uttar Pradesh (UP) and Jharkhand, even if the actual act of migration might have occurred decades or even a generation prior, are the subjects of popular disdain and discrimination. These people are popularly referred to with dismissive names like *bhaiyya* ("brother," a form of address common in Bihar and UP) and are sometimes called "North Indians" by antimigrant politicians, an overly broad category that indexes their outsider status in the western state of Maharashtra.

In addition to everyday acts of dismissal or discrimination, Bhojpuri speakers were targeted with political exclusion and vitriol, which reached its peak around 2008 and 2009, when I began my research into Bhojpuri migration and media production (Hardy 2014). The large population of Bhojpuri-speaking migrants to Mumbai was identified as a political problem, a social fact mobilized to encourage fear and distrust of "nonnatives" among Marathi-speaking "native" Maharashtrians (Kumar 2009). But in the decade that followed, Bhojpuri speakers were brought into vote-bank politics proper, held up as a *constituency*—an entity to be collectively addressed both denotationally (through explicit appeals to people from UP and Bihar as voters) and through politically performative appeals to Bhojpuri speakers—namely, by organizing stage shows and other public support[2] during Chhath Puja.

In this chapter, I examine the sonic practices of Chhath Puja stage shows on Juhu Beach to argue that it is sound itself, not language per se, that calls forth political imaginaries of migrant belonging to (or exclusion from) Mumbai. Bhojpuri speakers—conflated with "Biharis" and "North Indians," though these all comprise demographically different, albeit overlapping, groups—are primarily articulated in scholarship and the news media as linguistically and geographically specific communities. But political address on the beach depends not on linguistic particulars but on sonic choices that address migrants as either regionally distinct (primarily Bhojpuri) or regionally homogenized (primarily Hindu).

Although it is often politically hostile to migrant communities, Mumbai is home to a large community of Bhojpuri-speaking labor migrants from both UP and Bihar (Hardy 2010; Sharma 2009). Linguistic formations such as Bhojpuri, officially classed as dialects divergent from the official standard of Hindi, are popularly linked with rural illiteracy, migrant labor, and poverty. Even so, the rapid expansion of Bhojpuri commercial media industries in the 2000s have transformed a newly imagined Bhojpuri public into an object of national attention (Abbi 2013; Verma and Tripathy 2011; Tripathy 2007), including explicitly political attention, and the sounds of Chhath are intimately tied to these industries through the stage show. In 2010 the aesthetics of these stage shows were consistent with other Bhojpuri stage show aesthetics across North India, both visually and sonically. Often crossing sonic lines between the bourgeois categories of eroticism and devotion by using the language of bhajans (devotional music) alongside the sound of *chatpata* (spicy, erotic) songs, Chhath stage shows were aesthetically of a piece with other forms of Bhojpuri cultural production.

But more recently, along with the national rise of the Hindu nationalist Bhartiya Janata Party (BJP), the self-evidence of the Bhojpuri stage show performance aesthetic has splintered into divergent forms of political address. New stage shows sponsored by the BJP sonically interpellate Bhojpuri speakers as both pious Hindus and normative national subjects. The sonic qualities of the new BJP stage shows suggest a new kind of Bhojpuri-centered politics in which Biharis are simply figured as a local variant of homogeneous national Hinduism, part of an overarching political vision in which regional differences can be subsumed into essential (Hindu) sameness. Bhojpuri speakers are increasingly addressed as a plausibly Hindu nationalist collectivity, and the sound of regionality can be heard to shift as well. Politicians use sound to carve out meaningful political groups—emergent sonic publics—implicitly articulating complex projects of the nation and regional citizenship itself.

A Bihari Festival in Mumbai

Due in part to historic government underinvestment, and what is now identified as "underdevelopment," Bihar is one of the states with the most rural-urban outmigration in India (UNESCO 2013, 2). And when Biharis move the sights and sounds of Chhath Puja move with them. From Patna to Kanpur, UP, Mumbai, and Delhi, loudspeakers blast heavily autotuned bhajans in praise of the goddess Chhathi Maiyya, "Mother Chhath," both day and night. In Mumbai these songs are often in Bhojpuri, a language spoken in Bihar and neighboring UP. The sounds of Chhath bhajans are just as distinctive as the long, green sugarcanes with leaves still attached, and they telegraph Bihari identity to all who observe them.

Technically, Chhath is celebrated twice a year in Bihar—in the Hindu month of Karthik (October–November), after Diwali, and in the month of Chaithra (March–April), after Holi (Kantor 2016). But in Mumbai only the Karthik Chhath is publicly relevant. Sanjay Nirupam is a politician from Bihar who claims to have initiated the first Chhath celebrations on Juhu Beach in Mumbai. In 2016, he explained the gradual spread of Chhath, which is still most strongly associated with both Bihar and the Bhojpuri-speaking parts of UP) that abut it.

> Basically it's only a Bihari festival. But young women would get married and spread the practice of observing Chhath first to UP, then elsewhere—and when these families came to Mumbai for jobs, they would begin to celebrate Chhath there as well.

The festival is an unusual one. Many people took pains to tell me that Chhath is the only Hindu festival in which both the setting sun and the rising sun are worshipped. Chhath centrally involves an arduous fast over four days of gradually increasing difficulty, which culminates in more than twenty-four hours without either food or water. People who take part in the fast, mostly women, stand in water with carefully arranged fruits, flowers, lamps, and incense held in rice winnowers, which are offered to the sun itself in the evening and again in the morning. In Patna, Bihar, where Diwali, the national holiday, is treated as a mere lead-up to the more regionally important Chhath, families crowd around the ghats, the steps leading down to the River Ganga, holding on to specially constructed handrails in designated zones patrolled by police boats—the river is deep and can be dangerous. In Mumbai, where celebrating Chhath is an external sign of being a Bihari (or otherwise North Indian) migrant, Chhath is ideally celebrated by the ocean. Although Chhath is also observed at other public spaces on the water in Mumbai—Powai Lake, Aksa Beach—Juhu is the center of activity, called by one Bihari man living in Mumbai "the Times Square of Chhath Puja."

Fasting women arrive on Juhu Beach by the thousands, accompanied by their extended families. Since devotees must watch the sun as it sets and rises the next day, most families bring blankets and sheets, so as to stay on the beach through the night, in addition to food (for the nonfasting members) and elaborate puja materials, always including the all important *thekuas*, wheat- and jaggery-based dry sweets quite like buttery, cardamom-scented cookies. These are exchanged as prasad in the morning among families that get to know each other over the course of the night.

For these two days in autumn, Juhu Beach becomes a visible and audible sign of the sheer numbers of migrants from UP and Bihar, and thus of their possible political strength. Iconic images of Chhath are increasingly depicted in national newspapers and television spots, highlighting the diversity of regional Hindu festivals around Diwali. Cameras pan across the sea of sugar canes planted firmly in the sand in festive pyramids tied off with yellow or red cloth edged in gold spangles. Photographers capture pious women standing knee deep in ocean water with their bright orange *sindoor* applied all the way from the partings of their hair to the tips of their noses.

Chhath and its associated songs have social and political effects on Juhu Beach in Mumbai that differ from those in the Bhojpuri-speaking heartland of UP and Bihar, around fifteen hundred kilometers away by train. On the beach, visible signs of the migrant population and piety are inseparable from the sonic particularity of the beach festival, where political parties engineer carefully produced soundscapes dominated by stage shows that explicitly call forth Bhojpuri-speaking constituents.

Soundscapes and the Relativity of "Noise"

The soundscape of Chhath Puja is most notable for the vigorous opposition it has occasioned in Mumbai. As Chhath grew in popularity throughout the early 2000s, the increasingly audible disturbance to the regular soundscape of Juhu Beach was one of the main focuses of annual court cases against Chhath organizers. All the Chhath stage shows included music, usually categorized as bhajans. These bhajans were described as either regionally inflected but firmly Hindu songs or crass migrant noise. But the boundaries of acceptable and unacceptable publicly amplified devotional music are not constructed by the presence or absence of internally felt religious fervor. Rather, these limits are determined by social conceptions of what counts as "noise," which is, as David Novak writes, "not really a kind of sound but a metadiscourse of sound and its social interpretation" (2015, 12). Chhath has provided a reliable occasion during which the metadiscourse around "noisy" Bhojpuri soundscapes can be elaborated.

In ordinary times, the soundscape of Juhu Beach offers an aural panorama of leisure and labor in Mumbai. Semipermanent snack stalls crowd each entrance from the street to the beach. There popular Hindi film songs, from recent releases to vintage favorites, compete with patter from hawkers drumming up business for the visually similar restaurants, which serve fresh juice, hot buttery *pao bhaji,* icy *golas,* and Mumbai's iconic *chaats.* The hawkers can only be heard at close range over the clanging of metal utensils as they thrust identical menus in the faces of passersby, who stroll through without turning, as if not hearing them.

If the weather is calm, the waves of the Arabian Sea are gentle but insistent, and the soft roar of the ocean forms the backdrop of sound to all the other human interventions. International flights from the nearby Santacruz airport to the south take off at predictable intervals, booming over the ocean. Crows and pigeons take off in flocks of hundreds, their wings echoing the sound of the planes and waves. Building is prohibited near the waterline. In a city where space is otherwise regularly interrupted by human-made structures, two hundred meters of open sandy expanse from shoreline to city is unusual. The openness shapes the way people communicate. Although voices carry somewhat across these long, open expanses, their edges are muffled as they travel, lost in the oceanic rumbling. Eavesdropping is difficult; while wandering down the beach, conversations quickly drop in and out of audibility. The young couples who wander near the waterline at sunset can speak privately even under the gaze of hundreds of strangers.

The sea functions as a natural white noise machine, drowning out conversation except among intimates. The acoustic environment of the beach, measured in decibels, is far from silent. Chhath Puja shifts the aural environment substantially, as the beach fills with thousands of people from UP and Bihar, but the shift is not one of silence to "loudness," merely on the level of decibels.

In R. Murray Schafer's influential formulation of the soundscape, physical space and sonic space are aligned. "The soundscape is any acoustic field of study," he writes, and such an acoustic field can be examined "just as we study the characteristics of a given environment" (2012, 99). The distinct characteristics of an acoustic environment include both the physical characteristics of the material world—the percussive reflectiveness of marble or the soft, muffling, absorptive qualities of grass or piles of cloth—and the purposeful or unpurposeful production of sound in that environment. The soundscape includes birdsong and horns honking, waves lapping on the seashore, and music playing on a radio. The soundscape "consists of events *heard* not objects *seen*" (99). The Chhath soundscape, then, consists not just of music and its amplification but of the beach itself, the waves, passersby chatting, politicians giving speeches, and the songs that call forth the observers of Chhath, alongside all the other sounds that interpenetrate the music.

For Schafer the concept of the soundscape allows these nonmusical sounds to be taken as seriously as music. By "treat[ing] the world as a macrocosmic musical composition" (2012, 96), Schafer extended an increasingly expansive view of what music might be in the twentieth century, arguing that if music is merely arranged sound then the unarranged, incidental sounds of the world must equally be thought of as music. He asks, "Is the soundscape of the world an indeterminate composition over which we have no control, or are *we* its composers and performers, responsible for giving it form and beauty?" (96). For Schafer and many of those who followed him, the answer was clear. We are responsible for protecting our own ears and the ears of those around us, as well as the "natural" soundscapes that are increasingly under attack from human intervention.

The question of *which* sounds "truly matter" and which are "insouciant and distracting" served as a call to arms for later sound scholars and sound artists,[3] who considered the soundscape as something to be measured, recorded, preserved, and above all protected, reinscribing binaries between (pristine) nature and (human) culture and (authentic) sound and (overproduced, overly loud, out of place) noise. As William Cronon argued in his influential *Uncommon Ground*, "wilderness" was never ontologically distinct from places affected by human presence.

> [Wilderness] is not a pristine sanctuary . . . without the contaminating taint of civilization. Instead, it's a product of that civilization, and could hardly be contaminated by the very stuff of which it is made (1996, 69).

In a parallel formation, distinctions between (untrammeled) sound and (human-infected) noise also emerge socially. Emily Thompson describes how the category of "noise" evolved historically, identified in the late nineteenth century (and still recognizable) as a scientifically measurable distinction between sounds that are "discordant, irregular, and disorderly" as opposed to "harmonious, regular, and orderly" music (2004, 132). Laws and rhetoric around noise abatement, she explains, "typically identified relatively powerless targets, noisemakers who impeded, in ways not just acoustical, the middle-class vision of a well-ordered city" (123). Chhath-oriented bhajans were accused of being "noise" according to much the same logic. The interjection of Bhojpuri sounds into Mumbai's soundscape was adjudicated not merely in terms of decibel level but also in terms of what properly constituted the "devotional" in a bourgeois sense. Only properly domesticated, middle-class sounds could be considered "harmonious" and therefore not noise.

Stage Shows, Cinematic Sound, and the Sounds of Devotion

During Chhath Puja, the amplified voices and music of four or five formally distinct stage shows penetrates the roar of waves and planes. Even the music emanating from the stages closest to one another does not overlap much, for the sound of the sea dampens the amplification and limits the reach of each individual stage. Without exception, each stage belongs to a cultural organization tied financially and personally to a political party. Also without exception, each organization claims to be showcasing Bhojpuri bhajans.

The category "bhajan" designates a large and diverse set of religious song traditions with lyrics in Hindi, Marathi, Gujarati, Bengali, Punjabi, Bhojpuri, and any number of other languages found across the country. In temples, during festivals, at people's home shrines, or in the presence of auspicious bodies of water or other significant sites, songs praising various gods and goddesses are a familiar part of the North Indian soundscape. At the time of this writing, by far the most ubiquitous bhajans in India are technologically mediated—recorded in studios and disseminated in compressed file formats to be played on mobile phones (Manuel 2012; Doron and Jeffrey 2013). Bhajans are also broadcast over loudspeakers from temples, live performances, and recordings, making them an inescapable part of the ambient soundscape across India.

Prior to the 1980s, expensive and difficult to use long-playing record technology allowed a few companies to control the music business in India. This industrial consolidation, according to Peter Manuel, led to a musical landscape that was dominated by a few hegemonic sounds, eschewing "regional" languages—mostly in favor of Hindi, in North India at least—"in an attempt to appeal to a pan-regional market" (1991, 190). The hegemonic style of the bhajan—which I would argue connotes mainstream caste Hinduism—consists of a distinct set of sounds. Backing tracks rely on flutes and tablas (or their synthesized equivalents) with constant slow to midtempo beats, which fall into well-known "light classical" rhythm patterns such as the sixteen-beat *teentaal* or eight-beat *taal keherwa*.[4] The voices of typical male singers are soft, full, and round. Mainstream female bhajan singers have voices that are reminiscent of Lata Mangeshkar, the most prolific and popular film playback singer of the past many decades, whose iconic, nasal soprano set the norm for female sound over four decades of near-complete industry dominance (Sundar 2008, 147–48).

But by the mid-1980s the advent of the inexpensive, easily recorded cassette tape had revolutionized Indian popular music (Manuel 1991). Bhajans in many different languages were made available to consumers, often via small-time recording companies whose distribution networks had limited geographic reach. Now cassettes are another technology on the wane, and songs are more likely to be played on mobile phones than on tape decks. But bhajans in languages other than Hindi, including Bhojpuri, have become commonplace since this moment of technological shift in the 1980s. Along with a dramatic increase in the recording of these songs in nondominant languages, a concomitant shift in musical styles can be heard as well. Once they are recorded, bhajans are integrated into private and public soundscapes in India, as they are played on television programs, watched on YouTube, and amplified through loudspeakers in the city.

Bhojpuri recorded albums are divisible primarily into bhajans and *chatpata* ("spicy" songs), the racy songs considered necessary to commercially draw a Bhojpuri audience to a film or stage show, though recordings of genres such as *birha* and light classical *thumri* or *kajri* are also sold. Bhojpuri bhajans can sound quite different from the hegemonic model of normative Hindu sound, hewing closer to other forms of Bhojpuri popular music than to the soft, slower, flute-backed tracks normatively understood to "sound like" (middle-class) Hindi bhajans. Bhojpuri bhajans often feature very fast tempos (150 to 180 beats per minute) and racing drum tracks with the sharp, high-pitched staccato beats of the *dholak* hand drum, often played on a synthesizer, and distinctive sounds of distorting pitch correction or other vocal distortion. These bhajans "sound Bhojpuri" before they sound like bhajans, which has been a central problem for Chhath celebrations.

The politician Sanjay Nirupam claims to have started the formalized, public celebration of Chhath Puja in Mumbai on Juhu Beach in 1998. In a 2016 interview with me, he explained that from the beginning he wanted to make Chhath Puja a large-scale, popular festival with "glamour." The way to do this, he explained, was to put on a stage show.

> The first year, when we were planning it, in the beginning, we thought, look, there's 25 thousand, 30 thousand people [who were brought] together with five or six days' notice. We thought, look, this is very interesting, what if we heated this up? Next year we have to try to glamorize it. In Mumbai if you're going to glamorize something, the best thing is to call Bollywood. So what did I do? As many actors are from UP and Bihar, they're all from the north, starting from Amitabh

> Bachchan and Shatrughan Sinha, [so for] the second Chhath I called [the mainstream Hindi actor from Bihar] Shatrughan Sinha, with his wife. He knows what the importance of Chhath is. So Shatru came, and a certain atmosphere was formed. And because of that, "in Mumbai Chhath is happening," that became a news item.

The fact of the stage show, in other words, was central to the rapid up-take of Chhath across the country, as it led to national remediation of a Bihari festival, including its sonic worlds.

Stage shows in Bhojpuri, stereotypically high-energy and ribald, are central to the Bhojpuri music media ecosystem, as Ratnakar Tripathy has described (2012). Across North India, popular commercial stage shows have historically been more lucrative for singers than the recording contracts that follow from them, and the circulation of recorded music (which has been easy to pirate since the 1980s) is more important for a singer's publicity than for direct profits (Sundaram 2004). The Bhojpuri cassette culture that exploded in the 1980s grew out of, and also influenced, the sound and rhythm of stage shows, which in turn affected, and were influenced by, the songs of Bhojpuri cinema. Most of the personnel overlap throughout these three categories, and the rise of Bhojpuri cinema in the 2000s depended in large part on vocal and name recognition of the early heroes, most of whom were already well known on the stage show circuit before becoming film stars. Bhojpuri cinema in turn raised the profile of performers who then sang, danced, and joked in stage shows, often citing their own cinematic material and touting upcoming films. Artists such as Dinesh Lal Yadav, a hereditary Bihari *birha* singer and popular film actor, and Kalpana Patowary, who is originally from Assam, became household names in the Bhojpuri heartland, as well as in locations of migration such as Bombay and Delhi, through a combination of stage shows, recorded music, and cinema. Throughout the first decade of the twenty-first century, as Bhojpuri cinema's sonic aesthetics crystallized, the correlation of aesthetics and personnel among stage show, stand-alone music recording, and cinema soundtrack only increased.

The sound of Chhath stage shows emerged from and contributed to this multiply mediated sonic aesthetic concurrently with a new wave of cinema production. In fact Nirupam claims a direct relationship between the Chhath stage shows and early national publicity for the film that reintroduced the moribund Bhojpuri film industry in the early 2000s, *Sasura Bada Paisawala* (My Father-in-Law, the Rich Guy).

> In the second of third year, I started calling Manoj Tiwari, who's now a BJP MP [member of Parliament]. So nobody here knew who Manoj Tiwari was. He was from Banaras but he was a great singer, he sang in small programs [i.e., stage shows]. . . . This was in 1999 or 2000. So no one knew him then. At that time there had been no growth in Bhojpuri film. So he said, yes, I will sing, but listen, I have this film coming up, I need to do some promotion for that as well. Sasura Bada Paisawala. So I said ok, what's the problem with promoting Bhojpuri film? So he came, sang well, and told everyone that SBPW was coming, blah blah blah. When Manoj came, that was entirely live, across the whole country. So everyone heard and saw Manoj.

In reality, *Sasura Bada Paisawala* was released in 2004, so the promotion was not likely to have taken place in 1999 or 2000 but several years later. Nonetheless, by around 2006, Bhojpuri stage shows and cinema constituted a tightly wound aesthetic universe in which the existence of a coherent public of "Bhojpuri speakers" was assumed to stand apart from other mainstream Hindi speakers. That the people gathered to observe Chhath stage shows would also be interested in a Bhojpuri cinema revival was self-evident. Key to this aesthetic universe was primarily the *sound* of singers and stage shows, not the look of the films.

These sounds often troubled genre boundaries, transgressing bourgeois norms in which the devotional and erotic should be kept neatly separated. This melodic crossing of genres is not an uncommon practice. Ethnomusicologists across North India have long noticed that the same tune is often reused for many different sets of lyrics (Henry 2000). Some melodies align with a particular genre of song. There are dominant melodies, for instance, for the entire set of Bhojpuri songs called *sohar,* which are sung to welcome a newborn son into the family, and I have never heard those melodies transposed into *chatpata* songs. But melodies commonly migrate in the other direction, with *chatpata* songs recycled into bhajans. For instance, a family I knew in Varanasi invited a set of professional bhajan singers into its home to sing songs in praise of the goddess Shitala. One particular song was immediately identifiable as having the tune of an inescapably popular Bhojpuri *chatpata* song called "Lollipop Lagelu" (She's Like a Lollipop). The repetitive chorus, describing the woman's waist with the phrase "lollipop lagelu" (like a lollipop), was transformed by the bhajan singers to "bada neek lagelu" (it's very nice), describing the feeling of encountering the goddess. It would be difficult to describe the bhajan as a *chatpata* song as the so-called double-meaning sexualized lyrical content has been replaced with unambiguously pious devotional words. In the Bhojpuri recording industry and the singing practices that borrow from it, though, the boundaries between erotically charged *chatpata* songs and devotional bhajans are blurred at the level of melody, vocal timbre, and distortion. These fast-paced, autotuned bhajans are denotationally distinct, but they *sonically* connect devotional songs to sexually explicit ones.

Furthermore, in the context of stage shows, including Chhath stage shows, bhajans are mobilized as part of a much larger repertoire of *chatpata* genres. The singer Kalpana, for instance, explains her use of bhajans in her Bhojpuri stage shows as a calming tonic for a frenzied audience: "Then I would sing a bhajan. After the bhajan, people's gazes would become *saatvik*, very pure. And then I would sing a filmy song with many sexual innuendoes. So one minute the atmosphere would be very heated, then I would sing a bhajan and it would calm down" (Mullick 2015).

These connections between commercial popular music and bhajans are not new, nor have they been associated exclusively with Bhojpuri in particular. Manuel writes of an album of "disco-bhajans" using popular film songs, produced in the 1980s by film composer Bappi Lahiri and others. Journalist and film critic Subhash Jha declared the concept of a disco-bhajan "too ludicrous to be blasphemous," and Manuel's own interlocutors described the reuse of commercial tunes for bhajans as exclusively "for the front-benchers—the lower-class theater-goers who can only afford the cheap seats close to the screen" (Manuel 1991, 11). This differentiation of the "lower classes" as those who ludicrously take pleasure in listening to (or singing) songs with popular melodies and devotional lyrics has, in the sociohistorical moment I describe, been converted into a similar politics of audible distinction that differentiates based on language category.

The Sound of Addressing a Bhojpuri Public

By 2010 the recognizable Bhojpuri aesthetic of the stage show bhajan called forth a distinct sonic public on the beach, addressing Bhojpuri speakers as special and marginalized but nonetheless politically strong. Stage shows were already being explicitly used to carve out a Bhojpuri constituency by several political parties, both denotationally (by directly addressing a mass of presumably Bihari listeners) and aesthetically (by mobilizing Bhojpuri-sounding tropes). As Nirupam said several years later about this time period, Chhath "became a political statement."

The "political statement" of Chhath hinged directly on the sounds of Chhath stage shows, which were almost instantly a problem in Mumbai. Promoters (including Nirupam himself), city officials, and antimigrant politicians sparred over whether the shows were sufficiently devotional. As the shows took place during what was increasingly understood to be an important regional Hindu festival, it was difficult for the city to ban them outright; promoters such as Nirupam claimed repeatedly that the stage shows included only bhajans, which (taken at face value) accorded with the majoritarian municipal government's pro-Hindu stance. As discussed earlier, though, "bhajan" is a capacious category. The sonic practices that distinguished popular Bhojpuri bhajans from the hegemonic devotional sounds of normative national Hinduism, along with the interconnections between "Bhojpuri-sounding" aesthetics and other, nonsacred forms of music, seemed to be at the center of conflicts over space and sound on the beach. I now turn to those aesthetics in some detail based on a stage show I observed and recorded in 2010.

In 2010 the sound of the stage shows called forth a clearly demarcated Bhojpuri migrant public into the civic life of the city, often explicitly using Bhojpuri-specific sounds to challenge ideas about Bhojpuri migration. Every stage show was associated with a different cultural organization, each transparently linked to a political party. Regulations prevented the cultural organizations from using the names of parties directly, but large posters with recognizable faces of politicians were common that year. Temporary stages, constructed of bamboo and wood, were lashed firmly to seawalls in the back, facing the water. Intermittent stages roughly divided the beach into several zones. Groups of young men crowded the area in front of each stage, and in between thousands of families set up small temporary shrines, fixing long sugar cane stalks into pyramids directly over carefully arranged offerings of flowers, fruits, sweets, oil lamps, and incense.

Entertainment and devotion were demarcated spatially—no one mistook the stage shows for shrines and vice versa—but they intermixed easily, with no conflicts (or clear differentiations) between stage show audiences and devotees. Young men in particular moved easily and regularly from their families' puja sites to stage shows. Next to the largest stage was an enormous shrine covered in flowers, also on a stage. Throughout the night I spent on the beach in 2010, famous Bhojpuri actors, singers, and television personalities would occasionally walk up the steps to make offerings to the shrine, tracked as they went by camera operators on large cranes. Sprinkled throughout the beach were a series of water stations, improvised food stalls, and several giant monitors playing back the stage action on large screens to people slightly farther away. The cinematic qualities of the stage show were deliberately constructed to allow a seamless representation of the festivities on television throughout the country, but they also had a more proximal audience on the beach itself via the screens and loudspeakers set up alongside them. By turning a public puja into a mediatized event, the monitors represented migrants to themselves as a coherent migrant constituency even as they were being recorded for further representation throughout the country.

That year the sound of stage shows on Juhu Beach was fairly standardized; all, clearly, drew from the integrated system of recorded music, live music, and film music that defined the sound of Bhojpuri commercial music at the time. Like other Bhojpuri stage shows, Chhath stage shows in 2010 featured one main singer in addition to at least three different musicians playing live drums (either dholak or tabla or both), an electronic drum pad, and a keyboard synthesizer. Stage shows last many hours and cycle through periods in which the singer actively sings and dances alternating with interludes of spoken words, instrumental solos, and dramatic pauses. These shows explicitly addressed a collective of migrants from Bihar and UP in their denotational content, as well as their sonic particulars. A description of a few moments in one typical performance can illustrate this multimodal, regionally specific address, which is unmistakably Bhojpuri.

In a recording I made in the midst of a crowd of hundreds of men a few hundred yards back from a stage, the muscular voice of a female vocalist is mildly distorted with a deliberate echo effect and further warped by the amplification that transports her sound across the beach.[5] The stage show was clearly audible only within a few hundred yards of the stage and quickly faded into softer, muffled sound farther away. In the recording, the singer finishes a verse based on a popular melody well known across North India, "Chalat Musafir Moh Liya Re," from the 1966 film *Teesri Kasam* ("The Third Vow," directed by Basu Bhattacharya).[6] The two measures of the tune that directly precede the well-known chorus are repeated again and again as the singer increases in energy, pushing the listener's anticipation for melodic resolution. The crowd nearly drowns out the singer's words in the reworked lyrics of the song, but the chorus cuts through the chatter: "bolo jai jai Bihari" (say "victory to Biharis"!).

The singer belts the song from her chest in a style opposite the light near falsetto of Hindi film music popularized by Lata Mangeshkar.[7] The beat is driving, regular, and fast, staying steadily around 150 beats per minute throughout. The common four-beat *taal*, a cycle called *keherwa*, is kept by the bright, high-pitched dholak, an electronic drum kit, and the low swoop of the tabla's left-hand drum. The keyboard synthesizer follows the singer's melody, first mimicking the sound of a harmonium, and continues the incessant repetition of her two-measure phrase as the singer drops out for a few bars. The synthesizer switches to a variation in a high-pitched twangy *shehnai* modulation and then shifts again to imitate a violin following the original melody. The singer comes back in with standard Hindi lyrics, nearly shouting, "Rickshe chalaate hain, shaasan chalaate hain! Mehnat pe duniya ko paani pilaate hain!" (They drive rickshaws, they drive the government! When it comes to hard labor, they beat the whole world!).[8] Her voice trails off deliberately, and the music stops suddenly as the singer speaks clearly, above the din of the assembled viewers. "Lekhin bhaiyya," she says,. "jetnon se jetna qualification ba . . . jetnon se jetna kabiliyat ba . . . utna aadhar par apan Bihar, UP-Bihar ke log jil jahan ba, wahin jhanda kar lega" (But brother—whatever [educational] qualifications they have, whatever their capabilities, our Bihari and UP people, with that foundation, wherever they find themselves, they will plant their flag there [i.e., they will conquer that place].").

The interjection of speech described the loyalty of migrants from UP and Bihar to their home regions and was spoken in a mixed but iconically Bhojpuri form of speech (see, e.g., the Bhojpuri shibboleth *ba*). Even though the rest of the song was mostly sung in standard Hindi, this Bhojpuri spoken interlude made its regional address crystal clear. Finally, the singer ended the round with a rousing "Jai Chhatthi Maiyya ki!" (Victory to Mother Chhath!), the most common call of Chhath Puja.

In this short example, the hundreds of people gathered directly around the stage, and by extension the thousands of people on the beach on the night of Chhath, are directly addressed as Biharis with a familiar melody from a film (although, it should be noted, it was not a Bhojpuri film song and not in Bhojpuri). The lyrics of the song valorize the labor of North Indian migrants, interpellating them as Bhojpuri speakers (by addressing them in a stylized Bhojpuri during the spoken portion), workers, and Biharis. These identities were seen to invariably overlap in 2010, when controversies around Biharis in Mumbai—including the introduction of a new Marathi-language exam requirement for taxi and autorickshaw drivers that targeted migrant laborers, attacks on Bhojpuri-language cinema halls, and so forth—and general rhetoric assumed that North Indians in Mumbai were a unified bloc of Bhojpuri-speaking migrant laborers.[9] Language that centered Bihar (and sometimes UP) was echoed in other stage shows throughout the night as singers and politicians sang and spoke to their assembled listeners as "the people of UP and Bihar," "my Bihari brothers," and so forth.

But these overt, denotational references to Bihariness were equally echoed by the sonic particularity of the *nonlinguistic* sounds that issued from the stages. The fast-paced, driving beat of the dholak or its synthesized equivalent, the twang of a synthesizer standing in for a harmonium, the slightly warped, echoing modulation of the singer's throaty voice, the insistent repetition of the two measures before the chorus—all of these musical and sonic elements taken together unmistakably point to the aesthetic of Bhojpuri stage show music. Visual cues—the singer, in a well-spangled and tight-fitting *lehnga-chunni,* standing with mike in hand, pacing around the stage, raising her arms, and shaking her hips briefly in the moments between verses—provide further context to place the audiovisual performance as belonging to a specific regional performance stage show genre. The sonic environment of the beach allowed for multiple iterations of similar-sounding music, which together marked out the entire beach as a Bhojpuri, Bihari, and working-class space.

Sonic Conflicts

Conflicts around Chhath have centered on sound in particular. From the first decade of the twenty-first century, older, antimigrant, agonistic politics particular to Mumbai animated the discursive formulations of this festival. In the context of the pro-Marathi nativist politics that dominate the state of Maharashtra, Chhath often stands in for migrant politics *tout court.* This has been especially true for one of the most strenuously anti-Bhojpuri-migrant political parties, the Maharashtra Navnirman Sena (MNS).[10] Raj Thackeray, the leader of this party, wrote in an open letter to the city in 2008:

> Look at the people who come from Uttar Pradesh and Bihar: they enter the city with nothing and then after gaining a foothold they never mix up with the local people. In fact, after some time, they start organizing Chhath Puja and Uttar Pradesh Day and I object to this cultural hegemony. (Indo-Asian News Service 2008)

The way Chhath Puja publicly takes up space and resources shows off the numerical strength of the Bhojpuri-speaking community to the rest of the city. For a migrant community that is often disdained and certainly undercounted by official means (Bhagat 2015, 8), the large-scale observation of a festival that focuses on a rigorous fast demonstrates to the city that the community is pious, and also large enough to be politically important.

Even in the following years, regular political clashes annually threatened to prevent Chhath shows from taking place. In 2013 court cases challenged several of the cultural organizations that put on Chhath stage shows, arguing that they had violated the terms of their licenses in previous years by taking over too much of the beach and by amplifying music too loudly and far too late into the night. On November 9, 2013, the Mumbai-based *Business Standard* reported on the ongoing conflicts around Chhath stage shows as a conflict of interpretation. Were the Chhath shows religious or were they mere politicking? In a newspaper interview, Nirupam defended his commitment to Chhath, steadfastly casting the beach sounds as categorically religious.

> Dismissing political rivals' allegation that he uses the festival to garner votes, Nirupam said, "This is purely a religious and spiritual work." "This is a sacred occasion and there is no politics involved in it," Nirupam, who represents North Mumbai in Lok Sabha, said. (Press Trust of India 2013)

Another article from around the same time quoted Nirupam as saying, "Every Indian has a right to perform his religious duties and celebrate festivals" before explaining the ambivalently religious character of the celebrations: "To entertain the crowds, the organizers have hired Bhojpuri singers who will present devotional songs in Bhojpuri and Maithili—local dialects of Bihar." The debate in which Nirupam was intervening was not precisely over the connections between religion and politics in India, which are mostly taken for granted, especially under the current Hindu nationalist government. Instead, opposition to Chhath stage shows categorized them as noise, sounds out of place, unacceptable in the current sonic dispensation of public Hinduism and therefore entertainment, which could be collapsed into mere vote banking. The sounds of Chhath stage shows were too noisy, too fast paced, too Bihari, too *regional* to be acceptable as publicly consumable "devotional songs" despite the empirical elasticity of that category.

The situation was repeated in the following years. In 2015, in the weeks before Chhath, newspapers reported that Nirupam had approached the

Bombay High Court to challenge an order from the district collector's office. The controversy emerged when the district collector refused to issue a permit for the festival to the "cultural organization" headed by Nirupam "on the ground that it had violated noise pollution rules . . . laid down when permission was granted previously" (Press Trust of India 2015c). The earlier order had limited the size of stages on the beach and prohibited a fence between the stage and the spectators (ostensibly to discourage the practice of inviting celebrities to the stage). Most gallingly, the order from the district collector forbade Nirupam and his nongovernmental organization Bihari Front from inviting celebrities to the event, including singers. But the Bombay High Court upheld the order "after observing that an end needs to be put to celebration of festivals with songs and dances, instead of rituals" (Press Trust of India 2015b). After the district collector discursively categorized the soundscape of the beach as "noise pollution" to be discouraged, the High Court further singled out amplified devotional music in Bhojpuri as antithetical to authentic religious practice, which, it averred, should be marked with solemnity. The court's statements highlight the seeming bifurcation of cultural practices into "erotic" and "devotional," allowing for no overlap. One can imagine the soft sounds of normative Hindu bhajans playing in their minds as the members of the court censured the Bihari organization.

> With the Bombay High Court stating that song-and-dance events appear to have overtaken solemnity in the observance of Chhath Puja, various organisations involved in conducting Chhath Puja including those with political associations said Saturday they would abide by the court's orders while conducting the puja, an annual event for Biharis in the city. While the court said there was no restriction against assembling on beaches for the all-night puja and also that organisations could go ahead and provide assistance in crowd-management, mobile toilets and changing rooms, no mega event involving celebrity performers would be permitted. [Said the organizers,] "We have been assisting devotees for more than 12 years. We play devotional songs, we do not give our stage for film songs and dance. We should abide by the law so we will not play even devotional songs if the order says so." (Mishra 2015).

Nirupam ultimately prevailed again. The continued controversy has elaborated distinct sketches of "Biharis" or "Bhojpuri speakers" as aggrieved migrant collectives that are explicitly listening collectives. The issue of sound was central to both the court's opposition to the public practices and the politicians' claims of normative devotional legitimacy. The strict boundary claimed between "devotional songs" and "film songs and dance" allowed the collective of Bhojpuri attendees to be cast alternatively as pious Hindu devotees (posited by Nirupam) and an overexcited mass of celebrity-crazed young men (posited by the court). The idea of a "mega event with celebrity performers" was mapped onto the fast-paced, regional Bhojpuri sounds of Chhath stage shows past, which sonic connections to erotic *chatpata* film music made all too audible.

In the end, the Bombay High Court reversed its order and allowed performances to take place. According to a story published by the *Indian Express* on November 14, just three days before Chhath:

> Popular folk artistes and television stars are all set to be part of Chhath Puja celebrations in Mumbai even though the Bombay High Court had earlier observed that "celebrities" should not share the puja dais and "entertainment programmes" must not be staged. Bowing to demands from organisers, the Maharashtra government has permitted artistes to perform religious and traditional Chhath songs on the puja stage. (Ashar 2015)

Chastened, the Chhath organizers had to comply more carefully with restrictions on "noise," but the stage shows did go on. The optics of shutting down a Hindu festival completely were likely bad enough to cause the Hindu-nationalist government to pause, as became even clearer in subsequent years.

The Sound of Homogeneous, Empty Hinduism

In 2014 the BJP, ascendant in the early 2000s, again came to power on a platform of developmentalism and Far Right exclusionary Hindu nationalism. In addition to a major national electoral victory late that year, local and state-level political gains for the BJP swept across Mumbai and Maharashtra. The changes in the national political field have had far-reaching consequences for the articulation of a collective UP/Bihari migrant identity in Mumbai. Chhath has emerged as a central node through which pro-migrant politicians have addressed constituents not as migrants but as pious Hindus whose regional affiliation inflects, but does not overshadow, their nationally salient religious identity. It was in this climate of highly politicized support for Hinduness, or "Hindutva," that the outright suppression of Bhojpuri speakers' Hindu religious observances was untenable.

From October 12th to November 5th, voters in Bihar cast their ballots for members of the state legislative assembly in a five-stage election process that was reported breathlessly by the national media.: Bihar's election was widely seen to be a regional test for how well the national Narendra Modi–led BJP government was faring. Many newspapers carefully covered the "migrant vote," refocusing attention on Bihari and Bhojpuri-speaking residents of Mumbai as a recognized vote bank.

Thus, by 2015, even as Nirupam was battling the city of Mumbai in court to have his Chhath stage shows allowed on the beach, the BJP was changing its tune on targeting Bhojpuri migrants in general and using Chhath to do so in particular. For decades the party had been aligned with the state-level pro-Hindu Shiv Sena party, which was formed around antimigrant sentiment in 1966. But in 2015 the Shiv Sena was mostly quiet on the issue of migration, and a spokesman even explicitly claimed that it "never started any movement against any migrant from other states (including Bihari migrant [*sic*])" (Press Trust of India 2015a). The BJP at the time was both the national ruling party and the ruling party of the state of Maharashtra, and it went even further, declaring its intention to sponsor Chhath festivities of its own, also on Juhu Beach. From a little-known regional holiday, Chhath had become thoroughly synonymous with migrant politics on a national scale, as well as a normative locus for soliciting a Bihari migrant vote in both Bihar and Mumbai. Biharis would be "[key to the] Mumbai civic polls next year [in 2016], and parties are set to woo them with chhath pujas on November 17 [the date of Chhath 2015]. Sanjay Nirupam's pandal[11] on Juhu beach is an annual crowd-puller. For the BJP, Phool Singh said the BJP has plans [for] a grand show, including Bhojpuri stars. 'Even the Maharashtra CM [Chief Minister] is expected to attend,' he said" (Phadke and Ashar 2015). Perhaps its national plan for dominance, which was based on conquering UP, led the BJP to reconsider its strategy for dealing with migrants from the Hindi belt in Maharashtra (Vishvanathan 2014). Or perhaps the party was pressured by the demographic shift in Mumbai itself, where people from UP and Bihar were said to number more than 22 lakh (2.2 million). In any case, the political situation had lurched into a new alignment, and the sonic elements of this shift were immediately audible.

In 2016 stages were again erected across the beach, and most of them were aesthetically similar, both in look and in sound, to those I had observed in 2010. One stage show, organized by the Bihari Front and associated with the Congress Party, looked and sounded strikingly similar to the shows I had heard in 2010. Sanjay Nirupam, now president of the Congress Party in Mumbai, again organized the show. The temporary stage faced the beach, draped with red cloth and sporting a large sign inscribed with Nirupam's face and extending "to the fasting and the faithful of Chhath, a hearty welcome!" in large Devanagari letters. Although the words "Congress Party" were absent from the stage by court order, when asked, people in the crowd knew exactly which political party was paying for the entertainment. Just as they had in 2010, by late afternoon a crush of perhaps five hundred people, almost all men, surrounded the stage.

As before, musical accompanists were grouped at stage left—the tabla and dholak players seated, the men playing the electronic drum kit and synthesizer standing. The electronic drum kit and distorted synthesizer playing that familiar beat—*dhak dhakadhak dhakadha*—began to place the music even before the language of the song identified it as Bhojpuri. Performers cycled through, pacing, dancing and clapping across the stage. In front of the stage, two hundred or so men sat on a long, heavy-duty green cloth. Hundreds more stood, pushing into the two hundred meters or so between the bamboo fence near the stage and the edge of the ocean. Although it was not part of the overtly Bihari-identified ritual spaces made by families nearby, the stage show area was nonetheless lexically, sonically, and visibly marked as a Bhojpuri space by the linguistic content of the songs and the sound of the synthesized drum. The Bhojpuri film star Ravi Kishan paced in front of Nirupam himself, addressing the assembled people before him as *bhaiyyas* (brothers), here a reclaimed derogatory term used in Mumbai for people from UP and Bihar. ["One time, with love, raise your hands because everyone's a *bhaiyya*! Raise your hands!"] Over the resonant call of a conch, closely identified with public worship, Kishan shouted slowly and deliberately "har har Mahadev!," an invocation of the god Shiva that specifically indexes the Bhojpuri-speaking city Varanasi. In a video of this moment, which was widely disseminated online, the pan to the crowd audiovisually connected the film star, the politician, the hundreds of assembled men, and the festival itself—with sound marking the space as one of Bhojpuri political-religious assembly.

The *Times of India* reported that the BJP government was sponsoring twelve public Chhath celebrations in different parts of the city, including the all-important function at Juhu Beach, and the party did not disappoint (Times News Network 2015). A mere two hundred yards to the south of the Congress Party stage, another, quite different stage show was assembled. Whereas the Congress stage was red, the BJP's was draped in white cloth. Whereas the singers on the Congress stage *stood* and danced, the singers on the BJP stage sat while performing. And in contrast to the sounds of the Congress stage, the musicians on the BJP stage played tabla and harmonium with no synthesizer and no electric drum kit. A female singer sat in a rust-colored sari, singing with her hands in her lap, occasionally raising one of her palms with the midtempo beat for emphasis. Her voice stayed round, smooth, and measured, rarely leaving a single midrange octave in a recognizable bhajan to Chhatti Maiyya, the goddess of Chhath, ending with a thrice-repeated chorus (a *tihai*). Quite unlike the great pains taken by singers and politicians to directly address Biharis (as in the show described from 2010) or *bhaiyyas* (as in the show taking place on the same evening just down the beach), this singer came to the end of her song and, like all other performers, exhorted listeners to say, "Chhatti Maiyya ki jai ho!" (Victory to Mother Chhath!). After the singer finished, a man came onstage to introduce her as Shoba Bannerjee and then proceeded to speak in high Hindi, with no recognizable Bhojpuri inflection, despite the fact that the song itself used modified Bhojpuri grammar.

The look and feel of the stage brought to mind a semiclassical vocal concert of the sort often put on by colleges or arts organizations, and the sound matched this visually neutral performance context. The singer's voice and the instrumentation were surprisingly shorn of any regional Bhojpuri or Bihari sonic signifiers despite the fact that, linguistically, the performance was partially in Bhojpuri. Sanjay Nirupam's sounds of "glamour" were absent.

The visible markers of a Chhath Puja political appeal were also distinctly different. A large, well-policed, and rather empty VIP area was fenced off in front of the BJP's stage. Slightly closer to the ocean an area was fenced off exclusively for families conducting puja. To the right and left of the stage, the bamboo barrier fences abutted roads that were continually cleared of people by police patrolling the area. The masses of men crowding the stage that were addressed by the other Chhath shows were simply not physically allowed to assemble. The BJP stage refused to participate in the established visual or sonic sign systems of Bhojpuri political communication.

Conclusion: From Noise to New Futures

By convening and addressing the Bhojpuri crowd with the audiovisual particulars that bleed into other Bhojpuri stage show aesthetics, including the *chatpata* eroticized aesthetics of Bhojpuri cinema, other stage shows index their alignment with a certain form of pro-lower-class North Indian migrant politics. The group of families conducting puja collected in front of the BJP stage could not be read the same way. By definition, these families were not the all-male, lower-class crowd associated with Bhojpuri mass mediation. The white cloth, the sitting musicians, and the sonic diacritics of bourgeois, North Indian light classical music are all signs of a specifically *Hindu* propriety.

Absent "glamour," film stars, or indeed any recognizable aesthetic elements that configured the beach into a sonically regional Bihari space, the BJP's stage show instead addressed onlookers as primarily a middle-class Hindu collective. This was made denotationally explicit in a televised news clip in which the head of the Mumbai BJP said, in Marathi, "Every year in Mumbai, in Maharashtra, and in the whole country, there's Chhath Puja. . . . It's a very important part of Hindu culture." Not mentioning Bihar, and quite factually pointing out that Chhath is celebrated in Mumbai, he foregrounded the Hinduness of the festival above all else, expanding "Hindu culture" to include a regional element that his very party had worked against until recently. But he scarcely needed to make such a proclamation, for the sonic elements of the stage show had already identified the event as distinct from, or even diametrically opposed to, the other shows nearby.

Distinct sonic addresses do not necessarily shift the political commitments of the addressees themselves. People on the beach may have been moved or entertained or bored by any of the shows described here. But, by examining the politicized soundscape on the beach during Chhath Puja, distinct forms of political alignment come into focus in which Bhojpuri migrants are imagined as certain kinds of electoral potentialities. To tune our ears to the slight differences in tempo, timbre, and sound of these stage shows helps shed light on political difference, particularly on the novelty of the regional collectivity being ushered into the political arena by the BJP. The address of Bhojpuri speakers as normative Hindus does not come at the level of denotational speech or even the level of language. This new imagination of Bhojpuri migrants as part of a mainstream bloc of homogeneous Hindus is not encountered as a newly shared vision as much as it is made available to be heard as a distinct set of sounds.

Notes

1. Thanks very much to Laura Brueck and Jacob Smith for convening the Sounds of South Asia series and to all the other participants, especially Jayson Beaster-Jones, Praseeda Gopinath, Roanne Kantor, Neepa Majumdar, and Aswin Punathambekar for their incisive comments. Research for this project was made possible by a Mellon fellowship from Washington University in St. Louis, where I was buoyed by the scholarly support of Joseph Loewenstein. Earlier versions were presented at the Association for Asian Studies-in-Asia annual meeting in 2018, at a special talk given at the Indian Institute for Advanced Study in 2017, and at the Yale South Asia working group coordinated by Kalyanakrishnan Sivaramakrishnan. Thanks to everyone who engaged with the paper in these events, and especially to Dr. Sivaramakrishnan for his continued encouragement. Piyush Pandya offered nuanced second opinions on translations (though any errors remain my own). Finally, thanks to Ted Gordon for recent insights on sound, and to the anonymous reviewers for their helpful comments

2. In addition to stage shows, political parties and their associated cultural organizations sponsored water stations, portable toilets, changing tents for ladies (for use after their sacred dip into the sea), temporary beach-side temples, low-cost food stalls, and crowd control from the local police department.

3. In particular, this version of the soundscape was elaborated by scholars and artists connected to Simon Fraser University's World Soundscape Project, which began in the late 1960s, through projects on "acoustic ecology" and noise pollution. Later iterations of the "soundscape" steer away from questions around the moral imperative of a "clean" sound environment and toward ontological questions about sound itself (see Kane 2013), as well as social conditions of sound production and reception (see Samuels et al. 2010; Faudree 2012).

4. As Lelyveld (1994, 120–21) has described it, an appropriately bourgeois "light" classical music was developed and codified in part through All India Radio's experiments in the 1950s with broadcasting "light music to counter-blast bad film music" (120). Studios had "classical musicians along with poets to compose two songs a week" in regional studios (121). The "light" designation now falls on such melodic genres as thumri, chaiti, and kajri, all sung during particular times of the year and related to folk forms.

5. I had not originally planned to make field recordings during my 2010 visit to Juhu Beach during Chhath, so these first recordings were ad hoc and of fairly low quality. Nonetheless they help capture some of the sonic particularity of the event.

6. It is difficult to say whether the singer had in mind the song from *Teesri Kasam* precisely. The film version of the song has been remade and remixed many times since the 1960s, including an early Indipop hit by the Punjabi band Joshilay on Malini Awasthi's 2009 pop-folk album *Purbaiyya* and most recently in the 2017 Hindi film *Badrinath ki Dulhania* (dir. Shashank Khaitan). It is likely that the tune I recorded (and possibly its words) are a reworked folk song, plausibly from the Bhojpuri-speaking belt in UP and Bihar. It is telling that Surabhi Sharma (2009) describes the same song with very similar lyrics sung at a Chhath celebration on Juhu Beach a few years prior to this, a fact I realized only on rereading Sharma's article for the writing of this one. Apparently these lyrically pro-Bihari songs have been reused at least once.

7. See chapter 5, by Pavitra Sundar in this volume, for more on the distinction between "light" and "heavy" voices and the aesthetic, generic, and moral between these vocal qualities.

8. Literally, this line means "they make the world drink water"; however, idiomatically "to make [someone] drink water" can mean "to conquer" or "beat." Given the general tenor of the song, I have chosen this idiomatic translation. Thanks to Piyush Pandya for the suggestion.

9. This idea of a homogenized bloc of Bhojpuri speakers is contested, most notably by certain upper-class Biharis who have worked to redefine Bihari culture as (at least partially) upscale and urban. See Hardy (2017) for a discussion of a music video made for Chhath Puja that depicted Bhojpuri speakers as cosmopolitan consumers grappling with questions of urban-rural identity.

10. In 2006, Raj Thackeray split from his uncle Bal Thackeray's older nativist Shiv Sena Party, which was itself founded decades before on an antimigrant platform—a platform that targeted mostly Tamil-speaking South Indians. The Shiv Sena went on to align itself with anti-Muslim Hindu chauvinist policies in the 1990s. Raj Thackeray announced that his new party, the MNS, would continue to espouse the "sons of the soil" stances for which the Shiv Sena had been known. But unlike the older party, the MNS's antimigrant ideology was particularly centered on so-called Hindi-speaking North Indians, by which they explicitly meant labor migrants from UP and Bihar, a largely Bhojpuri-speaking population. From 2006 to 2008, Raj Thackeray established the MNS's antimigrant credentials by stoking violence against North Indians generally and Bhojpuri speakers in particular, circulating a series of incendiary letters and speeches, provoking attacks against cinema halls showing Bhojpuri films, and encouraging violence against "North Indians" themselves. In 2008 the MNS attained some political success, especially in cosmopolitan Mumbai and its outskirts, where ethnolinguistic xenophobia and a precarious tightening labor market has allowed a politics of communitarian mistrust to flourish. This success has been reversed in recent years, but it was at the center of anti-Bhojpuri migrant politics from around 2008 to 2010, and the political rhetoric continues to circulate.

11. A pandal is a temporary platform built for the purpose of publicly displaying and venerating a god or goddess, or for performing rituals. Here, "pandal" refers to the complex of stage, temporary ritual platform, and associated structures built for the purpose of Chhath on the beach.

Works Cited

Abbi, Kumool. 2013. "Politics of Linguistic, Cultural Recovery, and Reassertion: Bhojpuri Migrant Population and Its Films." *Economic and Political Weekly* 48, no. 33: 54–62.

Ashar, Sandeep. 2015. "Chhath Puja at Juhu Beach: Maharashtra Govt Permits Performances by Folk, TV Artistes." *Indian Express*, November 14. Accessed November 15, 2015. https://indianexpress.com/article/cities/mumbai/chhath-puja-at-juhu-beach-maharashtra-govt-permits-performances-by-folk-tv-artistes/

Bhagat, Ram B. 2015. *World Migration Report, 2015: Urban Migration Trends, Chal-*

lenges, and Opportunities in India. Mumbai: International Institute for Population Sciences.

Cronon, William. 1996. *Uncommon Ground: Rethinking the Human Place in Nature.* New York: Norton.

Doron, Assa, and Robin Jeffrey. 2013. *The Great Indian Phone Book: How the Cheap Cell Phone Changes Business, Politics, and Daily Life.* Cambridge, MA: Harvard University Press.

Faudree, Paja. 2012. "Music, Language, and Texts: Sound and Semiotic Ethnography." *Annual Review of Anthropology* 41: 519–36.

Hardy, Kathryn C. 2010. "Mediating Bhojpuriya: Migration, Circulation, and Bhojpuri Cinema." *South Asian Popular Culture* 8, no. 3: 231–44.

Hardy, Kathryn C. 2014. "Becoming Bhojpuri: Production of Cinema and Production of Language in Post-liberalization India." PhD diss., University of Pennsylvania.

Hardy, Kathryn C. 2017. "How to Do Things with Viral Videos: Spectacular Performativity, Global Networks, and the Region." Paper presented at the international seminar Regional Cultures and New Media Technologies, April 27, Indian Institute of Advanced Study, Shimla, India.

Henry, Edward O. 2000. "Folk Song Genres and Their Melodies in India: Music Use and Genre Process." *Asian Music* 31, no. 2: 71–106.

Indo-Asian News Service. 2008. "Thackeray Continues Tirade against North Indians." *Daily News Analysis,* February 16. Accessed September 2, 2010. https://www.dnaindia.com/mumbai/report-thackeray-continues-tirade-against-north-indians-1151247

Kane, Brian. 2013. "Eleven Theses on Sound and Transcendence." *Current Musicology,* no. 95: 7–26.

Kantor, Hayden. 2016. "'We Earn Less Than We Eat': Food, Farming, and the Caring Family in Bihar, India." PhD diss., Cornell University.

Kumar, Awanish. 2009. "A Class Analysis of the 'Bihari Menace.'" *Economic and Political Weekly* 44, no. 28: 124–27.

Lelyveld, David. 1994. "Upon the Subdominant: Administering Music on All-India Radio." *Social Text,* no. 39: 111–27.

Manuel, Peter. 1991. *Cassette Culture: Popular Music and Technology in North India.* Chicago: University of Chicago Press.

Manuel, Peter. 2012. "Popular Music as Popular Expression in North India and the Bhojpuri Region, from Cassette Culture to VCD Culture." *South Asian Popular Culture* 10, no. 3: 223–36.

Mishra, Santoshee Gulabkali. 2015. "Song and Dance Not Part of Chhath Puja: Bombay HC." *Indian Express,* October 25. Accessed November 1, 2015. http://indianexpress.com/article/cities/mumbai/song-and-dance-not-part-of-chhath-puja-bombay-hc/

Mullick, Disha. 2015. "'I Became Used to the Fact That When I Sing, Guns Go Off': Bhojpuri Star Kalpana Patowary." *Scroll.in,* September 15. Accessed October 10, 2015. http://scroll.in/article/751173/i-became-used-to-the-fact-that-when-i-sing-guns-go-off-bhojpuri-star-kalpana-patowary

Novak, David, and Matt Sakakeeny, eds. 2015. *Keywords in Sound.* Durham, NC: Duke University Press.

Phadke, Manasi, and Sandeep Ashar. 2015. "To Many, Their Work in Mumbai Comes before Their Votes in Bihar." *Indian Express*, October 26. Accessed November 1, 2015. https://indianexpress.com/article/india/india-news-india/to-many-their-work-in-mumbai-comes-before-their-votes-in-bihar/

Press Trust of India. 2013. "Thousands Celebrate Chhath Puja in Mumbai." *Business Standard*, November 9. Accessed November 12, 2013. https://www.business-standard.com/article/pti-stories/thousands-celebrate-chhath-puja-in-mumbai-113110900690_1.html

Press Trust of India. 2015a. "Never Took Anti-migrant Stand: Shiv Sena with Eye on Bihar Polls." *Hindustan Times*, October 10. Accessed October 15, 2015. https://www.hindustantimes.com/india/never-took-anti-migrant-stand-shiv-sena-with-eye-on-bihar-polls/story-0CaEsHAhtbU1fKBLuyWNqO.html

Press Trust of India. 2015b. "Stop Songs and Dances sans Rituals during Festivals in Public Places: Bombay High Court." *NDTV.com*, October 23. Accessed November 1, 2015. https://www.business-standard.com/article/pti-stories/thousands-celebrate-chhath-puja-in-mumbai-113110900690_1.html

Press Trust of India. 2015c. "Why Do You Want Celebrities for Chhath Puja: High Court to Bihari Front." *NDTV.com*, November 9. Accessed April 5, 2019. https://www.ndtv.com/india-news/why-do-you-want-celebrities-for-chhath-puja-high-court-to-bihari-front-1241856

Samuels, David W., Louise Meintjes, Ana Maria Ochoa, and Thomas Porcello. 2010. "Soundscapes: Toward a Sounded Anthropology." *Annual Review of Anthropology* 39: 329–45.

Schafer, R. Murray. 2012. "The Soundscape." In *The Sound Studies Reader*, edited by Jonathan Sterne, 95–103. New York: Routledge.

Sharma, Surabhi. 2009. "Bidesia in Bombay." *Inter-Asia Cultural Studies* 10, no. 4, 609–19.

Sundar, Pavitra. 2008. "Meri Awaaz Suno: Women, Vocality, and Nation in Hindi Cinema." *Meridians* 8, no. 1: 144–79.

Sundaram, Ravi. 2004. "Uncanny Networks: Pirate, Urban, and New Globalisation." *Economic and Political Weekly* 39, no. 1: 64–71.

Thompson, Emily. 2004. *The Soundscape of Modernity: Architectural Acoustics and the Culture of Listening in America, 1900–1933*. Cambridge, MA: MIT Press.

Times News Network. 2016. "BJP Pulls Out All Stops for Chhath Puja." *Times of India*, November 5. Accessed November 6, 2016. https://timesofindia.indiatimes.com/city/mumbai/BJP-pulls-out-all-stops-for-Chhath-Puja/articleshow/55251430.cms

Tripathy, Ratnakar. 2007. "Bhojpuri Cinema." *South Asian Popular Culture* 5, no. 2: 145–65.

Tripathy, Ratnakar. 2012. "Music Mania in Small-Town Bihar: Emergence of Vernacular Identities." *Economic and Political Weekly* 47, no. 22: 58–66.

Tripathy, Ratnakar, and Jitendra Verma. 2011. "Identities in Ferment: Reflections on the Predicament of Bhojpuri Cinema, Music, and Language in Bihar." In *Indian Mass Media and the Politics of Change*, edited by Somnath Batabyal, Angad Chowdhry, Meenu Gaur, and Matti Pohjonen, 93–121. New Delhi: Routledge.

UNESCO. 2013. *Social Inclusion of Internal Migrants in India: Internal Migration in India Initiative.* New Delhi: United Nations Educational, Scientific and Cultural Organization.

Visvanathan, Shiv. 2014. "Narendra Modi's Symbolic War." *Economic and Political Weekly* 49, no. 23: 10–13.

THREE | It's Rocking? Exploring Sound and Intimacy through Mumbai's Faltering Indipop Music Industry

PETER KVETKO

With a notebook and portable cassette recorder in hand, I headed off for my first formal interview with one of the trailblazing executives in the Indian popular music industry. As I stumbled over dusty, broken pavement and found shelter in the shade to await the next red double-decker bus, I reflected on the extraordinary physical transformation taking place all around me. It was the year 2000, a year that had animated my imagination since childhood. But in millennial Mumbai, the year 2000 represented not so much an achievement of living "in the future" as a hurtling movement toward the future.

The rubble surrounding my bus stop looked as if it were connected to a single, continuous trench running throughout the entire city. All of Mumbai, it seemed, was being dug up to lay down internet cable. This in turn was part of a broader reconstruction of the material contexts of everyday life, particularly in the city's more affluent western suburbs. But for people across India's vast geographic and social terrain, the rapid transformations brought on by liberalization at the end of the Cold War could be measured not only in economic terms but also in ways that were physical and environmental, corporeal and sensory, psychological and existential, visual and even aural.

The physical transformations and their impact on the corporeal experience were often the most immediate and included a growing expectation of air-conditioning, burgeoning modes of personal home entertainment, and privatizing experiences brought on by cell phones, ATM machines, portable music players, and video games. Similarly, the transformations of everyday life manifested themselves visually with every glance at the changing cityscape, the proliferation of satellite dishes and planned communities, and the diminishing and increasingly peripheral presence of state-run institutions and services.[1] And in the course of my ethnographic and historical research on the contours of nonfilm popular music in Mumbai since the 1960s, I found that these new modes of intimacy, embodiment, and citizenship emerging alongside India's neoliberal transformation could be listened to in daily life and were being sounded through the studio recordings of artists working independently of the film music industry and producing what had become known as Indipop music.

My bus journey that day was to take me to the headquarters of Magnasound, a record company that played a central role in producing "private albums" meant to compete with the Bollywood soundtracks that had dominated the North Indian market for decades. To get to the office, I descended past rows of auto body shops, cigarette stalls, and the ruins of an abandoned cotton mill. Like many of Mumbai's hip new businesses at that time, Magnasound had built its headquarters inside the walls of an old textile mill where during the nineteenth century much of Bombay's wealth was made. The physical presence of the city's history has continued to make itself felt in ways such as this, indexing the complex and enduring ties between a colonial past and the neoliberal present.

Passing through a guarded gate with the word Laxmi faded but visible above the guardhouse, I turned the corner and spotted a door with the Magnasound logo etched on a frosted glass window. As I entered, I was hit with a cooling blast of air-conditioning and met by two smartly dressed greeters who asked me to register at the welcome desk. Looking around, I noticed several televisions showing various music channels, a large tank filled with tropical fish, and a music-themed neon sculpture on the wall. The office of Magnasound's founder and director, Shashi Gopal, was in full view of the waiting area. The front wall of his office was made of glass, so while I waited I saw eager young employees slipping in and out of his office, Gopal answering a steady barrage of phone calls, and his executive assistant, whose office was in a loft directly above Gopal's desk, bouncing up and down the small staircase in the corner of Gopal's office.

Soon I was invited inside the director's office, and while Gopal continued a phone conversation I scanned the many photos hanging on the office walls: Gopal with Daler Mehndi, the Colonial Cousins, and other Indipop icons. I also noted a large photo of a smiling Shashi Gopal shaking hands with former president George H. W. Bush. Hanging up the phone, Magnasound's top executive greeted me warmly and began our conversation by contrasting the transparency of his office with what he saw as the typical behind-closed-doors or under-the-table activity of the film music industry establishment in Mumbai. Gopal's ambition and optimism were palpable, and I learned that Magnasound was planning to "go public" and offer stock on Bombay's Dalal Street market.

Within a few years, however, the Indipop bubble would burst. Despite the fact that Napster had been launched the previous year, neither Gopal nor I brought up the topic of the MP3 or its potential to transform both listening practices and the global music industry. And, while Apple released its first version of iTunes in early 2001 and sold its first iPods later that fall, the biggest concerns of artists and executives that I observed throughout my interviews at that time were that Indian music television channels were too focused on Bollywood to devote sufficient time to nonfilm artists and that the Indipop scene had grown too quickly and been inundated by aspiring acts with only mediocre talent. For the purposes of this chapter, then, I will focus my attention on the resonances of sound, citizenship, and intimacy in Indipop songs and videos, particularly those released by Magnasound during its heyday in the 1990s.

The Emergence of Magnasound and the "Made in India" Phenomenon

At its start, Magnasound had secured a deal to distribute and sell Western pop music from the Warner Music catalog. The company became the official intermediary between Indian audiences and global pop's biggest names, especially Madonna, Eric Clapton, and Phil Collins, along with classic groups like The Doors and Led Zeppelin. Thanks to its sales of international music, Magnasound was positioned to experiment with local talent. As Gopal explained it to me:

> The intention really was to deliver good quality music on a simultaneous release basis in India. Use their repertoire availability which was given to me on a royalty basis. Earn money. Send them royalties. And use the other money for investing into diverse programming. So we did business with Warner for about seven years. For seven years we did

> a lot for international music. What we did was we pioneered simultaneous releases in India, so to that extent people were happy with us. We uplifted quality. We gave them new heat-proof boxes, better recording quality. We gave them CDs, we gave them a lot of good marketing, proposals, merchandise, posters, you know, exactly as a company would service their products abroad, we did the same amount of service here. And we got a fairly good name for doing all that. Which is why we were in a position to start pop in India.

Two things stand out in Gopal's narrative. First, the dialectical relationship between India and the West is not only discursive but indeed built into the very business model of the company. As notions of Indian citizenship transform amid the flows of globalization, the West stands as a cultural Other for identity building, but the West also offers material resources for domestic industry building. This dynamic was somewhat optimistically referred to as "reverse colonization" during an MTV India–sponsored forum in 2000 on the state of the Indian music industry (see Kvetko 2004). Yet the discursive construction of "us" versus "them" also extends to the urban, cosmopolitan producers of popular culture such as Gopal discursively opposing themselves to the "them" of everyday Indian consumers whose lives are seen to be improved with these material and sonic innovations.

Thus, the second theme emerging from this quote has to do with Gopal's emphasis on the high quality of the sound, particularly in relation to what, for Indipop artists and executives at that time, was the much-maligned elephant in the room: the Bollywood soundtrack. With its unrealistically reverberant vocal tracks and ostentatiously large orchestration, the mainstream film music sound of the 1980s and 1990s didn't sit well with the newly emerging modes of privatized consumption that accompanied liberalization. Indipop offered a sonic experience that was more in line with the embodied experiences of music television, personal stereos, and private listening.

Yet, as this volume intends to prove, terms such as *sound, voice, resonance, space,* and *embodiment* are far from universal and must instead by understood within specific cultural and sociohistorical contexts. From Pavitra Sundar's chapter on the unique embodied voice of pop singer Usha Uthup to Neepa Majumdar's piece on late colonial era anxieties about female public performance in the "rage sequences" of Shanta Apte and Praseeda Gopinath's argument that Narendra Modi's political orations produce a distinctively embodied sonic neoliberal authoritarian masculinity, contemporary research has begun to reformulate some of the basic tenets of sound studies by grounding these ideas in particular ethnographic contexts. For many Indipop listeners at the end of the last century, the "global imagination" (see Appadurai 1990; Erlmann 1999; and others) evoked in the songs of Indipop artists such as Daler Mehndi, Alisha Chinai, or the Colonial Cousins created linkages that were rooted in embodied feelings and aural sensations of intimacy and citizenship in the context of specifically Indian experiences of globalization.

When I asked Shashi Gopal to tell me about his company's biggest hit song, Alisha Chinai's "Made in India," he immediately began his response by referencing Indian immigration amid the liberalization of India's formal economy and the information technology (IT) boom of the 1990s.

> With Alisha, we had this huge hit called "Made in India." Now what was the timing with "Made in India?" "Made in India" was actually recorded with Biddu in the UK. India was under a very protective environment for many, many years. The doors had to be opened. The world pressure on a country like ours was to open the doors and have free and fair competition, if you wanted support from funds like IMF and the World Bank. They wanted to see real demand. . . .
>
> I figured out that a lot of people, because I used to travel to England, didn't know what India was all about. Just like we didn't know what Russia was all about. A lot of non-resident Indians living abroad weren't really proud to be Indians. They were very submissive. They were very aware that, whether they were in England or they were in America, that they were immigrants, and that immigrants don't necessarily have to have a big say.

The release of "Made in India" coincided with the spread of satellite television in South Asia and the reentry of MTV into the Indian market, and its sounds and images offered an iconic reference to economic liberalization. Knowing that Magnasound's videos would be shown alongside those of Western superstars, Gopal invested heavily in the production of a quality video that could measure up to the "free and fair competition" of the global music market. Although he was then staying in the United Arab Emirates, he came back to Mumbai specifically to oversee Alisha's transformation from her earlier incarnation as an Indian version of Madonna to a *swadeshi* symbol of autonomy and confidence.

> I came from Dubai specifically on that product, and I said, "Hey listen, junk all that shit. You don't use that. Alisha has to be brought in as a princess. India is a land of princesses." And I said, "If need be, let's try to bring some people from the foreign lands coming here and trying to woo our princess." And [Alisha] says, "No, I want to go for an Indian. And let's make that Indian look very smart." And it worked. The video was all about leopards and snakes and Kathakali dancers, and you know . . . Alisha coming and looking gorgeous in that crown of hers. And eventually she gets a suitor, and the final suitor who comes out was Milind Soman, who was one of our best models in town—who really looked good, compared to everybody else. Hey, hey, hey, these Indians are pretty good, and listen I'm pretty proud to be an Indian.

The song and the video combine to function as both an orientalist fantasy for the foreign tourist and an act of nationalist propaganda for Indian consumers at home and abroad. "Made in India" can be read, therefore, as a marker of national origin as the song is exported to the global marketplace. Given the original context of the song, however (e.g., the Indian media was embarking on a project of national self-evaluation to coincide with its fiftieth year of independence), the label "Made in India" also articulates to Indians themselves an image of nationalistic pride and authenticity.[2]

The song itself has several features that were characteristic of Indipop music in the 1990s. First, the lyrics are a mix of Hindi and English, with the catchy chorus proclaiming, "Made in India, made in India / *ek dil chaahiye* (I need a heart) that's made in India." One of the most interesting features of "Made in India" is that the title is taken from the chorus of the song and not from the first line. This runs counter to the standard form of conventional Bollywood film songs (as well as many classical and folk music templates) in which the initial line of the song serves as the most memorable and most repeated line. In the structure of Chinai's song, the opening verse functions as a buildup to the refrain "Made in India." Alisha's vocal style enhances this affect. Her voice is deep and strong, and she practically chants the opening verse: "dekhi hai sari duniya, japan se le ke russia" (I've seen all the world, from Japan to Russia). The word Russia is given three distinct and aggressive syllables. As she concludes the verse, however, her vocal style changes to a more open, singing style. Her voice climbs higher as she sings "australia se le ke america-a-a-a," suggesting an iconic musical metaphor for the expanding narratives of freedom and celebrity in the countries she names. As she reaches the chorus, her articulation becomes smoother as the melody descends again. Musically, the producer Biddu uses melodic and harmonic materials (such as the climbing chanted verse and a jagged triplet riff) as a way to build tension, which will ultimately be released in the song's sing-along refrain. Like many Western pop songs, the piece employs a verse-chorus-bridge form, with "the hook" of the song designed to be its most enticing and saleable sonic feature.

The images in the music video for "Made in India" are equally compelling. The story is a classic one. Alisha is an Indian princess being wooed by male suitors from all over the world. Each man arrives at her court in stereotypical dress for his culture area. One by one, Alisha dismisses them with a wave. She then consults a fortune-teller whose crystal ball reveals her future. A brawny Indian man arrives in a wooden crate labeled "Made in India." After erupting from the crate shirtless and sweaty, he confidently sweeps Alisha off her feet and carries her off for a happily-ever-after ending. Rather than being shy or embarrassed, however, Alisha looks into the camera and smiles, perhaps implying that, although she is being carried, it is she that remains in control.

While the video produces a story just as escapist and fantastic as the Bollywood blockbusters of that era, some of the scenes in the video articulate a specifically nonfilmi orientation that amplifies the neoliberal messages in the lyrics and musical form. At the start of the video, Alisha expresses boredom with the dance being performed for her. I read this as an articulation of her (and by extension the aspiring Indipop movement's) boredom with the collective dance fantasy of Bollywood, as if to remind the audience that "we've seen it all before, and it's time for something new." After dismissing this collective ritual in the opening scene, Alisha wanders alone in vacant rooms calling for the product (an Indian-made heart) that she requires if she is to feel fulfilled. Alisha's costumes in the video provide another layer of symbolism. Typical of the fast-paced, changing world of music videos, Alisha's appearance varies radically from shot to shot. At the beginning of the video, she wears a wig of short blonde hair and sports a feathery stole. She is a true diva or, in the context of Indian filmic culture, a vamp. By the end of the video, however, Alisha is converted to, in her words, "a true Guju housewife" who wears the traditional sari and smiles when carried away by her man. The vamp is domesticated and becomes a carrier of authentic Indian culture. There's nothing new about this transformation, and it forms the basis of many a commercial Hindi film as well. However, what is interesting to me is that Alisha occupies a solitary space, individual rather than collective, and her transformation occurs without the explicit family approval that may be expected of Bollywood films in that era.[3]

Thus, the aural and visual components of "Made in India" draw on conventions of both Western pop and Bollywood, opening the space between the two to articulate a new orientation toward intimacy, embodiment, and citizenship in the neoliberal era. The song articulates an enthusiasm to join the global marketplace and a willingness to fetishize and objectify the local as a marketing strategy. It promotes a "new *swadeshi*"[4] nationalism and calls out to non-resident Indians ("NRIs") to look past the temptations of foreign lands and return to the perceived innate goodness of the Indian heart.

Sounding an Uneasy Boundary

While "Made in India" was exceptional in its sales and popularity, many Indipop songs and videos from this era share similar characteristics. On the Magnasound label alone,[5] one could point to the domestic space of middle-class youth consumerism evoked in "Aisa Hota Hai" by Shaan and Sagarika, the intimacy between celebrity and fan evoked in the video for "O Meri Munni" by Goan rocker Remo Fernandes, or the socially relevant lyrics and warm, enveloping timbre of the Colonial Cousins song "Krishna." Even the *bhangra* pop music icon Daler Mehndi, whose Punjabi songs suggest collective dance and public celebration, points to a sense of intimate, private consumerism through the tight headshots and direct eye contact into the camera lens in videos such as "Bolo Ta Ra Ra."

Yet, despite the Indipop industry's efforts to appeal to a broader audience, it has mainly been through the musicians' work as Bollywood playback singers that the voices of the artists mentioned here have found their way into Indian households. Thus the nonfilm industry's attempts to promote pop icons who unify both voice and corporeality were thwarted. This disjuncture between conflicting modes of production and consumption sowed the seeds for Indipop's seemingly inevitable downfall, providing yet more evidence that some of the basic premises of popular music studies and sound studies do not always translate across social contexts.

For example, Alisha Chinai described to me what she perceived as the limitations placed on her solo performance identity by the public: "If I get too Indian on them, they can't handle it either. Because I've always had music which is a blend, and it sort of goes with me. It has become my trademark. If I get too ethnic, they won't like it." However, when performing her "disembodied voice" as a playback singer in Bollywood,[6] for example, in the item number "Kajara Re" from the 2005 film *Bunty Aur Babli*, the same restrictions do not seem to apply.

The idea of voicing Indian authenticity was a common theme in my conversations with other Indipop singers as well. Shaan, another Magnasound artist who went on to lend his voice to the film music industry, took a more optimistic view of Indipop's potential to bridge the divide.

> You see, I really have no problem with Indian music. I mean obviously we have a great heritage, I mean so many years. The whole Indian scale. The ragas. The theory. It's intense. It's a lot more interesting in a lot of ways than maybe the music in the West. . . . But where I would think pop comes in is bridging the gap really. It's music of today. It has to be contemporary. It has to be progressive. So it has to be able to fuse the Indian essence and bring it closer to Western ideas for today's Indian, for today's educated youth, who are accepting, who are bound to accept so many things coming from the West, be it clothing, be it language. Various things, I mean, everything is coming to us via the West.

The tension between "the West" and an "Indian essence," along with the us-them dialectic mentioned above, were some of the more enduring tropes throughout my research. And despite the reality that popular film music was every bit the hybrid musical mongrel that Indipop was, I encountered far less concern with justifying the authenticity of Bollywood songs. Film music may have borrowed the rhythms and styles of rumba, waltz, tango, mambo, rock 'n' roll, disco, and rap,[7] but its hybridity seemed to be taken as natural and was largely unquestioned. Indipop artists, on the other hand, appeared to share the tensions experienced by musicians who mix the Israeli and Arabic musical repertoire, about whom Benjamin Brinner writes:

> None of these musicians seems to want to tout the fact of hybridity itself because it bears the mark of a bastard, of rootlessness, of artificiality. Musicians seek authenticity by establishing their credentials with

> regard to the various musical resources they use and by claiming an organic synthesis of those resources. (2009. 31)

Shaan and many other Indipop artists and producers emphasized their own creative agency, implying that they fully understood and manipulated both "Western" and "Indian" musical languages.

Yet, while for some this rhetorical strategy drew rigid boundaries between two distinct musical systems, others emphasized that this "organic synthesis" was foundational to all musics and that the very nature of "Western" music was already built on layers of hybridity and appropriation. This view deflected criticism of appropriation and defended an ideology of personal choice and creative authority. When I asked drummer and producer Ranjit Barot about his musical identity, he noted that, despite his deep connection to Indian traditional music and dance,[8] it was his embeddedness in rock music that helped him stand out among Indian producers.

> I'm thinking "Sympathy for the Devil" man, or the Rolling Stones, because my reference point is from the time that I was fourteen, I ate that music. I am really not doing anything new. I'm just regurgitating all the input that I had for the last thirty-six years. And I'm putting my spin on it, my DNA on it. After all, art is cannibalism. What are we doing? Are we going to take credit for a set of notes that may have been done by some obscure pianist, in Vienna in 1600? Who knows man? Cause really, all the information is there, with the masters, it's all there. And you have to listen, you have to deconstruct, find places in that music which reflect your ideology. It's like an actor who reads a script and he says, "Oh, there's a bit of this guy in me."

Barot's dialectical understanding of music, in which component parts such as "Western" and "Indian" are deconstructed and then synthesized in emergent and authentic ways, derives from his exceptional mastery of both jazz/rock and traditional Indian musics. Other artists, particularly those who existed not along the border between raga and rock but rather Indipop and Bollywood, moved with less confidence along an uneasy boundary, especially as the opportunities to promote nonfilm music through live performances and music videos began to dwindle in the early 2000s.

Conclusion

In listening to the soundscapes of late 1990s Indipop music, I have argued that the sonic textures created in computer-based recording studios, often using acoustic guitars, crooning vocals, and a warm timbral mix, were evocative of an intimate and personal relationship between a consumer and his or her media. In some cases, this sonic quality offered a contrast to the blaring, reverberating, sometimes piercing sounds of Bollywood productions coming from the traditionally large-scale recording sessions. As the new millennium unfolded, Indian film music absorbed this sonic sensibility, in no small part because of the growing significance of former Indipop and Indian rock performers and producers in contemporary Bollywood. In my conversation with Uday Benegal, the lead singer of Indus Creed (formerly Rock Machine) and an important figure in the growth of independent nonfilm songwriting in Indian popular music, he identified A. R. Rahman as among the first to initiate this change.

> Gone are those screechy, compressed, high mid-level soundtracks and now you got really nice, *sonically* interesting stuff. I think Rahman was one of the first people who changed that because he brought, what most people don't realize and really don't acknowledge is what Rahman brought, apart from change in style, was *a complete change in frequency*. You know because the *sound* of his music, he really explored the spectrum of frequency of sonic frequency that made it sound pleasant to the ear.

Benegal is far from alone in citing Rahman as a game changer for the Indian music industry. But while he is best known for his work as a music director in Tamil and Hindi films, what is less known is that Rahman got his foot in the door of the industry when he created the music for a nonfilm, English pop album by Malgudi Shubha called *Set Me Free*, which was released by Magnasound in 1991.[9] So, while few people think of Rahman as an Indipop artist per se, his approach to composition and, more important, sonic design had much in common with his nonfilm peers at Magnasound in the 1990s.

While I recognize the dangers of overdetermining the relationship between aesthetics and social context, I continue to think that changes in recording fidelity in millennial India might map onto larger changes in social organization and everyday practice.[10] What of the "sonically interesting" sounds recorded on computers, distributed on compact discs, and consumed by those with the means to engage in intimate, insulated listening? Might the sounds be homologous to other aspects of bourgeoisification brought on by neoliberalism? Studies from other cultures seem to corroborate this thesis. Writing about Turkish popular music after a similar neoliberal transformation in the 1990s, Martin Stokes describes the shift from cassettes to CDs. Because initially they could not be pirated, CDs offered "a means of distinction for middle-class consumers." He continues:

> The shift to CDs also made possible practices of musical and aesthetic distinction. If the cassette market and the predominant conditions of working class reception (e.g., noisy public spaces, public transport) favored a strongly focused melody line, the reception of CDs in middle-class (private and domestic) contexts favored textured instrumental sounds, acoustic depth, and polyphony." (2010, 126–27)

Interestingly, Stokes cites Peter Manuel's study of popular music in India, *Cassette Culture* (1993), in which Manuel notes that the cassette player itself was once an emergent symbol of privatized consumption when contrasted with the mass dissemination of film songs on the radio or in cinema halls.

As mentioned earlier, I have also argued that elements of musical form reveal something about the changing nature of the popular song as a fetishized object of consumerist desire. The arrival of Indipop coincided with a shift away from musical form based around a catch phrase, or *mukhra*, and more toward compositions emphasizing chord changes leading from verse to chorus. Indipop composers also avoided an approach to rhythm that was marked as particularly "Indian," the acceleration of tempo at the conclusion of a piece. Indipop songs that were recorded to a steady "click track" or programmed on sequencers emphasized the emotive power of harmony to dictate musical form, while the more filmi songs emphasized melodic expectations and tempo changes to create their own modes of affect. My research also led me to examine visual cues of these emerging new forms of intimacy and personal experience. Looking at Indipop album covers from that era, I noticed an emphasis on artists' faces, typically closely cropped and looking directly into the camera (and consequently into the consumer's eyes). This visual intimacy was reproduced in Indipop music videos, in which the artists often sang to the camera, thus evoking a sense of earnest self-expression and a televisual (rather than cinematic) mode of domesticity and intimacy.

The physical spaces from which Indipop emerged, such as recording studios and record company offices, offered some of the most striking visual examples. Recall the Magnasound office of Shashi Gopal, an air-conditioned glass box that was virtually iconic of the privatized "bubble" inhabited by the urban, bourgeois body and evoked through sonic fidelity and other musical and visual elements. And then, of course, there is the recording studio itself. Hermetically sealed off from the noise, heat, and activity of the public, the "project studios" from which Indipop emerged were a far cry from the bustling studios that captured the orchestral sounds of film music in past eras. In such small, computer-based recording studios, the recording process itself often unfolds in privatized, bubblelike segments. More and more, musicians work separately, laying down their parts in isolation sometimes days or weeks apart. As the recording grows more complex and filled out, the multitrack recording itself becomes the social context that holds together the creative labor of each musician.

Because of the ephemeral nature of pop music and the sudden and dramatic collapse of the private album market in India, Indipop might easily be forgotten. Reading William Mazzarella's work on advertising agencies in Mumbai during the same era has been helpful in putting my research and experiences into a broader context. In his exploration of the "cola wars" in India, Mazzarella describes local perceptions of the initial faltering of global corporations such as Coca-Cola and MTV during the early days of liberalization.

> Corporate consumer goods giants, lured in the early 1990s by the promise of the mythical 250 million-strong Indian middle class, had set up shop in India following the 1991 reforms of the Narasimha Rao government. Many, if not most, of them had found that early sales projections had proved chimerical. Much of the commentary on this phenomenon, after an initial phase of bewilderment, had taken on a triumphalist tone; it was as if the multinationals were being interpreted as a kind of recapitulation of the colonial encounter, in which Indians, approached this time as sovereign consumers rather than imperial subjects, were proving resistant to the best laid plans that the finest marketing minds in the West had to offer. (2003, 215–16)

He continues by comparing the universalist mind-set and "gentle global message" of Coke to the more spectacular, Bollywood-focused approach of Pepsi, writing, "The general feeling in the Bombay advertising industry was that while Coke's communications seemed 'arty' and 'obscure,' . . .

Pepsi had succeeded by understanding a deeply rooted Indian predilection for uproarious spectacle, for *tamasha*, preferably couched in quasi-mythological terms" (219–21). At the start of the new millennium, it appeared to me that the Indian music industry reflected a similar tension, with the neoliberal resonances of intimacy, embodiment, and citizenship embedded in Indipop failing to attract the notice of a mainstream audience accustomed to consuming music in cinematic contexts.

In an essay called "The Impact of Recording on Listening," Eric Clarke borrows the term *affordance* when thinking about the role of the musical recording in human life: "In the most general terms, when people perceive objects and events, they perceive what they can do with or about them—an idea that the psychologist James Gibson expressed in the term 'affordance'" (2007, 48). Hindi film songs, because of their long and established history, their many uses outside the cinema hall such as singing games like *antakshari* (see Kvetko 2017), brass bands at weddings (see Booth 1990), and culture shows or dance classes (see Morcom 2013), and their recycled identities as ringtones and even titles of soap operas, because of all of these uses film songs generate affordance for listeners. They connect the listener to a kind of social action or an act of recognition. They provoke intimate memories that recall the film scene, the gossip regarding the actor's real life, or material and embodied contexts where the film song recorded itself into the listener's memory.

Meanwhile Indipop fell flat at the turn of the millennium because, perhaps, people didn't know what to do with it. There was no affordance, no call to action. And, with the emergence of digital piracy and online file sharing, Indipop recordings came into the market at a time when the recording industry as a whole was struggling to evoke a sense of value for consumers who were sometimes duplicating CDs and hoarding more MP3s than they would ever have time to listen to. But the second decade of the twenty-first century has seen a reinvigorated scene for pop music authorship outside the context of cinema, for original songwriting and music production that makes me think the transformations of the Indipop era have a renewed relevance in contemporary India, and cultural critics will undoubtedly continue to explore the unfolding relationship among sound, intimacy, and citizenship in contemporary South Asia.

Notes

1. The tables piled high with handwritten ledgers at my neighborhood State Bank of India branch, for example, looked a world apart from the brushed metal

kiosks and sparsely furnished work spaces of the nearby bank operated by a private multinational corporation.

2. Although it bears noting that the album was made in England by Biddu, who left India many years earlier to embark on a successful career producing disco hits such as "Everybody Was Kung Fu Fighting," as well as bringing disco to South Asia with the Pakistani singer Nazia Hassan. Furthermore, Alisha's Indian suitor (who emerges bare-chested from a shipping crate stamped with the words "Made In India") was in fact born in Glasgow, Scotland.

3. Exploring the ways in which *filmi* love relationships are inevitably mediated through and condoned by parents, Sheila Nayar writes, "[Parental] permission and blessings are fundamentally necessary, and virtually always given on screen" (1997, 85).

4. See Mazarella's book, *Shoveling Smoke* (2003), for an analysis of the ways in which globalization and nationalism have been combined in the post-liberalization era of Indian advertising.

5. Related examples from other Indian record companies would include the whispering vocals and tight headshots in the music video for Sunita Rao's song "Pari Hoon Main" on HMV, the acoustic instruments, soft crooning, and remote landscapes in "Dooba Dooba" by Silk Route (BMG Crescendo), and the worldly wanderings of Lucky Ali in several videos released by Sony Music India.

6. See Majumdar (2001) for a closer analysis of the voice-body relationship in Indian film song.

7. See Beaster-Jones (2015) for a recent study of the "cosmopolitan" nature of the Hindi film song.

8. Barot's mother was the late Sitara Devi, a legendary *kathak* dancer, and Barot maintains a strong relationship with the tabla virtuoso Ustad Zakir Hussain.

9. At that time Rahman was still using his birth name, Dilip Kumar. By the time he became a celebrated film music director, he had converted to sufism and changed his name to Allarakha Rahman. Magnasound rereleased *Set Me Free* in 1996 to capitalize on the success of Rahman's Hindi-language debut, the soundtrack for the dubbed film *Roja*, which was also released by Magnasound.

10. In many ways this evokes a long-standing question in ethnomusicology. How does musical structure correspond to social structure? Steven Feld, responding to Alan Lomax's well-known "cantometrics" project (which attempted to show that song structures were manifestations of deep structures in societies), writes that comparison across time and place is a worthy endeavor but should be done in tandem with, not apart from, ethnography. He calls for a "comparative sociomusicology" whose goal is "elaborating not correlations of song structures and social structures, but coherences of sound structures as social structures" (Feld 1984, 406)

Works Cited

Appadurai, Arjun. 1990. "Disjuncture and Difference in the Global Economy." *Public Culture* 2, no. 2: 1–24.

Beaster-Jones, Jayson. 2015. *Bollywood Sounds: The Cosmopolitan Mediations of Hindi Film Song*. New York: Oxford University Press.

Booth, Gregory. 1990. "Brass Bands: Tradition, Change, and the Mass Media in Indian Wedding Music." *Ethnomusicology* 34, no. 2: 245–62.

Brinner, Benjamin. 2009. *Playing across a Divide: Israeli-Palestinian Musical Encounters.* New York: Oxford University Press.

Clarke, Eric. 2007. "The Impact of Recording on Listening." *TwentiethCentury Music* 4, no. 1: 47–70.

Erlmann, Veit. 1999. *Music, Modernity, and the Global Imagination: South Africa and the West.* New York: Oxford University Press.

Feld, Steven. 1984. "Sound Structure as Social Structure." *Ethnomusicology* 28, no. 3: 383–409.

Kvetko, Peter. 2004. "Can the Indian Tune Go Global?" *TDR: The Drama Review* 48, no. 4 (Winter): 183–91.

Kvetko, Peter. 2017. "Antakshari in *Maine Pyar Kiya*: Intertextual Pleasures and Musical Medleys at the Dawn of a New Era in Hindi Cinema." In *Music of Contemporary Indian Film,* edited by Jayson Beaster-Jones and Natalie Sarrazin. 35–48. New York: Routledge.

Majumdar, Neepa. 2001. "The Embodied Voice: Song Sequences and Stardom in Popular Hindi Cinema." In *Soundtrack Available: Essays on Film and Popular Music* edited by Pamela Robertson Wojcik and Arthur Knight, 161–81. Durham, NC: Duke University Press,.

Manuel, Peter. 1993. *Cassette Culture: Popular Music and Technology in North India.* Chicago: University of Chicago Press.

Mazzarella, William. 2003. *Shoveling Smoke: Advertising and Globalization in Contemporary India.* Durham, NC: Duke University Press.

Morcom, Anna. 2013. *Illicit Worlds of Indian Dance: Cultures of Exclusion.* Oxford: Oxford University Press. See esp. chap. 4, "The Bollywood Dance Revolution and the Embourgeoisement of Indian Performing Arts."

Nayar, Sheila. 1997. "The Values of Fantasy: Indian Popular Cinema through Western Scripts." *Journal of Popular Culture* 31, no. 1 (Summer): 73–91.

Stokes, Martin. 2010. *Republic of Love: Cultural Intimacy in Turkish Popular Music.* Chicago: University of Chicago Press.

FOUR | High-Fidelity Ecologies

India versus Noise Pollution in the Contemporary Public Sphere

SAMHITA SUNYA

> The combination of hi-fi equipment and the rock music which dominated the past decade, alone has probably affected the hearing of a whole generation of listeners. If these statements seem scary, they should. They are not exaggerations. Noise pollution is a growing menace, not just to boilermakers and jackhammer operators, but to all of us. The noise level we experience daily has increased so gradually that we fail to recognize its danger. But noise is a danger. It can result in a hearing loss that not only can be a handicap, but what is worse, a hearing loss that cannot be restored.
>
> United States Environmental Protection Agency 1972

> More attention must be paid to the problem in India as it is a noise loving country. On every occasion, from birth to death loud noise or *Band Baza* [band music] is part of our culture. Indian religion is also contributing a lot to noise pollution.
>
> Shastri and Trivedi 1988

Initially drafted as the "Noise Pollution (Regulation and Control) Rules" in 1999, under the auspices of the Ministry of Environments and Forests, the Supreme Court of India passed a judgment upholding measures to curb noise pollution on July 18, 2005 ("Forum" 2005a). Framed by the contemporary contexts for the judgment, this chapter examines perceptions, classifications, and public debates over noise as inextricable from gender, class, and communal politics that take recourse to classificatory binaries of noise versus music and other highly subjective criteria (e.g., that of "public disturbance") rather than expressly quantifiable measurements of decibel levels. This is no surprise, for, as sound studies scholars such as Emily Thompson and Mack Hagood have presciently noted in US-centered contexts, the politics and histories of the reduction and/or abatement of noise (i.e., sound that is undesirable and "other") frequently belie assumptions that certain (racialized, classed) bodies are the prime offending sources of undesirable sounds. What I hope to emphasize in this chapter are the sexual, caste, and communal notes that have rung through perceptions of, and debates over, noise pollution in post-Independence India.

In order to map a contemporary—and often contentious—public discourse over noise in India, I look at three films that are formally and thematically structured around motifs of noise: *Dastak* (Rajinder Singh Bedi, 1970), an older film, in addition to *Hulla* (Jaideep Varma, 2008) and *Loudspeaker* (Jayaraj, 2009). As audiovisual works emerging from contexts in which popular cinemas' hallmark song sequences have been both loved as music and lambasted as noise, these films afford opportunities to listen more closely to negotiations of sound, music, and noise both within and beyond their respective diegetic worlds (Attali and McClary 1985, 9–10). Through readings of these films, I note that modes of hearing associated with modern amplification have been central to the contemporary discourse of noise pollution in India, as techno-ideals of noise reduction and aspirations toward urban lifestyles of private consumption via high-fidelity (hi-fi) systems have become entangled with ideals of environmental protection and individual health.[1]

Ultimately, I show that "noise pollution" has become a conveniently floating target that not only betrays hierarchies of gender, communal identity, and class but also emerges from the very processes of industrial modernity and contemporary development to which sonic assaults are purportedly extraneous and excessive: "industrial activity, construction activity, generator sets, loud speakers, public address systems, music systems, vehicular horns and other mechanical devices [that] have deleterious effects on human health and the psychological well being of the people" ("Forum" 2005a). More specifically, as an issue that has been metonymic for the assaults wrought by urban living, the issue of noise pollution in India unfolds simultaneously as a problem of sexuality and modernity—that is, as a problem of maintaining patriarchal control of normative boundaries in city spaces, as bodies in perpetual motion jostle about in close proximity to one another.

As several scholars have noted, the Indian city as both a conceptual/

imagined and particular/lived space, has epitomized the site of encounter with postcolonial modernity and its concomitant (re)configurations of sexuality and nationhood (Chatterjee 1993; Gopal 2012; Kaarsholm 2006; Mazumdar 2007; Prasad 2001; Radhakrishnan 2017). Part and parcel of the (re)configurations embedded in the movement from rural to urban spaces were the social-cum-spatial transitions from dwelling in feudal, extended family units to cohabiting in nuclear family units defined by the heterosexual couple. As Brinda Bose writes:

> The city has occupied an ambivalent position in the Indian nationalist imaginary throughout the process of nation-building, often a confrontational, as well as contemplative space that signifies "modernity" and its concurrent promise as well as ills in relation to the "traditional" ethics of a very old culture, even while representing progress and development (presumably by Western frameworks of evaluation). Such progress has been traditionally perceived in India as a moral degeneracy of the nation (perhaps necessary but nevertheless demeaning), easily analogous with female sexual transgression/promiscuity—with the nation personified as woman (mother, goddess, mistress, prostitute). (Bose 2008, 36)

In this vein, I turn to cinema as a site that registers these tensions—often in a self-conscious way—as cinema, too, was intimately tied to the notional category of the city and held a similarly "ambivalent position in the Indian nationalist imaginary," as a thoroughly modern, mechanized medium for the masses that was renowned for its libidinal excesses of sensual, audiovisual pleasures—regarded, essentially, as noise from the perspectives of its redactors (Bose 2008, 36; Rajadhyaksha 2009).

Dastak and the (Sexual) Assaults of Noise

The initial 2005 judgment of the Supreme Court of India, aimed at establishing rules for curbing noise pollution, occurred in response to a pro bono publico petition by a citizen, Anil K. Mittal. As recounted in the opening statements of the judgment, Mittal was moved to file a petition by the rape of a thirteen-year-old girl in Delhi, whose cries for help "sunk and went unheard due to blaring noise of music over loudspeaker in the neighborhood," after which the girl immolated herself and died ("Forum" 2005a). The judgment's recounting of this tragic rape vilifies "noise polluters" as the assailants and the "blaring noise of music over loudspeaker" as their weapon, before going on to note that their other hapless victims include students who are unable to study ("Forum" 2005a).

That a tragic instance of violent sexual assault precipitated the Supreme Court's ruling on noise pollution occasions an initial exploration of the relationship between patriarchal state control, the policing of noise, and gendered violence. To this end, I turn to the older film *Dastak* and M. Madhava Prasad's keen analysis of the film in *Ideology of the Hindi Film: A Historical Construction*, a monograph that was groundbreaking for the subfield of South Asian—and especially Indian—screen studies, which has since burgeoned into a recognizable, robust avenue of critical scholarly inquiry. In revisiting Prasad's seminal text almost twenty years after its initial publication before going on to examine two much more recent films that are also structured around motifs of noise, I want to tug at an important thread in Prasad's reading of *Dastak*, with a view toward unraveling the tremendous potential for ongoing sound studies interventions in the historiography of Indian cinema and modernity.

Prasad's reading of *Dastak* situates the film in a broader historical discussion of middle-class cinema, whose major ideological project was that of constituting the nuclear family unit within a realist domain of conjugality. The problem of popular cinema, for the middle-class cinema that emerged alongside the establishment of the state-funded Film Finance Corporation in 1960, was that of the public woman who was readily available onscreen as an erotic object for the spectator's gaze in exchange for the price of a ticket. Prasad notes:

> As such the task that the film-makers undertook was not a confrontation with the popular cinema but an education of their audience in narrative form which could retain its integrity while absorbing the libidinal excess of the polymorphous popular film text. From the contracted voyeurism of the popular film text (and the brothel), the middle-class cinema turned its audience towards a "realist" voyeurism in which sexuality occurred in the depths of screen space, as an attribute of subjectivity. (2001, 186–87)

Indeed, the central narrative and formal tensions in *Dastak* revolve around the neighborhood's expectation that Salma, a newlywed who moves with her husband Hamid into a modest Bombay flat that happens to be in a red-light district, is a prostitute whose sexuality is on offer to any customer who is willing to pay. The camerawork, as well as the density and porosity of urban spaces, allows passersby within the diegesis—and spectators without—to readily intrude into the private domain of the couple as voyeurs and expectant clients, regarding Salma as a public woman even after they come to know better. Hamid and Salma's attempt to establish their middle-class respectability in a red-light district unfolds as an allegory of the middle-class cinema's attempt to establish its respectability in a popular medium associated with the raucous "libidinal excess[es]" of entertainment, spectacle, and sensual pleasure.

As Prasad notes, the constraints on the middle-class aspirations of the young couple in *Dastak*, whose private intimacies are threatened by the gaze of omnipresent voyeurs—including the spectator—are intensified by their marginalized Muslim minority status in a predominantly Hindu milieu (Prasad 2001, 183). While *Dastak* has since emerged as a quintessential film in discussions of middle-class cinema, the Indian New Wave, the genre of the Muslim social, and the recurrent, archetypal dichotomy of the virgin/whore in films from the same period, *Dastak* remains particularly ripe for an analysis that attends to sound as a fundamental motif, texture, and problem of urban modernity (Prasad 2001; Basu 2013; Bhaskar 2013).

For in *Dastak* it is the knock at the door, among other unexpected sounds of urban dwelling, that poses the most severe and uncontrollable threat to the privacy of the couple. The film's title itself, which means "knock," highlights the series of ongoing intrusions by strangers who come to the apartment and assume that Salma is, or is like, the woman who had previously occupied it and conducted her business of entertaining men as a singer and sex worker in the tradition of the courtesan-*tawaif* there (Booth 2007). While Prasad's analysis of *Dastak* highlights the voyeuristic gaze that is produced by the film's camerawork and then redirected by its middle-class, realist narrative as a libidinal excess (of popular cinema), the uninvited intrusions that violate the couple's conjugal domain are patently and thoroughly sonic, as much as—if not even more than—they are scopophilic.

The very first diegetic song sequence, *"Baiyaan na dharo,"* juxtaposes simultaneous expressive performances of feminine desire across the virgin/whore dichotomy. The faint background strains of the same lyrical composition, an offscreen sound, ostensibly float into Hamid and Salma's apartment from outside.[2] Salma's recognition of the composition as one she knows in a different melody motivates her own performance of the song for her husband. Belonging to the musical genre of the *thumri*, the song is coy and suggestive (Manuel 1990). The initial faint, offscreen background voice is throaty and low pitched, and the spectator recognizes that it very likely belongs to a sex-worker-cum-entertainer who is singing for her clients, given that the apartment is in a red-light district. Salma's naïveté is apparent in the fact that she does not pick up on this, and her rendition proceeds in the recognizably high-pitched, saccharine falsetto of star playback singer Lata Mangeshkar (Majumdar 2007). While Salma is expressing her romantic and sexual feelings for her husband, sideways pans and cuts reveal that she has an audience of which she is unaware, as the spectator is aligned with the men in the neighborhood, who perk up at the sound of her voice and approach her window aroused not merely as voyeurs but more specifically as eavesdroppers as well.

This opening song sequence thus characterizes the difference between the vamp and the virgin as a matter of the bodies, address, and spatial context for their expressions of sexual desire rather than as a difference in the genre of the expressions themselves. In *Dastak* this becomes, in turn, an allegory for the presence of songs—especially those performed by women—in a cinema that is addressed to a middle-class spectator. The implicit ideological argument is that the difference between the clatter of a vulgar popular cinema and the tunefulness of a middle-class cinema does not lie in the films' oppositional aesthetics per se—for example, the presence or absence, or even divergent genres, of songs—but rather in whether or not the songs emanate from a domain of propriety and respectability that circumscribes expressions of female sexuality and desire within the private space of conjugality.[3]

It is in the policing of the boundary between music and noise—of what sounds, from which bodies, and from where are acceptable and pleasing—that the ideological desires of the historical project of this middle-class cinema overlap with the ideological workings of a patriarchal state. In *Dastak* Hamid is utterly ineffective in blocking the sonic excesses—the knocks, for one thing—that continually penetrate the private space of his marital home. Despite the couple's resolve to maintain that Salma's sexuality is not available to the public, Salma is betrayed by the porosity of her private space, which can neither contain her desires nor protect her from desirous others, in a (cinematic) world where solicitations and sexual advances are expressed either as music, if properly middle class and respectable, or as the excesses of noise, if not.

When Salma sings desirously to her husband, her voice, unbeknownst to her, is audible to eavesdroppers, who hear her entertainments' availability to the public—even if inadvertently so—as proof that she is available as a woman of the night. The sounds that in turn enter Hamid and Salma's apartment as unwanted noise—knocks on the door, audible brawls, and the songs of the sex workers who entertain their clients in the red-light district—make Salma perpetually anxious over her actual sexual desires for her husband. At the same time, Hamid becomes enraged by his inability to prevent the breaching of boundaries by these various sounds despite mandating that Salma stay within the confines of the apartment, in the same way that he insists a bird he gives his wife must not be freed from its cage for its own good.

As Hamid's frustrations come to a head, it is amid the cacophony of the crowd's aural intrusion into the couple's intimate space that Hamid forces himself on Salma in an act of marital rape. Although Salma is newly wedded, the shy couple has had yet to consummate their marriage. Halfway through the film, after having gotten into a brawl with neighbors who yet again assume that Salma is available as a sex worker, Hamid seethes with anger and insists that he must have Salma himself before she is snatched away and enjoyed by another man. Hamid's act of aggression is driven by his inability to control the sounds that flout the boundaries between the private, intimate space that he shares with his wife and the space of the public bazaar outside. As the scene unfolds fully within the confines of the apartment, the audible tide of a roaring crowd below surges up as an offscreen sound into the frame of the couple's private space—the only sound besides the dialogue taking place between Hamid and Salma as he rapes her.

In this way, noise—as unwanted sonic intrusions and leaks—becomes a central motif in *Dastak* for sexual exchanges that spill over the boundaries of middle-class propriety. The *lakshman rekha*, or mythic, contractual barrier within which the honor of a married woman is impervious to any violation so long as she stays inside its lines, is apparently not soundproof. The problem of noise pollution in South Asia thus has been a problem of modernity and urban space, not merely because of loud industrial equipment and modern amplification but especially because of sound's ability to flagrantly violate the spatial and social autonomy of the modern, urban, nuclear family unit.

Dastak, like the much more recent films *Loudspeaker* and *Hulla*, dramatize noise as a conflict between the modern, urban organization of middle-class families into atomized nuclear units, on the one hand, and the population density and limited availability of affordable private housing in urban centers, which forces strangers to live in cramped quarters and close proximity, on the other (Bhaskar 2013). As noise from without crosses the bounded, private arena of the modern couple and nuclear family unit—an arena that is spatially depicted in *Dastak* and other films as that of the middle-class urban apartment—it becomes an issue that is inextricable from sexual politics of modernity in South Asia insofar as endogamy, or marriage within the boundaries of communities, continues to define social structures of caste, communal identity, and class. The issue of noise—and characterization of noise as a *pollutant*, moreover—highlights the conflict between the preservation of sociospatial boundaries of (sexual) purity that scaffold the modern lives of caste, communal identity, and class, on the one hand, and the demand for affordable urban housing that forces proximity to strangers and the omnipresent risk of (sexual) contact that sullies the purity of endogamous communities, on the other.

Loudspeaker and the Sonic Ecosystems of Concrete Jungles

Within the last decade in South Asia, the term *hi-fi* (short for *high fidelity*) has gained currency as a vernacular adjective for something that is desirable for its elite status. In addition to its ubiquity in colloquial speech, the neologism has made appearances in several hit film songs, such as "aiyanvii aiyanvii aiyanvii luut gayaa" from the popular film *Band Baaja Baaraat,* aka *Band Music and Revelry* (Maneesh Sharma, 2010). The simultaneity of the recent proliferation and prominence of both sonic terms—*hi-fi*, on the one hand, and *noise pollution* on the other—underscores the presence and significance of sound technologies and modes of hearing in a larger, current, South Asian public discourse. I show that notions of contemporary hi-fi lifestyles include a desire to remain cocooned in nuclear units and social segments that are free of the health hazards of noise pollution, namely, sonic intrusions emanating from undesirable class, caste, and communal locations.[4] The two terms' respective connotations of aspirations toward a certain class status, on the one hand, and healthy living in urban environments, on the other, point to the central themes of the recent, popular Malayalam-language film *Loudspeaker* (Jayaraj, 2009).

While *Dastak* was an attempt, in its own decade, to cull a middle-class address from the idiom of popular cinema, *Loudspeaker* is ultimately an exaltation of the raucous idiom of a longer genealogy of Indian popular cinema. This raucous idiom, manifest in *Loudspeaker* as noise, is prescribed as an antidote to the alienation of nuclear family units that emerges from the very desire for class segmentation in urban social spaces. Starring the Malayalam film star Mammooty, *Loudspeaker* is a comedy that exaggerates and critiques the contemporary atomization of social life, no more apparent than in the urban spaces of upper-middle-class apartment complexes.

The main character, played by Mammooty, is a golden-hearted villager with the given name Philippose, though he speaks so loudly that he has long since come to be known as Mic. Mic is in need of money to pay off a loan shark who is poised to snatch his ancestral land, to which Mic is attached solely because it holds the unmarked grave of his late father, who was killed and interred in the land by a mudslide. Mic comes to know of a racket for donated organs, and when he is identified as a match, he agrees to donate a kidney to Mr. Menon (Shashi Kumar), an elderly, ailing retired astrophysicist in Ernakulum City in Kochi. Mic must go to Ernakulum City for the transplant, and when Mr. Menon learns that Mic has no place to stay, he insists that Mic occupy his guest room and remain comfortable in the days leading up to the operation.

The ensuing comedy arises out of Mic's encounter with an upper-middle-class urban lifestyle, defamiliarized through his fresh eyes. Mic is a veritable and lovable bull in a china shop, and he is marked as out of place not only by his loud voice but also by the fact that he carries around a personal radio, which blares a hodgepodge of popular, mostly Malayalam, film songs. While the adults in the apartment complex, Mr. Menon included, find Mic's demeanor unrefined, embarrassing, and out of place, the children gravitate toward him, and it is in their company that Mic is most comfortable. Eventually, the adults, too, realize that they have much to love about the carefree villager in their midst, whose loud voice is but one way in which he constantly challenges their desire to keep to themselves. In befriending and regarding children and adults alike as his kin, he injects a sense of camaraderie and community into an apartment community that is rife with squabbles and domestic quarrels, both within and across the nuclear family units that had been more than happy to keep their distance from one another prior to Mic's arrival.

While noise, in *Dastak*, is painted as a motif for the unfortunate excesses that breach the propriety and spatial boundaries of modern, middle-class urban life, in *Loudspeaker* noise is instead painted as a welcome interruption that dissolves the social walls between residents who are not only organized in individual nuclear units but also—as in *Dastak*—deeply and reflexively tied to the excesses of popular cinema, whether Malayalam or Hindi.[5] Mic cannot comprehend that the residents do not embrace the kinship of their proximity, given that they all live side by side, and his loud voice and blaring radio ultimately erode the social walls that stand flush with their apartment walls. In *Loudspeaker*, this is apparent when, in the latter half of the film, several characters who live in the different units of the complex are drawn out of their private shells by Mic and celebrate Christmas together.

Early in the film, a child misremembers Mic's name as Loudspeaker. This moniker underscores the film's ensuing celebration of sonic excesses as a hallmark of popular cinema's ability to forge kinship between strangers from different social classes and generations. The associations among Mic's character, noise, and the egalitarian potential of popular cinema crystallize when, at one point in the film, he intervenes when he sees a watchman shooing away a group of homeless street singers who are busking outside the gates of the complex. Enthused on noticing their presence, he pays no heed to the watchman's protestations and excitedly opens the gates and welcomes them into the grounds of the complex. The gang of children in the complex joins, and the group joyfully sings a Hindi film song, the jazzy 1960s hit "mere sapnon ki rani kab aayegii tu."

While policy discourses aimed at controlling noise have framed noise pollution as an environmental and health hazard, *Loudspeaker* turns this around. The film self-reflexively reveals the potential of noisy popular forms to deeply pierce and rehabilitate the failing urban ecosystems of contemporary city spaces. As a villager from a forested area where wild animals roam, Mic repeatedly recalls and dramatically recounts encounters between his father and wild elephants. When Mic is initially making his way to the city, he stops at a tea stall and remarks that, just as villagers must contend with living alongside wild animals, so, too, must city dwellers contend with living alongside human animals. What Mic ends up contributing to apartment society is not merely the kidney that heals the ailing Mr. Menon but also, with his trusty radio at his side, a sense of communal living and affection for life—human, plant, and animal alike—which heals the alienation, greed, and materialistic priorities that plague relationships between neighbors, spouses, and people of different social classes and generations. Ultimately, the motifs of noise-producing paraphernalia—mic, amplifier, loudspeaker, radio, popular cinema—that congeal around Mic's character are connected to his (and the film's) uninhibited broadcasting of the ills of alienation rampant in contemporary urban societies in such an exaggerated, "loud," and comedic manner that they can neither be ignored nor shut out by walls.

Noise, through the character of Mic, aka Loudspeaker, and his radio, is characterized as not only loud enough to breach the walls of the apartments but also bighearted enough to bring joy to the residents and nonresidents in the vicinity. Difference, with Mic's loud voice and radio metonymic for other differences of class and age, is embraced as a way in which one individual's strengths can complement another's weaknesses. Just as Mic gives Mr. Menon a kidney and a nudge to make amends and renew ties with his estranged family by the end of the film, Mr. Menon ultimately decides to buy back Mic's ancestral land from the loan shark in order to return it to him. Similarly, when Mr. Menon's comely nurse Annie is angered that Mic has befriended her elderly mother and chides him for being a jobless wastrel, Mic defends his lifestyle, retorting that, despite all the time Annie spends toiling away at her work, her mother is utterly alone and bored without her companionship, an important resource that his very joblessness affords.

Loudspeaker's prescription for rehabilitating the atomized social formations of contemporary urban ecosystems insists on actively acknowledging and generously sharing affection, space, and other resources with the plant, animal, and human lives vying for warmth and happiness in the cold environments of concrete jungles. Throughout the film, Mic is shown not only to befriend humans, regardless of age and class, and speak of living alongside wild elephants but also to nurture plants as he fills Mr. Menon's apartment with indoor plants and teaches children to plant and nurture roses outside. While he is initially chided by Mr. Menon for making a mess and soiling his hands and garments, he and the other residents eventually express their gratitude for the blooms that brighten their environments as the plants grow.

Loudspeaker imbues not merely Mic's character but especially the noise of popular cinema, specifically, with an ability to connect urban audiences to nature as part and parcel of an ecosystem that includes "human animals" and "wild animals" as well. This occurs through the film's citation of the earlier Malayalam film *Rosy* (P. N. Menon, 1965), whose popular romantic song "Alliyaambil Kadivil" was rerecorded for *Loudspeaker* with the voice of playback singer Vijay Yesudas, who happens to be the son of the original singer, K. J. Yesudas. *Rosy* was one of the first Malayalam films to have been shot outdoors, and the song "Alliyaambil" is picturized in *Loudspeaker* over Mr. Menon's recollections of a love lost decades earlier in his ancestral village of Chelangad. The lush greenery of Mr. Menon's recollections colors his growing warmth toward Mic, to whom he confesses his sorrow over a tragic romance of bygone days that continues to eat at him.

Loudspeaker's citation of the old film song becomes the pivot around which Mr. Menon finally connects not only to Mic but also to his family, his village, and the natural beauty of the area after having been estranged from them for decades. A romantic image of a young Mr. Menon lining his beloved's eyelids with dew from a green twig, which appears as a memory during the song "Alliyaambil," is reprised by a tender, homosocial image of Mic performing the same gesture on Mr. Menon as the two are seated in a boat near Mr. Menon's village. While *Rosy* hit a technical milestone for being one of the first Malayalam films to have been shot largely outdoors, *Loudspeaker* hits another in being one of the first Malayalam films to have been shot largely with sync sound (Sidhardhani 2013). In the same way that *Loudspeaker* invokes *Rosy*'s formal connection to outdoor locations to make a thematic connection to the same, *Loudspeaker*'s attempt to use sync sound resonates, so to speak, with its overall thematic preoccupation with sound in both cinema and the world.

Loudspeaker's farcical comedy belies its deeper critique of the class biases that are inextricable from both a South Asian environmental discourse of noise pollution and a failure to consider environmental and health issues more holistically. In this way, *Loudspeaker* advances a critique that resonates with a debate among sound studies scholars regarding the notion of the "soundscape," initially theorized by R. Murray Schafer in *The Tuning of the World* (1977). The term *soundscape*, Ari Kelman (2010) and Jonathan Sterne (2015) have noted, has been as ubiquitous as it has been capacious. Kelman charges, furthermore, that it is frequently used with little regard for Schafer's original conceptualization.

While I am less interested in a prescriptive definition of the term, the debate itself—and a return to Schafer's notion of the soundscape—on the one hand illuminates Schafer's own assumption that industrial modernity precipitated mankind's fall from an Eden of natural harmony to a modern world plagued by noise pollution. On the other hand, this premise has at times been seized as Schafer's central intervention at the expense of the much keener insights that follow in his work. Kendall Wrightson presciently notes, "Like many issues emerging from the explosion of ideologies in the late 1960s, the profundity of Schafer's original message is hidden behind a single, soundbyte-friendly issue: noise pollution. This is unfortunate since Schafer has far more to offer" (Wrightson 2000, 10).

Indeed, Schafer's call in *The Tuning of the World* is not one that rails for noise abatement but rather one that advocates a positive discipline of acoustic design as a means of highlighting the relationship—through his concept of the soundscape—among sound, listening, and the rendering and inhabiting of spaces that are shared by humans and nonhumans alike. Schafer's reflections are deeply invested in the ethics of harmony, not merely in an aesthetic sense but in a sense of cohabiting spaces through practices of listening that are positively attuned to how humans shape—and can better—their environments for all inhabitants.

To this end, in calling for greater discernment on the part of listeners with better-tuned ears, who can craft their soundscapes by determining which sounds harmonize and belong in their respective environments, Schafer writes:

> Noise pollution results when man does not listen carefully. Noises are the sounds we have learned to ignore. . . . We must seek a way to make environmental acoustics a positive study program. Which sounds do we want to preserve, encourage, multiply? (1977, 4)

Schafer's astute sense of sounds' ability to render their concomitant spaces is picked up by Sterne as a keen insight that emerges specifically from midcentury Euro-American encounters with the technologies of radio, hi-fi, and stereo. Sterne identifies an indebtedness to technological processes and listening practices of recorded sound in Schafer's idealization of a "hi-fi" soundscape in which noise (e.g., industrial noise) recedes to make way for the full expressive potential of natural sounds that implicitly center the individual listener's position within a soundscape.

Sterne, who offers a genealogy that historicizes the emergence and circulation of the notion of soundscapes in "mid-century, bourgeois, Anglophone settler [media] cultures" of radio, hi-fi, and stereo, contrasts Schafer's "soundscape as natural environment" with Hagood's notion of soundscaping as the consumerist ethos of retreating from difference in his study of the marketing of noise-canceling headphones (Sterne 2015, 67). Crucially, Schafer's idealization of a high-fidelity soundscape is not staked on soundproofing strategies that block out unwanted sounds but rather on the ability to, first, hear difference with sensitivity and, second, implement practices of acoustic design that allow for the "tuning of the world" in ways that highlight difference and perspective.

Loudspeaker in a sense highlights tensions between critical discussions of soundscape/soundscaping as an antimodern environmental category and a privatized, commoditized space. As Sterne emphasizes, the essence of the soundscape, in either sense, "is a stable audioposition, one from which the entire world is available to be heard" (2015, 79). *Loudspeaker*, however, via its eponymous character, also known as Mic and his trusty radio blaring film songs, seizes the spirit of Schafer's soundscape as an *ethical practice of design.* Mic materializes as an emblem of the raucous modes of an everything-for-everyone Indian popular cinema—at once thoroughly modern and thoroughly imbued with lush images of nature and human emotion—that has the potential to overthrow the stable (audio)position of the atomized individual. *Loudspeaker,* in this manner, holds environmental issues to be inclusive of the cocooning "hi-fi" social ills of class and age stratifications and the concomitant inability to adequately nurture and show concern for human life—plants and animals notwithstanding.

Hulla and Capitalist Amplification

In its characterization of the victims of "noise polluters," the Supreme Court's quick jump from a woman who was raped before she went on to commit suicide to students who are unable to study raises the absurdity of even the slightest possibility of equivalence between the suffering of the former and the latter. The propensity to make such leaps, which gloss over the ordeals of the most vulnerable bodies and prioritize the utmost comfort of those with far greater resources at their disposal, lies at the core of the 2008 film *Hulla* (Noise). Over the course of the film, the issue of noise pollution makes apparent the clamor for insularity on the part of a younger generation of wealthy, educated, corporate professionals, who remain deaf to little beyond their aggressive pursuit of an urban lifestyle of unlimited luxury and comfort.

The narrative and formal prominence of noise in the dystopian visions of *Hulla* extend critical considerations of noise pollution and the spatial politics of gender, class, caste, and communal identity in modern South Asia into the arena of everyday systemic violence in contemporary global cities. The eponymous motif of noise in the film emerges as the inescapable roar of neoliberal development, characterized by an ever-widening chasm between educated, corporate professionals, small-time merchants, and wage laborers (Hagood 2011). *Hulla* portrays the "hi-fi" malaise of frenetic, corporate lifestyles that gorge themselves on lofty standards of living that are precipitously propped up by the normalization of lending and debt as engines of high-speed development.

Although *Hulla*'s initial box office reception and reviews were rather lukewarm at best, the film did garner some praise retroactively, especially after the director, Jaideep Varma, won the 2011 "Best Arts/Cultural Film" national award for *Leaving Home,* a documentary about the renowned

Delhi-based fusion rock band Indian Ocean, which had in turn composed music for *Hulla* (Ghosh 2013). While multiple critics of *Hulla* felt that the band's soulful, angsty music was out of place in a film whose plot and characters' dilemmas seemed superficially mundane, the recruitment of a well-known rock band nonetheless complements the *hatke* (offbeat), low-budget, indie aesthetics of Verma's debut feature (Ghosh 2013).

Hulla has since been included in journalist and film critic Avijit Ghosh's *40 Retakes: Bollywood Classics You May Have Missed* (2013), in which he justifies his inclusion of *Hulla* by noting that "few films have shown the urban mind's ghettoization so succinctly" (252). Ghosh singles out acclaimed director Anurag Kashyap's deep praise of the film for the freshness of its script in particular, despite the fact that audiences and critics seem to dislike the film for the same reason. Kashyap, according to Ghosh, chalks up the film's box office failure to the fact that many who went to see it were expecting a comedy, and as such the film did not deliver. Ghosh's postmortem is identical, before he goes on to summarize the film and finally conclude:

> *Hulla* can also be seen as a parable on intolerance. In these undemocratic times, when there is a general unwillingness to listen the other person's point of view, when there is a rapid vanishing of middle space, the whistle becomes a metaphor for everything we want to shut out of our lives. (258)

Ghosh's characterization of *Hulla* as a "parable on intolerance . . . [in] these undemocratic times" notes the protagonist's irritation with the noise of a nightly whistle and his desire for an impenetrable sonic environment as an allegory for an elite desire to keep the realities of poverty and inequality not only out of view but also, and much more ambitiously, out of hearing range. *Hulla*'s depiction of the difficulty of controlling and enforcing rules against noise pollution amounts to a larger critique of the undemocratic nature of legislation and law enforcement practices that hear only the petty complaints of upper-middle-class citizens if not a dark and indirect parody of the noise pollution ruling by the Supreme Court just three years earlier.

The protagonist, Raj Puri, is a newly-married stockbroker who moves into a Bombay flat with his wife Abha. Between the high-pressure environment of his workplace and gradual revelation to the spectator that all may not be well at home, Raj is shown to start losing sleep. We learn that he has helped himself to a loan from a client's investment fund for the sake of the flat, confident that he will be able to invest the remainder to quickly recover and return the amount he has skimmed. The flat is a dream for Abha, whose bespectacled, bookish father minces no words in expressing his condescension for Raj's career in an Indian investment firm in light of readily available opportunities to work for any number of multinational corporations. In this way, *Hulla* portrays the normalization of largely self-inflicted hi-fi pressures of lucrative careers in investment industries, of lifestyles that aim to make and spend large amounts of money in short amounts of time, and of the deification of multinational corporations as the holy grail of success, particularly among the upper-crust, educated intelligentsia.

Yet, when Raj starts noticing the repeated sound of the watchman's nightly whistles, he comes to regard this whistling as the ruthless robber of the sleep he blames for his stress. Never giving pause to question his career and lifestyle choices, he instead goes after the watchman and his whistle, for they constitute the easiest and most vulnerable target for Raj's frustrations. The watchman is a frail, elderly man named Roger Mathew, who is plagued by physical weaknesses that range from poor eyesight to a bad back that leaves him unable to lift things. Bereft of family support systems, Roger's livelihood is wholly dependent on his meager earnings as a watchman. Roger informs Raj that he must answer to the apartments' general secretary, Janardhan, who has mandated that Roger blow his whistle intermittently throughout the night for the sake of deterring potential thieves by announcing his wakeful presence. Roger apologetically lets Raj know that if he stops blowing the whistle, he may be assumed by Janardhan to have neglected his duties and fallen asleep and thus be removed from his job.

Ultimately, no single character in *Hulla* emerges as a clear hero or villain, although the film is unambiguously critical and stark in its portrayal of systemic inequalities that affect every character for the worse, albeit differentially so. Its parable for "these undemocratic times" portrays the issue of noise pollution as a red herring for a much more acute deafness to the everyday plight of those who struggle in deep poverty on the part of an increasingly segmented and privileged upper-middle-class, upper-caste citizenry. As *Hulla* proceeds, Roger the watchman becomes caught in power plays between Raj and Janardhan. Throughout the film, Janardhan is shown to be constantly squabbling with his wife, who chides him for his failure to acquire an apartment that is more like Raj and Abha's—larger and more luxurious. As Ghosh notes, Janardhan embodies an older, middle-class family man who has slowly and steadily worked and saved money with an eye turned toward the lofty ambitions of a much more luxurious lifestyle. Janardhan and his wife are shown to be indignant over the living standards that are taken for granted by Raj, who stands for a generation of young elites. As a result, Janardhan remains particularly cold and unsympathetic toward Raj's complaints about the nightly whistles. In an almost hallucinatory delirium, Raj escalates his complaints about the whistles to the apartment association, the police, the chief minister, and eventually the prime minister. The absurdity of Raj's snowballing obsession with the whistles takes on somber tones as the spectator witnesses a panoramic view of the fallout by the end of the film.

The leadup to the final scene occurs after Raj, not having slept well for days, badly bungles a stock trade at his workplace. His own shares in the stock, as well as his professional reputation, take a hit, alongside the investments of Janardhan, who had played the stock market in a desperate move to acquire a rapid windfall and raise his family's standard of living in order to please his wife. Parallel editing shows both couples packing up, having suffered their respective losses. Raj's marriage is fully on the rocks, and his trading fiasco at work is the final straw in his attempt to curb the noise pollution—that is, the watchman's whistles—which he regards as the stressor that has been rendering him sleepless. Thus, he makes the choice to leave the apartment complex and seek another—presumably quieter—residence. Janardhan, on the other hand, is unable to afford living in his apartment after his investments have plummeted, although he is unaware that it was Raj's error that resulted in this downturn.

The film's final scene, whose effectiveness arises from the omniscient perspective that it affords the spectator, brings into view the everyday suffering that is disproportionately borne by those who have the fewest economic resources. Panning and aerial shots show the two couples in their respective cars, inching along in slow-moving, congested traffic. They are not cognizant of their parallel departures from the apartment complex, their proximity to one another in the traffic jam, and the interrelatedness of the whistle dilemma, Raj's misstep, and their simultaneous setbacks. Most egregiously, however, neither Raj, Abha, Janardhan, nor Janardhan's wife has any sense of the setbacks borne by the frail, elderly Roger, who is shown standing in the middle of the road in the final scene, reduced to begging after having lost his job in the drama between Raj and Janardhan over the nightly whistling, despite the fact that Roger himself had no power to make any decisions affecting the matter.

The plots of *Hulla* and *Loudspeaker* are driven by noisy intrusions that rile up and affect entire upper-middle-class apartment communities in order to diagnose their *inability* to hear the much louder and more threateningly ubiquitous violence of rampant inequality and the dearth of concern for those beyond one's own nuclear family units and class segments. The two films, made within just a year of one another, share the mise-en-scène of a contemporary, urban, upper-middle-class apartment complex and its motley of archetypal characters (e.g., the watchman, the stubborn authoritarian secretary, the fun-loving young neighbors, and the uptight elderly neighbors) in addition to soundtracks whose respective music cites genres that have been frequently denigrated as noise for decades: popular film music in *Loudspeaker* and rock music in *Hulla*.[6]

In light of *Hulla*'s closing moments, as in *Loudspeaker* overall, a discourse of individual health, mindfulness, and stress management—which has also been at the heart of the Supreme Court's commitment to fight noise pollution—is shown to miss the mark in only further isolating individuals, as well as an elite, upper-middle-class, upper-caste segment that has the time and resources to spare for the hardly inexpensive wares of gurus, yoga studios, and the like.[7] To this end both films parody the faith and resources that are placed in such techniques of stress management through the highly caricatured character of a counselor who is little more than a drunken charlatan, which occasions moments of slapstick humor in *Loudspeaker*, and the repeated pronouncements in *Hulla* by Abha, Janardhan, and especially Janardhan's wife that the antidotes to Raj's sleeplessness lie in meditation, yoga, and diet. Parodying the health and stress management industries, these moments in *Hulla* point to systemic inequalities in a neoliberal era, as rapid development is shown to amplify not only the resources of those with access to lucrative corporate jobs and the capital to risk large credit lines but also the unprecedented degree of class segmentation that amounts to ever-widening gaps between upper-middle-class and working-class lifestyles and their concomitant experiences of day-to-day stress.

In *Hulla*, finally, there is no Mammooty/Mic who is loud enough to shatter the social walls that deafen the characters to the plights of those, like Roger, who are not only less fortunate but also so acutely affected by the decisions of people like Raj and Janardhan. As such, there is no sentimental feel-good note of closure at the conclusion of the film. Instead, the responsibility of grappling with the stark inequalities that remain at the end of *Hulla* is turned over to the spectator, and indeed the film's form and production contexts constitute an overall address to those who are perhaps a little, if not quite a bit, like Raj: a young generation of educated upper-middle-class, upper-caste professionals who might know and be lured by the promise of a soundtrack that features the fusion rock band Indian Ocean and who would go for such a debut, low-budget, actionless, starless indie film in the first place.

Noise Abatement Policies and Structures of Unbelonging

Policies concerning noise pollution, among other environmental issues, have seemed neutral in the rational voice of the state, which insists on taking action in the name of the public good. A closer look at *Dastak*, *Loudspeaker*, and *Hulla* highlights the segmentation of this "listening public" into bodies that carry gender, class, caste, and communal identities.[8] The comforts of certain (e.g., upper-middle-class and upper-caste) bodies are differentially and systematically prioritized by both a patriarchal statist discourse and an increasingly corporatized global market, just as the propensity of certain bodies (working-class, Dalit, Muslim) to engage in the production of pollution of various kinds is much more frequently assumed.

It is no surprise, then, that a recent controversy incited by the star Hindi playback singer Sonu Nigam spiraled out from a tweet that complained, "God bless everyone. I have to be woken up by the Azaan [Islamic call to prayer] in the morning. When will this forced religiousness end in India[?]" (Desai 2007). Several ordinary citizens, politicians, and Bollywood stars weighed in with various positions, some offering rejoinders that asked why Nigam chose to single out the *azaan* when "forced religiousness" emanated just as much from Hindu temples and festivals such as Ganesh Chaturti, Diwali, and Navaratri, among a host of industrial disturbances (Scroll Staff 2017).

Indeed, a follow-up judgment by the Supreme Court regarding noise pollution was issued in October 2005, three months after the initial judgment, which addressed precisely this aforementioned (communal) elephant in the room: a specifically Indian (if not South Asian) debate over the constitutionality of potentially curbing free expression and, more particularly, the free expression of religion with policies concerning the environmental issue of noise pollution. Fascinatingly, the follow-up Supreme Court judgment turned to an editorial published by the "Speaking Tree," a pop-spirituality column published by the *Times of India*. The judgment quotes the editorial at length, which notes the inauthenticity of loudspeakers in religious traditions as follows.

> Wait a minute. There were no loudspeakers in the old days. When different civilisations developed or adopted different faiths or when holy books were written to guide devotees, they did not mention the use of loudspeakers as being vital to spread religious devotion. So the use of loudspeakers cannot be a must for performing any religious act. Some argue that every religion asks its followers to spread its teachings and the loudspeaker is a modern instrument that helps to do this more effectively. They cannot be more wrong. No religion ever says to force the unwilling to listen to expressions of religious beliefs. ("Forum" 2005b)

The judgment goes on to reproduce the remainder of the editorial, which selectively quotes passages from the Bhagavad Gita, Qur'an, and Bible to argue that Hinduism, Islam, and Christianity all advise against preaching to those who are unwilling to listen and that loudspeakers are entirely irrelevant to these religious traditions due to their nonexistence when each of the three faiths were established.

In averring, "In our opinion [the quoted "Speaking Tree" editorial] very correctly states the factual position as to the objective of several religions and their underlying logic," the Supreme Court judgment thus exerts its own authority not only as an interpreter of religious texts (via the "Speaking Tree" no less) but also in promoting a conservative position that assumes the establishment of originary, monolithic traditions of world religions that become corrupted with any historical change ("Forum" 2005b). I point this out not to argue against the regulation of noise pollution per se but to push the point that the discourse over noise pollution in India—parallel to the politics of noise abatement elsewhere—has been deeply enmeshed with the normalization of problematic discourses and structures of gender, class, caste, and religion to the extent that they appear apolitical and merely factual (Thompson 2004).

I offer, in conclusion, the instance of the 1985 Kolahal Niyantran Adhiniyam (Noise Control Act) of the Indian state of Madhya Pradhesh, previously known as the 1951 Control of Music and Noise Act. In the same vein as the older version, the more recent state law offers a series of definitions that include the following for "loud music," "noise," and "soft music."

> (a) "*loud music*" means sound produced on or from band, bag pipe, clarionet, shahnai, drum, bugle, dhole, daf, dafda, nagara, tasha

or jhanj and includes any loud sound produced by any other instrument or means.

(c) "*noise*" means sound from any source whatsoever of such character as causes or is likely to cause mental or physical discomfort to a man of ordinary sensibility or susceptibility or causes or is likely to cause disturbance in the study.

(f) "*soft music*" means sound produced on or from any of the following instruments, namely:-

(i) sitar, sarangi, ektara, violin, bansi, dilrubam, bin, veena, sarod, jaltarang;

(ii) piano, harmoniyam, gramophone, tabla, khanjari, dholak and mridang;

(iii) transistor, record-player, stereo or radio in so far as musical programmes only are concerned. ("The MP Kolahal Niyantran Adhiniyam" 2017)

A number of things are striking about these definitions enshrined as law. For starters, the instruments that produce "loud music," and are thereby imbued with the propensity to create noise, are all associated with folk and brass band (e.g., nonclassical, nonelite) forms. By objective standards, for example, the daf (which supposedly produces loud music) and the khanjari (which supposedly produces soft music) are similar tambourinelike instruments. A major difference, completely unrelated to volume, is that the khanjari, also known as the kanjira, has been standardized as an instrument in South Indian classical music and dance performance. This, perhaps, merits its inclusion alongside the mridang, a barrel drum used for the same purpose. In this way, the law implicitly enshrines notions of propriety that privilege classical forms of expression associated with upper-class, upper-caste practices as authentic and inoffensive.

Among the earliest pamphlets that warn of the hazards of noise pollution is a 1972 publication by the US Environmental Protection Agency. Its opening line, reproduced as one of the epigraphs that opens this chapter, indicts rock music of the 1960s counterculture as the epitome of noise pollution, indicting "hi-fi equipment" and "rock music" as likely harming the health of all those who came of age within their ambit (United States Environmental Protection Agency 1972). This chapter has aimed to contextualize and analyze the stakes of state discourses over noise pollution—their widely acknowledged inefficacy notwithstanding in the case of India—within wider public debates over noise (Press Trust of India 2017). When cast as an object of state control, noise, I hope to have shown through the readings of three films, emerges by default as an unbelonging, sexually threatening outsider—a pollutant, an uncontrolled excess, a hazard. It has been the task of this chapter to show that even when noise is characterized as disembodied, atmospheric, and alien it often remains intimately tied to the bodies that are systemically and violently implicated as similarly unbelonging. Thus, it is often the regulation of the latter that occupies a central objective in the regulation of the former.

Notes

1. Regarding the notion of high fidelity, Michel Chion notes that fidelity "is a problematic notion from the start" since it implies a recording's *faithfulness* to an original sound, whereas even though so-called hi-fi recordings are able to reproduce a range of higher frequencies, what is usually meant by *hi-fi* is definition. To put a fine point on it, Chion asserts, "No one complains of nonfidelity from too much definition!" I retain *hi-fi as* a problematic term not only for its imprecision but also for the manner in which it has come to circulate with strong connotations of elite class status in South Asia (Chion 1994, 98–99).

2. Even in light of an emphasis on the mutually constitutive nature of images and sounds in cinema, Michel Chion's seminal text reminds us of the predominance of the visual in shaping the meaning of sounds. As Metz and Gurrieri (2008) note in their semiotic analysis of offscreen sounds, so-called, Chion's *Audio-Vision,* too, identifies the category of "offscreen sound" as a productive misnomer: "In the simplest and strongest relation, that of *offscreen sound,* the confrontation of sound with image establishes the sound as being offscreen, even as this sound is heard coming from the surface of the screen." (Chion 1994, 40).

3. Sangita Gopal's monograph (2012) is dedicated to the politics of conjugality in Hindi popular cinema, namely, in outlining prehistories and tracking shifts that mark the postmillennial New Bollywood cinema.

4. Shastri and Trivedi's *Noise Pollution* (1988), for example, was published as a scientific and legal survey of noise pollution in India as an environmental and health hazard. For an excellent analysis of the contemporary ideological terrain of hi-fi aspirations toward the reduction of noise, see Mack Hagood's "Quiet Comfort" (2011), an analysis of the marketing of Bose's QuietComfort noise-canceling headphones for privileged—namely, business-class—air travelers. For a deft historical contextualization of the soundproof study in Victorian era London, see John M. Picker's "The Soundproof Study," (2003), which connects the widespread concern over the "nuisance" of street musicians to the proliferation of middle-class professionals who worked from their homes—for example, writers—and felt a palpable need to isolate and legitimate their work(space) as a professional, masculine arena within the otherwise domestic sphere of the home. The perceived threat of noisy street musicians loomed as a threat not

only to distinguishing a space of precarious masculine professional identity but also to the British character of the city and the health of the environment. As anti-street-music campaigns professed a desire for noise abatement, they also betrayed xenophobic anxieties over foreign contagion and encroachment of outside contaminants on both the body of the individual professional and the character of the city and nation alike (Shastri and Trivedi 1988; Hagood 2011, 573–74; Picker 2003).

5. Ratheesh Radhakrishnan details a history of politics and the popular vis-à-vis Malyalam cinema in Kerala, particularly with respect to the history of leftist politics in the state. He "argues for the recognition of this form of the 'popular' [e.g., as leftover, unofficial narratives] as central to our understanding of politics and culture in Kerala . . . as a domain which is marked by contestations between various discourses of the political for hegemony," with one such discourse being that of popular cinema (Radhakrishnan 2010, 26).

6. Note, for example, the reference to rock music that headlines a 1972 pamphlet issued by the US Environmental Protection Agency, which appears as one of the epigraphs that open this chapter: "The combination of hi-fi equipment and the rock music which dominated the past decade, alone has probably affected the hearing of a whole generation of listeners." United States Environmental Protection Agency 1972.

7. For an analysis of the popularization and corporatization of yoga within a larger global culture of consumerism, see Andrea Jain's *Selling Yoga* (2014).

8. For a prescient theorization of listening publics that insists on attendant methodological emphases on listening practices in scholarly accounts of media publics, see Kate Lacey's *Listening Publics* (2013).

Works Cited

Attali, Jacques, and Susan McClary. 1985. *Noise: The Political Economy of Music.* Translated by Brian Massumi. Minneapolis: University of Minnesota Press.

Basu, Anustup. 2013. "'The Face That Launched a Thousand Ships': Helen and Public Femininity in Hindi Film." In *Figurations in Indian Film,* edited by Anustup Basu and Meheli Sen, 139–57. London: Palgrave Macmillan. DOI: https://doi.org/10.1057/9781137349781_8

Bhaskar, Ira. 2013. *The Indian New Wave.* London: Routledge.

Booth, Gregory D. 2007. "Making a Woman from a Tawaif: Courtesans as Heroes in Hindi Cinema." *New Zealand Journal of Asian Studies* 9, no. 2: 1–26.

Booth, Gregory D. 2008. *Behind the Curtain: Making Music in Mumbai's Film Studios.* New York: Oxford University Press.

Bose, Brinda. 2008. "Modernity, Globality, Sexuality, and the City: A Reading of Indian Cinema." *Global South* 2, no. 1: 35–58.

Chatterjee, Partha. 1993. *The Nation and Its Fragments: Colonial and Postcolonial Histories.* Princeton, NJ: Princeton University Press.

Chelangad, Saju. 2015. "The Changemaker." *The Hindu,* April 19. http://www.thehindu.com/features/metroplus/reeltime-the-changemaker/article7117110.ece

Chion, Michel. 1994. *Audio-Vision.* Translated by Claudia Gorbman. New York: Columbia University Press.

Desai, Mohua. 2007. "Sonu Nigam's Tweets on Noisy 'azaan' Spark Row." *Times of India,* April 18. http://timesofindia.indiatimes.com/india/sonu-nigams-tweets-on-noisy-azaan-spark-row/articleshow/58231599.cms

"Forum, Prevention of Environmental and Sound Pollution v. Union of India & Anv., No. 21851/03 (2005.7.18) (Noise Pollution) | ELAW." 2005a. Accessed July 2, 2017. https://www.elaw.org/es/content/india-forum-prevention-environmental-and-sound-pollution-v-union-india-anv-no-2185103–200571

"Forum, Prevention Of Envn. & Sound . . . vs. Union Of India & Anr on 28 October, 2005." 2005b. Accessed July 12, 2017. https://indiankanoon.org/doc/541057

Ghosh, Avijit. 2013. "Hulla (2008)." In *40 Retakes: Bollywood Classics You May Have Missed,* 252–59. Chennai: Tranquebar.

Gopal, Sangita. 2012. *Conjugations: Marriage and Form in New Bollywood Cinema.* Chicago: University of Chicago Press.

Hagood, Mack. 2011. "Quiet Comfort: Noise, Otherness, and the Mobile Production of Personal Space." *American Quarterly* 63, no. 3: 573–89.

Jain, Andrea. 2014. *Selling Yoga: From Counterculture to Pop Culture.* Oxford: Oxford University Press.

Kaarsholm, Preben, ed. 2006. *City Flicks: Indian Cinema and the Urban Experience.* London: Seagull Books.

Kelman, Ari Y. 2010. "Rethinking the Soundscape." *The Senses and Society* 5, no. 2: 212–34. DOI: https://doi.org/10.2752/174589210X12668381452845

Lacey, Kate. 2013. *Listening Publics: The Politics and Experience of Listening in the Media Age.* Hoboken, NJ: Wiley.

Larkin, Brian. 2008. *Signal and Noise: Media, Infrastructure, and Urban Culture in Nigeria.* Durham, NC: Duke University Press.

Majumdar, Neepa. 2001. "The Embodied Voice: Song Sequences and Stardom in Popular Hindi Cinema." In *Soundtrack Available: Essays on Film and Popular Culture,* edited by Pamela Robertson Wojcik and Arthur Knight, 161–81. Durham, NC: Duke University Press.

Manuel, Peter. 1990. *Thumri in Historical and Stylistic Perspectives.* New Delhi: Motilal Banarasidass.

Mazumdar, Ranjani. 2007. *Bombay Cinema: An Archive of the City.* Minneapolis: University of Minnesota Press.

Metz, Christian, and Georgia Gurrieri. 1980. "Aural Objects." *Yale French Studies,* no. 60 (January 1): 24–32.

"The M.P. Kohlahal Nityantran Adhiniyam, 1985." 2017. "Bare Acts Live: Central Acts and Rules Amended and Updated." Accessed July 3. http://www.bareactslive.com/MP/MP359.HTM

Picker, John M. 2003. "The Soundproof Study: Victorian Professional Identity and Urban Noise." In *Victorian Soundscapes,* 41–81. New York: Oxford University Press.

Prasad, M. Madhava. 2001. *Ideology of the Hindi Film: A Historical Construction.* Oxford: Oxford University Press.

Press Trust of India. 2017. "Noise Pollution Exceeds Permissible Limits in 7 Cities,

Including Metros: Govt." *Hindustan Times*, May 24. http://www.hindustantimes.com/india-news/noise-pollution-exceeds-permissible-limits-in-7-cities-including-metros-govt/story-6R0aO9pIuYpKl9Ko2NuZRL.html

Radhakrishnan, Ratheesh. 2010. "What Is Left of Malayalam Cinema?" In *Cinemas of South India: Culture, Resistance, and Ideology*, edited by Sowmya Dechamma and E. Satya Prakash, 25–48. Oxford: Oxford University Press.

Radhakrishnan, Ratheesh. 2017. "Guest Editor's Introduction." *positions: east asia cultures critique* 25, no. 1: 1–7. DOI: https://doi.org/10.1215/10679847-3710276

Rajadhyaksha, Ashish. 2009. *Indian Cinema in the Time of Celluloid: From Bollywood to the Emergency*. Bloomington: Indiana University Press.

Schafer, R. Murray. 1977. *The Tuning of the World*. New York: Knopf.

Scroll Staff. 2017. "Sonu Nigam Grumbles about 'Forced Religiousness' after Muslim Call to Prayer Wakes Him Up." *Scroll.In*, April 17. https://scroll.in/latest/834816/sonu-nigam-grumbles-about-forced-religiousness-after-muslim-call-to-prayer-wakes-him-up

Shastri, Satish, and Manjoo Bala Trivedi. 1988. *Noise Pollution: Its Scientific and Legal Perspective*. Jodhpur: Divyajyoti Prakashan.

Sidhardhani, Sanjith. 2013. "Kanyaka Talkies." *Times of India*, May 19. http://timesofindia.indiatimes.com/entertainment/malayalam/movies/news/Kanyaka-Talkies-set-to-break-sync-sound-barriers-in-Mwood/articleshow/20132956.cms

Sterne, Jonathan. 2015. "The Stereophonic Spaces of Soundscape." In *Living Stereo: Histories and Cultures of Multichannel Sound*, edited by Paul Théberge, Kyle Devine, and Tom Everrett, 65–83. New York: Bloomsbury Academic.

Thompson, Emily. 2004. *The Soundscape of Modernity: Architectural Acoustics and the Culture of Listening in America, 1900–1933*. Cambridge, MA: MIT Press.

United States Environmental Protection Agency. 1972. *Noise Pollution*. Washington, DC: Environmental Protection Agency.

Wrightson, Kendall. 2000. "An Introduction to Acoustic Ecology." *Soundscape: The Journal of Acoustic Ecology* 1, no.1: 10–13.

SECTION TWO

Voice

FIVE | Usha Uthup and Her Husky, Heavy Voice

PAVITRA SUNDAR

Introduction: "Skyfall is where we start . . ."[1]

On October 26, 2013, INK, an Indian organization modeled on the lines of TED, hosted the singer Usha Uthup (b. 1947) as part of its annual conference in Kochi, Kerala. Within a month of being posted, "Skyfall in a Sari" became one of the most watched videos on the INK website.[2] Uthup begins her performance reminiscing about her forty-four-year music career and then launches into "Skyfall," Adele's hit song for the 2012 James Bond film. That Uthup sings a Bond song should come as no surprise, for she has been regaling audiences with pop, rock, and jazz tunes since the late 1960s.[3] In her prelude to "Skyfall," Uthup reminds us that she has recorded all the Bond songs and has been compared to Shirley Bassey, the Welsh vocalist famous for "Goldfinger" and other early Bond songs. Uthup also makes reference to two of her other famous covers, "Fever" and "Feelings."[4] She tells of how she sang "Feelings" alongside one Mr. Boothalingam and the Cantopop singer Sandra Lang at the International Casino in Nairobi. Cringe-worthy as it is, her mimicry of her fellow singers and the venue's Italian manager secures her position as a cosmopolitan pop diva. Her story naturalizes her repertoire and demonstrates that her language, accent, and vocal style match her musical choices. What makes her seem incongruous is her sari. Indeed, the very title of her talk, "Skyfall in a Sari," suggests that what is distinctive about her performance is not her vocal prowess and repertoire so much as her appearance—the fact that she always performs in a traditional Kanjeevaram silk sari with a big *bindi*, a rich array of bangles, and flowers in her hair. Here I extend Uthup's argument about the perceived disconnect between the aural and visual realms of her performance—between her "husky heavy voice" and her South Indian look (Kumar 2003). This apparent mismatch was a mark of distinction on the live performance circuit, particularly at a time when nightclubs were taboo for middle-class Hindu women. However, it proved a liability in the world of Hindi cinema.

In what follows, I take a deep dive into print and music archives of the late 1960s and 1970s to flesh out Uthup's career as a live performer and recording artist.[5] Although Uthup's name is legendary, the details of her early career and the vibrant jazz and beat (rock) scenes of which she was an integral part are not well documented. As my citations and endnotes indicate, the information here is mainly pieced together from record covers; contemporaneous newspaper advertisements and articles; a Facebook page dedicated to rock music, "Indian Sixties and Beyond"; and a handful of recent blogs and print sources documenting the history of jazz and rock in India. The long lists of songs and collaborating artists I present are not simply acts of fandom on my part. They help me place Uthup in several overlapping sound cultures, all of which existed on the edges of the Bombay film industry. If we just attend to the history of Hindi film and film music, Uthup is largely missing. But if we listen more broadly, as middle- and upper-class Indians did in the 1960s and 1970s, to music wafting out of cafés and nightclubs, to sounds broadcast over Radio Ceylon, and to records brought back by relatives and neighbors who traveled abroad, then Uthup no longer seems like an anomaly. Her voice, her repertoire, even her sari make eminent sense. Through my analysis of Uthup's vocal sound and the discourse about her—articulated in ads, reviews, and images and liner notes of LPs—I demonstrate that both her bodily voice and a sense of "liveness" were critical to her stardom (Auslander 2008). But this extracinematic stardom complicated ideologies about voice and body in the Bombay film industry. I close this chapter with the argument that the problematic mismatch in Uthup's case is *not* between her voice and her look but between her star persona and the image of the (few) actors for whom she rendered playback. Her fame as a husky-voiced, sari-clad live performer meant that she could only render playback for the visually and aurally excessive disco numbers of the early 1980s or for songs in which she had a cameo as the nightclub singer she was. Uthup's voice was seen to belong to no-body but her.

Uthup's Early Career

Usha Uthup, who went by the last name Iyer at the start of her career, is known as a consummate live performer. Her fame is bolstered by the many albums and ad jingles she has recorded over the course of her career. She gave us some of the most memorable tunes on 1980s television, including ads for coffee ("Come alive to the taste of Nescafe"), orange soda ("Live a little hot, sip a Gold Spot"), cough drops ("Vicks ki goli lo, khich-khich door karo"), and noodles ("Maggi! Maggi! Maggi!").[6] Simple and catchy, these ads stick around as cultural earworms of a sort, but they belie Uthup's accomplishments. To grasp her versatility as a musician, we must attend to her early successes as a live singer and recording artist.

Print ads of the 1970s proclaim Usha Uthup as having been "born to sing."[7] Hailing from a middle-class Tamilian family in Bombay, she had role models in her older sisters Indira and Uma, who had been performing under their maiden names since the 1950s. The Singing Sami Sisters' repertoire of close harmony swing numbers was met with great acclaim in the clubs and gymkhanas of Bombay, Calcutta, and other cities (Fernandes 2011c). Uma Pocha (her married name) was also famous for her rendition of "Bombay Meri Jaan," which effectively tied her to the city's musical lore. By the late 1960s, Uthup was following in her sisters' footsteps. She got her start in the Nine Gems club in Madras in 1968 when she gave an impromptu performance of "Fever," the song that would become her signature number (Fernandes 2011c). That performance earned her a week-long gig at the Nine Gems, which led to longer engagements at the Savera (Madras), Ritz (Bombay), and Oberoi (Delhi) hotels. The turning point in her career came when Ellis Joshua, co-owner of the famed Calcutta nightspot Trincas, heard her in Mysore and invited her to be a regular artist at his Park Street venue. With a clutch of live music venues, including Mocambo, Blue Fox, Magnolia, Moulin Rouge, and of course Trincas, Park Street was where the elites of the city gathered for nightly entertainment. Despite entering a crowded field, Uthup quickly found her niche as a sari-clad diva (see fig. 5.1).

Uthup's first performance at Trincas was on August 1, 1969, and by all accounts her rise to fame was meteoric.[8] The liner notes on her first LP *Scotch and Soda* (also released that year) indicate as much:

> Usha Iyer just happened! There is no other way to describe this artiste who, in her simple saries and deceptively simple mannerisms bowled

Fig. 1. Album cover art depicting Uthup as a live performer

> the youngster over. For days after her Calcutta debut, her singing was the talk of the town. Never was there a young gathering where she wasn't discussed. And in what ecstatic terms![9]

Advertisements in the *Times of India* a couple months later also suggest that the newspaper's middle- and upper-class readership in Bombay had already heard about her. In an advertisement for a charity concert in the November 26, 1969, issue, a group called the Friends of Needy Children references her popularity in Calcutta: "USHA IYER who took Calcutta by storm At THE BEAT MEET" is clearly the star of the show.[10] The three bands scheduled to share the stage with her that night—the Savages, the Lightnings, and the Reincarnations—were fixtures in the country's budding beat or rock music scene, yet the ad presents them as secondary attractions. The reference to Calcutta is also notable. The city has always been known as an artistic mecca, but this was especially the case in the 1960s, when the music scene on Park Street was like no other. An ad three days later for the same charity show emphasizes, and implicitly laments, the fact that Uthup's hometown of Bombay was not her professional base that year: "USHA IYER appears in her One and Only Performance this year. . . . Hurry up. Don't miss this chance." The capitalization and font size, the fact that Uthup gets top billing, and the sense of urgency generated by these ads emphasize her star status.

During the summer of 1970, five months after the venue opened (and then again in 1971), Uthup was the in-house artist at a Bombay nightclub called Talk of the Town (TT). Friday, Saturday, and Sunday nights there were "Usha Iyer Nites." In addition, she hosted a Sunday morning session. Some TT ads are more hyperbolic than others: "USHA IYER *WILL* BLOW UP *THE* TALK OF THE TOWN TO-NIGHT DISCOTHEQUE NIGHT. . . . Come and groove along."[11] Another declares as confidently, "SUNDAY JAM SESSION WILL BE PACKED. USHA IYER. Last Jam Session. DON'T MISS IT."[12] Clearly, Uthup needed no introduction for Bombayites of a particular milieu. While she was joined at times by Ernest Ignatius ("the handsome singing discovery"), *her* name was clearly the draw. According to one report, Uthup was the highest-paid singer on the live circuit (Bose 2008). While it is hard to place when and how long this was the case, there is no denying Uthup's immense and immediate popularity wherever she performed.

By 1972, just three years after she turned professional, Uthup was the best-selling artist among Indian singers of Western genres (Chandra 1972, 21). A short *Times of India* piece on March 1, 1970, announcing an upcoming charity event hosted by the American Women's Club notes that her "hot numbers are sold like hot cakes everywhere" and deems her singing "Pop music at its scintillating best" (B. S. R. 1970). While her records were categorized as Indian, or in some cases international, "pop," her repertoire was in fact far more wide ranging. She was as comfortable with jazz standards as she was with blues, soul, folk, rockabilly, and pop. The songs on her early albums and the musicians who accompanied her on these recordings give us a sense of her vast expertise. Her first record, released by HMV in 1968, was a 45 rpm that included Hank Williams's "Jambalaya" and the Kingston Trio's "Greenback Dollar." She was accompanied by Hecke Kingdom and his jazz quartet, a distinguished group that was the resident band at Volga, a popular South Bombay music venue, in the 1950s and 1960s.[13] This single was followed by a set of two extended play recordings (EPs), also on the HMV label, entitled *The Fabulous Usha Iyer with the Flintstones* (1969; see fig. 5.1). She was backed in her energetic covers of "Blues Train," "Summertime," "Dizzy," and "The Trip" by the Trincas house band, which included Eddie Rynjah (lead vocals, guitar), Noel Martin (vocals, bass guitar), Rodney Thomson (guitar), and Steve Booth (drums) (Swer 2017; "Information on the Bands" 2011).[14] Each of these musicians, and Martin in particular, is now remembered as a legendary figure on Park Street.[15] Here's how one avid record collector, an Australian artist blogging in April 2016, describes the music on *The Fabulous Usha Iyer* record set:

> On the first single, the A sided The Trip is absolute killer material from both Usha and the band. With it's [*sic*] psychedelic brilliance, hard hitting break beats, snappy mod blues guitar work, and Usha's beautiful acidic jazz vocals, it's raw, dirty and dope, and for me, it feels like bathing in the richest soil of the Indian earth! (Sgro 2016)

Notwithstanding its orientalist whiffs, this review captures the musical prowess and depth of feeling that made Uthup's performances so compelling.

On her next record—her first LP, *Scotch and Soda* (Odeon, 1969)—Uthup was joined once again by two popular Bombay bands: the Ronnie Menezes Quartet and the Savages. Several songs on this album would become Uthup standards, including the title song, first recorded by the Kingston Trio in 1958; "Sunny," Bobby Hebb's 1966 song, which ranked high on the R&B and pop music charts that year; "California Dreaming," the Mamas and the Papas' 1966 hit; and of course "Fever."[16] The Ronnie Menezes Quartet accompanied Uthup on all but two songs on *Scotch and Soda.* On "Midnight Hour" and "California Dreaming," she was supported by the Savages. One of the foremost beat groups in India, the Savages gained fame (and a recording contract with HMV) on winning Best Performance and Best Original Composition at the prestigious Sound Trophy contest in 1967 (Singh).[17] They performed on a nightly basis to packed audiences at Trincas for about six weeks in 1969. For his part, Ronnie Menezes collaborated with Uthup on several occasions, including the Ward Rock 71 beat show (which also featured the Savages) and *To This Night . . . . A Dawn,* an anti-apartheid play staged in 1970.[18] Menezes and his fellow musicians backed her on at least two other records. One single in 1970 lists her as the "conductor" of the two songs by Ronnie Menezes and his Soul Sounds. Another single offers an ode composed by Uthup (on the spur of the moment according to one account) to a scooter of the same name released that year (Kulkarni 2013). With music arranged by Menezes and performed by his quartet, "The Lambretta Story" was "specially manufactured by the Gramophone Company of India for Automobile Products of India Limited," presumably as a promotional item for the auto manufacturer.[19] Uthup also recorded two EPs of Konkani numbers with the Goan bandleader Chris Perry: *Usha: Concanim Hits* (HMV, 1974), which included the fabulously funky "Paka Paka" (where she shows off her scatting chops), and *From Usha with Love* (EMI, 1976).[20]

Scrutinizing Uthup's early records drives home just how wide ranging Uthup was in the songs, genres, and projects she took on. She was (and is) an extremely talented singer who distinguished herself with an eclectic multilingual and multigenre repertoire. She is a stellar exponent not only of Western genres (with lyrics in English) but also of popular songs in Bengali, Konkani, Malayalam, and other languages. In several interviews, she recalls that she realized early on that audiences were thrilled when she switched from English to other Indian languages (see, e.g., Fernandes 2011c). In the 1980s, she would come to be associated with disco numbers in Hindi cinema, particularly those composed by Bappi Lahiri. This expansive repertoire and her decision to sing in a wide range of spaces and contexts—in jazz venues as well as beat shows and competitions; in concerts that included playback singers, dancers, and mimics; in nightclubs featuring other jazz and pop singers, but also striptease artists, magicians, and cabaret dancers—helped her tap into a broad middle- and upper-class audience in metropolitan India.

Uthup's prolific recording and live performance schedule also bears witness to the flexibility and porosity of the diverse sound cultures she inhabited. She collaborated with up and coming stars like Eddie Rynjah and Noel Martin, as well as such stalwarts of Bombay's jazz age as Hecke Kingdom and Chris Perry. It was not just "youngsters" at beat meets who were blown away by her; so, too, were older audiences at nightclubs and hotels. Her fellow musicians, like her fans, were based in different cities and thus moved in somewhat different (musical) worlds. Her records—and, as explained below, her concerts and radio as a medium—were spaces of conjunction for diverse audiences and sounds. The point is not so much that Uthup appealed to and gathered numerous "listening publics" (Lacey 2013). She did. What is even more interesting is how the rich aural milieu of India in the 1960s and 1970s, and the discourses about gender and postcoloniality operative in that urban milieu, enabled her impressive musicking.

Sound Cultures and Spaces

While the mythos of Uthup is that of an anomalous and pioneering figure, she was in fact part of a lively entertainment scene that spanned several cities. Many of her Bombay concerts took place at Shanmukhananda Hall, the biggest concert hall in the city at the time. Premier beat competitions, including the finals of the annual All India Simla Beat Contest, took place there.[21] So did performances by leading classical musicians and playback singers. On the very same page as the November 26, 1969, ad for Uthup's Friends of Needy Children concert, for instance, there is an ad for a Kishore Kumar show at the same venue the following night. In some concerts, Uthup shared the stage with playback stars such as Yesudas, Mukesh, Talat Mehmood, even the kathak maestro Gopi Krishna.[22] A March 25, 1970, ad for a benefit concert for the St. Mary's School, "Stars and Stars," has her performing alongside Mahendra Kapoor and Geeta Dutt. (Also on the docket that night were folk dances, skits, and appearances by film stars.) While the film singers are listed above Uthup, the ad describes her as "India's latest pop rage." We might read such ads as advertising her difference (i.e., she sings pop, *not* film music) or the fact that she can appeal to film fans despite specializing in nonfilm genres. Either way, what the ads certainly establish is that venues like the Shanmukhananda Hall and Birla Matushri Sabhagar (where "Stars and Stars" was held) were spaces where apparently disparate sound cultures overlapped, sometimes over the course of a single night.

The "variety" format of these concerts also clues us into why audiences, young and old, took to Uthup's performances. Located in the same performance venues and advertised alongside shows by film stars, English and Hindi films, and plays in myriad languages—all crammed onto the same page in the classified ads section—her performances jostled for the attention of (English-educated) Indians with a modicum of expendable income. These were middle- and upper-class people who were fans of Hindi film and film music, but who also tuned in regularly to Voice of America, the BBC, and Radio Ceylon to take in the sounds of popular culture around the world. Speaking of the soundscape of her own family home, Uthup says, "We heard varied kinds of music from Beethoven to Bach to Bade Ghulam Ali Khan, Kishori Amonkar and Cliff Richard and the Beatles and Frank Sinatra. . . . It was really mixed. . . . When people ask me who's your inspiration, I say Radio Ceylon" (quoted in Fernandes 2011c). Radio, then, nurtured the multiple, overlapping sound cultures of 1960s and 1970s urban India. While few singers straddled musical contexts to the extent that Uthup did, it is crucial to understand her versatility—and audiences' appreciation of that versatility—as being more than just about her vocal talent. Her musical and linguistic border crossings were both product and mark of an aural milieu that encouraged voracious listening. Musicians and audiences alike were exposed to, and sought out, a great diversity of artists and styles over the airwaves.

Another feature of the various sound cultures Uthup navigated is that women played an important role in them. In taking up singing as a career, Uthup was following the lead of not only her sisters but also other well-known women artists who were her predecessors and contemporaries. Women from Anglo-Indian, Goan, and Parsi communities and, to a lesser extent, from elite and anglicized Hindu families were a strong presence as live performers not just in Bombay and Calcutta but also in Bangalore, Delhi, Madras, Shillong, and other cities. Stanley Pinto, a nightclub pianist who cut his teeth on the Bombay jazz scene of the 1960s, writes of a British sextet called the Margaret Mason Band that played at the La Bella restaurant in the Kala Ghoda area of South Bombay. The group was led in its daily 11:00 a.m. "coffee sessions" by Margie Mason on the vibraharp. He also remembers being ushered into jazz circles by Dorothy Jones, a pianist who accompanied new singers on All India Radio's *Ovaltine Amateur Hour* hosted by Hamid Sayani, the older brother of Ameen Sayani of Binaca Geetmala fame. (Incidentally, it was the older Sayani who gave Uthup her first opportunity to sing on a children's radio show.) The Dorothy Jones Quartet played regular jam sessions at a small restaurant in Churchgate called Berry's (Pinto 2002?). Pianist Lucilla Pacheco was another well-loved performer who, beginning in the late 1940s, worked with such prominent musicians as Ken Mac, Mickey Correa, and Chic Chocolate, as well as the Bombay Swing Club.[23] She went on to play with Anthony Gonsalves, the most acclaimed violinist and arranger in the Bombay film industry, and made waves in the mid-1960s as the "first player of an electronic instrument, an electronic keyboard called the Solovox" in Hindi cinema. The name Nelly [Battiwala] and her band also comes up in accounts of the city's musicking past: Nelly (as she was known) led a highly successful twelve-piece dance band in Bombay from the 1960s to 1990 (Ranade 2006, 56). Pam McCarthy sang in her uncle Ken Mac's renowned dance band in the 1950s. Before her, in the 1940s, came singers such as Beryl Templeman, the Hutson sisters, and Maxine Steller. All three of trumpeter Chic Chocolate's daughters, Yvonne, Ursula, and Kittu Vaz, extended his musical legacy in their live concerts (Fernandes 2011e).[24]

But perhaps the singer most like Uthup in age and vocal style was Lorna Cordeiro. According to jazz historian Naresh Fernandes, she, too, was a "vocalist in the Shirley Bassey mould" (2011d). Her electrifying performances (and relationship) with the ace trumpeter and bandleader Chris Perry at the Venice, a restaurant in the Astoria Hotel in the heart of Bombay's jazz scene, were the talk of the town throughout the 1960s. Writing of how her story inspired Bardroy Barretto's award-winning Konkani film *Nachom-ia Kumpasar* (Let's Dance to the Rhythm, 2014), as well as Hindi film director Anurag Kashyap's less successful attempt to capture the city's jazz era, *Bombay Velvet* (2015), Dipti Nagpaul notes that Lorna Cordeiro was known as "the Bessie Smith of India." She dazzled audiences with "her full-throated voice . . . [belting out] jazz standards by Ella Fitzgerald and pop tunes by Connie Francis," as well as Konkani folk songs with a jazzy edge (Nagpaul 2015).[25] Around the same time, in Calcutta, it was Pam Crain who reigned supreme. An ardent fan of Betty Carter, Crain molded her voice and style to that of the great American jazz vocalist. Crain sang at two live-music institutions on Park Street: Mocambo, where she was the first singer hired by the club when it opened its doors in 1956; and Blue Fox, where she performed with the Louis Banks Brotherhood (Das and Paul 2013). Crain's performances and recordings with the legendary alto saxophonist Braz Gonsalves are especially well known.[26]

Other artists regulars recall from their Park-Street and Churchgate-Street days include Delilah, Eve (Eva?), Flora, Gerry Dee, Jenny, Molly (the first to sing at Trincas in 1961), Vivian Hanson, Brenda Lilley (and her sister Fay), Shirley Myers, and Linda Thompson.[27] Asha Puthli also moonlighted as a singer in Bombay in the late 1960s before emigrating to the United States, where she fashioned herself into an eclectic musician and socialite. The year 1969 saw the Jetliners make waves as the resident band at Blow Up, a discotheque in the Taj Hotel. The group from Ceylon had Mignonne Fernando as lead singer, and they recorded two albums during their time in Bombay (Fernandes 2011b). Sandhya Sanjana is another singer who began dabbling in experimental jazz bands with her husband Dinshaw Sanjana in the mid-1970s.

Beat culture in the 1960s and 1970s was more male dominated, but even there one finds a handful of women onstage (typically as singers, not instrumentalists). The "smoky-voiced," classically trained Radha Thomas joined Human Bondage in 1973, bolstering the group's experiments infusing Indian classical elements into rock (Bhatia 85–88).[28] Farida Vakil was the "lead lady guitarist" of the Bombay group Riot

Squad, which won the Simla Beat Contest in 1971. Vakil also founded one of the few all-girl beat bands in India, the Ladybirds, along with her friends Merlyn, Jenny, and Zarina in 1967. So novel and well-known a guitarist was Vakil that the alternative youth magazine *JS* (Junior Statesman) ran an interview with her in March 1971 (when she was just 19) entitled, "Determined to be Different—Could Farida Vakil be a Pop Jhansi Ki Raani?" (Ravi). Another Bombay-based girl band was the Pop-pets, composed of Frances Correa (niece to Mickey Correa), Jean Rocha, and twins Jacqueline and Jennifer Orton. As the name suggests, this band performed four-part harmonies of pop hits of the time. Frances went on to partner with Trudy Pagose on a go-go girl act at Blow Up (Bhatia 2014, 108–10). The Andrew Sisters (Delhi) and the Xavier sisters (Karachi) were also popular around the same time. Indira Gill and Anju Narayan formed a band called the Mixed Ups (Delhi) along with their friend Shekhar Singh (111–12). Madhuri Kamat sang with the Mixed Ups (and other bands) before she came to be recognized as a leading Indian "folk" singer alongside women like Kiran Dhar, Vanita Singh, and Radha Ramachandran (Makhijani 1971; "Delhi's Young Singers" 1975–76).[29] Photos from the era also indicate that various other bands had women singers, including the Neophiliacs (Allahabad) with Elizabeth McEvoy in the lead, Winglets (Gwalior), and Robert Xavier and his band ("Photos"). The sheer length of this list is mind-boggling, especially when one considers the decades-long vocal monopoly in the hegemonic cultural form of the time, Bombay cinema. With but a handful of essays and books charting the history of Western musical genres in India, the history of these women remains largely unwritten.[30] But that is a story for another day. The key point for our purposes is that although the various sound cultures Uthup traversed were male dominated, she was by no means the only woman performing. Neither was she alone in cultivating a bodily vocal sound akin to the best jazz and blues singers the world over.

Bodily Voice

In juxtaposing the words "body" and "voice" to describe Uthup's singing, I am challenging the binary configuration typically used to discuss these concepts. The sight of a body is not the only proof of its materiality. Bodies are tangible through their sounds, textures, and smells as well. Thus, the notion that voices are inherently disembodied entities when the person emitting the sounds is outside our view is just that—a notion.

Some voices may sound like they do not emanate from living, breathing entities; but others, like Usha Uthup's, do. Through manipulations of pitch, timbre, and style, and through the words she speaks and sings, Uthup constantly foregrounds bodily experiences, sexual or otherwise. From the very beginning of her career, Uthup explored a lower vocal range than did most of her contemporaries in cinema. But no matter the pitch or range of the song, there was, and is, a distinct fullness to her voice. Her vocal style is also distinguishable by the visceral emphases she incorporates into her songs. Grunts, growls, sighs, and other interjections of pleasure and pain have always marked her oeuvre. Writing about her in a Hong Kong newspaper in 1977, one enthusiastic reviewer gushed:

> I guess the reason I quite inordinately like Ms. Iyer is because she is one of the very few female cabaret singers I have seen who's willing to operate with some emotional intensity, to shout about a bit now and then, and to also show a bit of energy. ("Hot Chapati" 1977)

The image accompanying this review is captioned, "Usha Iyer . . . Coming on Strong," suggesting that the bodily sound of her voice was understood in sexualized terms.

The timbral and stylistic qualities of Uthup's performances complement the worldliness of her repertoire. Whether singing in a country or jazz idiom, the lyrics she chooses tend to highlight bodily whims and wishes. Uthup's trademark number, "Fever," for instance, voices the thrill of romance. The speaker in this song does not just invoke sexual intimacy but physical sensations thereof: the mere touch of her lover makes her body "sizzle" and "burn." Recorded at least twice and requested a thousand times over in live shows, this song showcases Uthup's bodily voice well. As early as her first recording of this song in *Scotch and Soda* (1969), Uthup had developed a vocal style apropos to the song's frank lyrics—a low, growling sound interspersed with sharp yells and occasional code switching to French. She gave the song a dark, dangerous edge. Bodily desire is even more audible in the funk-inspired iteration of the song in *Usha in Nairobi* (EMI, 1978). In this version, Uthup sounds like she is not singing so much as speaking in staccato fashion. The effect is as arresting: she whispers, she sneers, she spits out the lyrics.[31]

Another fixture in Uthup's repertoire also focuses on the body, if in more rough-and-tumble fashion:

I married a female wrestler
As massive as can be,
And she had bulging muscles
Which quite fascinated me.
She said she loved me truly,
She also said by heck,
If I ever catch you messing around
I'll break your lovely neck.[32]

Introduced on Radio Ceylon in 1969 by the famous broadcaster Vernon Corea, "I Married a Female Wrester" made songwriter Ernest Ignatius, a Goan musician who was Uthup's compadre in many Bombay performances, famous in households across South Asia. In this "jolly" song, we get a stricken male voice lamenting that his big-built wife constantly imposes her body on him, both in affection and in anger.

There is no dismissing such invocations of the body as mere requirements of particular genres or song lyrics. Quite the contrary—embodiment is integral to the way Uthup conceives of her work. Here she is speaking of how she chooses songs: "First of all, a song has to appeal to my heart and then to my head. The minute a song gives me that **'grrrr' feeling and makes my hair stand**, I know that it is going to be good for my audience" (quoted in Chatterjee 1981, emphasis mine). Uthup's main criteria for including a song in her repertoire is the physical effect it has on her. The mere "touch" of the song must make her body tingle, her hair stand up. In some early interviews, Uthup also makes fleeting reference to the calipers she wore on her partially paralyzed leg (Bohra 1970). In these instances, she speaks of her body as throwing up a challenge that she must transcend. Most often, though, Uthup presents her body as a site of pleasure. Here is a sound bite she often repeats about the place of her body in performance.

> I learnt something from that fantastic singer, Frank Sinatra, who wrote a little article many years ago in Time magazine, where he said that if you **use your microphone as your lover**, you will know exactly how to control your voice. Because, if you've got to say something loving, you just bring it closer. Every time you've got to say something powerful, you just take it far away. All these things only come through experience. (quoted in Bohra 1970, emphasis mine)

We might read in the word *experience* a veiled reference to the one scandal of her career. She met the man who would become her second husband, Jani Chacko Uthup, on her first night at Trincas. Her affair, divorce, and remarriage were marked by the shifts in her surname. But even if we interpret her words in more straightforward fashion, there is no denying Uthup's intense and embodied relationship with her material. While crooning in 1970s India did not provoke the anxieties around masculinity and sexuality that it did in the United States in the 1920s and 1930s, it is apparent from Uthup's comments that this style of singing raised the specter of sexual intimacy in India as well (McCracken 2015). Uthup's jazz cover of "If" demonstrates how well she put Sinatra's advice into practice.[33] Even in the contained context of state-run television (the Doordarshan network), Uthup's embodied presence is hard to miss. Her voice languid and seductive, she draws out her notes, dwelling in and extending the scene of pleasure. Eyes closed, lips pursed, she sways to the beat; with a subtle shrug and a wave, she opens her body as if to the lover addressed in the song. She also handles the microphone expertly, moving it close or far depending on the sentiment and sound she wants to convey.

What is apparent in this and other recordings, moreover, is Uthup's obvious pleasure in her vocal labor. Her bodily voice conveys more than just sex; it foregrounds her "musicking body." I borrow this term from Matthew Rahaim, who uses it to discuss the importance of Hindustani classical singers' physical gestures in performance. Far from being mere ornamental additions to their singing, vocalists' gestures and movements are markers of years of training under a particular teacher and in a particular style (Rahaim 2012, 3). Given that Uthup was an unschooled singer, her bodily movements do not reflect a specific musical lineage. But they do frame her body as a music-making entity. The way she carries herself onstage and moves as she sings demonstrate her obvious expertise and her joyous involvement in her craft. The image of her musicking body keeps in play all the worldly connotations of the words and sounds she renders without reducing her to the stereotypical figure of a nightclub singer.

The physicality of Uthup's vocal sound and performance style is fundamentally tied to her star persona as a *live* performer. In interview after interview, she speaks of how much she loves interacting with audiences. Singing, she says, is her way of connecting and "communicating" with fans; the sound of their clapping, her *nasha* or addiction (quoted in Sharma 2016). But as her reference to Sinatra and the handling of the microphone suggest, her connection to her audience is a thoroughly mediated one. Her success as a live performer depends on her facility with technology. In keeping with cover art of the late 1960s and 1970s, the images on her albums have her looking straight ahead (i.e., at her audiences or the fan in whose hands the precious recording rests) or engaged in the act of singing. For example, the double EP set *Fabulous Usha Iyer with the Flintstones* has *three* images of Uthup in performance (see fig. 5.1). The *Scotch and Soda* cover is from the perspective of the audience in the nightclub; the photo seems to have been taken from a table, with the camera placed between glasses. Uthup smiles broadly at the audience, mic in hand, as a trumpeter (likely Ronnie Menezes) plays behind her. Similar images of her in performance circulated in newspapers and magazines of the 1970s. More often than not, they showed her onstage surrounded by mics and music stands, and other performers. Despite her early and robust recording career (she has more than two dozen albums to her name), she is inevitably portrayed in relationship to her live audiences and not inside a recording studio (see fig. 5.2). One newspaper ad for Norge stereo has her beside the sound system, placing them in a relationship of equivalence: "BOTH TOP IN PERFORMANCE." Below the circular images of Uthup (mic in hand, of course) and the amplifier is an endorsement from the singer, affirming that she "was able to obtain the maximum quality from [her] AKG dynamic microphone in conjunction with the NORGE Stereo 40 amplifier." These early images of Uthup offer a very particular visual construction of liveness. They present her performances as fundamentally mediated events (Auslander 2008, 25). The mic is as important to Uthup's persona as it was to male crooners. It is not distinguished from her body, that is, these images do not invoke the body-versus-technology binary. To the contrary, the mic is a crucial means of evoking the body, of registering the power of Uthup's live presence onstage.

Uthup's bodily voice, repertoire, and stage presence also evidence the fact that she, like other young Indian artists of the era, drew inspiration from a number of international musicians. Visual and print discourse rendered her as an international figure, not a strictly national one. While she clearly highlights her Indian identity with her sari and has a history of performing with the most famous jazz and beat musicians in India, the genres she embraced, the imagery on her records, and reviews of her music link her to foreign artists and locations. For instance, on the cover of *Usha Sings Love Story and Other Hits* (Odeon), Uthup strikes a Joan Baez pose, guitar in hand, wearing a pensive expression and her

Fig. 2. Still from *Standing By* (2015) depicting Uthup onstage

hair long and loose. Assessing her first international show in 1977 as part of the Hong Kong International Food Festival, one writer hears shades of the American songstress Melissa Manchester, the reggae singer Hugh Griffiths, and (oddly enough) Ted Baxter, the comedic character played by Ted Knight on the *Mary Tyler Moore Show* ("Hot Chapati" 1977). This contemporary review of *Usha Sings Beautiful Sunday and Other Hits* (EMI) in the youth magazine *Dateline Delhi* brings up a few other names:

> Some six years after her take-off she's changed a bit: she's more **Helen Shapiro-ish** now if her latest album (EMI Stereo S/E MGE 21001) is some indication: *Beautiful Sunday and Other Hits*
>
> Now I'm keen on Don Maclean, like very many people. I can't imagine someone bettering him in his own numbers. Usha doesn't but she's no worse either with *If We Try*.
>
> *Seasons In the Sun* is similarly given a rich bass, slightly staccato interpretation by Usha. She is more in her element in *Never, Never, Never* and *Touch Me in the Morning*. Boone's *Beautiful Sunday* is also there, as are *When a Woman falls in Love* and *I believe in Music*. (Dewan 1976, 17, emphasis mine)

Likewise, in the INK talk with which I opened this essay, Uthup speaks of how she has been compared to everyone from Shirley Bassey to Frank Sinatra and José Feliciano.

As wide ranging as the comparisons are, there is in the discourse surrounding Uthup a consistent reference to black musicians. The cover art of *Beautiful Sunday* is particularly striking in this regard. The dark background and the image of Uthup on the album—head tilted up, eyes closed, mouth open as she sings into a mic—call up similar images of Billie Holiday. This visual reference is, of course, ironic, for Holiday was famous for her rendition of "Gloomy Sunday," not "Beautiful Sunday." Even as Uthup gives us a cover of the (white) British artist Daniel Boone's uplifting pop hit from 1972, the visual aesthetic of the LP recalls a more moody song and an emphatically black American genre and artist. The cover art on *Usha in Nairobi* (EMI, 1978) shows her in front of an Air India aircraft and in the presence of Kenyan dignitaries. She is famous for having shared the stage and recorded "Malaika" with the Kenyan singer Fadhili William.[34] In November 1970, she opened for "the Gatt Quartet, a Madras group specializing in Negro spiritual music" (Untitled News Item 1970). In May of the following year, she had the honor of performing with the great gospel singer Mahalia Jackson when she visited India on a tour sponsored by the US State Department. Two decades later, in 1995, she had occasion to sing with another musical stalwart, Miriam Makeba, in South Africa (Mojapelo 2008, 265). Stories and photos of such musical events, not to mention the antiapartheid play to which she contributed early in her career, amplify the more diffuse visual and aural gestures toward African and African American artists in her repertoire.[35]

Gender and Indianness

Given the myriad comparisons to international artists (especially black singers) and the fact that the sound cultures Uthup inhabited included many women artists (notably Cordeiro and Crain), it is curious that she stands out as "the one and only, Usha Iyer."[36] One explanation for this perceived exceptionalism lies in the way notions of gender and Indianness inflected her stardom.

The frisson and breathlessness of the aforementioned print ads and LP liner notes render Uthup as not just a singular performer but one who is visibly and *volubly* shaking up the music scene. So there is no doubt of her aural stardom, some ads list her name multiple times in quick succession. This textual representation of an echo is repeated on the cover art of some of Uthup's LPs, such as *24 Carats* (INRECO, 1981) and *Uncensored: Usha and The Sound* (Concord, 1984). While this trope is used in ads for other performers as well, it is fair to say that something notable is going on in her case. The reverberations of Uthup's voice were not just aural. They were physical, spatial, and cultural as well. "Fun lovers! Come in lungi . . ." reads one TT ad from June 7, 1970, assuring readers of the laid-back and festive atmosphere at her shows. With the reference to "lungi," the ad attempts to shed the notion that the club, and the songs Uthup sang there, were Western. One could enjoy her performance dressed in Indian garb, in something as casual as a lungi. Even as it does away with the notion that listening to "English" music requires a sophisticated dress code, this ad gestures to the fact that venues like TT were mainly frequented by men. Uthup insists that she disrupted this gender dynamic:

> "Where it was the prerogative of Anglo-Indians coming out in their slinky black dresses and singing in nightclubs, I changed it by just coming in a sari," Uthup recall[s]. "Slowly, the nightclub became a place that was not just frequented by men. It became a family thing because they found this very homely looking person singing there. People didn't hesitate to bring their wives or mothers or sisters. They figured that if Usha Uthup was singing, it couldn't be that bad." (quoted in Fernandes 2011c)

Uthup's claim is that she rocked the nightclub scene not just with her powerful singing but with her mere presence. By wearing saris—traditional South Indian saris no less—she simultaneously transformed the image of the nightclub singer and made clubs welcoming to women and families.

No doubt Uthup's unconventional sartorial choice brought an element of surprise to her performances. In one television show *I to I*, where she purports to interview herself, she introduces her "guest" as someone "who doesn't look like she sounds and she doesn't sound like she's supposed to look." Uthup goes on to attribute her longevity in the music business in part to the incongruity of her voice and clothing. But even her sartorial choice may not be as unique a feature as we are given to believe. Photos from cabaret and dance hall sessions in the first half of the century indicate that saris were not entirely uncommon attire for women in the audience. Playback singers like Asha Bhosle and K. Chitra, with whom Uthup occasionally appeared onstage, always performed in a sari. Her own sister, Indira Srinivasan (married name), had a full-page feature about her in the March 1972 issue of *Dateline Delhi* where she is pictured in a sari, just as Uthup was in a similar article in 1970 (Gupta 1972, 9; Prakash 1970, 1). The articles talk of how surprising it is to encounter "housewi[ves] who sin[g] pop," but both sisters brush off these comments; it is not at all strange to them to look and sing as they do (Gupta 1972). The pages of this youth magazine are filled with stories and photos of other middle- and upper-class women pursuing business and artistic careers and donning saris. *Dateline Delhi*'s fashion spreads also suggested that saris were not thought of as necessarily traditional or conservative clothing. In addition, Uthup and her audiences are likely to have known of Yolande Bavan, another sari-clad diva with a "rich range—from husky, knowing alto to door-squeak soprano" (Myers, 2007). Bavan was a contemporary of Uthup's from Sri Lanka (then Ceylon). On winning an amateur singing contest hosted by the Australian Broadcasting Company in 1956, she migrated to Australia, then England and the United States, where she was part of the acclaimed vocal trio Lambert, Hendricks, and Bavan in the early to mid-1960s (Fernandes 2013; Myers 2007).

Moreover, as the "star attraction" of many a beat competition, Uthup would have been in the presence of other young musicians and fans donning Indian clothes (see, e.g., Advertisement for the 3rd Simla Beat Contest Finals). The anxious notion that beat or rock was inherently Western—and thus inauthentic, immoral, and un-Indian—persisted for much of this music's history in India (Basu 2012, 9; Kumar 2016, 3111). One response to such accusations was to dress, speak, and act "Indian" while making and consuming beat music. Images of the Madras-based band the Pilgrims, winners of the 1971 Fortune Beat Contest, show them decked out in vests and hats with Indian embroidery ("Photos"). As Dubby Bhagat, a music journalist with *JS* in those years, observes:

> Young [people] were divided into the people who could afford the whole Carnaby Street apparel and those who deliberately (while listening to rock music) made it a point to be very, very Indian by wearing *khadi* [traditional handloom cloth, with nationalist, Gandhi ideological implications]. The *khadi* lot talked Hindi and the others English. (quoted. in Booth 2014, 218)

Thus, performing one's Indian identity—or pointedly *not* performing it—was an important aspect of early beat culture.

Uthup has always claimed that her choice to wear a sari was not a calculated or political one. It was the only way she knew how to dress, she says. That may be so, but it is worth remembering that she was married when she embarked on her career. She would have needed to, and did, present herself as modest and "homely" (in the British sense of the term, meaning "family woman").[37] When asked in a 1970 interview what her family thought of her unconventional career choice, she notes, "There was a little reluctance when [I] turned professional because of the stigma attached to nightclub appearances." But, she continues, she did have her mother-in-law's blessing throughout (quoted in Bohra 1970). Although Uthup is quick to assert that hers is a family of music lovers and everyone (especially her mother-in-law) supported her, one can discern in her response her family's anxieties around respectability. The sari may well have been a way to quell those anxieties rather than a performance gimmick. Consider this picture that the *Times of India* painted of the third Simla Beat Contest finals in August 1970:

> Neither the wet weather nor the taximen's strike (which persisted in the morning) could dampen the enthusiasm of the packed crowd of beat fans. From the word go, it was beat music with a swing and a zing. The crowd applauded its favourites and booed those it did not like, throwing on them paper arrows and showing [*sic*] "go home."
>
> **Weird** outlandish costumes on and off stage with bellbottoms, **guru shirts, lungis** and minis and maxis were seen to advantage [*sic*] and created the right atmosphere. Some musicians performed practically **bare-chested.**
>
> And to top it all, Usha Iyer, sent her fans into raptures with numbers like "Fever," "Mississippi Delta," "Dance of Love," "Scarborough Fair," "To Sir with Love," "Ode to Billy Joe," "Pata Patit" [*sic*], the ever-popular "Qantanamera" [*sic*] and **two slightly naughty songs** sung while she twanged the guitar strings. ("'Confusion' from Madras Prevails" 1970, emphasis mine)[38]

This was clearly a raucous and fun evening. Musicians and audience members alike were dressed in "weird" garb. There were so-called Western clothes like bellbottoms, minis, and maxis, but also Indian ones such as *lungis* and guru shirts (collared shirts or *kurtas* popularized by the film star Rajesh Khanna). That some artists took off their shirts is, for the writer, a measure of just how crazy an atmosphere it was. But Uthup's singing was even crazier. The quick transition from clothing (and lack thereof) to the night's song list is telling. The writer does not mention Uthup's sari, but it is a spectral presence in this paragraph. The unnamed sari clashes with the many Billboard-topping numbers from 1967 that Uthup charms the audience with that evening: Miriam Makeba's "Pata Pata," Bobbie Gentry's country classics "Ode to Billie Joe" and "Mississippi Delta," and Lulu's "To Sir with Love." The wonderfully mixed list is bookended by references to sexuality via her signature tune "Fever" and songs so "naughty" they must remain unnamed. If the boisterous energy of the show and the tunes Uthup sang that night cast her as something other than or more than a South Indian *amma* (mother or portly older woman) or a Bengali *didi* (older sister), her sari would have mollified those who doubted her traditional and conservative moorings.[39] Uthup often quips that women in the audience were her biggest fans because they knew that "with a face and a body like [hers, she] was not a threat" (quoted in "Conversations with Namu Kini" 2014). Tongue in cheek though this comment may be, it speaks to the discursive dangers for women in the profession.

Had Uthup been operating in the realms of film or classical music, the overdetermined sound of the body in her performances would have drawn the ire of cultural elites very early in her career. In fact, she did face accusations of Western decadence and promoting "cheap, perverted, disco culture" in a 1983 lawsuit by Jatin Chakraborty, the Public Works Minister of West Bengal at the time ("Marxist Leader Fails" 1983). But the notion that Western music was vulgar and promoted various social ills is only part of the story. By the mid-twentieth century, the dictum that women from "good," middle-class Hindu families do not to sing and dance anything other than Indian classical music was deeply entrenched. Such immodest public performances were left to women of other (i.e., socially marginalized) caste and religious groups. As historians of dance and music have argued, the classicization of certain genres and performance styles was part of broader processes of social reform and nationalism in the late nineteenth and early twentieth centuries. In the performing arts, as in other domains, "cleansing" national identity meant establishing the hegemony of particular caste groups and enforcing gender-caste-class ideologies. To use an example relevant to the Tamil brahmin community from which Uthup hails, as *sadir* dance turned into the "classical" form Bharatanatyam, traditional interpreters of the genre, *devadasis*, found their lives and lifestyles completely upended. Their repertoires and relationships with their audiences and patrons were stigmatized, even criminalized, in the name of banning prostitution (see, e.g., Soneji 2012). This process was rehearsed across the subcontinent, and other artist castes similarly lost access to performance opportunities, venues, and incomes that had traditionally sustained their communities.

The policing of bodies extended to voices and vocal styles—that is, to how and which bodies *sounded* in performance. In the North Indian (Hindustani) classical tradition, there was the marginalization of the *thumri*, a genre once associated with courtesans and now considered a "semiclassical" form (read "less serious and complex") (Du Perron 2007). Likewise, as Amanda Weidman's important work (2006) has shown, the centering of voice in South Indian (Carnatic) classical music was a means of staging both authenticity and a modern identity in the context of the colonial encounter. These and other struggles over what constitutes "national" music diminished the variety of sounds one heard on All India Radio (Lelyveld 1994; Huacuja Alonso 2019). The hegemony that playback singer Lata Mangeshkar established in 1950s Hindi cinema was another iteration of this process of fixing the sound of the nation. The Mangeshkar monopoly ensured that the heroines, the "good girls," could no longer sing in voices that sounded like Uthup's. The body could only be audible in the vamp's cabaret numbers. Later in this chapter I take up the question of why Usha Uthup was granted very few vampish numbers in the 1970s despite her mastery of vocal styles that would have been perfect for those songs. Here I want to emphasize the broader discourses that ensured that her voice was received as not—or at least, not entirely—Indian. While Uthup's performances might seem like a far cry from those of *devadasis* or classical musicians, or Mangeshkar for that matter, their histories are in fact entangled. Shared struggles over gender and nation in various sound and performance cultures explain why Uthup was seen and heard as a novel figure despite being surrounded by other women in the jazz, pop, and beat scenes. Hers was not the voice audiences in mid-twentieth-century India were disciplined to hear from a woman who looked and dressed like her.

Uthup was operating under a set of gendered expectations different from those of the singers Jennifer Fleeger discusses in *Mismatched Women* (2014). For one thing, cultural restrictions against marriage and motherhood did not apply to her in the way that they did for mismatched women singing in Euroamerican contexts. Those women also gained fame in the context of major shifts in technology; their bodies registered both the qualities of, and the ambivalence toward, emergent technologies. I do not read in Uthup's star persona marks of such historical turns (though India, too, was confronting major social crises in the late 1960s and 1970s). For me, the salient overlap between Uthup and the mismatched figures in Fleeger's book is in the way their performances are interpreted as "exceeding the limits of the female body" (14). Uthup's singing pushed the contours of the ideal Indian woman's body. As a middle-class Tamilian woman who wore her identity in the drape of her sari, she was positioned differently from her contemporaries who sang in nightclubs. The cultural politics that naturalized Anglo-Indian, Goan, and Parsi singers' proficiency in Western musical genres was precisely what made both Uthup and the "*khadi* lot" stand out. Otherwise put, it was the postcolonial history of the nation and the institutionalization of particular gendered (classed, sexual, caste, and racial) norms in the early to mid-twentieth century that cast Uthup as a mismatched woman. This perception of a mismatch is only possible if bodies are understood in both aural and visual terms: "Mismatched women must be seen before they can really be heard. Thus, bound up in every act of hearing is the image that catapulted this woman to fame" (17). Usha Uthup forces us think about the aural, visual, and gestural dimensions of vocal performance together, and this in turn helps pull apart the binary configuration of voice versus body. As distinctive as she is, she reminds us that all bodies are "sounding" entities and that the sound of bodies cannot be thought apart from what they look like and how they move.[40]

Cinematic Absence

This reframing of the voice-body relationship helps explain Uthup's relative absence in the world of the Bombay cinema. Despite her musical success and her interest in singing for Hindi films, Uthup remained relatively marginal in the film industry. By her own admission, her "husky, heavy voice" was considered perfect for Western genres but not for Hindi film music. Whereas Asha Bhosle sang for both risqué characters and modern (but good) young women in Hindi cinema, Uthup was deemed incapable of walking the tightrope of modernity and Indian femininity. Even as the gulf between heroines and vamps was narrowing in 1970s Hindi cinema, she did not get many opportunities to sing for modern heroines of the day. More baffling is the fact that she was granted relatively few vampish songs despite having the perfect voice, style, and repertoire for the role. Her strong, deep contralto voice was deemed unconventional not just for Bombay cinema's good girls but for most "bad" ones as well. In *Hare Rama Hare Krishna* (Dev Anand, 1971), she sang English verses mouthed by an unnamed white woman high on drugs.[41] (Her lines were limited to "I love you" and some scatting.) The few songs she was granted after that were duets with the music director Bappi Lahiri, who ushered in a disco wave in early 1980s Hindi cinema.[42] Some of her late 1970s and early 1980s numbers earned her Filmfare nominations, but no awards came her way. No doubt the competition she was up against had something to do with the paucity of film opportunities (Asha Bhosle was married to R. D. Burman). But, familial and romantic networks aside, I would venture to say that the Hindi film industry was slow to embrace Uthup because her bodily voice challenged the way the industry conceptualized sound and image in relationship to each other.

Two assumptions that Hindi cinema has historically mobilized (between the 1950s and 1990s) are germane here. The first is that all visible and aural manifestations of the body are potentially threatening. The second is that the singing voice is where the essence of a character lies. I have argued elsewhere that these interrelated ideas about voice and body persisted well into the 1990s, sustaining Lata Mangeshkar's vocal monopoly. Unlike Mangeshkar, Uthup was known for her bodily voice. Her vocal style and repertoire ensured that the image of her—specifically of her *as a live singer*—was always in the foreground for audiences. This conjunction of sound and image confounded Bombay cinema's usual assumptions about both "good" *and* "bad" women. Given Uthup's extracinematic stardom, the image of her as a live performer is never far away. Every time we hear that voice, we can practically see her, microphone in hand, taking delight in her singing and engaging with the audience. It becomes difficult to see anyone but her as we hear that voice. We delight in the dual star text that is Usha Uthup, that striking jazz and pop singer dressed like a South Indian aunty at a wedding. *This* is what sets her apart from Asha Bhosle. Bhosle also wore saris, after all, but she got to sing for Helen in her vampish roles, whereas Uthup didn't. Uthup's work as a singer in other venues in nightclubs, onstage, and later on television introduced a "mismatch" that Hindi cinema was not equipped to accommodate (even though it did deal with various other apparent disjunctures).

This explains why the few opportunities Uthup got to sing in films were either disco numbers or cameos in nightclub sequences. In the Bappi Lahiri disco songs, there is such a surfeit of *other* visual stimuli that it is hard to attend to the lip-synching of the dancers onscreen. (Indeed, it is sometimes hard to tell who the actors are in the first place.) That is, the "bling" of these song sequences, the excess of visuality, ensures that the sound of Uthup's voice does not automatically or necessarily point to the image of her musicking body. Examples of such numbers include "Hari Om Hari" (*Pyaara Dushman* [Beloved Enemy], Anand Sagar, 1980), "Ramba Ho Ho Ho" (*Armaan* [Desires], Anand Sagar, 1981), and "Koi Yahaan Nache Nache," sometimes called "Auva Auva"

(*Disco Dancer*, Babbar Subhash, 1982).[43] "One, Two, Cha Cha Cha," from *Shalimar* (Krishna Shah, 1978; music by R. D. Burman), is not as excessive as these other numbers, but it, too, centers bodily movements as a dance instructor (Aruna Irani) teaches people in Ferguson's Dance Studio while various nefarious transactions take place in the background. Also in this category of bodily bling songs is the James Bond–inspired opening sequence of *Shaan* (Pride, Ramesh Sippy, 1980), composed by R. D. Burman. "Shaan Se" (sometimes referred to by its opening lyrics, "Doston Se Pyar Kiya") depicts a woman in lycra dancing against a red background as the credits of the film roll. Her body is presented in fragments: eyes first, then a hand, her lips, her torso and butt, and so forth. Freeze-frames, fades, and superimposed images of fire and smoke make this song picturization as bizarre and excessive as the disco numbers. We hear Uthup's voice, but it becomes hard to "see" her. In these songs, the link between the sound of her voice and the image of her in performance is effectively broken.

Bombay to Goa Cameo

The second type of film song Uthup was granted was nightclub sequences in which she appeared as herself. Other playback singers of her time did not get such cameo roles. Uthup appears in two sequences in the English-language Merchant-Ivory film *Bombay Talkie* (James Ivory, 1970), having composed a couple of songs for the film herself.[44] In the Tamil film *Melnaattu Marumagal* (Westernized Daughter-in-Law, A. P. Nagarajan, 1975), she appears in a solo stage performance singing another English number, "Love Is Beautiful." These cameo numbers are diametrically opposed to the disco numbers in that they center *Uthup's* body.[45] She appears onscreen as herself, lip-synching to her own vocal performance. The song setting—usually a nightclub—is one that people already associate with her. In a sense, her stardom outside of cinema is the subject of these songs.

Consider the famous nightclub medley in *Bombay to Goa* (S. Ramanathan, 1972; music by R. D. Burman).[46] Uthup appears in the film as a popular nightclub artist who sings a string of requests by the hero and heroine, Ravi (Amitabh Bachchan) and Mala (Aruna Irani). Ravi begins the musical game by asking that she sing "Rain," Jose Feliciano's hit single from 1969. While this musical declaration of love comes out of an American pop context, it fits the Hindi cinematic convention of the "rain song," wherein lovers find intimacy when accidentally caught in a shower. It is only appropriate, then, that Uthup transitions, at Mala's request, to "Temptation."[47] Uthup sings the opening verse in a plaintive jazz/R&B idiom, not unlike the renditions of American singers like Bing Crosby, Perry Como, and Screamin' Jay Hawkins. By contrast, in true R. D. Burman style, the instrumental accompaniment to Uthup's "Temptation" has a more rhythmic funk/soul feel to it. Ravi counters Mala's satirical message with a surprise of his own: Ernest Ignatius's "I Married a Female Wrestler." Usha Uthup's obvious pleasure in this cheeky song appears to bring her out of her shell: instead of singing with her eyes closed, she begins interacting more with Ravi and the rest of her nightclub audience. As she smiles and waves a tambourine, her fans begin clapping and dancing in their seats. The next song is Uthup's signature number, "Fever." As with Mala's previous request, this song, too, mocks Ravi for his inability to seduce her by vocalizing the thrill another lover might inspire. Uthup's visceral rendition of "Fever" surprises Ravi, who then ups the ante (and the musical tempo) by offering the singer money to fulfill his next request, "Be Bop A Lula."[48] The final song requested by Mala is a Cole Porter classic, "It's All Right with Me."[49] In Uthup's hands, this song becomes a fast-paced number closer to Steve Lawrence's "Latin" interpretation on his album *Lawrence Goes Latin* (1961). The medley ends with Uthup shuttling between "Be Bop A Lula" and "It's All Right with Me" with increasing rapidity as the hero and heroine coax her to sing "their" song by waving money in her face. The tempo picks up so much that toward the end Uthup barely sings a bar or two before switching songs. She does not miss a beat or even catch her breath (it seems). Her virtuoso performance ends in exasperation: she throws her hands up and walks off, crying, "Wannnh! Stop it! I can't sing (any more)!"

The *Bombay to Goa* sequence foregrounds Usha Uthup's vocal performance in several ways. We have the introduction by the nightclub manager: "And now, ladies and gentlemen, we proudly present to you the one and only Usha Iyer! Usha Iyer!" The use of Uthup's own name (rather than some other name for her character) and the roaring applause from the audience even before she sings are acknowledgments of her talent and stardom outside cinema. The wide range of musical referents in this sequence—from jazz to bebop to rock and pop—highlights Uthup's versatility as a singer and her popularity on the nightclub and live performance circuit. Equally, the sequence exhibits a self-consciousness about playback and the role that songs (and singers) play as "go-betweens," means of communicating love. This is highlighted by the fact that Ravi initially approaches Mala and sings some nonsensical words to her himself in a bombastic, faux-operatic voice; when this overture fails, he changes tactics and asks Uthup to give voice to his desire. As Uthup sings, he lip-synchs the lyrics to "Rain" in a mock performance of his love. Uthup's position as the third term, the mediator, in this romantic transaction is also communicated visually as medium shots and close-ups of the protagonists are intercut with those of the singer. Toward the end of the song, Uthup stands in the middle as the two lovers fight to maintain control of the musical narrative. When she finally relinquishes her position as mediator and stalks off, Mala and Ravi are left hanging. They cannot communicate without the "playback" singer, and the sequence ends. Apart from unmasking musical technology and the labor of singing for films, this medley gestures to Uthup's fame in several overlapping sound cultures outside cinema. That audiences saw Uthup's musicking body, that they saw it all the time in print and visual media, mattered to the meanings associated with her voice. No other woman's body could be attached to the voice that sings this particular medley.

Conclusion

I have charted out in this chapter the diverse sound cultures and discourses that have fostered Usha Uthup's stardom as a mismatched pop diva since the late 1960s. It was not just her talent and versatility that made the sound of her husky voice stand out among a host of live-music performers. Her bodily vocal aesthetic was always understood in relation to her "Indian" look. Her silk saris and ever expanding *bindis* contained the sound of her voice in some ways, but they also pushed the limits of what constituted an "Indian" sound—be it the sound of Indian music or that of Indian womanhood. Further, the simultaneous invocation of sound technologies and liveness in the visual and print discourse amplified the power of Uthup's bodily voice, making her seem all the more distinctive. Her voice could only be attached to the image of her body. Thus, it is precisely her extracinematic stardom that kept Uthup from becoming the voice of the "bad girl" in Hindi cinema.

Notes

1. My deepest thanks to my research assistant, Anaidys Uribe, whose initiative and diligence led me to many of the print sources I cite here.
2. "Usha Uthup: Skyfall in a Sari" (2013).

3. During the first decade of her career, Uthup went by her then husband's last name, Iyer. The year 1978 is the earliest date of an advertisement I have located that uses the surname she took when she married Jani Chacko Uthup, whom she met during her very first performance at the Calcutta nightclub Trincas. For the sake of convenience, I use the name Uthup throughout this chapter except when quoting from primary texts that refer to her as Usha Iyer.

4. "Feelings" was a 1974 hit single by the Brazilian singer Morris Albert, who set English lyrics to a French tune composed two decades earlier by Loulou Gasté. "Fever" was an R&B hit in 1956, penned by Edie Cooley and Otis Blackwell. The original recording by Little Willie John was an instant hit; the song has also remained in popular memory via covers by several famous artists, including Peggy Lee, Elvis, and Ella Fitzgerald.

5. A note on one of my lesser-known archival sources: *Dateline Delhi*. Published by a cooperative of young journalists in the late 1960s and 1970s, it was one of the earliest magazines devoted to youth and music culture in India. In the 2015 documentary *Standing By* (episode 2), the journalist Aruna Das Gupta, who started her career with *Dateline*, and musician Manoj Pant (of the 1970s band Collegium) speak of how influential the magazine was and of the music events it (like the Calcutta-based *JS* magazine) hosted. Among the many music-related articles in *Dateline* are reviews of records and performances; features on upcoming bands, singers, newscasters, and other media personalities; ads for transistor radios, radio shows (Doordarshan's *Yuv Vani* [Voice of Youth]), radio and band fan clubs, music stores, and restaurants/clubs featuring live performances; and song lyrics sent in by readers. For the purposes of this chapter, I scoured the first decade of *Dateline Delhi* issues for such music-related entries.

6. Ambi Parameswaran notes the Nescafe and Goldspot ads in his *Nawabs, Nudes, Noodles* (2016, 215–16). While I have not been able to locate the particular ads he mentions, I did find an ad for another coffee product distributed by Nestle, Sunrise, which used Uthup's voice in a television ad ("There's a new sunrise in your life"). Uthup sings the hooks of the Maggi and Vicks ads when she discusses her reputation as a "jingle queen" on the NDTV show *I to I* (2003).

7. See, for instance, the ad announcing her show at TT in the *Times of India*, May 6, 1971, 3 (Classified ad 35).

8. Uthup cites this date as her Trincas' debut in a 1981 interview with Jayabrato Chatterjee (Chatterjee 1981).

9. The liner notes go on:

> Presenting an astonishing variety of songs in her soul voice, Usha Iyer touches every heart with her sincere and joyous delivery of each note. But no song is rendered the same way again for music is instantly created as she sings. She demands total concentration from her audience and she gets it. But such concentration is a small price to pay for the joy that one feels at her singing. Excitement is indeed the keynote of her performance and every finger that is clicking, every foot tapping and bodies sway along with her rhythm and blues.
>
> One can go on and on. We would rather do that with this album, to discover the wonderful world of Usha Iyer, as ecstatic and promising as the best brew from those Scottish highlands.

10. All emphases are in the original unless otherwise noted.

11. This ad was published in the Bombay edition of the *Times of India* on July 6, 1970, and is fairly typical of TT's advertising in the newspaper. On the same page, there is another ad for the Other Room, a jazz spot in the prestigious Ambassador Hotel right next door to TT. That bigger, quarter-page ad obviously represented keen competition, for it, too, advertised a "Discotheque Night" that very Monday in July 1970.

12. This ad was published on July 25, 1970.

13. Given that this was a late 1960s recording, we might assume that the baritone saxophonist was accompanied by Percy Isaac (bass), Richie Marquis (piano), and Max Mascarenhas (drums). In the absence of liner notes, though, I am unable to verify this information. As a single, the Kingston Trio's "Greenback Dollar" topped the Billboard charts in 1962. A recording of Uthup's first single can be accessed at "Usha Iyer 1968" (2014).

14. A dealer specializing in South Asian records from the 1960s and 1970s, hindustanvinyl, has posted three of the four songs on this set of EPs on YouTube. For "Blues Train" and "Summertime," see "usha iyer & the flintstones 1969" (2014a). For "The Trip," see "usha iyer & the flintstones 1969" (2014b).

15. See Pandey (2015) for a discussion of Noel Martin's decades-long music career. The Flintstones' phenomenal popularity is registered in two articles in a single issue of *Dateline Delhi*, following a highly successful beat show that the magazine hosted on August 3, 1969, The Knockout. The first article describes how the organizers refused to end the Goldspot Musical Knockout concert "early," before the Flintstones had performed: "Do you realize what you're asking us to do? If we close now, without the Flintstones having played, you're going to have a mad crowd on your hands, and they'll bring the house down" (quoted in Kumar 1969, 16). In the second, a feature article about the Flintstones, the writer gushes, "You saw the miniature storm they created among the audience in the jam-packed jam session [Knockout] with only four songs. And so you know that they're brilliant, dripping, soaking delightfully brilliant" (Gopinath 1969, 1).

16. *Scotch and Soda* was released by Odeon, a subsidiary of EMI. It was reissued in 2006 by Saregama India Ltd. and is available on YouTube. On this record, Otis Blackwell is credited with writing "Fever" using his pseudonym, John Davenport. For a sampling of the songs on this LP, see "Scotch and Soda" 2015; "Sunny" 2015; "California Dreaming" 2015; "Fever" 2015.

17. The Sound Trophy contest was organized by HMV at Nirmala Niketan, a prominent women's college in Bombay. In addition to the HMV contract, the Savages took home the princely sum of two thousand rupees for their wins.

18. The May 1971 beat show was organized by the Grant Medical College Students' Association, as noted in a *Times of India* advertisement on April 20, 1971. An ad for *To This Night*, published in the same newspaper on August 13, 1970, indicates that the play was written and directed by Imtiaz Khan and staged at the Tejpal auditorium. It was sponsored by the "Asian Mission, African National Congress South Africa." Intriguingly, the ad leads with *her* name: "USHA IYER Sings and composes music for an explosive play on racial discrimination." A review of the play clarifies that Uthup composed the music, penned the lyrics, and recorded the songs that are used in the play; she did not, however, make a live appearance. Menezes was in charge of the musical arrangement ("Pop Singer" 1970).

19. "usha iyer and the ronnie menezes quartet—lambretta" 2014.

20. For "Paka Paka," see "usha iyer & chris perry—conkani" 2014.

21. This most prestigious of all beat contests ran from the late 1960s (1967?) to 1972. It was sponsored by the Indian Tobacco Company (ITC) to advertise its Simla brand of cigarettes (NH7 2014).

22. Her concert with Yesudas (Jesudas) was mentioned in a short feature in the *Times of India* on October 9, 1970. An advertisement on June 7, 1970, announces her upcoming performance with the other artists as part of a "Variety Entertainment" stage show.

23. A photograph in Naresh Fernandes's *Taj Mahal Foxtrot* blog shows Pacheco (in a sari) with Duke Ellington on his State Department-sponsored trip to India (Fernandes 2011a).

24. Kittu also performed under her married name, Sequiera.

25. Nagpaul adds that on her opening night with Chris Perry at the Lido Room in 1963, Lorna Cordeiro "sang [Ella] Fitzgerald's Cry Me A River, taking each of the eight verses half a note higher. That night was magical. Within weeks, she had a loyal following" (2015).

26. Like Braz Gonsalves, several Bombay musicians also performed in Calcutta (e.g., Chris Perry).

27. In a 2008 interview for *The Tribune*, Uthup said, "Most of the crooners were Anglo-Indians then, and some of them like Eva and Gerry Dee were fabulous. Perhaps, I drew the most attention because I was the only crooner wearing a sari" (quoted in Bose 2008). Shirley Myers's name comes up in pianist Stanley Pinto's recollections; the other names listed here appear in Pandey 2015 and Bhatia 2014.

28. Human Bondage was talented and popular band that lasted from 1971 to 1976. Although it began as a collaboration among musicians from Madras and Bangalore, the group performed extensively in other cities as well, especially Delhi, where Thomas first encountered them. Bhatia uses the last name Ramaswamy to refer to the singer, but I suspect this is a mistake. There was a folk singer named Radha Ramachandran active around the same time, and she may be the person (later known as Radha Thomas) who joined Human Bondage. Thomas was married to a fellow musician in the band and went by her married name Shottam for a while. Today she heads her own jazz band called UNK (Bhatia 2014, 85–88).

29. On Kiran Dhar, see Makhijani 1971. Entries on Kamat and Singh, written by Pamela Juneja and Pradeep De, respectively, were part of a three-page special feature in *Dateline Delhi* entitled "Delhi's Young Singers Love Folk and the Folks Love the Singers" (1975–76). An article on the city's burgeoning folk scene a few years earlier lavish praise on Radha Ramachandran and Lata Mani, although Mani's oeuvre may have been closer to rock than folk (Lalit 1973). Given her South Indian surname and Bhatia's confusion (noted above), I suspect this is the same Radha who would go on to join Human Bondage.

30. Women in beat groups get one chapter, entitled "Sisters, O Sisters," in Sidharth Bhatia's *India Psychedelic* (2014), the only book so far on that musical moment and movement. However, even that chapter is mainly focused on Asha Puthli. Women's contributions to the beat scene get only passing mention in the

documentary series on independent music in India, *Standing By* ("Chapter 2," 2015), as if their struggles were no different than those of young men into beat music.

31. "Usha Uthup—Fever" 2011.

32. The song continues thus:

> Chorus:
> Aiyyo yo, what shall I do?
> How shall I save my skin?
> I married a female wrestler
> Now look at the mess I'm in.
>
> Sometimes to show affection,
> She takes me on her lap,
> And hugs me just little bit,
> I feel my bones will snap.
> Sometimes she hugs and kisses me,
> Until I'm out of breath,
> Oh my goodness, I'm afraid
> She'll strangle me to death. (Chorus)
>
> One day we were invited
> To a fancy dressing ball,
> She dressed up like Dara Singh,
> We wrestled in the hall,
> We wrestled through a fox trot
> I was powerless to resist,
> We wrestled through a tango,
> But I fainted in the twist. (Chorus)
>
> Now to make it worse I've fallen
> For that pretty girl next door,
> She is skinny but I love her
> like I never loved before
> But if my wife should find out
> The thought would make her rave,
> My friends you'll have to buy some flowers
> And put them on my grave. (Chorus)

For slightly modified version of these lyrics and a discussion of Vernon Corea's legendary status at Radio Ceylon, see Corea 2010.

33. "If-by-usha uththup-MPG." 2011. I have not been able to locate a date for this black-and-white recording, but it was likely part of *Pop Time*, an hour-long prime-time music show (which she claims to have helped initiate) on Doordarshan in the early 1980s (Kvetko 2005, 162). The song she performs in the segment was a 1972 hit by the American soft rock band Bread.

34. This Swahili song, written by the Tanzanian Adan Sami, was first recorded

by William and his band the Jambo Boys in 1960. Miriam Makeba's 1964 recording is one of the more famous versions of this song.

35. My research did not reveal any explicit comments about the "blackness" of Uthup's bodily voice in either the ads or the reviews. But given that racist discourse in a number of different contexts links black people to the body and emotionality, and that Uthup's singing called up voices, styles, and genres associated with black performers the world over, it is likely that these aspects of her voice and repertoire were intimately linked for her audiences.

36. See, for instance, a large ad for a concert in aid of the Dadar School for the Blind, sponsored by Wills cigarettes (Advertisement for the Bristol Show). Similar wording appears in an ad the following month sponsored by the Bombay International School Association.

37. Uthup uses the word *homely* to describe herself at times (see, e.g., Fernandes 2011c).

38. A review of the same event in *Dateline Delhi* names her as one of the highlights of the evening.

> And then, while the crowd relaxed and some rowdy elements in the balcony blew prophylactics into baloons and threw them on the crowd, Usha Iyer came and sang the songs she sings every time—*Guantanamera, Scarborough Fair, Mississippi Delta, Ode to Billy Joe.*
>
> **Welcome relief**. (Ramaswamy 1970, 13, emphasis in original)

39. She uses the term *amma* to describe how audiences perceive her the first time they see her (Chatterjee 1981). Having settled in Calcutta after her second marriage, Uthup is affectionately called "didi" by her Bengali fans.

40. Jennifer Stoever-Ackerman makes a similar argument in "Splicing the Sonic Color Line": "Aural signifiers of race are thoroughly enmeshed with the visuality of race [because] they never really lose their ultimate referent to different types of bodies" (2010, 65).

41. In an interview published in *Society* magazine (Chatterjee 1981), she notes that she had done some humming for *Purab aur Paschim* (East and West, Manoj Kumar, 1970).

42. Those Bappi Lahiri songs were in fact picturized on actresses typecast as vamps, Kalpana Iyer and Aruna Irani.

43. All these Bappi Lahiri compositions had Kalpana Iyer performing vampish dance moves. Kalpana Iyer is joined by Prema Narayan on the song for *Armaan.* The last song in this list also illustrates Lahiri's tendency to "borrow" generously from other pop hits. "Video Killed the Radio Star" is an obvious reference to the *Disco Dancer* number. For the song-dance sequences cited in the paragraph, see "Hari Om Hari" 2017; "Rambha Ho Ho Ho" 2017; "Disco Dancer (1982)—Auva Auva Koi Yahan Nache" 2011; "One Two Cha Cha Cha" 2015; "Doston Se Pyaar Kiya" 2018.

44. "Good Times and Bad Times" and "Hari Om Tatsat" are the two *Bombay Talkie* songs for which Uthup penned the lyrics. The music was composed by the film's music director duo Shankar-Jaikishen. The credits for the film do not list her as a lyricist, but the EP of these two songs does. The film acknowledges her

cameo performance by listing her name and an image of her in profile beside (and under) that of Helen, the famous actor-dancer typecast in vampish roles. An audio recording of first song can be accessed on YouTube ("Good Times and Bad Times" (2015).

45. "Love Is Beautiful." 2012.

46. For the nightclub sequence, see "Listen to the Pouring Rain—Amitabh Bachchan & Aruna Irani—Bombay to Goa" (2008).

47. "Temptation," written by Arthur Freed and set to music by Nacio Herb Brown, was first used in the film *Going Hollywood* (Raoul Walsh, 1933).

48. The rockabilly song "Be Bop A Lula" was first recorded by Gene Vincent and His Blue Caps and later covered by rock and rock 'n' roll stars as diverse as Elvis, the Beatles, and Queen.

49. Originally written for the 1953 musical *Can-Can,* "It's All Right With Me" was performed by Frank Sinatra in the film version of the musical seven years later. It also became a standard in the jazz repertoires of Rita Reys and Ella Fitzgerald.

Works Cited

Advertisement for Bombay International School Association concert. *Times of India,* November 30, 1970, 3 (Display ad 34).

Advertisement for the Bristol Show. *Times of India,* October 2, 1970, 12 (Display ad 1).

Advertisement for the Friends of Needy Children concert. *Times of India,* November 26, 1969, 3 (Classified ad 18).

Advertisement for the Friends of Needy Children concert. *Times of India,* November 29, 1969, 5 (Classified ad 21).

Advertisement for Norge Stereo. *Times of India,* April 12, 1971, 3 (Classified ad 25).

Advertisement for Stars and Stars concert. *Times of India,* March 25, 1970, 3 (Classified ad 26).

Advertisement for Talk of the Town. *Times of India,* June 7, 1970, 3 (Classified ad 5).

Advertisement for Talk of the Town. *Times of India,* July 6, 1970, 2 (Classified ad 22).

Advertisement for Talk of the Town. *Times of India,* July 25, 1970, 5 (Classified ad 17).

Advertisement for Talk of the Town. *Times of India,* May 6, 1971, 3 (Classified ad 35).

Advertisement for the 3rd Simla Beat Contest Finals. 1970. *Times of India,* July 30, 7 (Classified ad 35).

Advertisement for "To This Night . . . A Dawn." *Times of India,* August 13, 1970, 2 (Classified ad 1).

Advertisement for Variety Entertainment. *Times of India,* June 7, 1970, 3 (Classified ad 5).

Advertisement for Ward Rock 71. *Times of India,* April 20, 1971, 2 (Classified ad 2).

Auslander, Philip. 2008. *Liveness: Performance in a Mediatized Culture.* 2nd ed. London and New York: Routledge.

Basu, Sharmadip. 2012. "Between Rock and a Hard Place: Cultural Politics of 1970s Rock Music in Calcutta." *South Asian Popular Culture* 10, no. 3: 285–94.

Bhatia, Sidharth. 2014. *India Psychedelic: The Story of a Rocking Generation.* Noida, India: Harper Collins.

Bohra, Vikram. 1970. "Just Usha." *Times of India,* September 6, A11.

Booth, Gregory D. 2014. "The Beat Comes to India: The Incorporation of Rock Music in the Indian Soundscape." In *More Than Bollywood: Studies in Indian Popular Music,* edited by Gregory Booth and Bradley Shope, 216–37. Oxford: Oxford University Press.

Bose, Devaki. 2008. "Original Diva of Indi-Pop." *The Tribune,* magazine section, Saturday extra, November 15. https://www.tribuneindia.com/2008/20081115/saturday/main2.htm

B. S. R. 1970. "Miscellanea." *Times of India,* March 1, 7.

"California Dreaming." 2015. YouTube, uploaded by Saregama India Ltd., December 15. https://www.youtube.com/watch?v=AeV4oHqQ_HE

Chandra, Ramesh. 1972. "The Record Business." *Sound Systems* (special issue), *Times of India,* October 29, A18–21.

"Chapter 2: The Rise of Beat Music." 2015. *Standing By,* YouTube, October 21, 2015. Published by Red Bull Music and Culture. https://www.youtube.com/watch?v=K249emziwUs

Chatterjee, Jayabrato. 1981. "Usha Uthup: Up, Close, and Personal." *Society,* May.

"'Confusion' from Madras Prevails in Beat Finals." 1970. *Times of India,* August 3, 8.

"Conversations with Namu Kini." 2014. YouTube, January 24. https://www.youtube.com/watch?v=OmtSXS3o25E

Corea, Ivan. 2010. "Vernon Corea and Ernest Ignatius of 'I Married a Female Wrestler' Fame." *Vernon Corea. 1927–2002* (blog). November 9. https://vernoncorea.wordpress.com/2010/11/09/vernon-corea-and-ernest-ignatius-of-i-married-a-female-wrestler-fame/

Das, Mohua, and Mathures Paul. 2013. "Original Diva of Park Street Goes Silent." *The Telegraph* (Calcutta), August 15. https://www.telegraphindia.com/1130815/jsp/calcutta/story_17234483.jsp

"Delhi's Young Singers Love Folk and the Folks Love the Singers." 1975–76. *Dateline Delhi,* eighth year, no. 3 (December–January): 10–12.

Dewan, Parvez. 1976. "Rec-reation." *Dateline Delhi,* eighth year, no. 4 (January–February): 17.

"Disco Dancer (1982)—Auva Auva Koi Yahan Nache." 2011. YouTube, uploaded by TheBollywoodClassic, September 22. https://www.youtube.com/watch?v=-z-Uhx_af9w

"Doston Se Pyaar Kiya." 2018. YouTube, uploaded by Rohit Kumar NrK, February 19. https://www.youtube.com/watch?v=nrMNoVNdm9M

Du Perron, Lalita. 2007. *Hindi Poetry in a Musical Genre: Thumri Lyrics.* London and New York: Routledge.

Fernandes, Naresh. 2011a. "Battleground Bombay: Hot Jazz and the Cold War." *Taj Mahal Foxtrot* (blog). November 5, 2011. http://www.tajmahalfoxtrot.com/?p=961

Fernandes, Naresh. 2011b. "Bombay, It's Ours." *Taj Mahal Foxtrot* (blog). June 11, 2011. http://www.tajmahalfoxtrot.com/?p=246

Fernandes, Naresh. 2011c. "Dot Buster." *Taj Mahal Foxtrot* (blog). July 16, 2011. http://www.tajmahalfoxtrot.com/?p=507

Fernandes, Naresh. 2011d. "Morning You Play Different, Evening You Play Different." *Taj Mahal Foxtrot* (blog). July 23, 2011. http://www.tajmahalfoxtrot.com/?p=441

Fernandes, Naresh. 2011e. "Remembering Anthony Gonsalves." *Taj Mahal Foxtrot* (blog). August 27, 2011. http://www.tajmahalfoxtrot.com/?p=470

Fernandes, Naresh. 2013. "Sari-Clad Jazz Diva." *Taj Mahal Foxtrot* (blog). *December 28, 2013*. http://www.tajmahalfoxtrot.com/?p=3159

"Fever." 2015. YouTube, uploaded by Saregama India Ltd., December 15. https://www.youtube.com/watch?v=gLqOMfw4L2Q

Fleeger, Jennifer. 2014. *Mismatched Women: The Siren's Song through the Machine.* Oxford: Oxford University Press.

"Good Times and Bad Times." 2015. YouTube, uploaded by Shantanu, March 28. https://www.youtube.com/watch?v=HleG0gCObBs

Gopinath, C. Y. 1969. "The Flintstones: New Kind of Gems." *Dateline Delhi,* First year, no. 19 (August 17,): 1+.

Gupta, Nalini. 1972. "Housewife Who Sings Pop." *Dateline Delhi,* fourth year, no. 6 (March): 9.

"Hari Om Hari." 2107. YouTube, uploaded by Gaane Sune Ansune, December 15. https://www.youtube.com/watch?v=cOnLqQgD538

"Hot Chapati, She's Good!" 1977. *South China Morning Post,* January 9, 15.

Huacuja Alonso, Isabel. 2019. "Radio, Citizenship, and the 'Sound Standards' of a Newly Independent India." *Public Culture* 31, no. 1: 117–44.

I to I. 2003. NDTV. July. YouTube, https://www.youtube.com/watch?v=Na_CEeRDZdY

"If-by-usha uththup-MPG." 2011. YouTube, uploaded by Bobby Mudgel, July 11. https://www.youtube.com/watch?v=dH1Cqkgw6CM

"Information on the Bands." *Indian Sixties and Beyond.* Facebook. October 5, 2011. https://www.facebook.com/india60s/

Kulkarni, Mrinal. 2013. "Those Were the Days, My Friend . . ." *Exploring Cultural Frontiers,* September 22.

Kumar, Anuj. 2003. "Tea, Croissants, and Usha Uthup!" *The Hindu,* Metro Plus Delhi, December 4.

Kumar, Pramod. 1969. "Fabulous Knockout/An Unbeatable Beat Show." *Dateline Delhi,* first year, no. 19 (August 17): 1+.

Kumar, Sangeet. 2016. "The Global as the Postcolonial: Desire, Identity, and Liminality in Indian Rock." *International Journal of Communication* 10: 3106–23.

Kvetko, Peter. 2005. "Indipop: Producing Global Sounds and Local Meanings in Bombay." PhD diss., University of Texas at Austin.

Lacey, Kate. 2013. *Listening Publics: The Politics and Experience of Listening in the Media Age.* Cambridge: Polity.

Lalit, Naveen. 1973. "Delhi's Folk Scene." *Dateline Delhi,* fifth year, no. 4 (January): 6+.

Lelyveld, David. 1994. "Upon the Subdominant: Administering Music on All-India Radio." *Social Text* 39: 111–27.

"Listen to the Pouring Rain—Amitabh Bachchan & Aruna Irani—Bombay to

Goa." 2008. YouTube, uploaded by Rajshri, January 10. https://www.youtube.com/watch?v=jK_N2BAr4LE

"Love Is Beautiful." 2012. YouTube, uploaded by BravoTamizh, September 30. https://www.youtube.com/watch?v=Slfdp8eAQlA

Makhijani, Vishnu. 1971. "Folks Who Make Folk Music." *Dateline Delhi,* fourth year, no. 1 (October): 14+.

"Marxist Leader Fails to Silence Indian Singer." 1983. *New York Times,* September 4.

McCracken, Allison. 2015. *Real Men Don't Sing: Crooning in American Culture.* Durham, NC: Duke University Press.

Mojapelo, Max. 2008. *Beyond Memory: Recording the History, Moments, and Memories of South African Music.* Somerset West, South Africa: African Minds.

Myers, Marc. 2007. "Interview: Yolande Bavan (part 1)." *Jazz Wax* (blog). November 13, 2007. https://www.jazzwax.com/2007/11/a-chat-with-yol.html

Nagpaul, Dipti. 2015. "The Love Story of Lorna Cordeiro, the Inspiration behind *Bombay Velvet.*" *Indian Express,* May 25. http://indianexpress.com/article/lifestyle/the-love-song-of-lorna-cordeiro-the-inspiration-behind-bombay-velvet/

NH7. 2014. "Simla Beat Contest." *The Standing By Project.* December 16, 2014. https://www.redbull.com/in-en/simla-beat-contest

"One Two Cha Cha Cha." 2015. YouTube, uploaded by SEPL Vintage, February 6. https://www.youtube.com/watch?v=Aayds_7nLC0

Pandey, Jhimli Mukherjee. 2015. "In the Groove for 50 Years." *Times of India,* July 11.

Parameswaran, Ambi. 2016. *Nawabs, Nudes, Noodles: India through 50 Years of Advertising.* Macmillan.

"Photos." *Indian Sixties and Beyond.* Facebook, Accessed October 7, 2019. https://www.facebook.com/india60s/

Pinto, Stanley. 2002? "Bombay and the Swinging Sixties." *Upper Crust,* Special Section, April–June? http://www.uppercrustindia.com/oldsite/10crust/ten/mumbai6.htm

"Pop Singer Works for Play on Apartheid Issue." 1970. *Times of India,* August 2, 7.

Prakash, Renu. 1970. "Usha Iyer: The New Rage." *Dateline Delhi,* second year, no. 32 (May 17): 1+.

Rahaim, Matthew. 2012. *Musicking Bodies: Gesture and Voice in Hindustani Music.* Middletown, CT: Wesleyan University Press.

Ramaswamy, C. Y. 1970. "'Confusion' Wins at Simla Beat Show." *Dateline Delhi,* second year, no. 37 (September 13): 13.

"Rambha Ho Ho Ho." 2017. YouTube, uploaded by Gaane Sune Ansune, August 17. https://www.youtube.com/watch?v=MINo9f1hpz8

Ranade, Ashok Da. 2006. *Hindi Film Song: Music beyond Boundaries. New Delhi:* Promilla Publishers.

Ravi, Arjun S. 2016. "Meet the Woman Who Founded One of India's First All-Girl Band [*sic*] in the '60s." *Vogue.* November 28, 2016. https://www.vogue.in/content/meet-the-woman-who-founded-one-of-indias-first-all-girl-band-in-the-60s/#the-ladybirds-strike-a-pose-for-a-womens-magazine-in-1969

"Scotch and Soda." 2015. YouTube, uploaded by Saregama India Ltd., December 15. https://www.youtube.com/watch?v=Io2a0jnwYTI

Sgro, Piero. 2016. "The Fabulous Usha Iyer and the Flintstones." *Seven 45rpm* (blog), April 7. https://seven45rpm.com/category/garage/

Sharma, Yukti. 2016. "A Religion Called 'Happiness.'" *DNA (Daily News and Analysis),* August 20.

Singh, Priyanka. 2014. "The Savages." *The Standing By Project, November 10, 2014.* https://www.redbull.com/in-en/the-savages

Soneji, Davesh. 2012. *Unfinished Gestures: Devadasis, Memory, and Modernity in South India.* Chicago: University of Chicago Press.

Stoever-Ackerman, Jennifer. 2010. "Splicing the Sonic Color Line: Tony Schwarz Remixes Postwar Nueva York." *Social Text* 28, no. 1: 59–85.

"Sunny." 2015. YouTube, uploaded by Saregama India Ltd., December 15. https://www.youtube.com/watch?v=B-6YhPf7AzI

Swer, Mark K. 2017. "'It's You I Came Here For': Eddie Rynjah Story." *Raiot,* April 12. http://raiot.in/its-you-i-came-here-for-eddie-rynjah-story/

Untitled News Item on Usha Iyer and Gatt Quartet. 1970. *Times of India,* October 23, 5.

"Usha Iyer 1968." 2014. YouTube, uploaded by hindustanvinyl, July 8. https://www.youtube.com/watch?v=WD6lFV9ulQs

"usha iyer & chris perry—conkani." 2014. YouTube, uploaded by hindustanvinyl, June 29. https://www.youtube.com/watch?v=RsdsaLvmVBY

"Usha iyer & the flintstones 1969." 2014a. YouTube, uploaded by hindustanvinyl, July 8. https://www.youtube.com/watch?v=5k_QpDMs1QA&list=PLoGevWrcS3XJwt-PBkAdGUdxSshFwjiQ4&index=2

"usha iyer & the flintstones 1969." 2014b. YouTube, uploaded by hindustanvinyl, July 8. https://www.youtube.com/watch?v=3WDWuaMIle4&list=PLoGevWrcS3XJwt-PBkAdGUdxSshFwjiQ4

"Usha Iyer & Jesudas in Musical Evening." 1970. *Times of India,* October 9, 7.

"usha iyer and the ronnie menezes quartet—lambretta." 2014. YouTube, uploaded by hindustanvinyl, October 16. https://www.youtube.com/watch?v=cjNzkMiW7Bk

"Usha Uthup—Fever—Killer Indian version—Victor Kiswell Archives." 2011. YouTube, uploaded by Victor Kiswell, June 3. https://www.youtube.com/watch?v=F7vLHsKNQrA&start_radio=1&list=RDF7vLHsKNQrA

"Usha Uthup: Skyfall in a Sari." 2013. YouTube, uploaded by INKtalks, November 20. www.youtube.com/watch?v=QO3oILb1vSY

Weidman, Amanda. 2006. *Singing the Classical, Voicing the Modern: The Postcolonial Politics of Music in South India.* Durham, NC: Duke University Press.

SIX | Narendra Modi Speaks the Nation

Masculinity, Radio, and Voice

PRASEEDA GOPINATH

Narendra Modi's ascension to and retention of power has been predicated on the specific refashioning of a disciplined "ascetic" Hindu masculinity and its articulation with neoliberal gendered subjectivity. While his *chappan chhatti* (fifty-six-inch chest) circulated in the media as a metonym for his physical and phallic power, this ostensibly powerful male body is complemented and complicated by Modi's voice. This chapter examines how his various modes of address—public speeches and radio—embodied in gestures and voice, invoke the vastness of the Indian nation while including the nation-family in the intimate domestic. I examine how his strategic vocal practice in and through his massively popular radio broadcast, *Mann Ki Baat*, crafts a gentle everyman national savior even as it constructs a new national public. At the same time, I consider the ways in which his voice and words follow a distinctive rhythmic repetition, the rising breathless cadences at the end of repeated sentences both belie and reconfigure the visuals of the gestural performance of the speech-making body. The pervasive use of catchy advertising slogans in the midst of his exhortation of Hindu India's past greatness telescopes nation-time, creating anew in his voice-body and sound-body the Janus-faced masculine nation and collapsing the future tense of consumerist neoliberal modernity with the hoary past of Hindu magnificence. Focusing on Modi's voice, I examine how this embodied voice produces his affective masculinity and its imbrication with a national public, as well as the Hindu nation. I do so by examining Modi's resolutely lower-class voice-body and sound-body, including the vibrational quality of his voice, his gestural speechmaking body, and his speech and voice rhythms differently deployed in his speeches and radio broadcast show and podcast *Mann Ki Baat.*

Speaking (to) Power: Vocal Rhythms and Vibratory Affect

Narendra Modi's rise to power was built on the masculine idiom of a populist rhetoric articulated with the discourse of service. He was a man of the people, an outsider, not just in terms of Delhi's insulated and corrupt political insiders but also as someone whose class background (the oft-repeated narrative of the son of a *chai-wallah* [tea seller]) and linguistic domain automatically cordoned him off from the elite secular rungs of power. This narrative of the outsider, of the lower-class *pracharak* (activist and proselytizer for the Rashtriya Swayamsevak Sangh), who selflessly devotes himself to "Bharat Mata," was always implicitly couched in terms of ascetic, devoted masculine service to the nation-mother. Much of this carefully crafted narrative emerged in and through his speeches. Indeed, the narrative is not merely evident in the language of these speeches but in his voice (quality) and his speechmaking body. For instance, in one of his campaign speeches on corruption and the necessity of destroying the black market, it is possible to trace the embodied voice and gestural practice that invented Modi for the national stage. It is a modulated, theatrical, and powerful performance.[1]

Beginning with a confident call-and-response, Modi sets out a series of rhetorical questions about the flow of "black" money out of the country. *Black money* refers, of course, to illegally acquired money and money that is frequently not reported in tax documents. The call and response that prompts enthusiastic assent from his audience is accompanied by wide arm gestures in which he alternately points with his index finger or his whole hand into the distance, at and over the audience as if to encompass the nation with his voice and gestures. In that very decision to engage in a call-and-response there is the idea of collectivity and inclusivity. The confidence and certainty in his voice as he asks his rhetorical questions prompting ready responses is an index of his sense of belonging and assurance of the collective.

Modi speaks to his audiences in a colloquial, legible Hindi, accentuated by the regionalism of his Gujarati accent. He is of them, but also because he is of them he is uniquely positioned to serve and protect them. His voice quality is strident as he assures them that when the Bharatiya

Janata Party (BJP) comes to power the flow of black money out of the country will be arrested. Moreover, the *chor-lootere* (thieves and robbers) who stash their money in foreign bank accounts will be brought to account. Raising his voice, and indeed his whole body, he shouts angrily, embracing the crowd, the national collective, and "the poor" with his voice and words: "Yeh janta ke paise hain, ye ghareeb ke paise hain. . . . Wo dhan pe Hindustan ka adhikar hai, Hindustan ke koti koti ghareebon ka adhikar hai" (This money belongs to the people, this money belongs to the poor. . . . Hindustan has the right to that money; the poor have a right to every single penny of Hindustan). It is the anger in his voice-body that binds together the nation, the poor, and the public. Conflating the "the poor" with *janta* (the people/public) into Hindustan, Modi's voice rises to a crescendo as his voice-body sonically and visually renders his anger and aggression. As Caroline Wilkins points out, the "voice is a physical phenomenon. . . . [T]he body is the medium for experience. It communicates . . . through the voice to the listener by means of embodied affect" (2016, 119). The rise in volume is accompanied by more violent and assertive arm gestures. His voice-body becomes the vehicle through which to express collective anger on behalf of the exploited poor and the *janta* of Hindustan. Through his voice and body, he is the instrument of anger, the symbolic man who will fight on behalf of his people. He is them, as they are him. This is an obvious manifestation of his *chappan chati*, and his phallic power, signifying his hypermasculine ability to protect and lead the nation into a new future. However, this is only one dimension of Modi's performative political masculinity.

Shiv Viswanathan has argued, "Modi is a cultural construct whose semiotic grammar we have to understand." Semiotics, of course, draws attention to the visuality of signs and symbols. I want to draw attention to the aural and the auditory along with the visual in order to examine the production of Modi as political man. Evident in this speech is what Nina Sun Eidsheim calls the vibratory quality of the voice, where the vibration of the voice "stirs up" those within its sonic field. Explaining this process, Wilkins argues that the listener feels from within their own fount of "emotional experiences, one that is heightened by the physical vibration of sound waves on the body as they enter the ear" (2016, 119). Voice and sound work simultaneously at the affective and material levels. The affective is transmitted in the unconscious dialogue between the listening body and performing voice-body. Hence, the anger mentioned earlier is transmitted between Modi's voice-body and the listening audience in a feedback loop.

It also needs to be emphasized here that the affective also works discursively, that is, the listening body also constructs the performing voice-body. In Modi's case, the call-and-response works precisely because the audience hears discursively and affectively responds to Modi's voice, words, and accent. The discourses of class, region, and language in Indian national politics produce Modi as a distinctly lower-class, local voice, divorced from the elitism of English, and the elitism of brahmanical culture. The listening audience parses accordingly. Although he does use Sanskrit and Sanskritized Hindi, it is offset by his accent and body and peppered with colloquialisms and theatrical folksy mockery.

In the middle of his speech, his voice becomes condescendingly mocking and intimate, almost a joke between friends, when he makes fun of the *chor-lootere* who have the temerity to ascribe blame to Modi (he refers to himself in third person) when they are the shameless thieves. His vocal range moves from gruffly masculine to whispery and intimate: "Aur besharam hoke kehte hain, sarkar aap chalate ho. Aur poochte Modi ko ho." (And being utterly shameless, although these thieves are running the government, they ask Modi to answer). His gestures are modulated to this intimate mockery, incredulous wide-armed shrugs, pointing to himself when referring to himself in the third person. In this instance, the third-person reference coupled with a drop in volume, along with ironic pointing, creates a cocoon of intimacy. The body reinforces the incredulous irony in his voice. This intimacy contrasts with the loud angry voice at the end, but it reveals how effectively Modi modulates his voice. He is not just the strong man with the *chappan chati*; he is also the intimate friend who knows you well, who knows your desires. He draws you in, and the offscreen laughter that follows this performance only reinforces this sense of intimacy and camaraderie. It is almost as if a group of male friends are discussing the state of politics and their neighbors at the local tea stall or the café.

The rhythmic cadences of Modi's speech, as well as the breathy exhalations at the end of his sentences, also serve to emphasize the complicated vocal performance of his political masculinity. Adriana Cavarero, in her radical rethinking of the aural and the voice, argues that when "the human voice vibrates, there is someone in flesh and bone who emits it" (2005, 4). Indeed, Modi's voice foregrounds exactly this material human quality; the whispery, mocking voice and the smirking face foreground the flesh-and-bone body. The voice, for Cavarero, is both "hidden and most genuine" (4). Of course, political speeches and voices really complicate this idea: they are most carefully crafted and performed, but at the same time they are also meant to express the essence of the candidate. Modi's political voice combined with his oratorical performance brings together the "most genuine" with that which is crafted. His voice rises and falls in accordance with the emotion he expresses and/or replicates and those he wishes to "stir up" in his listeners. Accordingly, the rhythms of his speech rise and fall, but the voice climbs to a pitch when he makes his point, sometimes in the middle of word, only to fall off into what I call an intimate exhalation at the end of the sentence. An example of this is when he says, "Ek Ek pai Hindustan ki wapis layee jayegee, aur Hindustan ke ghareebon ke kaam lag jayegi" (Every single penny will be brought back and will be used for the poor of Hindustan). His voice rises with "layee jayeGEE" and falls off in the following clause, to a lowered tone fading to a whisper with "lag jayegi." Of course, there is a noticeable internal rhyme at the end of both clauses, a fact that he uses to great effect, going high and then fading to low. The breathy fading is theatrical and noticeable. The most immediate sonic memory that this whisperiness at the end of the line invokes is the dialogue delivery in Hindi cinema, a melodic sonorous grandeur. It lulls you and draws you in even as the rising pitch and repetitive cadences of his voice focus your attention, aurally signaling the importance and impressiveness of his speech's content. Whether he is mocking the opposition party, exhorting his listeners, affectionately joking among friends, or expressing anger at the state of the nation, the rhythms of his voice implicitly foreground the grandeur of his endeavor and his self.

A young mimic and fan zeroed in exactly on this aspect of Modi's voice. Shyam Rangeela's mimicry of Modi, which has since gone viral and garnered him attention from news and entertainment media, exaggerates this breathiness and clarifies it.[2] In his parody video, Rangeela, mimicking Modi's oratorical voice, speaks about the way Sonam Gupta (a fictitious girlfriend) has betrayed him. Indeed, the whole nation knows that she is treacherous.[3] Once again, it is an interesting juxtaposition of manly assertive strength and the appropriately humanly vulnerable. His vocal rhythms attend to humanity and strength, essence and affect. It is not merely an unmitigated sonic assault of aural virility but rather a modulation of patriarchal authoritativeness with the filial familiar.

Radio Voice: Feeling Everyman and the National Public

Modi fine-tunes this dimension of his persona in his popular radio broadcast and podcast called *Mann Ki Baat*.[4] In the soundscape of the radio, Modi's voice—with its roughish timbre and nonstandard Hindi and English pronunciation—is antithetical to the smooth and practiced professional radio voices on All India Radio (AIR)—the government-controlled national channel on which his show is broadcast. However, for all of his nonsmooth vocals, his voice, cadence, and style are that of an affectionate and beloved uncle, friend, and brother. Unlike in political speeches and rallies, the medium and microphone amplification make possible what Allison McCracken has called "the intimacy of live person-to-person" address on a mass scale (2015, 79). Through the form of the broadcast, Modi aurally brings into being a new persona, as radio enables and constructs intimate "affective engagement" and "sincerity of expression" through consistent personal address (21). He is able to create a personal intimate connection, crafting and consolidating a distinctive aspect of the caring everyman that undergirds his national savior persona: the benevolent patriarch and friend. Modi's radio performative voice, then, consistently centers his personhood and foregrounds his expressiveness. Through radio's "sociability factor," Modi re-creates himself as someone who speaks to individual listeners rather than at them (Scannell 1995, 24–25). The location, mode, and reach of the radio broadcast further cements his voice and persona as those of a familiar and benevolent patriarch who also happens to be prime minister of the world's largest democracy.

Inspired by the American president Franklin Delano Roosevelt's *Fireside Chats* (1933–44), radio addresses to the nation broadcast during the Great Depression, the New Deal, and US entry into World War II, Modi's deliberate choice of national radio, "a medium believed to be obsolete" (BlueKraft Digital Foundation 2017, 4),[5] reflects the blurring of the private and the public, the light and the heavy, and policy and affect. Broadcast from the comfort of his office, his private yet public domain, the show reaches into private and public spaces, rendering the private public and the public private. Jason Loviglio's theorization of radio's "intimate public" is instructive here. He argues that radio voices cross the "borders between the intimate worlds of domesticity, solitude, and one-on-one conversations, and the public world of politics, sociability, and mass communication" (2005, 16). Much like Roosevelt in his *Fireside Chats*, Modi, taking advantage of the radio's blurring of private and public, strategically mixes state authority and conversational intimacy, moving swiftly and easily across the national and the quotidian, the administrative and the personal with topics such as festivals, #Selfiewithdaughter, exam stress, global diplomacy with President Obama, Swachh Bharat

(Clean India) policies, "Sportsman Spirit," the Aadhar card (Unique Identification Card) policy, "Empowerment of Farmers," demonetization, how to maintain a travelogue, and exercise, among many others. His vocal and anecdotal style melds the state and personal with ease. Indeed, the title, too, encapsulates the content, tone, and persona of the speaker. The name, *Mann Ki Baat,* emerged from Modi's throwaway phrase, with which he describes his intention to "speak from the heart." Interestingly, the phrase he uses captures the layered nature of this endeavor: "kuch halke-phulke mann ki baatein," (some light conversation that emerges from the heart). The conversation is personal and light, but at the same time it is substantive and infused with affective intensity since it deals with matters close to his heart. Much of the *halke-phulke mann ki baatein* comprise the many government initiatives in which he encourages his listeners to participate. Modi's voice, then, speaking about newly instituted, as well as ongoing, government policies, about the state of the nation, about "Indian values," reverberates in the home, even as stories about his childhood, advice to young people about upcoming board exams, and *Panchantantra*-style (akin to Aesop's Fables) folksy homilies resonate in the public spaces of the markets, shops, and tea stalls.

Complementing the radio broadcast (and also broadcast on private radio), and in keeping with Modi's avowed commitment to India's digital future, the show streams in the digital form of the podcast, made possible by the internet and the smart/mobile phone. It is available on a web page dedicated to the show,[6] downloadable to one's phone, and streams on Saavn, a digital platform that aggregates and distributes English, Bollywood, and regional Indian music of multiple genres across more than two hundred countries.[7] Purported to reach more than eighteen million listeners via its app and online portal, *Mann Ki Baat* routinely features on Saavn's Hitlist (songs and podcasts with the highest number of plays and downloads), the only speech podcast to do so. The podcast format allows the listener to download and listen at will. It becomes an even more intimate medium as Modi's voice susurrates in your ear on your preferred electronic device (probably your mobile phone) or in your vehicle in the midst of traffic.

It's also important to point out the transmedial aspect of the broadcast of *Mann Ki Baat.* As mentioned, it is broadcast on private radio stations as well, indicating the exertion of governmental power in nudging them to participate in Modi's sonic propaganda. In addition, it is also excerpted and broadcast on Doordarshan News, the government-controlled national channel, as well as social media accounts of Doordarshan, All

India Radio, the national party and the Prime Minister's Office. It's a virtual sonic blanketing, spread across all media, old and new; the state's power is manifest in its attempt to control the airwaves through multiple technologies. Modi's radio voice channeled through visual and social media realms ensures that sonic Modi travels everywhere all the time. The reception of his voice on these platforms differs according to design and structure. For instance, an excerpt from an episode of *Mann Ki Baat* was played during the news on May 25, 2018. It concerned six navy women who had sailed around the world in 254 days on an Indian Navy sailboat, the *Tarini*. Rather than the news anchor relaying the news in a practiced and detached broadcast voice, it is Modi's voice and narrative that render the event. The excerpt then becomes extended philosophizing about the human spirit of adventure, moving from other "daughters" and their accomplishments to Modi's initiatives (such as Swachh Bharat and Fit India, a nationwide health and fitness campaign) and so on. The "News Flash" chirons, in both English and Hindi, indicate that what we are hearing is an excerpt from an episode of *Mann Ki Baat*. They then proceed to paraphrase the main points while a separate static chiron indicates that the text is from the forty-fourth broadcast of the program. The news then advertises the prime minister's show, reinforcing the seriousness of *Mann Ki Baat* even as it imbues it with a layer of "objective" truth. The visual consists of a demarcated screen, with Modi's photograph on one side looking out at the viewer and static images and videos of the six navy women on their boat, arriving at port, meeting the prime minister, and sitting with him while watching a video of their journey. It's show-and-tell, with Modi's voice enveloping the images, much like a narrator's, except it's not dispassionate narration of facts but Modi's voice and perspective as it interprets the images on screen. It is Modi offering his congratulation to the "daughters of India," shaping the event for the viewer-listener. Modi's voice, ringing with the quiet pride of the benevolent leader and patriarch, speaks of the superlative qualities and accomplishments of Indian women, "who are second to none."[8]

In the middle of the newscast, the broadcast showcases Modi performatively creating a celebratory and forward-looking India. The interspersal of Modi's *Mann Ki Baat* voice with the national news dialectically crafts the nation even as it produces Modi as the national architect and savior. The final effect of the transmedial presence is the ubiquitousness of Modi's voice, hailing the listener through all portals. The conjoining of old media (television and radio) and new (the digital realms of website portals, podcasts, and social media) expresses the omnipresence of the state—a state that decides what and who can be heard when. Modi, through the insertion of his vocal presence on the news and social media, arrogates to himself not just institutional state power but the moral authority to shape the nation in his image.

Through his radio address, podcast, and transmedial vocal presence, Modi constructs a national public and a national-personal identity.[9] I would like to focus on the specifics of the vocal practice in the radio show and podcast. Michael Warner argues that through public speech, and in this case the radio address, listeners recognize themselves as addressees but are also always aware that the "the speech is addressed to indefinite others" and in the process become cognizant of being part of a public (2005, 77). Indeed, Modi never fails to address his listeners as *mere pyare deshvasyion* (my beloved country-people) or, more literally, "my beloved inhabitants of the nation." This is, of course, a standard political designation, but coupled with the ritual listing of his country-people's participatory endeavors, accomplishments, spirit, and so on it creates what it describes, a sort of sonic citizenship. Listeners hear themselves as individually addressed, but they also hear themselves addressed as part of the national collective, producing a sense of "stranger relationality" (84) or an immediate sense of an imagined community of sonic citizens. Modi's "gentle persuasion" and "warm conversation" construct a national public that did not exist in quite the same fashion earlier (BlueKraft Digital Foundation 2017, 13). In his September 2016 episode, in honor of the show's first anniversary, Modi specifically addresses this newly created national public, the mobilized jan shakti (power of the people), which over the course of the year had involved itself in a "silent revolution" in response to his specific hailing. He details the success of media-friendly initiatives such as #IncredibleIndia, #Selfiewithdaughter, "Give-It-Up," LPG gas subsidies, "Khadi for fashion," and the ongoing success of Swacch Bharat. Seamlessly melding the analog and the digital, radio and social media, he represents himself as the voice of the past and the future, signaling his omnipresence. At the same time, through this blending of media, he also vocalizes into being a supposedly vast national enlightened and enthusiastic citizenry. His imagined radio/listening community is also a digital community whose most pronounced feature is civic participation. He characterizes the mood and tone of this awakened national public when he describes fifty-five thousand calls that his show has received from all corners of the country. Describing these calls as being "in the shadow of *Mann Ki Baat*," he points out that "they were totally positive, suggestion-oriented and constructive. Just see how the citizens of the country are moving with a positive spirit; this is the nation's greatest wealth."[10] The spirit of Modi's address imbues the national public hailed into existence by *Mann Ki Baat.* He is the indispensable fount and creator of this national public, the origin and source of sonic citizenship. In true Modi fashion, he draws attention to himself as the creator while also rendering himself as an awed servant of the nation who is consistently "amazed" and "astounded" by the power of "the people." In and through the show, he emerges as the devoted public servant, indispensable national savior, neighborhood uncle, and benevolent patriarch who creates a public with his voice.

Modi's *Mann Ki Baat* remakes his listeners into a participatory national public. Warner is again instructive here when he writes that a "public is constituted through mere attention" or, more specifically, through "active participation" and "renewed attention" (2005, 87, 89). At the beginning of each episode, Modi speaks without fail of the many messages, questions, and suggestions he gets on various platforms—voicemail (both mobile and otherwise), web page, text, letter, Twitter, and specially installed kiosks (BlueKraft Digital Foundation 2017, 11). Modi offers anecdotes sent in by listeners in which individuals, neighborhoods, or groups inspired by a previous address have enacted national policy at the local and personal level. In one episode, he speaks of a young man who rallied his peers to clean up the trash in their neighborhood, carrying out Modi's Swacch Bharat initiative, which is predicated on the participation of citizens. The show's immediate intimacy reforms citizens as people "who want to drive the change themselves because they place immense faith in the government" (Modi quoted in BlueKraft Digital Foundation 2017, 12). Modi's voice generates the listener as the ideal citizen, his performative utterances bringing into being people who "drive change." In other words, Modi's address interpellates his listeners as agents of change, constituents of the development narrative that he describes. Indeed, in describing citizen participation in his "Give-It-Up" campaign, in which listeners voluntarily gave up their gas subsidies for the sake of those less fortunate, he deems the initiative a success just by virtue of people's participation. Whether it accomplished anything substantive is moot, for participation itself becomes a matter on which to congratulate his listening public and himself for being altruistic, for serving/leading the nation, for being good citizens, and for moving the country forward by doing all the above. *Mann Ki Baat* crafts a national public around jan shakti (people power) but a jan shakti that can only be mobilized, understood, and sustained by Modi's charismatic and regulatory voice.

The February 2016 episode of *Mann Ki Baat* reinforces the coalescence of the private-public and familial-national in terms of both content and vocal tone. The episode, immediately preceding the nationwide month-long stress coma known as the "Board exams," was entirely devoted to offering comfort and perspective on what are widely perceived as life-defining exams for students. The Board exams are national public examinations that all students in the tenth and twelfth grades must take in order to advance to higher secondary education in the case of tenth graders or, in the case of twelfth graders, to determine their chances of admission to universities, professional courses, or training institutes. These exams are simultaneously administered across the country and graded through a centralized system run by the Central Board of Secondary Education, the government organization that oversees and administers secondary education across the country. The very fact that the prime minister of the nation decided to focus an entire national show on this most quotidian of events was itself noteworthy. It indicates that he is part of the national family, an everyman who shares in every familial trial. Taking on the vocal note of the avuncular relative and/or old family friend, Modi's voice is understanding and familiar: "Aap radio pe meri mann ki baat sunte honge, lekin dimaag iss baat pe laga hoga ki bachchon ki exams shuru ho rahi hai. . . . MAIN BHI aap ke iss yatra main sharik hona chahta hun." (You might be listening to the thoughts from my heart/mind on the radio, but your mind is focused on the fact that the children's exams are about the begin. I, too, want to share this journey with you). The capitalization marks the emphasis he places on these words. His voice becomes emphatic and registers an up-rhythm in his desire to be a part of the national family journey, while the rest of the sentence slips back into a down rhythm. The colloquial tone, the affectionate and soothing timbre, and the wish to be a part of the parent-listener's life implicitly carry within them the idea of the shared familial burden. Modi, through his radio address and vocal tone, creates a sense of the intimate, domestic, and familial. Indeed, the radio show succeeds because of the consistency of this tone.

Unlike his speeches, when broadcasting Modi never raises his voice, nor does he vary his pitch toward upper registers. As he speaks from the heart, he uses the same soothing narrative and vocal style, one brimming with concern and gentle exhortation. If there is any deviation, it is toward tenderness, humility, and service, all reflected in the lowering of pitch, the whispery breath, or the intimate exhalation noted earlier. To take another example, in a March 2015 episode of the show dedicated specifically to farmers and their concerns, the tone is even gentler than the one that is manifest in the show about exam stress. While I do not want to digress too much from my analysis of Modi's vocal practice and strategic tonal deployments, I do want to point out that he characterizes farmers as separate and distinct from his usual "brothers and sisters." He takes pains to ethnographically situate his farmer-brothers as part of the nation but nevertheless different from the nation-family that he has so far been addressing. In drawing attention to "farmers" as a special interest group different from his regular audience, or the show's populist elite, he makes a statement of inclusion, which nevertheless is predicated on their exclusion from the normative. His voice immediately signals the uniqueness of his subject matter. The gentler, low-pitched timbre transmits his sense of humility as he speaks to and of his farmer-brothers, reflecting his awe at the endurance and stoicism of the village, the brother-farmer, and the mothers and sisters who work in the fields.

Modi's vocal practice—and it is a very well trained bodily voice modulation in tandem with technology and the radio form—conveys empathy, sincerity, and the enormous sense of duty he feels. His vocal practice here denotes an authentic and selfless political masculinity. I am using *vocal practice* in the way Nina Sun Eidsheim describes it, as an "internal choreography" that reveals the bodily knowledge and training required to produce certain kinds of voices and sounds. Vocal practice draws attention to the materiality of the voice, not just in terms of the body but also in terms of technology and space (2009). As noted earlier, his voice is lowered to an almost whispery pitch, hinting at a quiver or a break suggesting intense emotion. More important, his strategic use of microphone technology enables the crafting of a soft yet gruff masculine voice that the listener discursively receives as quiet authenticity. The listener's ear discursively hears the low-key vibrational creakiness as genuine, produced as he or she is within the cultural discourses of Indian masculine vocal expressiveness, where a low-pitched, nearly breaking voice indicates genuine emotion. He is the quiet and authentic political man who is touched beyond measure by the endurance of his fellow countrypeople. While describing how he felt as he received the unexpected, wide-ranging messages, suggestions, and questions from his farmer-brothers living in faraway corners of India, Modi's voice vibrates with emotion. The vocal disintegration signifies an empathetic embodied political masculinity whose entire being is directed toward national service.

Marking the condescension implicit in his surprise, I want to unpack the quiver and hiss of Modi's voice as it is produced within the radio show.

According to Wilkins, "through the medium of technology both the performer's and the listener's relation to the 'reality' of a voice is altered," leading to the emergence of a mediatized voice, material in terms of both the body that produces it and the technology that alters it (2016, 128). The timbre of Modi's mediatized voice here signifies more than his deep empathy and concern for farmers; it signals his capacity to feel for the disenfranchised. The performative mediatized voice, "freed of any physical presence," becomes Modi's voice of feeling. As Wilkins points out, the listening body responds not to Modi, the performing voice-body, but to the vibrations of the mediatized feeling sound-body in the "realm of abstract sounds," which is nevertheless discursively produced in terms of affect, masculinity, and the traditions of political speech (2016, 128). Microphone technology and the intimacy of the radio/podcast format amplify and create his hushed, creaky voice, both rendering and enabling its reception as authenticity, sincerity, and concern. Here technology creates a space where a listening body responds to a vibrating sound-body via the circuits of affect. Sound technology and the form of the radio show, then, engender intimacy and sincerity, or McCracken's "affective engagement" and "sincerity of expression." This kind of hushed, low-key affect is only possible within the compressed sonic space created by the radio show, of which Modi is aware, as evidenced by his differential vocal practice in this medium as opposed to the extreme vocal shifts in his public speeches. *Mann Ki Baat* adds a dimension of affective familial sincerity to Modi's carefully constructed political masculinity, which has served to expand and cement his autocratic power, both sonic and otherwise.

Serving the Mother

The breaking and creaking of his voice to signify intense affect and sincerity is also manifest on the many occasions when Narendra Modi has cried during his speeches. One of the most famed of such occasions occurred on his entering the Indian Parliament for the first time after being designated the head of the BJP and the prime minister of India in the wake of a triumphant national electoral victory in 2014.[11] Following a show of excess humility, in which he bends down and touches his forehead to the steps of the Parliament in a gesture of obeisance, he speaks to the Parliament for the first time. Responding to senior party leader L. K. Advani's expression of gratitude to him for being instrumental in the BJP's return to power, Modi breaks down in surprising tears. He cries at the moment when he insists that Advani should not use the word *kripa* to describe Modi's actions. *Kripa* in this context means "favor"; Modi's response is to dismiss the very idea of a favor, which locates him in a hierarchically superior position that enables him to dispense favors. Instead he casts himself as the righteous and dutiful party servant and son: "Kya ma ki seva, kabhi krupa ho sakti hai? Katai nahi ho sakti. Jaise Bharat meri ma hain, waise he BJP bhi meri ma hain" (Can serving the mother ever be a favor? It can never be that. Just as Bharat is my mother, so, too, BJP is my mother). Not only does he have to pause in the middle of this to collect himself, but even after he does so his voice breaks and descends into a whisper, overcome by the idea of his duty to honor both party and nation as mother. The pause is long and awkward, but the visual of the bent body, of his hiding his tears, makes the silence all more the potent and emotional. The vocal disintegration and silence here do not signal weakness. Rather the breakdown is discursively entrenched within Indian patriarchal structures, where selfless filial service to the symbolic and idealized mother undoes the confident strongman. The mother is habitually constructed as "self-sacrificing," 'innocent," and the bearer of "unconditional love," and the mother figure is never far from the discourses of femininity and nationalism in India (Thomas 1995, 167). The broken voice and bent body signify his righteous and selfless masculinity as the devoted son who will sacrifice himself for his nation-mother. Indeed, in both religious and popular discourses, this is the highest and most appropriate form of masculinity. His appropriate masculine affect is manifest in his tears and breathy, broken voice. As an aside, the "authenticity" of his voice and emotion are emphasized by his use of his native Gujarati in *katai nahi* instead of the standard *kabhi nahi*, as well as in his pronunciation of *krupa* instead of the standardized Sanskrit of *kripa*. The transcendental intensity of the mother-son bond is, of course, a familiar narrative in the annals of Hindu mythology, folktales, and plays and is disseminated through various iterations in Indian cinema, particularly Hindi cinema. Not surprisingly, he has broken down on other occasions when speaking about both his mother and his filial duty to the nation. He casts himself in the mold of the mythological Hindu man but one who brings in the future.

Chanting Global (Hindu) India

Shiv Viswanathan and Sanjay Srivastava have variously pointed out that "[Modi-masculinity] combines the idea of an Indian essence with the notion of global comity (Srivastava 2015, 21). Modi's embodiment of such a particular iteration of masculinity is produced within a discourse of an essentialized version of Indianness, one that had been promulgated by both the BJP and the advertising and media industries since the 1990s. In fact the BJP's return to power in the 1990s and the "liberalization" of the economy were built on the intersection of traditional Hindu essence and neoliberal consumerism. William Mazzarella calls the latter the "new consumerist ontology," wherein the market and "the affect-intensive power of advertising images" selling foreign brands reflected the deep truth of the individual citizen's desire and simultaneously provided a "sounding board for the national community" (2003, 13). This consumerist desire (produced and sustained by media and advertising) refracted the emergence of an aspirational new India, one where the cultural particularity and integrity of the country were reinforced by the discourses of global consumerism. This new 1990s globally-oriented Indian, usually upper-caste Hindu, "essence" steeped in aspirational consumerism, or the "Indian soul with international feel," proliferated in cultural texts of the time (Arathoon 1996), in iconic hit films like *Dilwale Dulhaniya Le Jayenge* (1995) and *Kuch Kuch Hota Hai* (1998), and in popular television commercials such as Cadbury's "Kya Swadh Hai," the National Dairy Development Board's "Dhoodh Dhoodh," and Pepsi's "Ye Dil Mange More."[12] Modi mobilizes precisely this marriage of consumerism, advertising, essentialized Indianness, and globalization through his masculine stylization and vocal address.

In the episode of October 2014, Modi spoke about his initiative called "Khadi for Nation, Khadi for Fashion" (simultaneously advertised on Twitter, on his web page, and in newspapers and, of course released through news broadcasts).[13] He is gently persuasive, but at the same time he describes the "youth of the nation" as already far more forward thinking than is cynically believed. Inhabiting the role of the supportive, proud father who sees potential in the young, Modi encourages young people to contribute to the nation by buying khadi. It is hard to miss the catchy advertising zing of the program's name. It is a direct appeal to the Indian citizen as consumer; indeed, it is precisely through appropriate consumerism that the listener becomes an Indian citizen. Calling it a khadi revolution, Modi rebrands Mahatma Gandhi's symbol of anticolonial, anticapitalist, *swadeshi* (national, local) self-reliance. While retaining khadi's symbolic value of the quintessential national fabric, he resignifies it as a fashionable commodity to be purchased alongside other brands or "products from companies." Modi makes it both a quintessential local/national fabric and a global commodity. He recognizes that if khadi is to become an Indian global brand it must be rooted in the Gandhi's *swadeshi* discourse, hence the invocation of him, but if it is to signify the new global India of the twenty-first century, it has to be rendered as fashion.[14] While arguing that it is a tribute to "Bapu" (Gandhi), Modi, through the resignification, also constructs himself as a leader of the future, updating and perhaps replacing the "Father of the Nation." Speaking as the benevolent uncle-father-friend-leader addressing all "his brothers and sisters," he nevertheless constructs his listeners as a popular elite since he argues that through their consumerism his listeners are "lighting the lamp of Diwali in the house of the poor." As with the farmers episode, the *ghareeb* (the poor) here are part of the imagined community of the nation but do not quite fit into the intimate public of this particular address; they are the objects on which the agentive consumerist citizen-listener will act to strengthen and sustain the nation.

And yet, even as he distinguishes between "the *ghareeb*," "the *kisan*-brother" (the farmer-brother), and his listening public, Modi's own voice-body performatively brings into being a new classed, regional iteration of the Hindutva-neoliberal man. His nonstandard accent, his rough timbre, and his body sonically and visually repudiate the upper-class, upper-caste elitism of government and political institutions. As this chapter demonstrates, his voice-body, sound-body, and the political masculinity they produce are distinctive. He embodies a populist iteration of Indian/Hindu neoliberal masculinity, and his charismatic oratorical and sonic performances enable him to position himself as both everyman and national savior. His speeches and his voice-body performance telescope nation-time at the instant of their delivery. His public performances sonically embody ancient Hindu grandeur with the future tense of neoliberal capitalism. In his speech to Parliament in 2015, where he offers up his "Idea of India," he brings his signature rhythmic voice patterns to flow through a number of aphorisms about India. Indeed, the speech crescendos in an aggressive series of unbroken chants melding English with Sanskrit slokas (verse).[15]

Each melodic intonation of the Idea of India in English is followed by a new aphorism in Hindi or Sanskrit, but most often in Sanskrit. The up-down wave of Modi's voice is superimposed on the sonic palimpsest of Sanskrit *slokas*. He gathers momentum the longer he speaks, and he does not stop to explain the Sanskrit. This is a deliberate attempt to create the Indian Parliament as a Hindu space, where Sanskrit/Hindu/India collapses and the Hindu philosophical/civilizational past is implicitly understood as a through line in the genealogy of the nation. It is an interesting aural invocation of both Sanskrit prayer/*slokas* and the rhythms of advertising copy. It is important to note here that the Idea of India works precisely because it has the cadence of a commercial tagline. At the same time, it invokes the television campaign for Idea Cellular, which also circulates narratives of an aspirational and driven nation that is nevertheless situated within a long historical past. The commercials routinely represent the nation as poised at the intersection of the local-global and the past-future.[16] Modi's repetition of "Idea of India" ensures that the jingle and its associations will run through the listener's mind, replicating the music of advertising—consumerist desire coalesced with the nation as a new brand—but the sonic haunting of *slokas* and the use of Sanskrit ensures that the perennial present-future of advertising is articulated with the hoary mists of Hindu brahamanical civilization. This is a perfect political sonic fusion of consumerist ontology with Indian-Hindu essence rendered by a virile, nonelite everyman voice. His voice quality is rhythmic but rough around the edges, forceful, and dynamic. He gesticulates and moves around constantly as he aggressively sing-speaks his Idea of India.

> *Satyamev Jayate,* Idea of India,
> *Ahimsa Parmo Dharma,* Idea of India
> *Vasudhaiv Kutumbakam,* Idea of India
> *Paudhe mein bhi parmatma,* Idea of India,
> *Sarva panth sambhav,* Idea of India . . .
> (Victory of Truth, Idea of India
> Respect for All Living Things as Primary Duty, Idea of India
> The World is Family, Idea of India
> God is in Vegetation, Idea of India
> Everything is Possible, Idea of India)[17]

Here there is no trace of his softened radio voice; it is a voice-body that announces its virility, strength, and power. The ancient Hindu philosophical ideals that are projected into the future Idea of India speak to universalism, globalism, environmentalism, and nonviolence, and yet the voice that chants them is intimidating, loud, and angry. His vision of India, channeled through his moving voice-body, is of a resolutely male and Janus-faced regional man, yet an everyman. However, it is a regional everyman that will not brook any opposition, nor one that will yield to any but this particular breathless and forceful idea of India.

Each time he reiterates his Idea of India, Modi's voice rises and then falls again when he indexes what that idea is in Sanskrit or Hindi. The rising voice in English calls attention to India as a brand and the envisioned future of the nation-brand. At the same time, the falling yet firm assertion indicates that which has always already structured this forward momentum of neoliberal futurity. The rising and falling cadence then replicates the sonic architecture of the imagined projected nation. The thick Gujarati accent and the gruff voice that structure English, Hindi, and Sanskrit match his stoic, aggressive posturing, indexing his voice-body as regional, local, and not delocalized urban elite. This embodied voice IS the India that he, along with BJP, is in the process of consolidating.

In this chapter, I have offered suggestive analyses of the ways in which Narendra Modi's voice-body and sound-body produce a distinctively embodied sonic political masculinity that moves between the affectionately intimate and the violently public, the emotional and the stoic, the affective and the material, the local and the global, the past and the future. Through the simultaneous use of both analog and digital media, his voice travels everywhere, all the time, emerging as a form of sonic power and control. Through his vocal practice as a familiar and sincere patriarch on the radio and in podcasts, he brings into being a national public that responds directly to his idea of the imagined community—a form of sonic citizenship sutured to his voice. His voice quality and gesturing speaking body, along with the ways in which rhythms, stresses, pauses, and the constantly shifting pitch of his voice, complicate the simplistic narrative of masculinity, which focuses on the optics of his *chappan chatti* and aggressive posturing. Narendra Modi's careful and deliberate construction of an aural and indispensable political masculinity is imbricated with the creation of a national (Hindu) public through his voice.

Notes

1. See "Shri Narendra Modi Promises." 2014. YouTube uploaded by Narendra Modi, January 9. https://www.youtube.com/watch?v=i1Lw53W_AkM

2. In India there is a long history of political mimicry, and now fan culture, which merits exploration. Here it is important to note that Rangeela's appearances on television indicate that, even as his ability to hyperbolically re-create Modi's vocal rhythms and speech patterns produce his second-order celebrity, the impact of this mimicry lies precisely in his ability to exaggerate the patterns and not the faithful rendition of them. In the process, the mimicry, even as it registers the repeatability of vocal patterns, reinforces the recognizable fixity of

Modi's voice. I am indebted to Neepa Majumdar for this insight. For a sophisticated analysis of star mimicry and stardom in cinema, see Majumdar's forthcoming essay, "Embodiment and Stardom in Shahrukh Khan's *Fan.*"

3. See "Sonam Gupta Bewafa Hai." 2016. YouTube uploaded by Shyam Rangeela, November 19. https://www.youtube.com/watch?v=2cd5VQ0d8gI

4. While there are no definitive numbers from independent research organizations, there are several piecemeal indications of the popularity of the show. However, it is not possible to know with any degree of accuracy whether the show continues to be popular or has plateaued since All India Radio refuses to release any data as part of the propaganda arm of the Modi government. For an objective perspective, see Suma Saha. 2016. "Mann Ki Baat: Modi's Pet Platform." *The Hoot,* January 2. http://www.thehoot.org/media-watch/media-practice/mann-ki-baat-modis-pet-platform-9824

5. *Mann Ki Baat: A Social Revolution on Radio,* by the nonprofit BlueKraft Digital Foundation (2017), is clearly a government issued propaganda text that celebrates Narendra Modi's radio show/broadcast. Published as a response to the "widespread keenness about the origin and evolution of this programme" (viii), the text functions as a useful look at Modi's multipronged strategy of government marketing and self-mythification. The book offers various paeans to Modi's genius as a communicator, transcribes the praise for various initiatives he talks about on his shows, and, most important, explains how he keeps the show "detached from politics" (viii). The preface was written by Shinzo Abe, while the blurbs are from Bill Gates, the now infamous Aung San Suu Kyi, and Sri Ravi Shankar.

6. The webpage dedicated to Mann Ki Baat is part of Modi's official website, where his "accomplishments" are laid out in excruciating detail. See Narendra Modi. Mann Ki Baat. http://www.narendramodi.in/mann-ki-baat

7. There is an entire article to be written about Modi's use of social media platforms, the internet, the mobile phone, and the podcast format as a way to consolidate his persona as a future-oriented leader and concerned service-oriented everyman. More important, this self-mythification emerges in a dialectical process with the crafting of a savvy future-oriented, neoliberal national public. Through strategic corporate and state advertising on different virtual sites, apps, and platforms, Modi (and it is usually advertised as the "brainchild" of "India's most tech-savvy politician") builds a pervasive digital network that draws in constituencies that would not ordinarily consider the virtual and digital a terrain for either nation building or self-definition *(BlueKraft Digital Foundation, 2017,* 4). For more on the ways in which Modi uses new media, especially social media, see Nitin Govil and Anirban Kapil Bashya, 2018. "The Bully in the Pulpit: Autocracy, Digital Social Media and Right Wing Populist Technoculture."

8. See "Mann Ki Baat: PM Modi congratulates all women crew of ISNV Tarini." 2018. YouTube uploaded by Asia News International, May 27. This is also available on the The Doordarshan News website, but its search function is fairly ineffective. The Doordarshan News website is more or less dedicated to Modi in the guise of news. Nevertheless, in the links to Doordarshan shows, the first link is a picture of Modi (with no indication of the name of the show), which takes you to a page dedicated to *Mann Ki Baat* on Doordarshan, where you can scroll through the dates and watch videos of *Mann Ki Baat* excerpts on the news.

9. It's no accident that the time slot for the broadcast was Sunday, 11:00 a.m. Before the advent of satellite television and cable, the national television service, Doordarshan, the only game in town, would beam the televised adaptations of two beloved Hindu mythological tales, first, the *Ramayana* (1987–88) and then the *Mahabharata* (1988–90). Streets would empty and life would come to a standstill for the duration of the hour because everyone would be watching television. The shows and that particular timeslot have accrued cultural and national significance.

10. An English rendering of the text of the episode aired on September 20, 2015. See Mann Ki Baat. 2015 "Episode September 2015." http://www.narendramodi.in/mann-ki-baat

11. See "Narendra Modi in Tears: Modi Emotional Speech." YouTube uploaded by Mango News, May 20. https://www.youtube.com/watch?v=Q3dJ0dAOTdA

12. For Cadbury's "Kya Swad Hai, see "Cadbury's Kya Swad Hai Zindagi." 2013. YouTube uploaded by Chobi O. Bigyapon, April 21. https://www.youtube.com/watch?v=GaBU-9Dw9VM. For the National Dairy Development Board's "Doodh, Doodh," see "Doodh Dhoodh Dhoodh." 2013. YouTube uploaded by Food and Beverage Commercials, December 18. https://www.youtube.com/watch?v=1nZzSAzHmzk. For Pepsi's "Yeh Dil Maange More," see "Pepsi, Sachin Tendulkar, Yeh Dil Maange More." 2017. YouTube uploaded by Great Indian Advertising, June 18. https://www.youtube.com/watch?v=wy20ENgHaYQ

13. He has returned to it several times in his show, marking it as an ongoing successful program, which has apparently brought a 125 percent increase in khadi sales along with reviving a failing khadi industry (October 2016).Other initiatives were given media-friendly, advertising jingle-style titles: Minimum Government, Maximum Governance; Start-up India, Stand Up India; Sab Ka Saath, Sab Ka Vikas; and Toilets before Temples. Whether these initiatives have achieved any degree of success, other than generating reams of press, is a matter of debate.

14. There is a special page dedicated to the success of "Khadi for Nation, Khadi for Fashion" on Modi's website. See "Khadi for Nation and Khadi for Fashion: A Tribute to Bapu," 2016. http://www.narendramodi.in/khadi-for-nation-and-khadi-for-fashion-tribute-to-bapu-532457

15. See "When Lok Sabha Reverberated with PM Modi's Idea of India." 2015. YouTube uploaded by MataramVande, November 27. https://www.youtube.com/watch?v=lAtQUpWa6K4

16. See Idea Cellular commercials at "Idea Cellular INN (Idea Internet Network)." 2015. YouTube uploaded by Sachin Parashar, April 12. https://www.youtube.com/watch?v=JpF_xHpj29Q and "Idea 4G: Transforming India." 2016. YouTube uploaded by Idea, December 1. https://www.youtube.com/watch?v=EyNAKfvtGzU

17. This loose and literal translation is mine.

Works Cited

Arathoon, Marion. 1996. "Think Indian in Global Terms." *Economic Times*, February 21.

BlueKraft Digital Foundation. 2017. *Mann Ki Baat: A Social Revolution on Radio.* Gurgaon: LexisNexis.

Cavarero. Adriana. 2005. *For More Than One Voice: Toward a Philosophy of Vocal Expression.* Trans. Paul A. Kottman. Stanford, CA: Stanford University Press.

Chobi O. Bigyapon. 2013. “Cadbury's Kya Swad Hai Zindagi.” YouTube, April 21.https://www.youtube.com/watch?v=GaBU-9Dw9VM

Dilwale Dulhaniya Le Jayenge. 1995. Directed by Aditya Chopra. Yash Raj Films.

Eidsheim, Nina Sun. 2009. “Synthesizing Race: Towards an Analysis of the Performativity of Vocal Timbre.” *Trans 13. Accessed on September 27, 2017.* http://www.sibetrans.com/trans/articulo/57/synthesizing-race-towards-an-analysis-of-the-performativity-of-vocal-timbre

Eidsheim, Nina Sun. 2015. *Sensing Sound: Singing and Listening as Vibrational Practice.* Durham, NC: Duke University Press.

Food and Beverage Commercials. 2013. “Doodh Dhoodh Dhoodh.” YouTube, December 18. https://www.youtube.com/watch?v=1nZzSAzHmzk

Govil Nitin, and Anirban Kapil Bashiya. 2018. “The Bully in the Pulpit: Autocracy, Digital Social Media, and Right Wing Populist Technoculture.” *Communication, Culture, Critique* 11: 67–84.

Great Indian Advertising. 2017. “Pepsi, Sachin Tendulkar, Yeh Dil Maange More.” YouTube, June 18. https://www.youtube.com/watch?v=wy20ENgHaYQ

Idea. 2016. “Idea 4G: Transforming India.” YouTube, December 1. https://www.youtube.com/watch?v=EyNAKfvtGzU

Kuch Kuch Hota Hai. 1998. Directed by Karan Johar. Dharma Productions.

Loviglio, Jason. 2005. *Radio's Intimate Public: Network Broadcasting and Mass-Mediated Democracy.* Minneapolis: University of Minnesota Press.

Mann Ki Baat. 2014. Episode 1. All India Radio, October 3.

Mann Ki Baat. 2015a. Episode 4. All India Radio, January 27.

Mann Ki Baat. 2015b. Episode 5. All India Radio, February 22.

Mann Ki Baat. 2015c. Episode 6. All India Radio, March 22.

Mann Ki Baat. 2015d. Episode 12. All India Radio. September 20.

Mann Ki Baat. 2016. Episode 25. All India Radio, October 20.

Mazzarella, William. 2003. *Shoveling Smoke: Advertising and Globalization in Contemporary India.* Durham, NC: Duke University Press.

Mango News. 2014. “Narendra Modi in Tears: Modi Emotional Speech.” YouTube, May 20. https://www.youtube.com/watch?v=Q3dJ0dAOTdA

McCracken, Allison. 2015. *Real Men Don't Sing: Crooning in American Culture.* Durham, NC: Duke University Press.

Modi, Narendra. 2014. “Shri Narendra Modi Promises.” 2014. YouTube, January 9. https://www.youtube.com/watch?v=i1Lw53W_AkM

Modi, Narendra. 2015. “When Lok Sabha Reverberated with PM Modi's Idea of India.” 2015. YouTube, November 27. https://www.youtube.com/watch?v=lAtQUpWa6K4

Narendra Modi. 2016. “Khadi for Nation and Khadi for Fashion: A Tribute to Bapu,” 2016. Narendra Modi Website, October 2.
http://www.narendramodi.in/khadi-for-nation-and-khadi-for-fashion-tribute-to-bapu-532457

Parashar, Sachin. 2015. "Idea Cellular INN (Idea Internet Network)." YouTube, April 12. https://www.youtube.com/watch?v=JpF_xHpj29Q

Rangeela, Shyam. 2016. "Sonam Gupta Bewafa Hai: Shyam Rangeela–Modi Mimicry." YouTube, November 19. https://www.youtube.com/watch?v=2cd5VQ0d8gI

Saha, Suma. 2016. "Mann Ki Baat: Modi's Pet Platform." *The Hoot*, January 2. http://www.thehoot.org/media-watch/media-practice/mann-ki-baat-modis-pet-platform-9824

Scannell, Paddy. 1995. *Radio, Television, and Modern Life*. New York: Routledge.

Srivastava, Sanjay. 2015. "Modi-Masculinity: Media, Manhood, and 'Traditions' in a Time of Consumerism." *Television and New Media* 16, no. 4: 331–38.

Srivastava, Sanjay. 2016. "Natives, Subjects, Consumers: Notes on Continuities and Transformation in Indian Masculine Cultures." *Masculinities and Social Change* 5, no. 1: 1–27.

Thomas. Rosie. 1995. "Melodrama and Negotiation of Morality in Mainstream Hindi Cinema." *Consuming Modernity: Public Culture in a South Asian World.* Minneapolis: University of Minnesota Press.

Visvanathan, Shiv. 2013. "The Remaking of Narendra Modi." *Seminar* 641 (January). http://www.india-seminar.com/2013/641.htm

Warner, Michael. 2005. *Publics and Counterpublics.* New York: Zone Books.

Weidman, Amanda. 2014. "Anthropology and Voice." *Annual Review of Anthropology* 43: 37–51.

Wilkins, Caroline. 2016. "From Voice-Body to Sound Body: A Phenomenological Approach to the Voice." *Journal of Interdisciplinary Voice Studies* 1, no. 2: 117–30.

SEVEN | Voice of the Voiceless

Audiobook Performance and the Meaning of Sound in New Nonfiction from India

ROANNE L. KANTOR

Introduction: A Sound to Drown Out the World

> While Abdul knew little of music, he had been enchanted by the concept [of the iPod]: a small machine that let you hear only what you wanted to hear. A machine to drown out your neighbors.
>
> Katherine Boo, *Behind the Beautiful Forevers*

In the middle of Katherine Boo's book about slum life in India, *Behind the Beautiful Forevers*, her informant Abdul dreams of acquiring an iPod.[1] Hearing this startles me so much that I nearly trip on the wet, leafy ground. I slow to a walk, pull out an earbud, press pause. Through the very technology of which Abdul dreams, I am able to hear him run for his life from the police in 2008 while at the same time I am running for my leisure in 2016. In this moment I am using Boo's book to do precisely what Abdul wants to do—to drown out the noise of one's own world with the sounds of another world, far away.[2] Across this distance, we are connected through an imaginary of sound technology. More than that, we are connected by a voice: Abdul's voice, which is also Boo's voice, which is also, in this moment, the voice of Sunil Malhotra, the actor hired by Random House to read the audio version of the book.

This chapter tells the story of those voices as they travel and are transformed across space, time, and medium. Audiobook performances recall the many layers of remediation in books like Boo's—from the moment of recording an interview to the moment of transcription, translation, and curation to the moment of written creation and finally rearticulation in the audiobook form. The materiality of Malhotra's voice reanimates and complicates questions around subjectivity, methodology, and representation that are already woven into the fabric of narratives like *Beautiful Forevers*.

Audiobooks are always at least one additional layer of mediation removed from the source of a nonfiction text. Yet in a compelling reading it can be all too easy to forget that the text is mediated at all. Until the moment recalled above, I had temporarily allowed myself to forget that Abdul does not speak English, does not sound like Malhotra—a "neutral" American accent for interior monologue, a drawling version of Indian-English for reported speech. At the moment I recalled these things, my attention also returned to Boo's third-person omniscient style, an intentional and, in some circles, controversial choice that works like Malhotra's voice to erase the reader's awareness of a mediating presence. When I spoke with Malhotra some months after this incident, I was struck by how carefully he had considered Boo's methodology in the crafting of his own performance style for the text. The audiobook voice actor became, for me, a fascinating figure because of his triple identification with the book's subjects, its author, and its readers and the way these identifications and choices become so naturalized as to be invisible (or perhaps inaudible) within the product that results.

Yet, for all that Malhotra's voice becomes "invisible," there was one feature of his narration that began to catch my attention. That is, he tended to mark the speech of slum dwellers with particular vocal cues that not only set them apart from the narration but also linked his representational choices to those of another audiobook actor, Vikas Adam, who had narrated another story of pavement dwellers in another major Indian city, Aman Sethi's *A Free Man*. In addition to elements of a "brown-voice" Indian-English accent, why did both actors reach for features like nasalization, gravelly timbre, and dynamic prosody to distinguish these voices from other characters and narrators? In texts whose original processes of transcription and translation had largely denuded character utterances of their nonverbal qualities, how did Malhotra and Adam come to know how Abdul and characters like him "really sound"? And how, in an equal but opposite fashion, did they come to know what authors Boo and Sethi "really mean"? What, in short, does voice performance have to do with the *real*?

Voice operates at the interstices of the metaphorical and literal. As

Amanda Weidman reminds us, Western thought has long made an equivalence between voice and subjectivity, in which "voice is a guarantor of truth and self-presence," and the site of claims about "personal agency, cultural authenticity, and political power."[3] At the same time, she notes, these theories of voice are explicitly disinterested in the material qualities of such voices. In audiobook performances, though, it is precisely the material presence of voice that sets to boil certain tensions already simmering in the source narratives.

These tensions attach to two subject positions—the narrator and the character—which divide what follows. First, I draw on interviews with Malhotra about the process of representing Boo's methodologically significant "nonpresence" in *Beautiful Forevers*. Using volume and tone to create her authorial persona, he exposes disagreements about the relationship between narrative voice and authorial identity in the two disciplines where *Beautiful Forevers* and *A Free Man* are often studied: anthropology and literature. Second, I speak to Adam about developing the character voice for Sethi's protagonist, Ashraf. The resulting performance, I show, uses timbre and prosody to reanimate socially significant aspects of Hindi dialect in English. Just as Malhotra's performance reveals tensions between disciplinary audiences, Adam's approach reveals schisms in the expected cultural unity of his listeners. In the conclusion to the chapter, I suggest how the resulting fractures open new space for audiobooks as part of a larger shift in the expected audience for narratives about what has often been called the subaltern experience in India.

The name "Voice of the Voiceless," draws attention to the way we use the shorthand of "voicelessness" to denote the subject position of members of an economic underclass to which Boo's and Sethi's protagonists are understood to belong. In a context where such subjects are assumed to be unable to "speak for" or represent themselves in various arenas—the political, the economic, the epistemic—there is a long and controversial tradition of middle-class writers who attempt to "give voice" to them and their circumstances. Questions around the ethics of such representational projects become even more urgent as books like these cross lines of language and culture, especially when moving from locations and languages formerly subjugated under colonialism into locations and languages of colonial power. And, of course, all these concerns relate to questions of citizenship. How do prospective audiobook listeners and the books' subjects relate within different political units—the city, the nation, the globe? Can the project of "giving voice"—whether that of actors or authors—have any impact on that imaginary? It is my hope that the turn to literal voices will refresh arguments over the stakes of the larger project of "giving voice," of which *A Free Man* and *Behind the Beautiful Forevers* are a part.

The Sounds of Silence

> A good narrator will know . . . when to become . . . invisible.[4]

Behind the Beautiful Forevers and *A Free Man*, both published in 2012, are both book-length nonfiction texts about the precarious lives of impoverished slum and pavement dwellers in major Indian cities (Mumbai and Delhi, respectively). Both hover at the interstices of traditional journalism and an embedded long-term research that Orin Starn calls "for lack of a better word, 'anthropological.'"[5] Both, not coincidentally, focus on protagonists who follow the typical migrant trajectory to those cities from provincial areas of North India—people from the states of Uttar Pradesh and Bihar who speak Hindi inflected with Bhojpuri or related regional languages. Both sets of protagonists are further marginalized by their identities as Muslims. In these senses, both books are bound up with much larger discourses about migrant workers and slum dwellers in India.

Although Boo's main character, Abdul, and Sethi's protagonist, Ashraf, share similar roots and routes, they are quite different in attitude. At seventeen, Abdul is the de facto patriarch of a hardworking slum family trying to bootstrap its way into a marginally more stable existence through a thriving garbage-collecting business in the slum of Anawadi. In the audiobook, his voice is soft and slightly whining, a reflection of his generally laconic nature and perhaps also his tender age. At the time the book begins, Abdul's family is saving money to pay in installments for a plot of land in a new development beyond the slum. Through a series of petty conflicts and bad luck, they become embroiled in a criminal case that decimates these middle-class aspirations.

The much older Ashraf, by contrast, is an apparently single man who lives on the streets in the Bara Tuti market in Delhi. He works part time in construction, mostly in order to pay for his vices—tobacco, alcohol, and hash. Ever philosophical, he classes this lifestyle as a commitment to the titular "freedom" (*āzādī*). Like Abdul, his voice has a nasally drawl, but it is held taut between dynamic shifts in tone and a pinched, gravelly, or scratchy timbre. Like Ashraf himself, shifting incessantly between voluble and taciturn, wide open and clammed up, these conflicting vocal elements seem to underscore a contradictory character. As in Boo's book, Ashraf's story is about the death of a dream as his desire for *āzādī* comes into conflict with his rapidly deteriorating health, underscored in the audiobook by his increasingly wheezy voice.

Sunil Malhotra, who voices Boo/Abdul in *Beautiful Forevers*, and Vikas Adam, who performs Sethi/Ashraf, are likewise a study in small but significant differences. Both are actors living in Los Angeles who support themselves primarily through forms of voice acting. Both are of Indian descent but were raised in North America, and both have spent months or years in India traveling and visiting family. Like Abdul and Ashraf, both are involved in a kind of gig economy—although, of course, a much plusher one—which externalizes risk and insecurity onto the individual worker. Audiobook narration is much less structured than other types of acting, even other types of voice acting. Pay reflects recording time, not any of the preparatory research the actors discuss later in this piece. Moreover, audiobooks, unlike other voice-acting formats, are only compensated by the finished hour, not total studio time. For a challenging job, an actor might get only get an hour of usable material from up to two hours of recording.

The most time-consuming aspect of recording an audiobook has to do with filling in the tiny missing pieces that inevitably appear in any recording—a word dropped, a name mispronounced. For each of these errors and elisions, it's necessary to review up to seven seconds of the existing recording to find and correct the mistake. The process is tedious—time adds up. For this reason Malhotra, who narrates audiobooks as a supplement to voiceover work, will only record in a studio where a director or producer is responsible for tracking errors. Of course, additional participants and studio space dramatically increase the cost of producing an audiobook. Adam, on the other hand, now makes his living primarily through audiobook performance. He tends to record independently in a soundproofed studio space set up in his apartment. As we will see, both actors' process of amending, correcting, and condensing raw audio into a finished product reflects way that Boo and Sethi went about curating their massive troves of primary-source recordings into a finished research narrative.

Both actors narrate their entry into audiobook performance through their facility with accents. For Malhotra it was a lucky break. Another Indian American voice actor was forced to turn down a contract to read Abraham Verghese's 2009 novel *Cutting for Stone* and passed it along to him. Written by an author in the Indian diaspora and set in Ethiopia among a diverse group of Indian, African, and British characters, the novel allowed Malhotra to show off a range of accents. It became a critical and popular success, winning Malhotra an Audiophile Earphones award for narration and putting him on the roster at Random House Audio. He has gone on to be the voice of several well-regarded best sellers about the subcontinent and its diaspora, including Jhumpa Lahiri's *The Lowland* (2012) and Paul Kalanithi's *When Breath Becomes Air* (2016). Landing the latter role involved another strange stroke of luck. Kalanithi's widow, who was involved in the production process, apparently felt that Malhotra's voice resembled her late husband's, thereby reanimating one of the earliest imaginaries for sound recording as a "resonant tomb."[6]

Adam's trajectory was more mundane: Some years ago he happened to stop by a series of college workshops for voice actors hosted by Audible.com, and the casting crew asked if he could do an Indian accent. He could. Tellingly, the first project to call on this particular talent was a narration of the Raj nostalgia saga *The Far Pavilions* (2012), while more recent performances include *A Long Way Home* (2013), the book that inspired the 2016 film *Lion*. Even within this small sample, it is possible to see how the same performer is called on to use his identity position and voice to authorize many different kinds of representations.

It cannot be overstated that Malhotra and Adam were chosen to read for Sethi and Boo because of their facility with "Indian" voices. This is despite the fact that, during these interviews and in recorded interactions on YouTube, both actors sound, to the untrained ear, like the folk notion of American "neutral."[7] No study of this form can avoid the cultural context in which Asian American actors are called on to represent a homogenized, ersatz version of the "self" through accent work. Nor should it ignore the larger Hollywood ecosystem in which Asian American actors have been consistently marginalized—perhaps pushed into less secure forms of work, like narration, that rely on their ability to alternate stereotypical presence with strategic invisibility. And yet it's essential to remember that America is not the only context in which Boo's and Sethi's writing circulates, nor for which Malhotra and Adam perform. Scholars such as Purnima Mankekar and Rajinder Dudrah have taken up the way in which cultural performance moves and changes between India and the diaspora in the United Kingdom and United States.[8] Still, it has been the general tendency of Asian American studies to treat performances like these as if they exist only within the matrix of American racial politics. Although they originate in the United States, prominent aspects of Malhotra's and Adam's performance can only be understood in a transnational frame.

In this sense, they inhabit a counterform of world literature, an identity position that Francesca Orsini calls the "multilingual local." For Orsini, this is "an approach to literature and space that takes multilingualism within society and literary culture as a structuring and generative principle and holds *both* local *and* cosmopolitan perspectives in view."[9] Usefully here, the ideas of "local" and "cosmopolitan" are not markers that necessarily divide an audience by space—as Mankekar and Dudrah do—but instead by orientation. While producing an audio version of the text for readerships that the actors themselves conceive of as majority white/American/non-Indian—the cosmopolitan orientation—Malhotra and Adam make performance choices that are differentially legible to a "local" audience of readers familiar with North Indian language and life worlds. Malhotra and Adam also toggle between cosmopolitan and local orientations as they try to inhabit the subjectivity of both the globetrotting journalists-narrators and their marginalized Indian subjects.

Let us associate Orsini's concept of "cosmopolitan" and "local" positions with two prominent theorizations of Indian and Indian American accent work: Shilpa Dave's concept of "brown-voice" and Weidman's examination of the Tamil humor tradition of *vikatam* performance. Dave coined the term *brown-voice* as the vocal analog to the stereotyped visual performances of black/yellow/brown-face. As with those forms, its primary purpose is to reinforce "a static, racialized position for South Asian Americans" in which they appear as "one undifferentiated group who are saddled with *one* accent and *one* voice."[10] The vocal imitation that Weidman studies is also highly stereotyped, but it is aimed at an Indian audience familiar with many more subtle markers of class and caste than with the broad contours of race.[11] Instead of a univocal accent that remains unassimilable to American culture and thus "cosmopolitan," traditional *vikatam* performers demonstrate virtuosity through the production of multiple, distinctly "local" voices. And yet, just like brown-voice, the purpose of *vikatam* humor is to reinforce the social positionality of relatively elite listeners vis-à-vis marginalized others.

Is this the exclusive social utility of imitation? Is the best we can say of Malhotra and Adam is that they manage to negotiate two apparently incompatible forms of cynical social ventriloquism? This feels insufficient. We might instead turn to Rey Chow's recent work on the "xenophone," a foil for the idea of a native speaker that reveals the "copresence" of multiple language experiences within a single utterance. In my reading, these audiobook performances reveal "linguistic—or shall we say, accentual—plurality" even where those aspects have been obscured in the written text.[12] Chow's more generous framework also makes space for both actors' earnest investment in the ethical projects of Boo's and Sethi's texts. They consistently reported using voice to convey something culturally and socially "real," the knowledge of which might likewise have positive impacts among listeners in the "real" world.

The fuller scope of Weidman's analysis suggests that performance in a purely audio format—that is, in the absence of a visibly raced or classed body—has the power to impact precisely this sense of realness. Originally, *vikatam* highlighted the talent of physically present performers who were manifestly not of the social and gender positions their voices imitated. Once these performances were recorded for the gramophone, however, the technology itself—"the perception of the gramophone as a machine that faithfully reproduces sounds"—eventually lent the form "the status of faithful representation."[13] We are likewise conditioned to understand today's audio players, increasingly embedded within mobile phones, as unproblematic conveyors of sounds from the "real" world. Indeed, Sethi used his own mobile phone to record many of the interviews that make up the text of *A Free Man.*[14] Without the visual presence of Malhotra and Adam, we might imagine that what we hear is the direct transfer of that recording from his phone to ours.

Perhaps we already know at some deep level that the illusion of realness is dependent on erasure. Just as the gramophone in Weidman's account simultaneously erases the speaker and authorizes his or her speech as "real," researchers have historically edited out the presence of recording technology from their accounts in order to produce a sense of greater accuracy. As we will see in the next section, certain writers do the same thing to their own presence in search of the same results. This may go some way toward explaining why audio performance is so often described in a relentlessly visual idiom: invisibility, transparency. Most consumers of audiobooks—including most academic critics of audiobooks—perpetuate the idea that voice performance is most powerful when it disappears. For all that sound studies scholars like Sterne rail against the "audiovisual litany"—the notion that sound is more immediate, immersive, emotional, and subjective than sight—these commonsense ideas remain salient for both lay readers and scholars of audiobooks.[15]

As scholars report becoming immersed in the form, moreover, previously notable aspects of the voice performance are consistently imagined as "invisible/inaudible." In fact the less "visible" they become the better they are, the more "real" they are. Defining a good narrator,

Smiljana Komar suggests that they will know "when to become an invisible channel of words."[16] Discussing the initially awkward mismatch between socially salient characteristics of performer and writer, D. E. Wittkower writes, "In less than a minute, I noticed that I was no longer listening to a woman reading Nietzsche but was instead listening simply to Nietzsche."[17] Sara Knox notes that in an ideal reading, "The 'voice,' previously to the fore in the reader's encounter with the printed text is dropped to the rear."[18] According to scholars like Komar and William Irwin, nonfiction books especially should be read most invisibly of all, "without" performance. Yet we do well to remember that what we hear in Malhotra's and Adam's performance is more than a specific interpretation of the text; it is also a specific interpretation of the construction of that text. In the following section, I show how negative concepts shared by audiobook actors and scholars—"nonperformance," "nonpresence" and "invisibility"—are used to reproduce "realness" in Malhotra's performance of Boo's research method.

Method Acting

> She's this white lady in India, right? But the book isn't in the first person. She's there but she's not.[19]

It seems perfectly natural to most scholars of literature to talk about Abdul and Boo's narrator as having voices. While this is true of almost all literary narratives, it is doubly true of nonfiction narratives like *Beautiful Forevers* and *A Free Man*. Both purport to reproduce actual conversations between researcher and subject, both of whom are real people whose subjectivities are assumed to be independent of—but also isomorphic with—their representation in text. What's more, even as we acknowledge admonitions by the authors that their texts take a certain amount of license with literal truth in favor of narrative coherence, we also believe that such accounts retain their value as repositories of social scientific fact. Indeed, journalists would not devote the enormous amounts of time and resources necessary to produce this type of narrative unless they were equally committed to its sociological truth. Still, the resulting texts exist somewhere between anthropology and literary study, their interpretive communities and methodological assumptions. The potential conflicts between these groups condense precisely around the question of voice and its relationship with a "real" world outside the text.

Because we understand narrators to have "voices," they are often imagined as having an identity whether or not they appear as characters in the text. Cognitive literary studies suggest that the identification of narrative discourse with a voiced character is inherent to the way we process text: we actually construct this persona in the same way we do for a real person with whom we are having a conversation.[20] Even a field like narratology, which is scrupulously careful about distinctions between narrative discourse and narrative perspective, ultimately falls back onto the "mimetic illusionist assumption about the nature and status of the narrator" coded through Gerard Genette's question *qui parle* (who speaks)?[21]

And yet narrative voice is a metaphor insofar as it is not literally manifest as a sonic presence within written text. Instead, for literary study, the concept of "narrative voice" is a means of condensing discussions about styles of narration and their relationship with types of subjectivity. In the case of *Beautiful Forevers* and *A Free Man,* those types of subjectivity are quite different. One of the most striking and frequently commented on distinctions between the two books is the presence/nonpresence of the investigator's persona in the narrative voice. *A Free Man* has a homodiagetic narrator while *Beautiful Forevers* has a heterodiagetic one, to borrow terms from Genette.[22]

Although Boo and Sethi both engaged in the kind of long-term reporting we might call "fieldwork," they represent that research quite differently in the final account. Sethi conducted the reporting for *A Free Man* more or less alone, and his writing style foregrounds his own presence as a witness or listener at most points in the story. Through this style, we usually know what kinds of questions Sethi asked to produce what kinds of answers, what he saw firsthand versus what was reported to him later, and how certain he is that one or another bit of information is true. Boo takes the opposite tack. Unlike Sethi, Boo employed translators and research assistants to help her with the process of reporting. She also gave informants recording devices and allowed them to collect some material themselves.[23] Partly as a reflection of these multiple research forms and partly according to the author's own stylistic preference, *Beautiful Forevers* is written in a third-person omniscient style. The style does not allow her reader to trace how information was gathered, who witnessed what, or how truth is being verified. The person of Katherine Boo herself does not appear at all until the book's afterword. Commenting on their contrasting methodologies in a joint interview, Boo remarked, "Unlike Aman I keep myself out of my story, except for at the end in a long author's note where I explain my so-called methodology for reporting. But what I love is the way that Aman keeps, in a very honest, wry, funny way, the whole absurdity of the enterprise at the foreground—you know, the experiences we have as journalists."[24]

Even without a character named Katherine Boo, there remains a stylistically consistent "voice" narrating the textual version of *Beautiful Forevers.* To this, Malhotra adds his own forms of vocal characterization to distinguish the narrator from other voices in the text. This makes the narrator, for the first time, a "real" voice. But whose? The separation or unity of the character of the researcher, the voice of the narrator, and the real identity of the author is a huge distinction between the fields of literature and anthropology—two fields to which long-form journalism like this might be understood to belong.

Literary study insists on a rigorous separation between authorial identity and narrative voice. Within the school of narratology, the character called Aman, who asks questions within *A Free Man,* provides the narrative perspective (*qui voir*), which is often held to be separate from what we think of as Sethi's voice, the discourse that describes the action (*qui parle*), which is always held to be separate from the person of Sethi, journalist in Delhi.[25] Even those literary scholars who do not subscribe to narratology will still have been drilled, following Roland Barthes's "The Death of the Author," to avoid the fallacy of assessing the text for authorial intent or of assuming that literature conveys "through the more or less transparent allegory of fiction . . . the voice of one and the same person, the author."[26] Since, as we have seen, Boo intentionally removes her persona from the narrative action, there is no conflict between the first two subjectivities, but the question of identification between discursive and authorial perspective remains and is, indeed, highlighted by Malhotra's literal voiceover.

Since the reflexive turn of the 1980s, ethnographic writing has been explicitly committed to the homodiagetic manifestation of the narrator as researcher, both of whom are necessarily identified with the author in the real world. It is tremendously important for contemporary anthropological methodology that these three are understood as one and the same person. This is part of a larger project to make manifest the "partiality" (here in the sense of both limited and committed to a particular perspective) of ethnographic research, decentering the authority of the anthropologist over their subjects.[27] In James Clifford's figuration, this is also a shift away from metaphors of unified omniscient sight and toward the hearing and voicing of multiple subjectivities. Essential to this shift is the idea that the writer's "voice"—what literary studies calls the narrative voice—"pervades and situates the analysis, and objective, distancing rhetoric is renounced."[28] Homodiagetic narration is, effectively, the only appropriate form for modern ethnographic writing.

These two approaches to narrative voice are fundamentally incompatible. The narrator is either a person or a construct, either present or absent. So, too, are concepts of the "real" to which these interpretations of narrative attach. In literary study we talk about a literary genre called "realism" and its qualities of "verisimilitude." Yet verisimilitude, in its very etymology, is only the quality of being similar to the real. It is actually opposed to any sense of the real external to the text, what anthropology attempts to access. It is also quite different from "realness" as a quality of performance, something both Malhotra and Adam consistently invoke.

We can now begin to see the way in which this disjuncture between literary and anthropological orientations to narration sets up a conflict around Boo's text. While *A Free Man* roughly follows the contours of the reflexive turn in anthropology, *Beautiful Forevers* manifestly does not. It is not merely that Boo removes her persona from the text; she also narrates the hopes, dreams, and thoughts of her characters from a subjective location to which modern ethnography would not claim access, though literature would. It is also fair to say that Boo's text is more invested in the omniscient visuality Clifford critiques. Even the title recapitulates a common perception of journalists as voyeurs, a visual metaphor in which we peek behind a barrier that ought to keep us out—in this case an invitation behind a wall of advertisements built to block the view of a slum.

Boo is not an anthropologist, and she has no obligation to write like one. Indeed, by referring to her "so-called methodology," she goes so far as to interrogate the idea of rigor in her writing.[29] Why, then, does it matter that her approach to narrative might throw a wrench in these relatively recondite arguments over genre? In part it matters because, despite evincing some discomfort with the implications of Boo's narrative method, anthropologists like Erica Bornstein also recognize its value as a type of social scientific text that looks anthropological, again "for lack of a better word."[30] Moreover, Bornstein notes, the shift to omniscient narration seems to have been particularly successful with a general audience, which finds her "unmediated" storytelling tremendously engaging.[31] Like Starn, Bornstein suggests that anthropology's long-term viability may require more flexibility in narrative style.

Bornstein reports finding Boo's book immediate, as if, in contrast to academic anthropology, Boo's text has never left the realm of the sensual. Bornstein imagines the book as a body that moves free and "unfettered" across disciplinary lines.[32] Somewhat unconsciously, she cues this sensual immediacy as particularly aural. In addition to "speaking," the book is also more than once imagined to "sing."[33] These aural metaphors are more than merely turns of phrase. They force us to ask the question: What does methodology sound like?

For Malhotra, Boo's method is the sound of silence. There's a remarkable echo here between how Boo and her critics discuss her narrative voice—"unmediated," "immediate," "keeping [herself] out"—and the characteristics that are most valued in the voice actor's invisible presence. Indeed, the first thing Malhotra remarked about *Beautiful Forevers* was her narrative nonpresence: "She's this white lady in India, right? But the book isn't in the first person. She's there but she's not." Here Boo's "out of placeness" as a foreign woman is mitigated by her nonpresence in the narrative, the sense of "not-thereness" that contrasts with the presence of her characters. Perhaps despite her identity position, in Malhotra's telling, Boo's book is exemplary nonfiction, "truthful," and "honest" and "real" in its depiction of Mumbai slum life.

When it came to Boo's own presence, Malhotra worked hard to replicate her choice to be "there but not." He "backed off," creating a quieter, less emotional voice, which he said conveyed a "journalistic" neutrality that said in every utterance, "This is what happened." Incidentally, this is also an American-accented voice, as opposed to the Indian-English accents of his characters, one of the few places where we might recover Boo's outsider presence in the text. On the other hand, Malhotra and his primarily American audience may read this "neutral" American accent simply as replicating the "journalistic neutrality" of the narrative style. In either case, for Malhotra the power of the book lies what he calls "duality," the fact that there is already a high degree of relief between the characters and the narrator in the original text. It's also the same observation made by Bornstein in another of her aural metaphors: "The book is written in two registers [characters and narrator], almost in stereo."[34]

Malhotra imagines a contrast between presence and nonpresence through an idiom of spatial proximity in which vocal characterizations are closer or farther away, more or less distinguished from an imagined background. His rendering of *Beautiful Forevers* is characterized by high contrast between the narrator and the characters. In his experience of reading the book, Malhotra found the characters jumping out at him. "They're there!" he said emphatically, "alive," "colorful," and "separate," both from each other and from the overarching narrative voice.

The choices he made about how to represent these voices were informed by interpretive inferences about Boo's authorial identity and its relationship to his own—the kind of insights that literary scholars have, for decades, scrupulously pushed beyond the bounds of the knowable. "She's painting a picture for people who have no idea what this world is," he told me. That is, Boo's job is to build a bridge between her own deep knowledge of the context of Anawadi and an audience that is perceived to be very distant from the book's subject. His own role was to underscore Boo's project by layering over it his own situated knowledge of India—as someone who has been to Mumbai and "seen that." Throughout, Malhotra seemed to understand his Indian American identity as a hinge between the Indian context of the book and its American audience, in keeping with the more cosmopolitan orientation described by Orsini.

Malhotra's Indian American identity does something else in relation to Boo's narrative style and its relation to method. While a potentially "white-sounding," female voice actor would have drawn attention back to Boo's own identity position, the presence of a male narrator of South Asian descent literally speaks over whatever is left of Boo's authorial voice. Malhotra's presence does not just reproduce but actually furthers Boo's intentional erasure of her persona and research process from the body of *Beautiful Forevers.* As Malhotra notes, and as Boo herself has affirmed in interviews, continual reference to her outsider identity might distract from the content of *Beautiful Forevers* or even its truth claims. It would certainly remind readers of the additional layers of mediation in her text: her lack of fluency in Indian languages, her literal absence at key narrative moments. Because we tend to experience audiobooks as more immediate and less mediated than their textual predecessors, however, Malhotra's voiceover actualizes Boo's self-erasure in a way that her prose style alone never could. Depending on whether we treat *Beautiful Forevers* as literature or anthropology, this is the best or the worst thing to ever happen to it.

The Ghost in the Machine

> "So is everything I say being recorded?"
>
> Yes, it is! Not only is it being recorded, I will be forced to listen to it when I review my tapes, forced to transcribe it in the hope that someone would have said something memorable, and forced to relive this moment when I review my transcripts. Over the last few months, my tapes are full of conversations like these.[35]

There is a strange harmony between the final moment of voice performance in the audiobook version of *Beautiful Forevers* and *A Free Man* and the original moment of voice capture in the research that produced them. The idea that narrative discourse forms a "voice" may be a convenient fiction, but the same is not true of the voices of characters/research subjects in Boo's and Sethi's books. The utterances attributed to them in the text really were vocalized to the researcher at some point, recorded on phones or tape recorders, and then put through multiple processes of review like the one described in the epigraph that opens this section. Even so, the relationship between character voices and subjectivity is even more fraught than that between narrative voice and method. As we shall see, the process of getting character voices on the page includes several layers of erasure. In what ways does voice performance, as another layer of mediation, further that erasure, and in what ways may it be used to recover some of the features that have been lost?

The existence of audio and video files tantalizingly suggests that there is a conclusive answer to the question of how Boo's and Sethi's informants "really sound." As we can see in the epigraph, however, the raw material itself is already mediated by its capture. The presence of the audio equipment distorts and changes what is "real," even as it is frequently occluded in the final research account.[36] At the same time, the initial research and the audiobook production are sort of inverse processes. That is, Sethi and Boo put their original recordings through three steps—transcription, translation, and curation—steps that progressively denuded them of culturally significant sonic elements. Readers mostly learn about the characters' class and regional origins through narrative description or, at most, they infer them from such things as vocabulary and syntax. With few exceptions, neither author retains features of dialect—phonetic spellings, italics, or other markers of emphasis—that might be reproducible in an audiobook version.

Transcription is the moment when all those qualities of the voice—its timbre, its accent, its fluidity or brokenness—are flattened into a set of characters that represent standardized patterns of sound (letters) and silence (the punctuation between them). Scholars of voice have amply demonstrated the ways we read nonverbal vocal cues for information about gender, age, class, race, and region of origin, not only from more obvious forms like accent but even from relatively ambiguous qualifiers like timbre.[37] Nor do these features arise solely from membership in discrete identity categories. As Nina Sun Eidsheim reminds us, "Each person is born with a physical body which, throughout its lifetime, is never left to its own devices—and even if a particular pressure on that body is eased, physical imprints of the trauma remain; and these become integral aspects of the body's sounding."[38] When nonverbal characteristics were denuded through the process of transcription, did Boo and Sethi find ways to reallocate characteristic "imprints" elsewhere in the book or were they simply lost?

Linguistic translation accelerates the process of erasure initiated by transcription. Here, again, Sethi and Boo are distinguished by methodology. Sethi spoke directly with his informants in Hindi and tended to preserve more Hindi terms in the final version of the book. Indeed, his glossary for the anticipated non-Indian reader—the *angrezi murgī* ("white hen," a white person but also a generic outsider)—is a delightful excursion in an otherwise uninspired genre. Yet "untranslatable" words tend to fall into a few discrete categories: blue language and street slang, on the one hand, and on the other what we might call philosophical terms like *lāwāris* (orphan/unclaimed one) and *āzādī* (freedom). These are mostly Persian-derived words that would remind a subset of readers familiar with India of the main character's Muslim identity. While certain features of identity thus remain visible in translation, other features associated with accent and vocalization, features that would be full of socially indexical meaning to Hindi speakers, do not come through.

Boo's use of translation is quite distinct. For her, the process of translation appears to precede transcription, since she communicated with her informants primarily through interpreters. Here the language itself is always already mediated, not only by technology but by linguistic limits. Unlike literary translators, interpreters cannot reflect on their choices at leisure. Their purpose, instead, is to convey the most accurate version of source utterance, often without conveying the particular intonation, word choice, turns of phrase, or twists of syntax that make one speaker different from another. Although Boo's author's note is relatively thorough, it does not tell us, for example, if she always used the words exactly as they were conveyed to her by interpreters or tweaked them later. Nor does it tell us whether she was able to attend to things like dialect and tone.

Finally, like the actors who would eventually perform their work, Boo and Sethi went through a tedious process of double-checking and hole filling as part of their research. What is represented as a single utterance in the final text was often the accretion of several moments in the research process, just as, in the audiobook form, it is often the result of several takes in the recording booth. Boo writes, "I came to my understanding of [my informants'] thoughts by pressing them in repeated (they would say endless) conversations and fact-checking interviews, often while they worked. . . . Abdul spoke for many of his neighbors when he protested one day, 'Are you dim-witted, Katherine? I told you already three times and you put it in your computer.'"[39] This conflict between the recorder and its subject is even more clearly dramatized in *A Free Man*, where Sethi displays a similar tenacity when attempting to construct a timeline for Ashraf's life. Ashraf's stories proceed thematically, tangentially, while Sethi's imperative is strictly chronological. When Sethi attempts to impose his sense of order, Ashraf rebuffs him with much less diplomacy than Abdul does with Boo: "Fuck your timeline."[40]

By the end, however, Ashraf seems to have acquiesced to a style of recounting dictated by the recorder: "Our voices all locked in your recorder. . . . Now you know everything."[41] Abdul and Ashraf read the remediation process as a permanent one. Boo's information is final and solid because it has been written into the computer, and by submitting to Sethi's recordings Ashraf and his friends have been securely "locked" into his device. This is an orientation that we, as the audience, tend to share. We see the written and audio formats of these books as final, permanent, and fixed. It is only by attending to these two instances of mediation in tandem that we can see these forms as fluid, repeated over and over with small but important changes, and the process of perfecting each record itself inevitably producing more and more variation.

As Christi Merrill observes, "The most frequently repeated riddle of postcolonial theory" is one framed in the idiom of voice: Gayatri Spivak's essay "Can the Subaltern Speak?"[42] Voice and speaking here are at once literal—the failure of colonial archives to record the experiences of oppressed peoples—and figurative—the inability of elites to apprehend the subjectivities of non-elites. Even more than narrative voice, character voice, here the voice of the subaltern informant, is a shape-shifting metaphor for all kinds of anxieties about subjectivity and alterity. In the case of *Beautiful Forevers* and *A Free Man*, the question is whether well-intentioned researchers have the right—or perhaps even the capacity—to represent the needs and feelings of their socially distant subjects. As we saw in the previous section, anthropology attempts to address this question by making visible the researchers' positionality and the method through which they come to know their subjects. Even these forms of reflexivity, however, generally gloss over the processes through which these utterances of research subjects are made comprehensible to an English-speaking audience in a textual medium. How might the imposition of a literal voice force us to think through this process anew?

Speak for Yourself!

> My job is to convey, *through voice*, that extra thing that isn't on the page.[43]

It was the suggestion of dialect specificity that partly caught my attention in both actors' rendering of character voice. It forced me to ask what the specific "extra thing" is that both Malhotra and Adam seem to convey in the voice of a slum dweller, a day laborer, a migrant from North India. How do Asian American actors with family connections to middle-class India come to know the sound of internal migrants and pavement dwellers with whom they might have next to no interaction beyond haggling over fares, wares, or alms? In short, when these actors talk about the "realness" of Sethi's and Boo's characters, what do they mean?

Vikas Adam, the voice of *A Free Man*, helped me understand how "realness" appears differentially in different kinds of texts and how his interpretation of authorial and readerly knowledge inflects it. "If I'm doing a romance novel, and the character is from the South," Adam explained, by way of an example, "is it important that I do the research of a particular place or just a southern drawl because that's what the author was thinking?" Notice again that authorial intent is considered fair game by audiobook readers; understanding themselves at interpreters, they feel a kind of fidelity to the author that literary scholars do not. Perhaps this is a natural outgrowth of their association with audio recording and audience obsession with a shifting standard of technical "fidelity."[44] But in the case of the audiobook in particular, the performer is torn between two forms of faithfulness: to the social world he or she knows independently and the specific intentions of the author who renders it. In the example above, Adam felt that an accurate accent was not warranted because a specific sense of place was neither evoked by the author nor expected or discerned by the reader. A nonfiction book, on the other hand, deserves more care because the actor is rendering not only a social reality but also the relative effort of the author to make that reality manifest.

Here Adam also reminds us that our understandings about the relationship between sound and social identity are not always precise. In fact, as Asif Agha argues, almost all of us work with a "folk concept" of accent rather than a linguistically precise one.[45] That is, among the many differences of pronunciation and intonation that distinguish one speaker from the next, only some features are "salient," based on what we perceive as contrasts from a "norm." These deviations are then assigned a social value, a process that linguistic anthropologists call “enregisterment.” As media artifacts, Malhotra’s and Adam’s audiobook performances both draw from and contribute to this process of enregisterment. To see how this happened, I look closely at the way Adam researched the accents for his role in *A Free Man.*

“With *A Free Man,* I was adamant about speaking with Aman Sethi, trying to get ahold of him, and get his thoughts on some of the voices, because it was real,” Adam recalled. Because, in contrast to Boo, Sethi’s persona is very present in the pages of *A Free Man,* I first asked Adam whether he was interested in trying to recapture Sethi’s deep, resonant voice and relatively deadpan affect in his narration. Adam considered for a moment. “If we’re doing something with audiobooks that is real life,” he said, “there can be a temptation to imitate to the point of extra authenticity, but if it’s not easy, it can come across forced.” Here we see an interesting contrast between the “real” and “real life” as ontological facts and “extra authenticity,” which is merely a quality of performance, and not always a desirable one. While authenticity and “flavor” are things to be applied, realness is something to be conveyed.

In the end, Adam retained “just a flavor” of Sethi’s voice. Since Sethi is an Indian national and appears as a homodiagetic narrator who participates in plot action, Adam chose to render both narrator and character voices as “Indian.” To produce the “flavor” of Sethi’s narrator/character role, Adam spoke with a few consonant and vowel shifts common to brown-voice. The performance has less dynamic prosody than Adam’s cheerful and emphatic conversational voice, and thus sounds deeper, although it is actually similar in timbre.

Yet Sethi’s voice in the audiobook was also developed in explicit contrast to Ashraf’s. “Because these guys are the two biggest presences” Adam explained, “they should be as different as possible.” Here we see precisely the concept of enregisterment that Agha describes: “a system of contrastive social personae stereotypically linked to contrasts of sound.”[46] While Malhotra’s narration of Boo is a contrast between different levels of presence, Adam’s narration of Sethi is a contrast between two strong but distinct presences—what scholars of literature would call “foils.” At the same time, Adam, like Malhotra, understood himself to owe an additional debt of performative “authenticity” because the subject material was “real”: “I was so touched by the book, I recall, and since these were real people, Ashraf, I wanted to know his voice—and Sethi gave me a description, and he gave me this actor reference from this one movie [*Gangs of Wasseypur II*].”

The *Gangs of Wasseypur* series is very much a story about a particular region of India. It takes place in Dhanbad, the second-largest city of what is now Jharkhand, formerly Bihar. In the minds of most urban Indians, the large swath of North India to which Jharkhand belongs is associated with stereotypes of underdevelopment, corruption, and massive migration within India and abroad. Although this area is home to many separate dialects, these various languages are often spoken of collectively as Bihari or sometimes Bhojpuri, one of the most prominent dialects in the region. And, indeed, much of the film's dialogue is in Bhojpuri-inflected Hindi, reflecting the region near Varanasi where it was produced. For the purpose of this chapter, I refer to a "folk" concept of Bhojpuri held by Modern Standard Hindi speakers, which encompasses a broad—and growing—swath of North Indian dialects across several states. These sonic features work together to connote both region (a "backward" part of the North Indian, Hindi-and-Bhojpuri-speaking "cow-belt") and class (uneducated, underworld, "rough").

Now Ashraf really was from Bihar. In fact we know from Sethi's text that Ashraf was raised in Patna and thus probably spoke a dialect closely related to Bhojpuri. Perhaps Abdul's family, which Boo tells us is from somewhere in the neighboring state of Uttar Pradesh, is also from the Bhojpuri-speaking eastern part of that state where *Gangs of Wassyapur* was filmed. Adam and Malhotra might then reasonably assume that the protagonists of both books really spoke with this kind of accent. They may also be drawing on a tradition of broader "rural" accent work that has long been a staple of popular Hindi cinema.

The question then becomes how one conveys stereotypes about a Hindi dialect in an English-language performance. While there are probably myriad features that distinguish a folk Bhojpuri-speaking accent from a Modern Standard one, only a few are "salient" or stereotypically recognizable to Modern Standard speakers and an even smaller number are "translatable" in any significant way. Only a small subset of these might be conveyed specifically and solely through the voice. First, speakers of Bhojpuri and related dialects tend to shift certain consonants vis-à-vis their position in Modern Standard Hindi: sha → sa, ksha → cha, va→ ba, za→ ja. Second, the folk notion of Bhojpuri holds that its speakers use more dynamic prosody—length and tone of speech units—than Modern Standard speakers do. Third, speakers of folk Bhojpuri are understood to use a different vocal timbre—gravelly, whiny, or nasally compared to Modern Standard norms.[47]

While it is theoretically possible for a voice actor to employ consonant shifts when rendering a character—saying *jeero* instead of *zero*, for example—there are two reasons why this is unlikely to happen. In the first place, if the authors had wanted to represent these dialect characteristics, they would have been able to do so orthographically. Since they did not, the audiobook performer might betray his primary fidelity to the text and his perception of authorial intention by inserting them. In the second, those choices are marked enough to draw the attention of the audiobook reader yet not particularly salient as class or regional markers in English. They might then come into conflict with the injunction to maintain "invisibility/inaudibility," which, as we have seen, is of enormous importance to audiobook readers. What is needed, then, is a type of vocal characterization that, first, does not contravene the existing textual representation of speech, and, second, carries a socially indexical meaning for both speakers of Hindi and speakers of English.

Given these constraints, Malhotra and Adam both turn to vocal texture and tone as primary vehicles of characterization for the slum- and pavement-dwelling protagonists in *Beautiful Forevers* and *A Free Man.* In Adam's performance, Ashraf's brown-voice features are slightly more pronounced than Sethi's. This is a choice based in part on ease of pronunciation, since Ashraf is more likely than the narrator to code-switch between English and the select Hindi vocabulary Sethi leaves untranslated in the text. But the primary distinctions are in vocal texture. Although Adam's Sethi has some degree of characterization, he voices Ashraf with much more emotional range, similar to though less dramatic than the way Malhotra developed Abdul and the other characters as "there" in contrast to the narrator as "not-there." Most obviously, though, Adam used features of prosody and timbre to build Ashraf's vocal character.

We can see this in the passage in which Ashraf defines the acronym LLPP for Sethi.

> In the super-specialized world of today everyone needs a degree. Some are BAs, some are MAs, some are CAs, and the truly unfortunate are PAs. The really well read are PhDs, but here on the chowk, ninety percent of the mazdoors are LLPPs—the universal degree that we are all born with. . . . Yes an LLPP—Likh Lowda Padh Patthar.[48]

Adam conveys this monologue in a particularly emphatic way, underscoring through vocalization Ashraf's characteristic love of pontificating. He stresses and elongates the first letter in each acronym "*Bee* Ay," "*Em* Ay," "*Cee* Ay," "*Pee* Ay," some of which are further marked by the dramatic up-and-down tones of folk Bhojpuri prosody. Performance makes obvious the implicit rhyme in the letters *B, C,* and *P,* minimal differences that nevertheless signify totally distinct levels of education, adding ironic force to Ashraf's expressed disdain for credentials. The phrase "everyone needs a degree," which has no special markings in the textual version of *A Free Man,* offers an even more dramatic example of dynamic prosody in Adam's performance. The word *everyone* stretches out, its tone curving up and then sharply down, while the momentum of its falling forces out the rest of the phrase as if it were a single word. In concert with this tonal dynamism, Adam ruthlessly compresses his vocal apparatus inward and upward until it sounds like he is dragging the words over a bed of sandpaper and then forcing them through his nose. Again, to a reader with knowledge of the Indian context, performance choices like these might convey the specificity of folk Bhojpuri vocal conventions. But to a generalist it can also suggest a hard life, the effects of smoking, drinking, and crushing labor on a vulnerable body. The particular scratchy, wheezy texture of *everyone* in this phrase may even be interpreted as the voice of a smoker who has just taken a hit, which is, indeed, what the narrator tells us Ashraf has done.

What Adam does here is develop a character voice that produces different levels of meaning for differently situated listeners. Following Goffman's discussion of conversational "footing," we might think of Adam's use of accent to initiate "collusion" with a certain subset of his audience, "using allusive words ostensibly meant for all participants, but whose additional meaning will be caught only by some."[49] In this context, nasalization and intonation are at once specific and "real" markers of folk Bhojpuri speech and general cues to nonexpert listeners about class difference between character and narrator. These folk accents may not be accurate—they may not sound very much like the "real" Ashraf—but they nevertheless rehabilitate a layer of "realness" for Asian and Asian American readers familiar with regional differences in India, or at least their representation in popular Hindi cinema.[50] The audiobook reminds us that a certain representational detail, like accent, can be at once authentic (he really was Bihari) and ersatz (just a drawl) depending on who is listening.

Unmediated Access

So who is listening? How does a perception of audience—the writer's perception, the actor's perception, the critic's perception—inflect our reading of both these projects' ethics and form? Should we read them merely as a recapitulation of Tamil *vikatam* performance, that is, a way for middle-class audiences to shore up their own identity position by consuming lower-class subjects? Or, by moving us away from literacy as a barrier to entry for reading, might audiobooks potentially democratize the market for literary knowledge?

The MP3 player that Abdul dreamed about in 2007 is now a standard feature of mobile phones, which abound even in the poorest communities in India. Not only do these technologies allow relatively poor South Asians to consume audio media, but they increasingly allow them to produce it as well. In rural Bihar, for example, a very different version of the "multilingual local" might consume pirated serials in Modern Standard Hindi produced in Mumbai, low-budget devotional video compact discs (VCDs) in Bhojpuri produced in Patna, and even lower-budget Magahi-dialect MP3s made in the nearest city with a heavy dose of autotune.[51]

We are not so far, in the end, from the world of Boo's informants, narrating their own adventures with GoPro cameras. It is precisely the potential of technological mediation that may, in due time, allow for a project of testimony like *Beautiful Forevers* or *A Free Man* whose audience is the same as its subject—a project that speaks for itself.

And yet we have made the mistake before of assuming that newer and better media forms will automatically overcome the problems of rendering subjectivity externally legible. As Rebecca Lemov shows, American social scientists once believed that changing technology was on the cusp of granting them total access to the subjectivities of research participants from India and other parts of what was then known as the Third World.[52] But these projects never came to fruition. In fact their spectacular failure occurred more than fifty years ago.

Instead these issues might force us to rethink our desire for or belief in "unmediated" access at all. I suggest, following Kate Lacey, that listening can be an ethical imperative in the creation of a public sphere. To do so, however, listening must have a specific orientation away from the hearer, "travelling between spaces of familiarity and strangeness" and 'listening to others' stories and other ways of telling stories."[53] As we have seen, this orientation carries risk. If the idealized future of technological democratization does bring with it an expansion of testimonial forms, then the collaborative nature of these multiply mediated projects ensures that there will be, if anything, a growing role for interpreters of various types. As Fabiola Hanna points out, digital recording and archiving technology have led to an explosion of testimonial projects, and yet it often seems that the only "witness" for these stories is the computer itself. Archives, it seems, cannot "speak for themselves."[54] Instead they require curatorial and interpretive projects to make them accessible to potential listeners. And these projects include, of course, the actors who perform such stories, quite literally giving voice to others who might otherwise remain "voiceless."

Notes

1. Katherine Boo, *Behind the Beautiful Forevers* (New York: Random House, 2012), 86.

2. It is a commonplace about contemporary audiobooks that they allow us to create private space in public, a quality that is almost universally derided as anticivic. See, for example, Deborah Philips, "Talking Books: The Encounter of Literature and Technology in the Audio Book," *Convergence: The International Journal of Research into New Media Technologies* 13, no. 3 (2007): 293–306; D. E. Wittkower, "A Preliminary Phenomenology of the Audiobook," in *Audiobooks, Literature, and Sound Studies*, ed. Matthew Rubery (New York: Routledge, 2011), 216–32. What these critics have not acknowledged is that audio media are able to create private space not only for middle-class American consumers but, increasingly, for people all over the world. People like Abdul live in cramped and insecure conditions that defy a typical American imaginary of privacy and often possess a concept of public versus private space that is quite distinct. What would it mean for them to have access to a space of seclusion between headphones?

3. Amanda Weidman, "Voice," in *Keywords in Sound*, ed. David Novak and Matt Sakakeeny (Durham, NC: Duke University Press, 2015), 233.

4. Smiljana Komar, "Listened to Any Good Books Lately? The Prosodic Analysis of Audio Book Narration," *ELOPE: English Language Overseas Perspectives and Enquiries* 3, nos. 1–2 (2006): 94.

5. Orin Starn, ed., *Writing Culture and the Life of Anthropology* (Durham, NC: Duke University Press, 2015).

6. Jonathan Sterne, *The Audible Past: Cultural Origins of Sound Reproduction* (Durham, NC: Duke University Press, 2003).

7. I use this term advisedly with the realization that the folk notion of neutrality encodes not only a regional identity—vaguely associated with the California milieu in which both actors live—but also a racial one, the idea of a "white-sounding" voice that has been explored by Eidsheim, among others. Those interested in a reference point for what I mean here might look to Malhotra's voicing of Prince Wu on Nickelodeon's *The Legend of Korra*, the character who, I think, sounds closest to his naturally upbeat and California-accented speaking voice.

8. Rajinder Kumar Dudrah, *Bollywood Travels: Culture, Diaspora, and Border Crossings in Popular Hindi Cinema* (London: Routledge, 2012); Purnima Mankekar, *Unsettling India: Affect, Temporality, Transnationality* (Durham, NC: Duke University Press, 2015).

9. Francesca Orsini, "The Multilingual Local in World Literature," *Comparative Literature* 67, no. 4 (2015): 345–74, emphasis in the original.

10. Shilpa Dave, *Indian Accents* (Champaign: University of Illinois Press, 2013), 40, emphasis added.

11. Amanda Weidman, "Sound and the City: Mimicry and Media in South India," *Journal of Linguistic Anthropology* 20, no. 2 (2010): 296.

12. Rey Chow, *Not Like a Native Speaker* (New York: Columbia University Press, 2014).

13. Weidman, "Sound and the City," 308.

14. Aman Sethi, *A Free Man: A True Story of Life and Death in Delhi* (New York: W. W. Norton, 2012), 109.

15. Sterne, *Audible Past,* 15.

16. Komar, "Listened to Any Good Books Lately?," 85, 94.

17. D. E. Wittkower, "A Preliminary Phenomenology of the Audiobook," in *Audiobooks, Literature, and Sound Studies,* ed. Matthew Rubery (New York: Routledge, 2011), 226.

18. Sara Knox, "Hearing Hardy, Talking Tolstoy: The Audiobook Narrator's Voice and Reader Experience," in *Audiobooks, Literature, and Sound Studies,* ed. Matthew Rubery (New York: Routledge, 2011), 131.

19. Sunil Malhotra, personal communication. March 21, 2016.

20. Bortolussi and Dixon 2003, cited in Uri Margolin, "Narrator," in *The Living Handbook of Narratology,* n.d., http://www.lhn.uni-hamburg.de/article/narrator

21. Margolin, "Narrator.".

22. Ibid.

23. Katherine Boo, "Afterword," in *Behind the Beautiful Forevers* (New York: Random House, 2012).

24. Chiki Sarkar, "A Conversation with Katherine Boo and Aman Sethi," *Brick,* 2012.http://brickmag.com/conversation-katherine-boo-and-aman-sethi

25. Margolin, "Narrator."

26. Roland Barthes and Stephen Heath. *Image, Music, Text* (New York: Hill and Wang, 2009).

27. James Clifford and George E. Marcus, eds., *Writing Culture: The Poetics and Politics of Ethnography* (Berkeley: University of California Press, 2010), 10.

28. Ibid., 11–13.

29. Sarkar, "Conversation with Katherine Boo and Aman Sethi."

30. Erica Bornstein, "Stories of Poverty in India: An Ethnographer Reviews Katherine Boo's 'Behind the Beautiful Forevers'" *American Ethnologist* 41, no. 1 (2014): 180–86.

31. Ibid.

32. Ibid., 182.

33. Ibid.

34. Ibid., 181.

35. Sethi, *A Free Man,* 109.

36. Erika Brady, *A Spiral Way: How the Phonograph Changed Ethnography* (Jackson: University Press of Mississippi), 199, 60.

37. See, for example, Nina Eidsheim, "Synthesizing Race: Towards an Analysis of the Performativity of Vocal Timbre," *Trans: Transcultural Music Review,* no. 13 (2009); Nina Eidsheim, "Voice as Action: Toward a Model for Analyzing the Dynamic Construction of Racialized Voice," *Current Musicology,* no. 93 (2012):

9–33; Jody Kreiman, Diana Vanlancker-Sidtis, and Bruce Gerratt, "Perception of Voice Quality," in *The Handbook of Speech Perception*, ed. David B. Pisoni and Robert Ellis Remez (Malden, MA: Blackwell, 2005); Norie Neumark, "Doing Things with Voices: Performativity and Voice," in *Voice: Vocal Aesthetics in Digital Arts and Media*, ed. Norie Neumark, Ross Gibson, and Theo Van Leeuwen (Cambridge, MA: MIT Press, 2010), 95–118.

38. Eidsheim, "Voice as Action," 18.

39. Boo, "Afterword," 250, 252.

40. Sethi, *A Free Man*, 93.

41. Ibid., 217.

42. Christi Merrill, *Riddles of Belonging: India in Translation and Other Tales of Belonging* (New York: Fordham University Press, 2008), 29–30.

43. Sunil Malhotra, personal communication, March 21, 2016.

44. Sterne, *Audible Past*, 284–85.

45. Asif Agha, "The Social Life of Cultural Value," *Language and Communication* 23, nos. 3–4 (2003): 232.

46. Ibid., 241.

47. Kathryn Hardy, "Becoming Bhojpuri: Producing Cinema and Producing Language in Post-liberalization India" (PhD diss., University of Pennsylvania, 2014), 62–63.

48. Sethi, *A Free Man*, 20.

49. Erving Goffman, *Forms of Talk* (Philadelphia: University of Pennsylvania Press, 1981), 134. One might ask what distinguishes a general idea of "collusion" from more specific practices of resistant communication such as Henry Louis Gates Jr.'s concept of signifying. In this case there are two answers. In the first place, treatments of signifying have tended to explore the layering of linguistic meaning, excluding other aspects of vocal expression. In the second, these actors consistently report using vocal effects to support and amplify, rather than ironize or otherwise resist, the textual content they perform.

50. The use of accent to "collude" with differently acculturated audiences was brought home to me in a recent example from Rebecca Walkowitz's *Born Translated*. Walkowitz cites an extended passage from Junot Díaz, one of the best and most frequently cited exemplars of dialect writing in contemporary American fiction. In praising Díaz's innovation of a Dominicanized Spanglish—as contrasted with Standard American English—Walkowitz apparently misses the fact that the passage is contrasting two speakers of *distinct* Dominican dialects. The less standard, or *campesina*, dialect is marked, in the passage, by the dropping of *d* sounds from participles (ado→ ao) and consonant shifts v→b and r→l, markers that convey much the same socially indexical knowledge for Dominican Spanish speakers as consonant shifts in folk Bhojpuri do for speakers of Modern Standard Hindi.

51. This example is taken from my field site in Nalanda district, Bihar. The 2008 film *Supermen of Malegaon* shows how the democratization of technology encouraged similarly low-budget, subregional film production in Madhya Pradesh. P. Sainath's *The People's Archive of Rural India* (PARI) and Neelesh Mishra's *Gaon Connection* are other examples of recent multimedia projects that seek to give marginalized people a platform through which to tell their own stories.

52. Rebecca Lemov, "Towards a Data Base of Dreams: Assembling an Archive of Elusive Materials, C. 1947–61." *History Workshop Journal* 67, no. 1 (2009): 44–68.

53. Lacey here references theories of listening by Romand Coles and Tanja Dreher. Kate Lacey, ed., *Listening Publics: The Politics and Experience of Listening in the Media Age* (Cambridge: Polity, 2013).

54. Fabiola Hanna,. "Share Your Story—but Who Will Listen?" *Sounding Out! The Sound Studies Blog,* https://soundstudiesblog.com/2016/08/22/18160/

EIGHT | From Punjab Trilogy to the BBC Eastern Service

The Political Critiques and Cultural Mediations of Mulk Raj Anand

SEJAL SUTARIA

The writer, journalist, and activist Mulk Raj Anand, long committed to India's anticolonial nationalism, found himself compelled to engage in antifascist activism in response to the violence unleashed during the Spanish Civil War. But in 1941, when the BBC's Eastern Service asked Anand to contribute to British propaganda programs aimed at garnering Indian support for World War II, Anand initially refused. As a colonial subject living in London, Anand was torn; he was unwilling to support British colonization of India (Ranasinha 2010, 57), yet he was aware that the British government had grown increasingly anxious about seditious Indians following the 1940 hanging of Udham Singh (MacClean 2016, 23). Melissa Dinsman explains that for many South Asians like Anand—whose home was destroyed by bombing in 1941—the decision to accept work on the BBC was partly dictated by financial strain and other shortages that hindered their ability to write. Ultimately, Anand's own ethical commitments to combat violations of democracy only heightened his urgency to act. So, when India Talks producer George Orwell renewed this request in early 1942, Anand agreed. Through his radio programs, Anand sought to promote understanding between Britain and India in hopes of building solidarity in the fight against fascism (2015, 113).

This chapter considers selected episodes from Anand's radio programs *New Weapons of War* and *Meet My Friend* in conjunction with his novel, *The Sword and the Sickle,* to investigate how his modes of mediating between conflicting political commitments emerged out of his experience as an Indian colonial subject loyal to anticolonial nationalism required to confront the material realities of wartime Britain. I investigate Anand's representations of sound, orality, and time in both sets of texts to contend that he subversively folds his critique of Britain's colonial, capitalist exploitation of India's peasants into bold commentary on Germany in his radio broadcasts. Anand constructs a novel that gives voice to the Punjabi peasants—so rarely represented in dominant narratives—by delivering their enunciations of protest in language that echoes the cadences of speech patterns born of their oral culture and thus granting them ownership of that protest. When producing radio propaganda programs, Anand employs a combination of what Paddy Scannell describes as "Broadcast Talks" when delivering critiques of fascism or conversations between himself and an English guest designed to promote affirmative portraits of British people and culture. By choosing Indian voices to broadcast such content, the BBC sought to create intimacy with listeners in colonial India and so win their trust.

This work engages with the recently growing body of compelling scholarship around Anand's contributions to modernism by expanding on the uncharted intersections between his literary work and his less frequently explored radio programs. Daniel Ryan Morse poignantly explores how Anand frames his position as an outsider on George Orwell's radio magazine *The Voice* (2015, 83–98). In her work on the "intermodernists" of the 1930s, meanwhile, Kristin Bluemel, astutely attends to Anand's relatively underdiscussed shift away from the members of the Bloomsbury Group—whom he found insufficiently critical of empire—to connect with the "radical eccentrics" George Orwell, Stevey Smith, and Inez Holden (2004b, 67–102). Critics such as Ulka Anjaria (2012), Sonali Perera (2004), and Toral Jatin Gajarawala (2012) productively challenge the imposition of dichotomies such as realism and modernism in their respective analyses of how Anand portrays the complexities of caste, class, or religion as they are represented in literature about the experiences of India's disenfranchised communities (Gajarawala 2012). I intervene in this discourse by connecting my analysis of anticolonial, antifascist attitudes expressed in Anand's radio programs to his use of techniques I identify as sonic resistance and aesthetic interruption in his relatively underexamined Punjab Trilogy to understand what they reveal about the role of the Indian diaspora in multivalent activism in 1940s London. In turn I distinguish what his vital contributions tell us about Britain, its diaspora, and the workings of resistance in India. To accomplish this, I employ Kate Lacey's concept of listening publics to consider the ways in which Anand and the Eastern Service built propaganda programs that reveal their imaginings of India's audiences and what they suggest about Britain's anxieties around the colonial encounter during World War II. Conversely, Anand's presence as an Indian broadcaster delivering a series of anticolonial and antifascist programs on the Eastern Service marks the BBC's defining of itself, however unwittingly, as a hybrid unit with space for dissenting voices that reflected the realities of the British public in 1940s Britain.

New Weapons of War and Echoes of Empire

Reading Anand's radio productions in tandem with his literary work reveals a series of ambivalences and seeming contradictions as he navigates between his antifascist commitments and his concerns about British colonial capitalism in India. Anand's earliest commentary on this first appears in the novel *Coolie.* In her poignant reading of the novel, Jessica Berman examines the geopolitics of the narrative to demonstrate how Britain's involvement in managing industry led Indian owners to exploit already disenfranchised laborers (2011, 108–9). Accordingly, Anand addresses these tensions through what I term aesthetic interruption and strategically deployed sonic representation in his literary and radio productions.

His *New Weapons of War* series, aired from March to April 1942. The series was proposed by George Orwell who approached Anand to write five fifteen-minute episodes. Each talk was to define and contextualize nomenclature frequently employed in news of the time; Orwell requested segments on "The Fifth Column," "Lebensraum," "New Order," "Pluto Democracy," and "Propaganda." Anand met this request by developing talks that began by defining the central term, explaining its relevance to German, Italian, or Spanish fascism, and then implicitly alluding to British replications of similarly oppressive measures in India. (Anand 1942b)

In the second episode, Anand subtly challenges Britain's colonial capitalism in India's agrarian and industrial sectors through his more explicit critique of Hitler's use of the rhetoric of Lebensraum to legitimate his exploitation of Jews and German peasants. Anand begins by defining the title term of the episode, "*Lebensraum*," which is literally translated as "living space" (1942c). He explains that Hitler devised this slogan to support his argument that Germany needed more land to support a population of 18 million citizens, growing by 900,000 each year. Having primed listeners to expect further cultural and historical explanations, Anand shifts their attention to the dangerous consequences of Hitler's rhetoric by exposing the unspoken implications of his agenda. After explaining Hitler's claim that Germany needed more land to "build new farmsteads, rear more pigs, fatten more calves, and grow more grain," Anand clarifies that, while Hitler doesn't state his ends explicitly,

> he had in mind that [the German peasants] should become earth serfs, Boors, and slaves of the soil for essentially Hitler does not like our urban civilization with its big industrial cities but wants people to revert back to the land so that they can remain wedded to the narrow, self-centered, daily life of the small farm, contented with their lot while he and his like can keep them in their place and fatten on their labours. (1942c)

Having captured the attention of his Indian listeners by exposing Hitler's intention to subordinate his "Nordic German peasants," Anand follows by anticipating, then answering, the questions that he imagines might arise naturally in a conversation as people process what they hear. Given that colonization was the primary mode through which European nations sought to increase their wealth, audiences might have questioned Germany's efforts to expand its landholdings at home rather than abroad. Accordingly, Anand challenges Hitler's claim that pure-blooded Aryans are unsuited to the tropics; he suggests instead that Germany's lack of sufficient naval power to seize distant territory led Hitler to pursue acquiring European land from nations deemed culturally inferior such as Austria, Czechoslovakia, Poland, and the Balkan states.

Anand's disgust and rage are evident when he draws attention to the irony that the lands sought to support an expanding German population have "become the biggest graveyard of Germany where the excess population that troubled him, the extra souls he was so concerned about have been finding their abiding peace" (1942c). This reference to graveyards unmistakably conjures images of the Holocaust, even though it does not speak directly of the Jews. Anand's insertion of this image subversively alludes to the Bengal famine that was concerning Indian listeners at the time, exacerbated by Britain's draining of resources to support the war effort. It also gestures to the exploitation of Indian peasants by a corrupt feudal system—after World War I—which Anand represents in his 1942 novel the *Sword and the Sickle.* The reference is ambivalent, as if to ask why India would hesitate to stop Hitler from inflicting similar privations on others yet also asking why India would consent to participation in another war that threatens the same collateral damage. Hitler claims that abolishing a feudal system—overseen by landlords who he argues were largely opposed by the Jews—would constitute internal colonization and damage Germany's prestige abroad. The use of such rhetoric to rationalize exterminating the Jews and securing his own power is alarming and unconscionable; explaining this to Indian audiences helps Anand emphasize Britain's commitment to stop Nazi and fascist mobilization and urge Indians to support similar efforts. For astute, progressive listeners in India, the allusion would have resonated with their growing objection to India's involvement in the war and to the strain placed on Indians as their resources and raw materials were redirected to fuel the war effort.

Since recordings of broadcasts by Anand and his contemporaries, such as Una Marson (Whittington 2018. 180–81) and Venu Chitale, have not survived, critics face a unique challenge when analyzing the affective impact of these programs. We can, however, look to the BBC Eastern Service's stated intent to deliver war propaganda to Indian listeners for insights about how such programs were constructed. The urgency to convey messages so directly linked to the sociocultural moment would have been accentuated by the intimacy of the talks format regularly employed during the war. As Scannell explains, Hilda Matheson—the first Director of Talks at the BBC—conducted experiments that revealed that listeners wanted to be addressed intimately, as if being addressed "man to man" (Scannell 1991). As George Orwell, the *India Talks* producer for the BBC Eastern Service, explained, the network's programs were designed to be delivered almost exclusively by Indian presenters whose aim was to share something of British life and thought with listeners in India (Anand 1992). For listeners in India, hearing Anand as a fellow

Indian speaker would have offered them a sense of familiarity helpful in inspiring trust. Like the laugh tracks that Jacob Smith suggests were used in early American recordings to ease anxiety about engaging with disembodied sound from an unfamiliar technological device, the individual voice of an Indian broadcaster like Anand would have been personal, intimate, and perceived as an authentic, credible representation of Britain (Smith 2008, 17).

The knowledge that Anand appeared as a spokesperson for the Indian diaspora combating fascism on the Eastern Service also marks the BBC's tacit acknowledgment of him as a hybrid part of Britain itself. As Ian Whittington explains, Marson's presence as a black British woman on the BBC introduced strains of dissent into the British propaganda narrative through her presence and the attention to race in her broadcasts. Although Anand's messaging was somewhat more covert and subversive, the fact that he presented programming in his accented English and spoke as he did entails an act of self-assertion by a colonial subject and the British acceptance, however unwittingly, of his dissent.

The other significant question about how to understand these broadcasts involves a 1943 listener research report conducted by Lawrence Brander in India which revealed that very few Indians listened to these broadcasts (Lodhi, Orwell), making the delivery of pro-British propaganda largely ineffectual.[1] Even if there are those who counter the Brander Report by suggesting that listenership was inevitably hard to measure accurately, the absence of any accounts by possible listeners requires us to consider its implications. Lacey's concept of the way developments in sound technology changed what it means to listen as much as it shifted the way institutions like the BBC imagined their listenership offers an opportunity to rethink what such broadcasts reveal (Lacey 2013, 10–12). Anand's broadcast reveals how the BBC—as an arm of the British government—perceived its Indian audience, how this perception shaped strategies for propaganda messaging, and how such broadcasts reveal as much or more about Britain and the precarity of its colonial diaspora than it does about Indians in India.

At a moment when the Bengal famine was escalating and a number of Indian activists were growing increasingly critical of Britain's depletion of India's raw materials and food to sustain its military efforts, the British government feared Indian loyalties would turn to Germany, Italy, and Japan. The BBC's Monitor records and Brander's report confirm that all three were engaged in radio propaganda that reached Indian listeners far more effectively than British broadcasts did. Many Bengali youth were captivated by Subhas Chandra Bose's Indian National Army, which joined the Japanese forces as a rebellion against the British colonizers. The efforts to define significant terms as an entry point into the threats to democracy, freedom, and security presented by the conflicts of World War II signal British assumptions that Indians could or even should be convinced that the threat facing Europe might affect the subcontinent with just as much intensity. These programs were primarily directed toward the Indian intelligentsia and activist students and assume both a certain level of historical, political knowledge about and interest in the everyday lives of Europeans confronting the realities of war. Anand's emphasis on the inhumanity of Hitler and the effectiveness of German propaganda suggests that Britain both needed India's support and felt enough uneasiness about failing to secure it to enlist the Eastern Service in a project to broadcast a steady diet of propaganda presenting British culture and people in an affirmative light. A brief look at a fellow broadcaster involved with producing World War II propaganda programs offers a valuable context for Anand's work. In his work on the American broadcaster Norman Corwin, Tim Crook explores Corwin's success in collaborating with the BBC's Home Service to produce programs free of Allied government interference so as to "tell Americans exactly what [he] saw in England" (Crook 193). Admired for his ability to dramatize "the theater of the mind," Corwin had the support of the director of productions and head of features on the BBC's Home Service. While Corwin and Anand worked with different audiences, forms, and remits, they shared a commitment to present the truth, vivifying it to impress its urgency on the listener. Their transmissions in 1942 indicate parity between the BBC's Home and Eastern Services; both focused on creating listening publics in the United States and India, respectively, through intimate diplomacy crafted to convey urgent truths about the realities of wartime. As the episodes from *Meet My Friend* will demonstrate, the construct of friendship, so celebrated by the Bloomsbury Group as a mode for connecting across difference, became the BBC's mode for characterizing its relationship with India as if to overlook or transcend the realities of the ongoing colonial encounter in the interest of antifascist solidarity. But, first, exploring Anand's fiction reveals his critique of this encounter and how he implicitly folded it into "New Weapons of War."

Sonic Resistance and Aesthetic Interruption in Anand's Fiction

Anand's "New Weapons of War" aired in March 1942, just months after the postscript concluding the *Sword and the Sickle*, "Devon, 1941," was published and five months before Gandhian nationalists launched the

Quit India movement. Yet the three novels that narrate the character Lalu's experiences as a young agrarian peasant span the years leading up to, during, and just after World War I. *The Village* (Anand 1939) introduces Lai Singh and reveals how his falling in love with the landlord's daughter Maya results in his downfall and forces him to flee to protect himself and his family. *Across the Black Waters* (Anand 1940a) would have been published at the time of Dunkirk and focuses on Lalu's experiences as an Indian soldier fighting for the British on the Western Front in World War I. In *The Sword and the Sickle* (Anand 1942d), the primary novel I address in this essay, Lalu returns to India—after being held as a prisoner of war in Germany—in hopes of continued service in the army and a possible medal of honor—only to find himself unceremoniously discharged after having been tricked into admitting exposure to seditionist Marxist revolutionaries. This segment of the plot is confined to the first ten pages; the remainder of the novel traces the consequences of Lalu's decision to join the very same seditionist revolutionaries he was falsely suspected of supporting as a prisoner and reuniting with his forbidden love Maya. More than any of Anand's other novels—with the exception of *Coolie*—*Sword* reveals the author's deep concerns for Indian peasants amid Britain's capitalist-driven colonialism coupled with its depletion of India's human and material resources during and after World War I.

On September 19, 1914, just months after the beginning of what would become World War 1, the *London Illustrated News* published a spread lauding the first Indian troops deployed alongside British soldiers to ward off the German forces along the Western Front. The headline read "India on Active Service in Europe: Splendid Aid for Britain," with photographs of Indian soldiers in British uniforms, prepared for battle, directly beneath it. These photos were a sharp contrast to the more exotic picture found farther down the page. High army officials in loincloths were shown cooking around a fire with a caption "Picture of a typical Gurka." The accompanying text notes that their facial features resemble those of the Japanese. The characterization of their contribution as "Splendid Aid" is striking, given that many Indians were either unaware of the reasons for the conflict or ambivalent about being drawn into a war they saw as a British and German matter. Yet the consequences of involvement were significant for India. On the front, losses would be rapid and catastrophic, with only eight thousand Indians surviving by December 1914 (Das 2011, 15). In India the redirection of resources to support Britain's troops coupled with the impact of industry on farming contributed to famine across large swaths of India.

I contend that Anand's commentary about the time after World War I speaks directly to the repetition of this phenomenon taking place at the height of World War II when he wrote this novel.

Accordingly, the trilogy implicitly addresses debate as to whether World War II was ever India's to fight at the very moment when Britain was striving to secure Indian loyalty and support for the war. As my reading of Lalu's discoveries in the third novel illustrates, Anand employs sonic elements to give voice to the novel's Punjabi peasants as they enunciate their struggle to survive amid capitalist exploitation that parallels the plight of German peasants oppressed by Hitler's Lebensraum policies.

The alternating noise and silence that reverberate across the novel's increasingly depleted landscape contributes to the reader's visceral understanding of the desperation Lalu's family and fellow peasants experience when they are stripped of their lands and livelihoods. While these sonic elements appear to give Anand's prose an overwritten quality, the affective qualities they capture and the ways they inflect the speech of the semiliterate peasants account for the cadences of a spoken Punjabi shaped by its emergence as part of their oral tradition. Rather than more intellectually articulated analyses of the kind employed in his radio broadcasts, Anand interrupts the reader's anticipation of such a narration with dialogue or vocal expressions of emotion voiced directly by the peasant characters. In contrast, he also employs bouts of silence when representing devastated landscapes in order to critique the gritty socioeconomic realities his characters face due to the economic decline. The introduction of industry, as much as the modern, technology-driven capitalism imposed by Britain's industrialists, disrupts the agriculture and artisan economies that once sustained the laborers that Anand presents as alienated from their traditional ways of life. I suggest that the multivalent impact of such colonial capitalism manifests aesthetically through the relationship between the laments of the characters and the way their natural world alternatively echoes their despair or meets it with a silence conveying the weight of forces the peasants cannot surmount.

Many, like Lalu's uncle, view themselves as an extension of the land they once owned. In a scene that lays out the central conflicts that will proliferate throughout the novel, the narrator points out that Lalu's uncle, Harnam Singh, "felt not only that the land he had to mortgage and forfeit belonged to him but that he also belonged to the land" and that the "earthiness of generations in him was calling him to accept serfdom rather than wage slavery in the brick factory" (Anand, 1942d, 60). Harnam Singh justifies this choice, however, suggesting that as a nationalist agitator, working on the land would permit him to serve his "real lord and master" rather than a factory master or the British sarkar (60). The narrative highlights the centrality of farmland to peasant identity, subsistence, and autonomy. We, along with Lalu, learn how Harnam Singh and peasants from their village first find themselves forced, during the years of World War I, to sell their grain at prices too low to yield any profit. Unable to sustain themselves sufficiently to pay rent, they lose their land to their landlords, who collude with British cotton mill owners and the sarkar in exchange for large plots of land and ever larger bungalows. A fellow villager, Faislu, who initially benefits from pouncing on Lalu's family land only to lose it, alludes to the damaged livelihood of artisan weavers unable to compete with the faster, cheaper bulk production of factories. With this association established, the impact of the violence is conveyed largely through sound or silence on the landscape these characters experience as an extension of themselves. Speaking of Harban Singh, the landlord chiefly responsible for the demise of Lalu's family, Faislu, exclaims:

> [He] has left no small farmer in these parts alive. The breath of famine is in his mouth, the spirit of the storm is in his behind, and his feet create an earthquake wherever they tread. Thieves! Carrion! Traitors! Hounds! Miscreants! He and his likes do not fear God! (62)

While the descriptors indicating famine and devastation initially appear as visual images, the analogies they evoke are embodied, sonic, and charged. The unsettling—and eschatological—winds of storm, the rumble of an earthquake triggered by the feet of Harban Singh, and the cries of birds of prey swooping on a landscape that has little but decay to scavenge may be largely metaphorical. Yet they emerge out of the traditions of orality and allow the characters agency to voice the visceral impact caused by damage to their farmland. The references to sounds make the desolate silence of the aftermath even more poignant. The imagery invoked to convey India's plight also seems to intensify a sense of desolation in its return to an entirely visual mode absent of sound. "This country is like a lean bullock that has been reduced to the bone by the Angrezi lion, son" (63–64). The only sonic reference is to Britain, likened to a lion whose roar leaves the colony emaciated. The final gesture to what Harnam Singh concludes is a sense of "pain, a disease which you can't even diagnose by feeling the pulse, a belly-ache for which there does not seem to be a remedy," comes in the form of aesthetic interruption (64). The reader, presented with the view of a silent, desolate landscape, is jarred by a reference to a lone donkey calling—possibly to a potential mate—while a security guard drives off parrots with his stick (64). These banal, irreverent references to donkeys or parrots punctuate a discussion between Harban Singh and Faislu as if to remind readers about the material privations imposed on villagers in a landscape that retains markers of its former condition as a source of fertility and sustenance. The interruption of animal sounds highlights the landscape as a force and character that is marred but inescapable. Anand's distinctively crafted modernist aesthetics are designed to represent the specificities of India's colonial modernity.

If poignant sections of the novel portray the ability of Lalu and his friends to speak despite their relatively limited power, they also enact the aporias of the peasants who Anand portrays as too completely oppressed to view themselves as being in any position to challenge their oppressors. While the relative absence of accessible voices from these communities makes them difficult to represent, Anand again devises experimental narrative practices that either connect Lalu and the readers to these characters or emphasize that they are silenced or unseen through narrative negation, which erases them just enough to leave the faintest trace. When Lalu and his fellow revolutionaries try to draw a group of Hindu pilgrims, engaged in a posteclipse purification ritual, into their Marxist rally, they instinctively appeal to sonic signifiers that mimic the religious practices of the pilgrims. The "dhum, dhum, dhum" of the drums, which play a "one two" beat at Lalu's urging, evokes the rhythm of a heartbeat as well as the backdrop of chanting or singing associated with religious ritual (125). The nonverbal nature of this communication arrests the attention of "hundreds of startled pilgrims," making it far more potent than the speeches Lalu and the Count will deliver to the captive crowd (125). Similarly, Lalu's comrades urge their listeners to hail them as they would typically hail a deity to achieve a similar effect.

> "Bolo Sri Ram Chander ki jai!" Ram Din suddenly called the cry of religion, and then continued: "Come, brothers, come friends, come and see the new incarnation of God, the saints, who bring you a new message, a new hope. . . . Come."
>
> This kind of incitement made Lalu impatient. He hoped he would not have to raise his voice so dishonestly and so loudly. . . . But this call seemed to confirm the familiar feelings of the crowd, to stir the memory of an age-old cry in their blood, specially with the pressure

> of the deep rhythmic sound of the drum which came behind it. They rushed towards the focal point of the dais on which Ram Din was standing as if he were the God King Rama himself, who had appeared and was talking to them. (126)

The pilgrims are drawn in by the familiar cadence and sensibility of music and words conventionally associated with their religious practice rather than any conscious engagement with the political message being conveyed to them in messianic terms. While Lalu objects to such forms of incitement, which seem disingenuous to him, he, like Anand, recognizes that gaining one's attention is often rooted in affective appeals of the familiar. The assessment of these tactics is delivered to us through free indirect discourse, which blurs Lalu's thoughts with those of the narrator.

> [The crowd] reached out to the platform, pulsing to the throb of the dhum, dhum, dhum.
>
> Sheikh, sure of touch on the undertones of a sitar, as well as on the overtones of the tabla, ingeniously improvised an imitation of the heart-beat on the dholki and then led up to a crescendo of shrillness till the crowd had almost become a compact mass. Then he dropped the handle suddenly and caught the crowd in a torment of interest. (126–27)

Despite the visceral, affective appeal that excites the pilgrims, the disconnect between them and their awareness of the agency that would enable them to engage and deploy the ideas presented to them is again emphasized by narrative instances in which Lalu and his comrades employ affective appeal or even answer the very rhetorical questions they pose to their dumbfounded listeners. Although Anand cannot represent their German counterparts as fully on his radio programs, his reference to them on the "New Weapons of War" broadcast evokes the helplessness we see in the Indian peasants represented in print. While the disenfranchised peasants of the novel would not have had access to this narrative or the radio programs, both provide us with evidence of the implicit connection between Anand's critiques and the programs subversively addressing the peasant struggle of the novel. Lalu and company take on the work of mobilizing resistance through sonic strategies much as Anand does in his Eastern Service broadcasts. The latter, however, may be comprehensible to the less disenfranchised Indian nationalists, such as the Count and his fellow landlords, but they fall short in conceiving and solidifying a unified listening public. Anand's narrative describes Lalu's tone as conversational, one that the pilgrims note as they settle in to listen to the revolutionaries. Lalu begins by asking questions like "What are the things that hinder the life of a peasant?" with the intent of rallying the pilgrims into animated answers (127). But he quickly discovers that it "was too sudden a blow: the crowd looked dumbfounded," uncertain about what this had to do with the eclipse festival (127). Lalu subsequently supplies the answer, "poverty" (128). When a restatement of the question produces another bewildered silence, Ramdin restates the question: "What makes a camel walk slowly?" (128). An answer from the crowd, "a heavy load," is quickly picked up by Lalu, who makes a passionate analogy between the heavy load on a camel and debt on the backs of peasants (128). This opens a space where Lalu can speak about his own disenfranchisement, which in turn aligns him with the peasants he engages by identifying his sorrows with theirs.

> Knowing that it was touch and go whether the audience scattered or remained intact, he let loose his words, trusting his instinct to guide him. He knew the effect of debt in his own bones. His father had died of it, and his whole family had been ruined by it, so his emotions welled up and he shrieked. (128)

Here shrieks and cries indicate anguish or emotion that Anand presents as visceral rather than assigning words to it, as if to suggest that it cannot be fully articulated, understood, or translated. These calls, which jar us as readers, alert us to the real distance between ourselves and the disenfranchised, who can be partly embodied yet not fully spoken for. Still, the response of the crowd remains indifferent, suggesting that there is only a partial connection between the pilgrims, who are too downtrodden to view themselves as agents able to resist their landlords, and the revolutionaries who seek to mobilize them.

These exchanges are notable in their representation of peasants, who Anand suggests are ill equipped to speak for themselves. While I do not address the extent to which such groups engaged in subversive activities that the dominant accounts of history rarely address, Anand's critique here is twofold. First, the exchange emphasizes how much the landlords, in complicity with British capitalists or industrialists, depend on the suppression of their tenants and agricultural laborers to sustain their own wealth; for Anand, such tactics resemble Hitler's treatment of peasants in Germany. Second, while Anand supports the nationalist allegiances of his revolutionaries, the ruptures in their protests reveal how an inability to recognize their privilege, relative to those they seek to mobilize, often heightens their vulnerability to the oppressive forces Lalu and his friends urge them to challenge.

We see this in the novel when Indian police, complicit with the British sarkar, collude with the landlords to incite disturbances in the name of preserving order or deflating threats to colonial authority. For instance, we eventually learn that Captain Affendi, the son-in-law of the chief nawab and landlord in Raj Ghar. where the revolutionaries establish their home base, incites Hindu Muslim tension when urging Hindu priests to confront the rally for defiling their festival while simultaneously inciting Muslim peasants to disrupt the rally by claiming that hailing Hindu deities excludes and offends them. As Frank Schulze-Engler shows in his reading of Anand's *Coolie* (2015), a similar sectarian disturbance breaks up a union gathering of Indian laborers working in a British cotton factory. Munu and his fellow workers, uncertain of what they are being invited to support, find their meeting disrupted by news that a Muslim has abducted a Hindu child. The pilgrims Lalu rallies and the laborers who work with Munu are thwarted by sectarian violence instigated by British sympathizers who stir old animosities or patterns of mistrust. Such representations might suggest that Indians themselves thwart their own progress due to their inability to make peace or build solidarity among themselves. While Anand might not dismiss this entirely, his novels address the way the hegemony of colonial capitalism diminishes indigenous cultural practices as much as it exacerbates peasant poverty. Coupled with the impact of anti-imperial nationalists like the revolutionaries in *The Sword and the Sickle* and the well-meaning union organizers in *Coolie*, who act without considering how liberal humanist values might fit into the world view of India's disenfranchised, most of the efforts to mobilize result in failure or at times cause damage to those the agitators aim to serve.

Although Anand's written work allows for detail and specificity that radio cannot provide, viewing the two together sheds light on the intersecting and conflicting commitments that drive his work. The communities of landless laborers in Anand's novels are, for him, like the German peasants oppressed by Hitler. His novels and radio broadcasts vivify the struggles of the marginalized, depicting the ravages on their bodies, minds, and geopolitical landscapes to awaken the empathy and imagination of his audience.

Meet My Friend: Diplomacy, Realism, and Resistance

Anand arrived in England to study philosophy in 1925, and his encounters with members of the Bloomsbury Group awakened him to these realities.

> My mood at the time was existentialist, brought on by the agony of suffering as an innocent involved in the struggle for freedom in India. I had, after all, received seven stripes after the Jallianwala Bagh shooting in Amritsar. That incident coloured my approach to the Bloomsbury circle in London, which I entered through the courtesy of E. M. Forster and Leonard Woolf. No one in the Bloomsbury group mentioned anything about Indian freedom or even about British politics, but never the less at the regular Wednesday evening "At Homes" I found myself reacting against the "art for art's sake" attitudes of Clive Bell and Roger Fry. (Anand 2000, 78)

Kristin Bluemel explores Anand's shift away from Bloomsbury toward writers like George Orwell and Inez Holden, whom she identifies as "radical eccentrics" whose politics were more aligned with his own (94). I read these vexed exchanges between British and Indian writers as ones Anand enacts in his interviews with George Bishop and Inez Holden, although he adapts them in service of his ambivalence around torn loyalties. In 1990s scholarship by critics like Meenakshi Mukherjee, the work of Mulk Raj Anand, Raja Rao, or R. K. Narayan came to be coined twice born fiction (Mukherjee 1971). In debates around how to situate it in contrast to high modernism, critics suggested that the social realism aesthetics of these texts, very different from high modernism's claim to autonomy and hermetic insulation, was essential for responding to the unique conditions of both external and internal oppression in India. More recent critics have argued that it employs aesthetics typically associated with Anglo-American modernist practice and embeds these into social realism in sophisticated ways.

If "New Weapons of War" enabled Anand to convey critiques of fascism and colonial capitalism by speaking directly to Indian listeners, then "Meet My Friend" engaged these increasingly tense issues through the personal mode of dialogue between Anand as an Indian in Britain and his left-leaning British friends. Like his previous broadcasts, this series was proposed by Orwell, written completely by Anand, and subject to the BBC's censor. Although the recordings have not survived and we lack evidence about listener responses, I contend that Anand's delivery of the sonic transmission performs a speech act that marks an embodied enunciation of Indian diasporic resistance, even as it fulfills the BBC's mission to disseminate propaganda and enhance diplomacy. Julie Cyzewski offers a compelling reading of how BBC Eastern Service programs such as "Meet My Friend" engaged in cultural diplomacy by employing the interview format to model British Indian friendships (2018, 22). My analysis now turns to examining how episodes from the series mark Anand's speech act as an embodied enunciation of resistance to the complaisance or disengagement of his Bloomsbury associates. These episodes also indicate that he and the Eastern Service imagined that Indian listeners would find a reformed character like Bishop or an activist like Holden far more persuasive than British speakers delivering an India Talks program like Anand's in "New Weapons of War."

Anand opens the first episode of "Meet My Friend" by identifying as a fellow Indian who has "stood between Europe and Asia now for some years as a kind of interpreter" and "tried to tell the English people something about life in India . . . to reveal [Indians] as the human beings in the lanes and alleys of Hindustan (Anand and Bishop 1942). This allows him to heighten listener empathy and openness toward the English friends he wants to "present to India . . . so that men do not remain the collective they or the great British nation of the Anglo-Indian controversy, but as human beings" (1).

Anand and Bishop then agree to engage in a charade, with Anand pretending to speak as his friend's conscience and Bishop responding to Anand's questions about his life and outlook. Quick to stress that he does not want Bishop to feel guilty and that he defines conscience as "social anxiety," Anand begins by inviting Bishop to explain his relationship with his conscience.

> George Bishop, you often talk to me, your still small voice, your conscience (on the way from home to work and back from work again), on tops of houses and in tubes, you ask me how to understand this world involved in the most terrible convolutions (in history). I believe in your integrity and your zest for life. But why didn't you ever consult me before? (5)

Explaining that he didn't even know his conscience existed until he discovered it in 1937, during the English War (5), Bishop attributes this to his impulsiveness and desire to live in the moment. Yet a sentence crossed out in the transcript captures his retrospective thoughts about the mood that contributed to his inattention to conscience: "I wanted to live life as I found it. I did not want to think, take the path of least resistance. I was young" (5–6). Anand completes Bishop's unfinished sentence, "and handsome?" (6). This lighthearted teasing softens his earlier, more critical question in response to Bishop's statement that he lived life much like an actor possessed as he throws himself passionately into his role onstage, only to forget the words after the play ends: "Ought not an actor . . . aspire to be both an actor and a spectator of his work?" (5). The metaphor invoked by Bishop and extended by Anand references Bishop's literal profession. The implicit question also gently yet firmly points to what Anand, as Conscience, sees as an individual's responsibility: to be aware of the implications his or her actions have on others. Bishop's candid response that he was not ashamed then makes more poignant his revelation that he subsequently did develop a commitment to greater political engagement and came to recognize the error of his earlier attitudes.

Such an opening frames the meeting of friends as a playful performance in which Anand serves as a mirror for Bishop's organic development, carefully steering away from the perception that listeners are hearing an Indian colonial subject acting as a judge passing judgment on an English friend. Although Anand asks gently probing questions, he never offers explicit judgments on what Bishop shares; the mild traces of affect embedded in the questions are subtle, such that listeners, who make an apostrophic third, are left to draw their own conclusions. While the conversation format lends itself to creating intimacy, and by extension heightens familiarity with and trust in potentially foreign British perspectives, it also allows Anand to engage in subversive play to emphasize ambivalence when the views of guests like Bishop prove insufficiently critical of British colonialism or capitalism. The sonic conveyance of the exchange emphasizes that it is a dialogue in ways that a written text might not allow as fully. The mode leaves open the potential for multiple coexisting interpretations, largely because the meaning drawn by BBC production teams and audiences in India would have been separated by distance and the contextual filters through which each heard the broadcast. As we see in subsequent parts of the exchange between these friends, the matters they discuss are sensitive and potentially heated. Yet the spirit of their conversation is friendly and honest, with hints of damning commentary on Britain's colonial apparatus—aimed at

Indian listeners—cloaked as a playful performance for British officials at the BBC. Anand's sense of an Indian listening public concerned about Britain's continued depletion of India's resources to support British war efforts prompt his questions about Bishop's initial inattention to what his choices imply.

His questions about Bishop's experiences in colonial New Zealand and Nigeria, coupled with his work on engineering projects supporting World War I efforts, draw out the actor's nonchalance about the political implications of his privilege. Bishop explains that he decided to board a ship to New Zealand as a lark, to have an adventure, only to tire of it after time spent enjoying the open-air life doing odd jobs on a farm (Anand and Bishop 1942, 7). When pressed by Conscience to offer reflections about his experience, Bishop replies, "I didn't give myself time to think" (8). Similarly, when speaking about his work in Nigeria building the Baro-Kano railway, Bishop reflects, "It was so new and exciting, something impelling you to work and there was a race to finish the survey and get the railway built. Of course if I had let myself think of the things around me and not worked hard, I should have gone to pieces" (8–9). His descriptions offer almost no commentary on the people he encountered or the politics of the colonial enterprise. He barely reflects on his feelings about the realities around him, holding them at bay through absorption in hard work and efficiency as he engages with his mission to complete the survey and build the railway. The exchange between Conscience and Bishop about his emergence physically and emotionally unscathed by his work as an engineer on the front is equally telling.

> BISHOP: I was involved in the war and knew we should win. I did my job and was indifferent to the rest.
>
> CONSCIENCE: You mean you were asleep and woke up like Rip Van Winkle after the war?
>
> BISHOP: No, I didn't wake up until much later. When you have the kind of valour I had then, you don't wake up easily. Questions of life or death don't enter your mind if all that you are interested in is having a good time and making money. . . . You must remember we were the victorious generation and so cultivated a complacency. What was the use of regretting this or that or the other thing? (9–10)

Like much of the detail shared throughout the interview, Bishop's acknowledgment that privilege kept him from questioning the impact of his colonial service speaks to the larger scale of complacency among British citizens. In part this signals British unawareness and carelessness about the forces that underpin India's colonial subjugation. Heard in another light, however, Bishop's candor is disarming, particularly in light of his later disclosure that he does explain, retrospectively, why people of his generation approached matters as they did. Responding to questions from Conscience about his activities and what inspired him to choose the path he did, Bishop exclaims, "My dear fellow, I'd grown up from the Edwardian era to the Georgian my friend. You didn't have to do anything in that era. You sat around and ate and drank and talked and could be complacent. . . . I didn't ask questions or answer any" (8). Initially, Bishop resists efforts by Conscience to invite him to express remorse, introspection, or signs of awakening. He ultimately responds to Anand's charge that his prolonged adolescence was a void rather than a magnanimous, courageous, purpose-driven surge forward with a confession: "I don't mind admitting that today, but I should have protested strongly to your imputation at the time" (11). Through a focus on Bishop's awakening, Anand opens space for listeners to experience a parallel awakening about the urgency to address fascism. Their alertness to anti-imperial nationalism would have been long-standing. Anand's own anxieties and outrage about the rise of fascism were inspired by the Spanish Civil War, where he initially sought to serve in the International Brigade but switched to journalism when he found himself unable to tolerate the sight of blood. Although the interview provides an opening for censure, it simultaneously lauds Bishop for his honest appraisal of his lack of political engagement, envisioning Indian listeners who are likely to appreciate the critique while being mollified, if not inspired, by Bishop's transformation.

The interview concludes on a redemptive note as Bishop explains how his eventual awakening—inspired by the activism of his son—leads him to discover that commitments to causes are the means of maintaining youth, explaining that those who believe in causes remain young due to their "faith in living" and their willingness to "cast off lies and illusions" (Anand and Bishop 1942, 11). He is humble when articulating what he describes as the inevitable yet mistaken heedlessness of his generation, the difficulty of inspiring the transformation he experienced, and the urgent need to do so.

> Now I know that every human being has inalienable rights to food, freedom, and work. The happiness of dreams. Now I know that fas-

> cism means the negation of all these things. Only a prisoner knows the taste of freedom. Having escaped from the slavery of spacious houses and apparent ease the dullness of the senseless mind, tortured and mangled by self-interest and taboo, twisted under the charred ruins of traditions which are the outer disguises of death. Now I know the misery of the poor and I can hear in their anguished cries the very call of life. (12–13)

Rather than offering any direct statement of his political position as he does in "New Weapons of War," Anand relies on a story-based format in which listeners engage in the transformation or awakening Bishop experienced, inviting their complicity in supporting antifascist efforts. In his final statement, speaking as Bishop's conscience, Anand explains that he wouldn't wish his friend to feel guilty. By framing Bishop's final soliloquy as the episode's ultimate message, Anand endorses the actor as an important symbol who might awaken others from sleep to realize their dreams. This establishes Anand's support for antifascist war efforts while allowing Bishop's words to resonate with Indian listeners, who can extend them to apply to Britain's capitalist colonialism, which has much the same effect on India's poor. The medium of radio, then, allows Bishop as an agent of the political views he expresses to speak to issues that Anand as an Indian colonial subject would not have been able to address through the platform of the BBC's Eastern Service.

If Anand's exchange with Bishop reconstructs a narrative of personal and political awakening, his conversation with Inez Holden examines political and aesthetic questions about who writes and reads narratives about marginalized voices. Moving away from the performative play in George Bishop's episode, the more conventional conversation format Anand employs with Holden frames their dialogue as one between writer-activists comparing British and Indian modalities of literary representation. Such a pairing allows Anand to legitimate his unconventional, even revolutionary, focus on India's peasant and laborer communities as ethical. For Anand this parallels the British literary turn to middlebrow writing, which Virginia Woolf refers to as the novels of the Factory Acts (Anand and Holden 1942).

Anand and Holden make a compelling case for the importance of realism, suggesting that it bridges an already existing political and aesthetic consciousness in the British working class of Indian rural communities that engage with cultural production representing their experiences. Speaking of her experience working in disguise at a factory in which her fellow workers were unaware she was a writer, Holden observes that many industry operatives are politically conscious because politics affects their own lives (Anand and Holden 1942, 3). She recalls a conversation between two workers discussing a Soviet film they were watching in the factory canteen during a lunch break (4). While one points out, "It must be wonderful there, officers and men talking freely to each other like brothers," another notes, "It's beautiful, the snow and the tanks moving like ghosts through the trees" (4). The example demonstrates that the first speaker has an affective response to a social ideal the film portrays as a consequence of a political practice, while the second speaker is drawn into the political through an appeal to the harmony he experiences through the aesthetics of the narrative presentation. Anand offers a similar example from India, noting the beautiful poetry composed by peasants who carry on the oral traditions of the village bards (4). As their conversation turns to the recognition that many in the working classes and armed forces write poetry, a good amount of which is "bad," Anand attributes "the lack of intensity" to the destruction of the old culture by the Industrial Revolution (4–5). Although his comment responds to Holden's reflection about British working-class poetry, it applies equally to the peasants he depicts in novels like *Coolie* or *The Sword and the Sickle,* who find their traditional modes of life and livelihood destroyed by industrial capitalism. Holden corroborates Anand's support for realism as a viable mode, noting that many factory workers combine their reading of escapist detective fiction with realist novels by Shaw, Wells, and Bennett and "the modern writers who are intensely political" (6). Anand's response, "Good luck Mrs. Brown," refers unquestionably to Woolf's essay, "Mr. Bennett and Mrs. Brown," which argues for fiction driven by character rather than plot (6).

Considering Anand's experience of the Bloomsbury Group's failure to address empire, Holden's open support for his commitment to bridge aesthetics and politics through the modes of realism he employs in *The Sword and the Sickle* demonstrates political solidarity. The conversation establishes their realist British and Indian writing as a departure from the aesthetics of Bloomsbury's high modernism and claims it as world citizens writing for world citizens.

Anand as Insider and Outsider in London

The final section of this chapter considers how Anand's position as an Indian colonial subject living in wartime London inflected his choices about how to balance his commitments to Britain's antifascist resistance with his allegiance to a sovereign India. As Carolyn Steedman suggests (2001), the meaning conveyed by the archive is inextricably linked to the materiality involved in producing, recovering, and interpreting it. If dust and crumbling paper determine which pieces of the print archive are accessible, the faded microfilm scripts that are entirely unreadable in places shape our understanding of their story. Our awareness of historical outcomes that Anand and his peers could not have known—for instance, the outcome of the war, the Brander Report's findings about limited listenership, and Indian independence—invariably influences our reading of this narrative.

As Shompa Lahiri explains, although Indians resident in Britain for two years or longer were "liable" for military service, many declared themselves conscientious objectors on the grounds that they were unwilling to support an imperialist war (2007, 152). Others maintained that "the war was not their business and that their stay in Britain was only temporary" (153). According to surveillance reports, the Indian Workers Association served to protect Indians from conscription on political and economic grounds, supporting their efforts to delay enlisting as long as possible. The India Office, however, was quick to emphasize that "for every one Indian serving in the Pioneer Company, there [were] at least six earning a livelihood in Great Britain who have not been conscripted" (161–62). Meanwhile government officials, fearful that Indian disloyalty could pose domestic security threats, developed a "contingency plan" to intern six Indians, although such measures were never ultimately taken.

For Anand, however, the realities of living as an Indian colonial subject concerned challen fascism in wartime London were not just political but material. On three separate occasions, in 1934, 1937, and 1940, he applied to the Royal Literary Fund, requesting financial support to help him meet his living expenses and complete his novels (Anand 1934). The descriptions of his situation are direct, earnest, and humbling. Each application was supported by letters from friends, including Eric Gill, E. M. Forster, and Rosamond Lehrman, and each was granted by the fund. In the last of his letters, Anand describes the impact of London bombings on his financial struggles. In a letter dated November 25, 1940, he explains that the damage from bombing had required him to evacuate to Ilfracombe in Devon and had led to the cancelation of lectures he had planned to give in London to generate income (Anand 1940b). His wife's experience with shock and his own struggle to adjust to the damp Devonshire weather indicate the extent to which his dislocation from India to Britain and the daily threats of air raids imposed by bombing shaped his material reality and security. Work for the BBC's Eastern Service also contributed to his subsistence.

In part, then, we can read Anand's support of antifascist war efforts as closely linked to his belief in democracy as an ideal and a condition that ensured the safety and stability of his world in Britain. The governmental anxiety about disloyalty among Indians filtered into the BBC's remit of which forms of propaganda could or could not be broadcast. While Anand refused to support Britain's colonial policies on or off the air, his radio programs allowed him space for subversive commentaries on colonialism while simultaneously working to secure his own well-being as a colonial subject living and working in the metropole.

Despite the absence of program recordings and the likelihood that very few Indians heard Anand's transmissions, they offer his strategic constructions of himself as a passionate, informed colonial subject who develops modes for enunciating a resistance that boldly, subversively honor his conflicting commitments. The BBC's airing of programs like "New Weapons of War" envisions an Indian listening public that can be persuaded to contribute to fights for a democracy denied them by the nation enlisting their services while Anand constructs it subversively, envisioning an audience he believes will recognize both the irony and the urgency to act in spite of it. Similarly, "Meet My Friend" imagines an Indian audience that might be drawn in by Anand's strategic performance of cross-cultural diplomacy and friendship even as he playfully challenges Bishop's lack of awareness of his complicity in the colonial project. Although my reading of both programs relies on an awareness of his literary work and personal experiences, I propose that the BBC's understanding that these passionate, affective, and intimately delivered transmissions would circulate to the Indian public, whose solidarity it sought to concretize, makes them essential to understanding the complexities of Anand's sociohistorical moment, which I illuminate through my reading. Similarly, attending to the sonic elements in novels like *The Sword and the Sickle* entail a valiant effort to introduce the voices of India's most disenfranchised citizens to an international readership in ways that preserve the orality of their culture and modes of communication. It simultaneously acknowledges the struggle for India's peasants to speak and the limits elite writers face when representing them. Even if they didn't reach their intended audiences, Anand's acts of embodied enunciation—using his own voice to deliver transcripts written by him on the BBC—marks his own multipronged resistance and the BBC's acceptance, however unwittingly, of the underlying subversion of Anand's speech acts.

Notes

Special thanks to funding through King's College London and the Marie Sklodowska Curie Individual Fellowship that has made the archival research for this project possible.

1. Information about the Brander Report comes from conversations I had with Aasiya Lodhi about research she is conducting for future publication.

Works Cited

Anand, Mulk Raj. 1934. "MS Loan 96 RLF 1/349 Mulk Raj Anand: Application to the Royal Literary Fund," January 27. British Library Western Manuscripts.

Anand, Mulk Raj. 1939. *The Village: A Novel.* London: Jonathan Cape.

Anand, Mulk Raj. 1940a. *Across the Black Waters: A Novel.* London: Jonathan Cape.

Anand, Mulk Raj. 1940b. "MS Loan 96 RLF 1/349/28 Mulk Raj Anand: Application to the Royal Literary Fund," November 25.. British Library Western Manuscripts.

Anand, Mulk Raj. 1942a. *Letters on India.* London: Routledge.

Anand, Mulk Raj. 1942b. "New Weapons of War." Original transmission, BBC Eastern Service, April. BBC Written Archive Centre.

Anand, Mulk Raj. 1942c. "New Weapons of War No. 2, Lebensraum." Original transmission, BBC Eastern Service, March 22. BBC Written Archive Centre.

Anand, Mulk Raj. 1942d. *The Sword and the Sickle.* London: Jonathan Cape.

Anand, Mulk Raj. 1979. "Why I Write." In *Perspectives on Mulk Raj Anand,* edited by Kaushal Kishore Sharma, 1–7. Ghaziabad: Vimal.

Anand, Mulk Raj. 1981. *Conversations in Bloomsbury.* London: Wildwood House.

Anand, Mulk Raj. 2000. "A Writer in Exile." In *Voices of the Crossing: The Impact of Britain on Writers from Asia, the Caribbean, and Africa,* edited by Ferdinand Dennis and Khan Nassem, 77–82. London: Serpent's Tail.

Anand, Mulk Raj, and George Bishop. 1942. "Meet My Friend—George Bishop." Original transmission, BBC Eastern Service, May 26. BBC Written Archive Centre.

Anand, Mulk Raj, and Inez Holden. 1942. "Meet My Friend—Inez Holden." Original transmission, BBC Eastern Service, May 26. BBC Written Archive Centre.

Anjaria, Ulka. 2012. *Realism in the Twentieth-Century Indian Novel: Colonial Difference and Literary Form.* Cambridge: Cambridge University Press.

Berman, Jessica. 2011. *Modernist Commitments: Ethics, Politics, and Transnational Modernism.* New York: Columbia University Press.

Bluemel, Kristin. 2004a. *George Orwell and the Radical Eccentrics: Intermodernism in Literary London.* Basingstoke: Palgrave Macmillan.

Bluemel, Kristin. 2004b. "Mulk Raj Anand's Passage through Bloomsbury." In *George Orwell and the Radical Eccentrics: Intermodernism in Literary London,* 67–102. Basingstoke: Palgrave Macmillan.

Cyzewski, Julie. 2018. "'Making Friends': The Geopolitics of the Interview on the BBC's Eastern Service." *Biography* 41: 322–43.

Das, Santanu, ed. 2011. *Race, Empire, and First World War Writing*. Cambridge: Cambridge University Press.

Dinsman, Melissa. 2015. "Orwell and his BBC 'Voice': Propaganda, Literature, and New Networks." *Modernism at the Microphone: Radio, Propaganda, and Literary Aesthetics During World War II*. London: Bloomsbury Academic.

Gajarawala, Toral Jatin. 2012. *Untouchable Fictions: Literary Realism and the Crisis of Caste*. New York: Modern Language Initiative.

Lacey, Kate. 2013. *Listening Publics: The Politics and Experience of Listening in the Media Age*. Cambridge: Polity.

Lahiri, Shompa. 2007. "From Empire to Decolonisation, 1901–1947." In *South Asians in Britain: Four Centuries of Peoples from the Indian Sub-Continent*, edited by Michael H. Fisher, Shompa Lahiri, and Shinder S. Thandi, 127–58. Oxford: Greenwood World.

MacClean, Kama. 2016. "Revolution and Revelation, or, When is History Too Soon?" In *South Asia: Journal of South Asian Studies* 39, no. 3: 678–94. https://doi.org/10.1080/00856401.2016.1191536

Morse, Daniel Ryan. 2015. "An 'Impatient Modernist': Mulk Raj Anand at the BBC." *Modernist Cultures* 10, no. 1: 83–98. https://doi.org/10.3366/mod.2015.0099

Mukherjee, Meenakshi. 1971. *The Twice Born Fiction: Themes and Techniques of the Indian Novel in English*. New Delhi: Heinemann.

Orwell, George. 1997–98a. "All Propaganda Is Lies." In *The Complete Works of George Orwell*, edited by Peter Hobley Davison. London: Secker & Warburg.

Orwell, George. 1997–98b. "Two Wasted Years." In *The Complete Works of George Orwell*, edited by Peter Hobley Davison. London: Secker & Warburg.

Perera, Sonali. 2004. *No Country: Working-Class Writing in the Age of Globalization*. New York: Columbia University Press.

Ranasinha, Ruvani. 2010. "South Asian Broadcasters and the BBC: Talking to India." *Journal of South Asian Diaspora* 2, no. 1: 57–71.

Scannell, Paddy. 1991. *Broadcast Talk*. Thousand Oaks, CA: Sage.

Scannell, Paddy. 1996. *Radio, Television, and Modern Life*. Hoboken, NJ: Wiley-Blackwell.

Schulze-Engler, Frank. 2015. "Once Were Internationalists? Postcolonialism, Disenchanted Solidarity, and the Right to Belong in a World of Globalized Modernity." In *Reworking Postcolonialism: Globalization, Labour, and Rights*, edited by Pavan Kumar Malreddy, Birte Heidemann, Ole Birk Laursen, and Janet Wilson, 19–35. Basingstoke: Palgrave Macmillan.

Smith, Jacob. 2008. *Vocal Tracks: Performance and Sound Media*. Berkley, CA: University of California Press.

Smith, Jacob, and Norman Corwin. 2016. *Anatomy of Sound*. Berkley, CA: University of California Press.

Steedman, Carolyn. 2001. *Dust*. Manchester: Manchester University Press.

Whittington, Ian. 2018. "Calling the West Indies: Una Marson's Wireless Black Atlantic." In *Writing the Radio War: Literature, Politics and the BBC, 1939–1945*. Edinburgh: Edinburgh University Press.

Woolf, Virginia. 1924. *Mr. Bennett and Mrs. Brown*. London: L. and V. Woolf.

SECTION THREE
Cinema Sound

NINE | # Between Rage and Song

Voice, Performance, and Instrumentation in Shanta Apte's Films of the 1930s

NEEPA MAJUMDAR

Indian cinema's song and dance performances may be said to belong to roughly two periods. The years between the coming of sound in 1931 and the mid-1940s was the era of singing stars, when actors sang their songs in their own voices. This gave way in the 1940s to the era of the "playback" singer, when actors lip-synched to the voices of singers, who also over time became stars themselves. Thus, in terms of the performance and reception of film songs, there were arguably two major moments of transition. The first was the transition from silent to sound film in 1931, when all the nonsonic forms of female performance of the silent era, such as dance, stunts, and acrobatics, all involving a great deal of movement, gave way instead to vocal performance, usually accompanied by relatively minimal movement. The second moment of transition, from singing star to playback singer, was marked by a drastic reduction in the range, timbre, and tonality of the female playback singing voice. The technology of playback singing, which separated singing and acting, emerged in the mid-1930s and spanned both eras, allowing even singing stars to record their songs separately.[1] As female actors no longer needed to sing in their own voices, and sound no longer needed to be recorded at the time of shooting a scene, bodily movement reemerged in the form of dance and other movement.

In this chapter, I discuss the first moment of transition, when actors still sang in their own voices and new anxieties over female public performance focused on the relation between the female voice and the female body in the technologically mediated space of the cinema. The unprecedented scale of public visibility afforded by the cinematic medium in its early years at the turn of the twentieth century had been a social hindrance to women's screen performance in many national contexts around the world, including India. The coming of sound had a similar impact on actresses who were now also singing, once again renewing the disreputability of female screen performance through its associations with the paid private performances of courtesans.

Shankerrao Damle, the sound recordist at Prabhat studio in Poona, remembers that in sound films in the early 1930s, songs had to be filmed in a single take with a static or minimally mobile frame.

> . . . only one microphone was used and was focused on the actor singing in front of the camera. Sarangi, harmonium and tabla players were given positions outside the camera frame. It used to be a tight frame composition and the actor was not allowed to make any movements because the microphone was fixed and so was the balance between voice and the musical accompaniment. You move the microphone to the left—the tabla sound will dominate the voice, you move it to the right—the harmonium will sound very loud. (Thakkar 1980, 15)

While technological constraints led to the immobility of actors who were singing, we could also argue that there were additional pressures on female actors. With the female star now also audible in her own voice, we find 1930s cinema working initially to decouple singing from dancing and the singing voice from the performing body, with the restraint in movement during song sequences coded as a form of modesty, distancing the singing voice from the erotic charge of the female body.

In this context, I explore anxieties over female vocal and bodily movement and performance in the early sound era with a focus on Shanta Apte, a major singing star at Prabhat Film Company, whose song sequences were marked by what I read as a tension between the resistant female roles she embodied both on- and offscreen and the codes of modesty marking vocal female performance on screen at this time. I compare voice-body relations in song sequences with those in what I call "rage sequences," which were a second type of performative scene that specifically marked Shanta Apte's star persona. Analyzing Apte's song sequences in her two most popular films with Prabhat studio *Rajput Ramani* (Rajput

Maiden, 1936) and *Kunku* (Vermilion, 1937), I argue for a split dynamic of the female voice, in which the distinction in performing the raging voice and the singing voice demonstrates the tension mentioned earlier between female resistance and modesty. Because of the distinction between voice and movement, it is fruitful to analyze song sequences side by side with rage sequences in her films. In the context of the cinematic medium, I understand "performance" to be the product of the intersection of voice with bodily expression and movement. And, although such performances appear to be organic, they are of course technologically mediated and fragmentary. In *Kunku,* in particular, voice expands to the body as instrument in both types of sequences as the sounds of breathing, slapping, kicking, and hitting produce a continuum of instrumentation accompanying human gesture. Drawing on Richard Dyer's work, Jean Ma points to "the immediate, visceral, and sensuous impact of song performance" (10) which can be extended to other vocal performances such as the rage sequences I discuss here, especially when one considers the voice and vocal timbre as an instrument or conversely, instruments as voice.

What was it about the female singing voice in the early sound era that provoked new calls for modesty in cinematic performance, one that minimized bodily movement? While one can think of the voice in terms of notions of the authentic self, especially in Western thought, my interest is in cinematic discourse of the 1930s and 1940s in India, which worked to render voice as a pure, bodiless form of identity and communication, somewhat indicated by the term *ghost voice* given to playback singers (Majumdar 2009, 185–89). Cinematic norms from the 1950s onward would draw on this ideological distinction between the pure, disembodied voice and the sexualized, material body through its reliance on playback singers and the split between the actor and the singer. Arguably, such attempts to separate the singing voice from bodily association stem precisely from the fact that the voice is physiologically anything but disembodied for either the singer or the auditor. While one may distinguish between the live and the recorded voice, both kinds of sound have a greater material presence and impact than the visual image on the screen. Andrea Hammer points to "sound's fluid, even synaesthesic relation with all modalities of sensing, particularly with the haptic." As she puts it, "We hear with our teeth" (2007). Moreover, unlike cinematic vision, sound is also spatial and three-dimensional. Registered in the body and surrounding us in space, the star voice has a material presence in a way the star body, a mere flickering image on a flat screen, does not. The absence-presence of stars, the paradoxical intimacy without substance that has been argued to be the heart of cinematic stardom, refers implicitly to the visual rather than aural register. Resonant within the sounding body, every form of the star voice—singing, speaking, laughing, coughing, screaming—exists in a bodily relation with the listener in a way that the star's body does not. It is the material resonance of the voice and its impact on the body that renders it "intrinsically and unignorably relational." As Brandon LaBelle says, the voice "leaves a body and enters others" (2012, 468). But when the voice articulates song, rather than speech, the power of this bodily relation is further enhanced through rhythm, melody, vocal timbre, and lyrical emotion. It is this greater material and affective resonance of the singing voice that arguably led to a disavowal of the female singer's performing body in the case of cinematic singing stars.

In 1932, at the age of sixteen, Shanta Apte began a five-year contract with Prabhat Film Company, with her first major role in the 1934 film *Amrit Manthan* (The Churning). Apte's peak years with the studio were 1936 and 1937. In 1936 she released two films that launched the two major aspects of her star persona. *Amar Jyoti* (Eternal Flame) established her as a major singing star, while *Rajput Ramani* (Rajput Princess) was the first film to reveal her as the woman with the fiery temperament, which was both lauded and criticized at different moments in her career. *Kunku*, made in 1937, combined these two aspects in a starring role. In her earlier films, Apte played a secondary role to the main star while performing more song sequences than the main star. In other words, the acting and singing roles were already beginning to be divided between two actresses. Clearly, Apte was initially cast for her singing voice and hence in a secondary role. Film magazines at this time were full of complaints regarding the poor acting skills of singing stars and vice versa whenever they saw mismatched acting and singing abilities. This could have been one reason why the primary star in *Rajput Ramani*, Nalini Tarkhad, was not given as many song sequences as Apte. In a song sequence that comes early in the *Rajput Ramani*, there is a sharp spatial and visual distinction between the singing star, Apte, and the dancing bodies of anonymous women, who are framed in fragmentary and partial ways, with parts of the body cut off. They are also rendered ornamental, with the dancing bodies forming patterns after the manner of Busby Berkeley's choreography in Hollywood musicals of the 1930s. The sequence gives relatively little screen time to Apte, who is also more or less still as she sings, while all the movement provoked, desired, and induced by the song is displaced onto the bodies of the anonymous female dancers, with her singing voiceover floating over them. The sequence is intercut with shots of listeners, who turn around to look. But are they looking at the singer or the dancers? We are meant to understand that, while they hear the singer, they look at the dancers; in other words, there's a separation between the visual and aural, the body and the voice, looking and listening, and this is emphasized by the restraint in the singer's accompanying body movement. As viewers, the diegetic and extradiegetic audience are invited to view the song and dance as separate perceptual experiences.

But it was not only her singing in *Rajput Ramani* but also her scenes of fiery performance, of speaking truth to power, that made Apte overshadow Nalini Tarkhad. She plays Kesar, the younger sister of Taramati (played by Tarkhad), who has been married off to a tyrant king, Mansingh. The only one willing to tell Mansingh how much his subjects hate him is Kesar, who is also the object of the lecherous advances of one of his henchmen. Her response to the latter's lewd suggestions is one of the rage sequences in the film. In this scene, her anger is dynamically represented through only her facial expressions and figural movement as she slaps the man, then walks off the frame, where we hear her voice offscreen complaining to Mansingh about his servant. Once again there is a clear separation of vocal and bodily responses. But in *Kunku*, where director V. Shantaram was invested in sound experimentation, it is not so easy to separate the sonic aspects of vocal and bodily responses, as we will see.

In 1937, one year after *Rajput Ramani* established Apte's star persona as a singing actress who also voiced outrage against injustice onscreen, she starred in her most famous film, *Kunku* (Vermillion, released in English as *The Unexpected*). In this film, which was initially released in two languages (Marathi and Hindi), she played a young bride of an old man who famously resists his advances, refusing to consummate the marriage but nonetheless standing up for him when his worthless son insults him in her presence. The film's reputation for progressive gender politics rests largely on the performance of Shanta Apte, rather than on the narrative outcome of the film, which ultimately co-opts her resistance in favor of pious widowhood after her repenting husband commits suicide. Here her role as Neeru, the fiery young bride, provides the occasion for multiple rage and song sequences, which together constitute the alternating and contrastive scenes of spectacle that structure the film. Apte's vocal work in the film goes beyond rage and song sequences to include a third type of scene, one that is far more common in melodrama, the performance of weeping. Such scenes of weeping and despair can similarly be paired with scenes of joy and laughter with the young girl she befriends in her husband's home.

Although Apte came to be known as one of the first female singing stars to move her body while singing,[2] in *Kunku*, this movement is still highly constrained, in striking contrast to her performances of rage in various scenes of gender and political resistance. As we have seen, this restraint in song sequences is absolutely essential to the narrative interest in enabling her to violate norms of wifely behavior. It is worth noting that we see her in song sequences with relatively greater movement in *Amar Jyoti*, a 1936 film in which she plays a young princess who lives in close attunement to nature. In one song sequence, for example, as she moves from shrub to tree to rock, picking off thorns, touching leaves, and even briefly twirling around in one close-up on her skirt, closeness to nature alleviates anything that might be construed as disreputable in the scene. Although we do not know the specifics of *Amar Jyoti*'s production history, it seems clear that the song sequences in this film used the playback technique, enabling greater freedom of movement and distance from the camera in each shot.

In *Kunku*, it is worth considering a rage sequence and a song sequence side by side to reveal several sets of voice-body relationships. Many of the songs Apte sang belong to the devotional genre of religious music, which drew on regionally specific folk musical forms. In a scene that occurs soon after Neeru, Apte's character, moves to her husband's house, she is in her room with a young girl who is her husband's relative. Offscreen, we hear the sound of an itinerant musician's voice, and they turn their heads toward the window in response to the sound. The girl then asks Neeru to sing a song, which launches a song sequence. The entire song is framed in the domestic context of her bedroom, and the only movement is when the camera pans slowly to follow Neeru as she walks a short distance to a window and stands in front of it. The rest of the song shows her in a long shot standing and singing while swaying very slightly. In every possible way this song sequence establishes Neeru's singing as one befitting a wife as opposed to a woman who sings in public, the cinema actress, a figure that is repeatedly invoked in the dialogue of the film as the antithesis of all that is decent. In order to make room for her scenes of rage, while maintaining a sense of her character as a good wife, her song sequences require a greater level of restraint than we saw in *Amar Jyoti*. Not only is she singing a devotional song, inspired by the off-screen singing of what is assumed to be the voice of a wandering holy man, but her restrained body movements, her upward gaze, the private space of performance, and the young girl as the sole auditor within the sequence all work to contain any hint of disreputability in the performance.

By contrast, in the vocal performance of rage scenes, the bodily elements of voice, such as heavy breathing, infuse the sonic space of the scene, and where the voice is absent, Foley sounds of other objects stand in for the voice and the body itself also becomes an instrument of noise. In one of the first scenes of rage in the film, on her first night in her husband's house, Neeru is tricked into going up to the bedroom to get a copy of the *Gita* for her husband's widowed sister, who then locks her in the bedroom for her husband to come to her. From begging to be let out, Neeru's manner changes to rage as she locks the door from the inside and, despite the threats and entreaties of her husband, refuses to open the door. In the first shot, a long take, the entire frame of the screen is used to highlight her wild bodily movement as she repeatedly kicks the door, moves to the bed, grabs the pillows, and throws them to the ground. As the scene progresses, her movement becomes more contained and is transferred to facial expression as her speech also becomes reduced, and she threatens to burn down the house by smashing the oil lamp in the room. Anger in her spoken inflection in this and other rage scenes is expressed not so much in intonation as in panting and bodily performance. In rage scenes, voice, breath, and body work in tandem, taking over and complementing one another. This transforms the body into a kind of corpophone, producing a spectacle that is as much sonic as visual. While singing is accompanied by bodily immobility, scenes of anger present other kinds of constraints. Given that Apte's rage scenes are always some form of protest against injustice, their expression is carefully modulated to elicit viewer support for what might otherwise be perceived as outrageous behavior. Thus, in rage scenes, bodily movement and expression are often combined with a restrained vocality. Not only is there no shouting in these scenes, but anger is dramatically enacted in ways that transfer the work of the soundtrack from her voice to her breath and then from her breath to other elements, some of which are naturalistic sound effects, such as the sound of the door being kicked or a metal pot rolling over, or they are symbolic audio effects, such as the sound of a train over the action of driving her sister-in-law from her house in a later scene.

The epithet "fiery," which was so often repeated both positively and negatively about Apte's screen persona, became a malleable term that very easily could be read as rude and immodest behavior in offscreen contexts. In fact, regardless of whether one considered her immodest or a fighter for justice, the continuities between Apte's on- and offscreen image were significant to her star persona. Many recent accounts leave the fiery image of a resistant woman at its most generalized. But a closer look at specific moments in the film *Kunku* shows a split between the gender resistance marking the scenes of anger and the religiosity and modesty marking Apte's song sequences. *Kunku* constructs a family that was highly unconventional in cinema, not only because of its negative representation of a young girl and her old husband but also because of the emphasis given to the reactions of the old man's two adult children, who both find his remarriage repugnant but are in complete contrast in their attitudes toward the young bride. The son is associated with a rage sequence, while the daughter is associated with a song sequence. The son is a lecherous fool who gets his comeuppance, while the daughter is a feminist activist whom the young wife admires and looks up to.

In a key scene in her room in which the grown stepson flirts lecherously with his stepmother Neeru, calling her Maharashtra's Greta Garbo, his insults center on the idea that female performance is equivalent to availability to all men. He chooses to read her anger, enacted only vocally and in facial expression so far, in terms of film acting, choosing to read her heavy breathing as a sign of dramatic performance. Neeru's response, that he should remember that he is not in the theater with a prostitute, but in his stepmother's room, encapsulates the effort of cinema to separate its female performers from such associations. Here the son's comments about her dramatic performance come through with a knowing self-referentiality as in rage sequences such as this one Apte's bodily performance of righteous anger works to simultaneously refute and corroborate his insults about her talents as a dramatic actress in the movies. As his insults settle on comparisons with film actresses and snide references to his father's marriage in old age, Neeru picks up a stick and proceeds to thrash him in a single take as the camera follows her movements, the soundtrack dominated by the sound of the stick. Her dynamic bodily movement, framed in a long shot, shows her wielding the stick with athletic vigor and nimble steps. This scene, despite the work it does to refute negative comparisons with film actresses, would have had resonances later with Apte's offscreen persona, specifically with a much-reported incident a few years later when she went with a riding crop to the office of Baburao Patel, the editor of *filmindia*, to whip him for his negative reviews of her films.[3]

The opposition between political resistance and female modesty, divided between speaking voice and singing voice, between rage and song, finds its resolution in one of the most famous of Apte's song sequences in *Kunku,* in which she sings "A Psalm of Life," a poem by Henry Wadsworth Longfellow. This song sequence may be considered a parallel to the rage sequence with her adult stepson as the song is sung at the request of her adult stepdaughter, who is a highly respected social worker whom Neeru idolizes. Apte's rendition of this English song in a Western vocal style provides a comparable resonance to the devotional songs she sang earlier for the young girl. Although she once again sings in a private domestic space with another woman as her sole auditor, this song is marked by an ardor of expression that enables a reinterpretation of the song in light of Neeru's personal predicament. Framed mostly in medium shots in long static takes as she sits on her bed facing the gramophone that has accompanied almost all her songs in this film, this song sequence further mirrors her ardor through shots of her stepdaughter as she listens to her. In this, as in other song sequences, in addition to Apte's restrained bodily movements, the film effaces corporeal associations of the voice through various other devices, such as frequent cutaways in editing so as to create a disembodied voice, placing the song performance in private and quotidian spaces such as the kitchen and bedroom, and transferring the camera's gaze onto diegetic *listeners,* who are always female. In this sequence, during an instrumental segment played on the gramophone, a dramatic cutaway takes the camera to various pictures on her walls, moving upward from portraits of her deceased parents to pan across three framed pictures of gods. Apte's voice resumes as the camera pans over these images of deities, to sing "Lives of great men all remind us / We can make our lives sublime." Over the course of the song, the contrast of these words with her actual life circumstances produces a change from simple ardor to tears as both Neeru and her stepdaughter begin to weep. The images of deities serve, alongside her mode of performance, as a kind of inoculation against her clear rebellion against domesticity. She may be expressing outrageous levels of resistance to domesticity, but that doesn't mean she isn't also a pious woman. The scene ends with a conversation between the two women about Neeru's parents, who had raised her to want much more out of life than marriage but had died before they could protect her. The embrace of the two women at the end of this song sequence highlights the cruel irony that she is married to a man who allowed his own daughter freedoms that he denies the young woman he has married.

Kunku is unusual in its attempt to foreground its sound choices, primarily by refusing to include any nondiegetic instrumentation. This means that the film made the rare choice for its time of not including a background score, something that many early sound films relied on as a way to cover up sound recording mistakes or the ambient crackling of an unrecorded scene. In an even more noteworthy move, the film shows Apte's character, Neeru, the young bride in the film, taking a gramophone with her to her husband's home.[4] With one exception, in every song sequence, she always first places a record on the turntable and plays the gramophone, which provides her with instrumental accompaniment, and then sings. The film is keenly aware of the distinction between live and recorded music while also undermining such distinctions, as I will argue. In the sequence discussed earlier in which the young girl asks her to sing, as she heads to the gramophone the girl insists, "I don't want a recorded song. I want you to sing." This slyly refers to the fact that even as other studios were beginning to separate the function of singing voice and acting body through playback technology, in this film the actress is indeed singing her own songs.

In song sequences using the gramophone for instrumentation, it is always centered in the frame so that its presence cannot be ignored, and its sound cannot be thought of merely as "background" nondiegetic music. In one song sequence, most of the framings place Apte next to and facing the gramophone, while in another it is placed between the characters in the center of the frame. In an article titled "Media or Instruments?" Jonathan Sterne asks us to question the assumed hierarchy between "live performance and performance for reproduction" or performance in a recording studio. He questions the distinction between recording media and musical instruments, arguing that recording media need to be "played" the same way as musical instruments and technological instruments such as microphones and phonographs because "players," those who are recording or being recorded, need to know how to work around the limitations and affordances of each recording medium. To make the case for questioning this distinction, he points out that it "takes only a passing glance at contemporary musical practice for one to conclude that the boundary between musical instruments and media of transmission or reproduction has long been ruptured. . . . [T]his intermixture among recording, reproduction, and musical production goes all the way back in the history of sound recording. In fact, one can reasonably argue that it *predates* the successful invention of sound recording in 1877" (2007). In this context, Damle's description of microphone placement and its constraints on bodily movement can be reread as the microphone itself functioning as an instrument of musical performance.

We can draw on this expanded notion of what it means to play an instrument to consider the range of instrumentation in the film, which would include the gramophone, kitchen pots, clocks, birdcalls, and other sources of sound that accompany the human voice or gesture and function as repetitive, rhythmic Foley sounds in lieu of a score. The spectrum of noise to music in the arena of instrumentation is deliberately and remarkably fluid in the film, forcing a consideration of instrumentation in both technological and musical senses of the term. *Kunku* quite literally demonstrates for us how to play the gramophone like an instrument, even as it makes its distinction between live and recorded music. This is a reference not only to the fact that records played on the gramophone provide the instrumentation for Neeru's songs but also that the machine itself occupies the center of the frame, right next to the singer, and has to be played by her before she can start singing, thus blurring the distinction between technological and musical instrument. The gramophone is a technological instrument like a microphone or camera, but it is also a musical instrument like a *shehnai* or sitar. Sterne insists that we should consider "the intermingled history of media and instruments" because that "conjoined history exists in the human ear itself" (2007). In the context of *Kunku*'s choices regarding the gramophone, we hear in our ears the diegetically live voice and the diegetically recorded instrumentation in one seamless mode, with the singer essentially playing an instrument and singing to its accompaniment.

Because the film deliberately has no background score, the entire range of Foley sounds in the film serve as instruments. When associated with Apte's character, the sounds of birdcalls, conch shells, clinking pots, cows mooing, cats meowing and caterwauling, bells, coins, and sticks create a feminized sonic spectrum. In turn, the husband also has his sonic spectrum, including train whistles, bus horns, his walking stick, and the clock's ticking. In Apte's rage sequences, she bangs on doors, kicks beds, and throws things around in ways that render her body into an instrument of noise. In the film's only song sequence in which she herself doesn't sing, she becomes the source of instrumentation as she uses kitchen pots and utensils as percussive instruments to accompany the young girl who sings in this sequence unaccompanied by anything else. The gramophone, with its lid shut, is notably framed in the center of even this scene. Across the range of instrumentation, the only scene that uses actual musical instruments is one that makes their function more symbolic than real. Early in the film, we see wedding musicians tune their instruments. As soon as they start playing, a cut shows the first of many repeated scenes in which Neeru hesitantly and reluctantly applies vermillion (the *kunku* of the title) to her forehead, producing a disjunction between wedding music and a bad marriage.

Several scenes in the film suggest that the world itself provides instrumentation to accompany human gestures and voice.[5] One striking example is a scene in which Neeru's uncle visits her in her husband's house. As he arrives at the house, his speech is intercut with, and therefore accompanied by, a donkey braying. This dual-voiced human-animal speech by the uncle actualizes Neeru's act of defiant listening, rendering her uncle's words inaudible as a response to his treachery in essentially selling her into this marriage. This is a scene that recasts instrumentation as an act of audition by Neeru. In another scene, the world provides a bird, and in sync with its call Apte and the young girl raise their teacups to their lips. As its calls get louder and faster, they try to keep pace, eventually dissolving into laughter. Even the characters themselves notice the use of everyday noise as instrument. When the sister-in-law complains that the resistant bride argues about everything, the clock chimes in unison with her, and she says "even the clock agrees with me," which also does double duty in associating the clock with the husband and his side of the family.[6] In all of these cases in which the world, it seems, provides instrumental accompaniment to voice and gesture, what we also get is a visualization of the act of audition. For example, we see a choreographed rhythmic bodily movement as visualization of the act of listening to the bird as Apte and the girl raise and lower their cups in sync with the bird's call, their faces expressing laughter and joy, as well as the faraway look that comes from listening.

The film's intentions in foregrounding the source of every kind of musical sound, as well as its strong sense of its own newness in relation to older sound recording technologies, explains its central use of the gramophone as image and design in its opening credit sequence. It begins with a hand reaching out and putting a needle on a gramophone record. As the machine begins to turn, the record whirls out to the screen with the credit titles written on it. Every subsequent credit title emerges in a similar manner as a turning record that whirls up and faces the camera. Eventually, as the film itself begins, the gramophone turns out to be diegetic as a hand stops it, and we see its role in a children's theater show that is itself about an old man who wants to marry a woman young enough to be his daughter.[7] The centrality of the gramophone as both metaphor and material object is unmistakable. As metaphor it stands for the audiovisual technologies undergirding the cinema, and as material object it is a musical instrument that Apte plays, but it also performs for the camera in the same way as Apte, indirectly reminding us of the camera that has placed us in the position of spectators to a private performance that is ultimately the epitome of public performance. In its careful modulations of movement, voice, breath, instrumentation, and noise in rage and song sequences, the film walks a careful line that keeps in balance female resistance and modesty, private performance in a public medium, and domesticity alongside aspirations other than marriage for women. *Kunku*'s investment in the voice in both song and anger is enhanced by its unusual reliance on diegetic sources of instrumentation to accompany the voice, as well as its striking use of the gramophone record in song sequences. Instead of the usual practice of including background instrumentation to accompany the onscreen singing in song sequences, here we have what might seem to be a rather strange obsession with realism, so that the gramophone provides an explanation for the instrumental accompaniment to the songs. But it is more than that. Given how rare it was for films to show or include gramophones and other technologies of mechanical reproduction, including cameras, the decision to do so here suggests other ways to understand the gramophone. For one thing, the visibility of the technologically mediated source of the musical accompaniment helps corroborate the authenticity of Apte's own singing voice since the first experiment with playback singing had taken place in the previous year, 1935, in the film *Dhoop Chhaon* (Sun and Shade). But her use of the gramophone also models another way of using entertainment technologies, one that emulates and acts on the stimulus they provide. Thus, rather than using the gramophone as a passive listener or a source of comfort in her unhappiness, Apte's character uses it as an accompaniment to her own musical expression and, more importantly, in order to strengthen her relationships with other women in the film. There is the young girl who looks up to her and might someday emulate her resistance to social pressure, and there is her mentor, whom she looks up to and emulates in the private sphere of the home and the family. It is in the interests of this private sphere of domestic resistance that Apte used her voice both on- and offscreen and in both song and speech. The film's unusual use of the gramophone prepares viewers for the film's choice to render the world as an instrument, making no distinction between the human, machine, and natural worlds as sources of sonic accompaniment and expressive enrichment.

Notes

1. *Dhoop Chhaon* (Sun and Shade) made in Calcutta's New Theatres studio in 1935 is generally accepted as the first film to use playback technology, although all the songs were sung by the actors in the film.

2. Here I consider a singing actor a "singing star" if he or she was popular enough to also be able to release gramophone records. The *Encyclopaedia of Indian Cinema* (Rajadhyaksha and Willeman 1999), notes, "In *Amritmanthan* [1934], as the hero's sister Sumitra, [she] caused a box-office sensation with her songs, which became popular in the North (Amritsar and Lahore) leading to a distribution breakthrough for Prabhat. Although music director Keshavrao Bhole had doubted whether she could adapt to his light classical style . . . her ability to counterpoint musical rhythm with gestural spontaneity proved a refreshing departure from the then prevalent ponderously stagey style" (44).

3. For further details, see Majumdar 2015.

4. According to Stephen Putnam Hughes (2002), "gramophone players got significantly less expensive by the end of the [1930s] decade. During 1928–1929 gramophone machines manufactured in Japan flooded the Indian market for the first time and effectively created a price war, which drastically lowered prices" (451–52).

5. Shankerrao Damle, the sound recordist for the film, said, "I had many challenges during 'live' mixing of effects while the shooting was in progress. The film *Kunku* for instance—there was no re-recording and yet the sound effects are there on the track" (Thakker 1980, 17).

6. P. K. Nair (2002) and others have discussed the allegorical relation between the old man and the intermittently functioning grandfather clock.

7. For more on the play they perform, which is also the source of this film's story, see Meera Kosambi.

Works Cited

Hammer, Andrea. 2007. "Audible Evidence: On Listening to Places." *Jump Cut*, no. 49 (Spring). https://www.ejumpcut.org/archive/jc49.2007/Hammer-Audio/text.html.

Hughes, Stephen P. 2002. "The 'Music Boom' in Tamil South India: Gramophone, Radio, and the Making of Mass Culture." *Historical Journal of Film, Radio, and Television* 22, no. 4: 445–73.

Kosambi, Meera. 2015. *Gender, Culture, and Performance: Marathi Theatre and Cinema before Independence*. London: Routledge.

LaBelle, Brandon. 2012. "Auditory Relations." In *The Sound Studies Reader*, edited by Jonathan Sterne, 468–74. New York: Routledge.

Ma, Jean. 2015. *Sounding the Modern Woman: The Songstress in Chinese Cinema*. Durham, NC: Duke University Press.

Majumdar, Neepa. 2009. *Wanted: Cultured Ladies Only! Female Stardom and Cinema in India, 1930s–1950s*. Champaign: University of Illinois Press.

Majumdar, Neepa. 2015. "Gossip, Labor, and Female Stardom in Pre-

Independence Indian Cinema: The Case of Shanta Apte." In *Doing Women's Film History: Reframing Cinemas, Past and Future,* edited by Christine Gledhill and Julia Knight, 181–92. Champaign: University of Illinois Press.

Nair, P. K. 2002. "A Closer Look at Director V. Shantaram's Prabhat Film *Kunku/ Duniya Na Mane (The Unexpected).*" *South Asian Cinema* 1, nos. 3–4: 19–35.

Rajadhyaksha, Ashish, and Paul Willeman, eds. 1999. *Encyclopaedia of Indian Cinema.* New rev. ed. Oxford: Oxford University Press.

Sterne, Jonathan. 2007. "Media or Instruments? Yes on Hybridization." *Offscreen* 11, nos. 8–9 (August–September). http://offscreen.com/view/sterne_instruments.

Thakkar, S. B. 1980. "The Challenge of Sound." *Cinema Vision India* 1, no. 2: 13–18.

TEN | Have Mandolin Will Travel

Musical and Affective Themes of DDLJ

JAYSON BEASTER-JONES

Few Hindi films exemplify the category "film musical" more concretely than *Dilwale Dulhania Le Jayenge* (*DDLJ*). Released in 1995 at the beginning of the Bollywoodization of Indian cinema for national and international audiences,[1] *DDLJ* richly integrates the melodies from the foregrounded film songs into the musical textures of the background score, thus reinforcing the affective and narrative themes of nostalgia, duty, and sacrifice. This chapter provides a close reading of these musical themes in *DDLJ* and their use in generating the emotional subtext in significant scenes of the film. I argue that through its musical-historical contiguity with early periods of Hindi cinema, *DDLJ*'s music composers provided a musical template that heavily influenced the genre of "family films" of the late 1990s and beyond. The chapter concludes with a discussion of the reuse of musical themes in a variety of filmic contexts and the relative stability of these themes as an index of *DDLJ* in later Hindi films. By focusing on the score of *DDLJ*, I highlight the ways in which music directors supply melodic themes in the films to covertly develop the film narrative. I suggest that melody carries additional associations of the film to extrafilmic contexts. These consistent aural codes in the film operate as a kind of aural "co-text,"[2] which the filmmaker and music director utilize to transform the subtexts of scenes within a film as narrative time passes. If the "sound bridge" enables potent modes of social and political encounter, as Punathambekar and Mohan suggest in chapter 1 of this volume, this chapter illustrates how the melodies in the film score are spatial and temporal bridges not only to earlier epochs of Indian cinema but to particular evocations of desire and nostalgia.

There are several reasons why I have chosen *DDLJ* for this close analysis. First, the year 1995 is a musical inflection point for Hindi films. It is the year after R. D. Burman's death in 1994 and near the end of Laxmikant-Pyarelal's and Kalyanji-Anandji's long careers as the dominant music directors of the 1970s and 1980s. Thus, this is a useful historical moment to consider a musical change in trajectory as musical production processes shifted away from what Gregory Booth (2008) has called "Old Bollywood," to the practices of "New Bollywood," which heralded the contemporary practices of Indian film song production. That said, following from the widespread discussion of Bollywood as a historical epoch and marketing category, I tend to think about this issue in a different way from Booth, insofar as I consider the practices-cum-marketing category of Bollywood as an era of Hindi cinema that came into being at about the same time as *DDLJ*, that is, the moment when Hindi cinema began to step up its global marketing campaign in earnest. Indeed, it has been argued that *DDLJ* was the first global hit of Bollywood in its contemporary incarnation (Chopra 2002), and it is a landmark film in Indian cinema, as the many twentieth-anniversary celebrations indicate. *Dilwale Dulhania Le Jayenge* is an exemplar of the "family film" genre, that is, films that emerged in the late 1980s that explore the roles and resilience of the Indian family, especially with regard to love, marriage, and women's sexuality. These films thus portray newly revamped norms and social expectations that are oriented both to India's urban and diasporic populations (see Dwyer 2000; Ganti 2013). I have found that these films are an important touchstone for my students and the basis for their expectations for how a Hindi film *should* look and sound, while the narratives bridge the (hetero)normative social values of the post-liberalization nation-state and diasporic self-fashioning.

Second, there are parallel mainstream Bombay film industries and logics that are operating concurrently in the present day that stem from some of the dynamics I discuss in this chapter.[3] One way to begin to address the question of parallel film practices is by way of sound and music aesthetics in film through a close reading (listening) of family films of the 1990s. This period of Hindi cinema features the decline of the large orchestra in films (i.e., Old Bollywood), though not necessarily the decline of the big orchestra sound. As such, I see the music directors A. R. Rahman and Jatin-Lalit as also evocative of parallel trends of music composition in and for Hindi cinema that emerged in the 1990s and continue in the present moment. In particular, one might understand Jatin-Lalit (along with Raamlaxman) to be one of the musical progenitors of the "family film sound." If we were to catalog the most important big budget family films of this era (table 1), we would see that Jatin-Lalit are largely responsible for this musical approach, a set of practices that continued into the 2000s by way of music directors such as Shankar-Ehsaan-Loy. In short, one might argue that Jatin-Lalit created a fusion of the R. D. Burman rhythm section and the Laxmikant-Pyarelal violin section that had—and still has—distinct musical and affective resonances in this period of Indian cinema.

Film Scores in Hindi Cinema

How does one approach the meanings of musical sounds when they are operating in multimedia contexts? Film scholars have noted that music cooperates as a part of a film narrative; it might reference dialogue or important moments of character development; it works in tandem with visual dimensions like lighting, camera movement, or choreography, which provoke afterimages of the sound; it might reveal a character's origins or social class; and so forth. Accordingly, it makes little sense to discuss the music—and sound and the meanings they generate—in isolation from its affiliated media, much less the social and historical contexts of its emergence.

Musical sound is, among other things, important for establishing and reproducing enduring social connections; manifold social practices are consistently intertwined with musical practices in multimedia contexts. For instance, certain instruments retain their cultural associations even in contemporary contexts (e.g., certain Indian instruments, such as the *shehnai*, sarangi, and sitar are associated with weddings, melan-

Table 10.1: Landmark Family Films of the 1990s

Film	Year	Film Director	Music Director
Maine Pyar Kiya	1989	Sooraj Barjatya	Ramlaxman
Jo Jeeta Wohi Sikandar	1992	Mansoor Khan	Jatin-Lalit
Hum Aapke Hain Koun . . . !	1994	Sooraj Barajatya	Ramlaxman
Dilwale Dulhania Le Jayenge	1995	Aditya Chopra	Jatin-Lalit
Dil To Pagal Hai	1997	Yash Chopra	Uttam Singh
Kuch Kuch Hota Hai	1998	Karan Johar	Jatin-Lalit
Mohabbatein	2000	Aditya Chopra	Jatin-Lalit
Kabhi Khushi Kabhie Gham	2001	Karan Johar	Jatin-Lalit

choly, and Indian tradition respectively). Indeed, cultural associations among instrumental sounds, timbres, rhythmic styles, and so on have been strengthened, if not created, through their mediation in film and other media. This is certainly the case with the folk genre of bhangra, as the sound of the *dhol* and a particular drum pattern index not only bhangra as a musical genre but the entirety of the Punjab and its cultural and regional associations. Similarly, as I suggest later, some of these associations exist between the mandolin as an instrument and the "family film," in large part due to the importance of *DDLJ* in Indian film history.

Although I make this point in *Bollywood Sounds* (2015), it is worth reiterating the distinction between "film music" (*filmi saṅgīt*) and "film song" (*filmi gīt*) as categories of music in Indian cinema. While scholars and fans often treat these terms as synonymous categories of musical sound, people involved in the production of musical sound for film carefully distinguish between them. From a production perspective, "film music" is the typically nondiegetic background music—or the "film score"—that, among other things, helps to create the underlying affective, spatial, and geographic contexts of particular moments in a film, even as it frequently operates as a sound bridge in the classic film studies sense. While it is relatively common for some composers of background scores to use the human voice as a component of their scores, particularly in the era I describe in this chapter, the musical uses of the human voice only rarely have lyrics. On the other hand, "film song" in an Indian context denotes the music foregrounded in the film narrative that have conventional song forms (e.g., the *mukhda-antara* or the verse-chorus form), and they have lyrics performed by playback singers.[4] In the vast majority of cases, film songs are distributed by film and music companies as a way to promote a film. Like Hollywood films, orchestral scores have been present in Indian cinema since its earliest moments, yet, unlike Hollywood films, the scoring is not distributed separately on the film soundtrack.

There is almost no systematic writing on Indian film scores, principally because film scholars, critics, and fans have focused on films songs.[5] I would speculate that this elision is due to the visual spectacle of song sequences and because songs are the most visible products of the Indian music industry and deeply implicated in Indian social memory. Moreover, it quite rare for music from background scores to be distributed on film soundtracks on their own. However, music of the background score sometimes makes its way into the recorded soundtrack through covert inclusion in the musical interludes. At other times, instrumental and/or remixed versions of the key songs from a film are included on a soundtrack, but these versions are rarely mentioned by music scholars and reviewers, likely because they are perceived to be a kind of "filler" for soundtrack recordings that might not otherwise have enough original music to justify separate sale (see Morcom 2007). Although they have always been a fundamental component of the Indian cinematic experience (even in the silent film era), background scores receive minimal attention from audiences, and score composers themselves are marginalized within the filmmaking process. Indeed, score composers are frequently commissioned to write music for film cues without any direct consultation with the film director or music director (Tubby, Hindi film score composer, personal correspondence, July 2016). This issue has been particularly relevant in the era that followed the death of the music director Laxmikant, who was known for his score writing (Booth 2008). Even from the perspective of Filmfare Awards (India's analog to the Academy Awards), the category for Best Background Score was only created in 1998 and is considered among the technical categories rather than among the artistic categories, which provides further evidence of its marginal status within the filmmaking community. For this reason, music directors often decline to write the background scores of the films for which they have been commissioned to write songs. Instead, a different composer might be subcontracted to write the film score, and, while they might work closely with film director or editors on a project, they might have minimal interaction with the music director(s) beyond sharing the digital project files of certain songs.

In many films, melodies derived from songs are a subset of the material of the background score, and these themes and motifs are one way in which filmmakers index characters, situations, and affect in the narrative. As such, music directors and their assistants sometimes use melodies from the *mukhda (i.e., the primary repeated melody)* of songs as a repository for the background score. The release of the soundtrack in the months preceding the film's release often enables the film director and composer to gauge which melodies have the most traction for the film based on the information they receive from radio and television airplay. Composers are directed by film directors to make the popular melodies more overt in the film narrative, thus facilitating cross-promotion of the film and its soundtrack (Tubby, personal communication, 2016). That said, it is safe to say that these melodies are not always used well or consistently within films and the use of popular melodies in the background score certainly provides no guarantee of success for the film or the music.

Musical interludes of film songs are another melodic repository for the background score. Interludes are oriented to the song situation, and like a background score, they might emphasize some aspect of the visual-cinematic narrative and help establish place created by a picturization. Interlude melodies frequently reappear in the background score in meaningful ways, albeit in ways that are typically divorced from their song meanings. Thus, the music in the interludes might indicate the location where the film was shot or was purported to represent (e.g., a particular country or Indian region), some element of the social context of the song (e.g., a nightclub or religious observance), or other onscreen action (e.g., the aging of a character or a love or fight scene). Like the background scores, the sounds incorporated into many of these interludes often have a rhythmic intensity to them, with sharp musical hits or violin sweeps that work in tandem with the camera to emphasize action or movement. Many of the interludes and background scores bear the traces of the cinematic era in which they are composed. For example, the score of *Teesri Manzi* has a strong flavor of the style of Hollywood composer Henry Mancini, which foregrounded brass, Latin percussion, and a mediated rendition of the Brazilian bossa nova, even as films like *Sholay* and *Deewar* each incorporated incidental music that sounded like the scores of 1970s international films such the Western and gangster film genres. Interestingly, iconic indexes of Indian tradition continue to be represented by the sitar, sarangi, and santoor, especially when the narrative touches on institutions and rituals of the family. These classical instrumental utilizations are similarly present in *DDLJ* and within most family films of the 1990s and beyond.

Beyond the Indian context, I want to take this opportunity to connect my argument here with discussions of film music from the perspective of writers on the Hollywood film score. Film music scholar Kathryn Kalinak has succinctly summarized the manifold roles of music in film.

> The classical Hollywood film score revolved around a core set of functions: music to sustain unity by covering potential gaps in the narrative chain occasioned by editing (such as transitions between sequences and especially montages); music to emphasize narrative action through coordination of music and image, often through "mickey mousing," matching screen actions explicitly to the rhythms and shape of the music (so named because it was distinctively developed in Disney cartoons); music to control connotation by fleshing out mood and atmosphere, establishing time and geographic place,

> and delineating characters' subjectivity; music to accompany dialog, called *underscoring*, through the subordination of music to speech; and music to connect the audience to the filmic world through an appeal to emotion. Music was rendered unobtrusive by masking its entrances and exits, but it was none the less powerful because it was relegated to the perceptual background. (2010, 62)

It is safe to say that each of the uses of music she describes in the classical Hollywood film score have made their way into Indian film scores; indeed, there are plenty of examples of every one of these devices. Kalinak goes on to note the psychoanalytical approaches to film music (described in the work of Claudia Gorbman, Caryl Flinn, and Michel Chion) and the constitution of filmic utopias by way of film sound.

One kind of classification Kalinak presents that I would like to transcend, however, is the reduction of Indian film scores to the category of "bricolage scores." In discussing film musical practices distinct from the classical Hollywood film score in other parts of the world, Kalinak refers to bricolage scores as scoring practices that incorporate Hollywood and indigenous musics into their distinctive compositional practices and sounds. Indian cinema, she argues, is a prime case study for this label. While it is certainly accurate to describe cosmopolitan Hindi film-scoring practices as drawing from multiple musical traditions, this language presumes that Hollywood film practices are not themselves emerging out of the same aesthetic as bricolage scores. That is, to define the bricolage score as an Other to the classical Hollywood score as a practice that has a set of established conventions and is somehow the progenitor of cosmopolitan scores (rather than mediating musical sound itself) is disingenuous. Kalinak acknowledges that many cinematic traditions have developed their own set of long-standing conventions but overlooks the arbitrariness of musical signs in Hollywood, as though Hollywood composers were not themselves incorporating musical ideas, timbres, textures, and so on with diverse origins in precisely the same way that other cinematic traditions have been doing.[6] I prefer to think of these practices as a kind of mediation wherein every set of conventions is always already mediated by the musical resources/affordances of the time. That said, I am not trying to deny the hegemonic, if not cultural imperial, power of Hollywood film emerging from its global distribution networks and immense marketing apparatus. Certainly, Hollywood film scores have been a powerful influence on other cinematic traditions, those of India included. Composers I have interviewed have noted the ways in which Hollywood scores have influenced their own practices, often on the basis of the expectations of Hindi film directors and editors. Nevertheless, even if certain Hollywood conventions have been adopted by Indian composers, Indian film scores have always been mediated to attend to the expectations of local audiences. Accordingly, they have histories, logics, and discourses that need to be addressed in their own right.

The Music of *DDLJ*

For the reasons stated earlier in this chapter, Hindi film scores have not—and are still not—taken seriously as an object of attention, but they are nevertheless an indispensable component of the film for precisely the same reason of enabling plentitude and suspension of disbelief that Gorbman (1987), Chion (1994), and Vernallis (2013) describe in the context of the classic Hollywood film score. In Indian cinema, as much as any other cinematic tradition, one of the key differences between a "commercial film" and an "art film" is the presence of the background score, in addition to the amount of narrative time that is filled with music. To that extent, there is even differentiation within commercial cinema between heavyhanded uses of music to underscore all interactions (e.g., in a melodramatic mode) as compared to the relatively sparse use of music in contemporary upper-middlebrow Indian cinema (Dwyer 2016). In short, *DDLJ* falls well within this category of melodramatic background score.

In the sections of this chapter that follow, I turn to a close analysis of the film score of *DDLJ*. For readers who may not have seen this film, or perhaps need a refresher, *DDLJ* is about Simran (Kajol), a girl of Punjabi parents living in London who, after finishing college, is reminded of her engagement to the boy Kuleet Singh (Parmeeth Sethi) in her father's village back in the Punjab. She meets the rich but lazy hero, Raj (Shah Rukh Khan), while traveling in Europe. They fall in love. When Simran returns from her trip, her father (Amrish Puri) overhears Simran telling her mother (Farida Jalal) about the boy she has met. Her father gets angry and moves the family back to the Punjab to marry her off. Raj arrives in the Punjab a short time later and ingratiates himself with the families. However, Simran's father discovers that Raj is the boy she met in Europe. Her father is angry but eventually relents at the end of the film and allows their marriage. *Dilwale Dulhania Le Jayenge* is the consummate family film of the 1990s, insofar as it explores gender, sexuality, and family roles in contemporary India. It is also noteworthy that it represents Indian families living comfortably and "traditionally" abroad, as opposed to the earlier trope of "foreign-returned" Indians having been corrupted by the West.[7]

Along with the film *Hum Aapke Hain Koun . . . !*, *DDLJ* has been an exemplar of the sound of the family film of the 1990s. The title of the film borrows the name of a film song from the 1970s, which is referenced several times within the film, along with many other important intertextual elements. Like the melodies used in A. R. Rahman's score for the films *Bombay* and *Taal*, *DDLJ*'s background score is a fundamental component used for indexing characters' interior emotional states. Also, like Rahman's approach to scoring, Jatin-Lalit drew liberally from the palate of song melodies written for the film when composing the background score for *DDLJ*. As such, there is a deliberate and coherent use of melodies in the film as they relate to the themes of the film.

Beyond addressing the larger issues about film scoring in India, I have several goals in this analysis. First, I want to unveil the tight use of musical themes in developing narrative themes within *DDLJ* in ways that might be surprising to much of the audience for this film. There are few films that have as iconic a background score as does *DDLJ*, so much so that ten pitches sounded on a mandolin is a sufficient index of the film. Indeed, the mandolin melody operates as a concise musical metonym of the entire film that is transferrable to other films. As I argue later in this chapter, this mandolin melody invokes the specific memories of this film while also invoking the potential to operate as a sound bridge through its displacement through mediation. Beyond this mandolin theme, I point to the consistent use of musical themes within the film, which in the case of this particular film, are largely derived from song melodies. As a result, they are *baptized* (to borrow a term from linguistic anthropologist Michael Silverstein) into meaningful, relatively stable (indexical) relationships within the film narrative, often incorporating musical foreshadowing. What is largely overlooked by critics and fans is the way these themes are gradually deployed to accrete new sets of meanings within the film narrative. The remainder of this chapter provides analytic insights into four principle musical themes, each of which is derived from a song but nevertheless indexes a particular nostalgic mode within the background score of the film. For that reason, I have assigned each of them a three-letter acronym derived from each of their song titles (see table 2).

Like other family films of this period, *DDLJ*'s background score is very dense, and there is very little "empty" musical space in the narrative. I would speculate that part of the reason for this busy score is that Jatin-Lalit, like other composers, had a limited time to score the film, which may have led the duo to overuse music.[8] That said, insofar as common practice in Indian films is for the film director and editor to dictate the musical cues, it is more likely that the heaviness of the score owes its origin less to the wishes of the music director duo and more to the desires of the filmmaker. Some of this narrative space is filled by music that I do not discuss in much detail here, as it is fairly generic incidental music used as underscoring for dialogue and to provide emotional cues for scenes that are similar to those of other family films of this era. For example, there are a number of moments (e.g., when actor Amrish Puri's eyes are bulging in anger) in which a dramatic orchestral hit, sometimes with a violin tremolo leading to a string melody in a low register of the violin, is used to emphasize some point of dialogue, to underscore a festive moment, or as interstitial music that sutures two scenes together. Similarly, the composers frequently use the sound of a strummed acoustic guitar in moments when characters are faced with a decision. *Dilwale Dulhania Le Jayenge* features a notable amount of diegetic music in the form of Punjabi women's folk songs. Some of these songs, journalist Anupama Chopra notes (2002), were sung by Pamela Chopra, the mother of Aditya Chopra, *DDLJ*'s director. These songs accompany wedding preparation activities, as well as inflecting the marriage ceremonies later in the film. Other moments in the postintermission film sound like adaptations of grooves developed in the song "Ghar Aaja Pardesi" and evoke an otherwise (ephemeral) Punjabiness. This regionality is signaled in the instrumentation and orchestration of these sections, particularly harmonized flutes, which evoke the sound of the Punjabi *johri* flutes. Finally, there are noteworthy moments in which flute and sitar played in an Indian classical style make their way into the soundtrack, particularly in scenes that

Table 10.2: Background Score Melodies Drawn from Songs in *DDLJ* (in order of frequency)

Song	Acronym	Number of Uses in Score
"Tujhe Dekha To"	TDT	40
"Ho Gaya Hai Tujhko"	HGH	19
"Mere Khwabon Mein"	MKM	12
"Ghar Aaja Pardesi"	GAP	12
"Mehndi Laga Ke Rakhna"	MLK	0
"Zara Sa Jhoom Loon Main"	ZSJ	0
"Ruk Ja O Dil Deewane"	RJ	0

reflect the sentimentality of—and the nostalgia for—the Indian family and family life writ large.[9]

Dilwale Dulhania Le Jayenge is also noteworthy for the number of intertextual musical (and nonmusical) references in the film, including Simran singing the bhajan "Om Jai Jagdish"; Raj's song parody of "Ham tum ik kamre mein band ho" from *Bobby*; songs in the sing-along with Baldev's mother, including songs like "Ichik dana" from *Shree 420*; Raj's rendition of "Pyar Kiya to Darna Kya" from *Mughal-e-Azam*; Simran's rendition of "Kahin Pe Nigahen" from *C.I.D.*; Baldev's rendition of "Meri Zohra Jabeen" from *Waqt*; and, most prominently, "Le Jayenge Le Jayenge" from *Shor Machaye Shor*, which was the film's namesake and is sung by Raj in a couple of prominent moments in the narrative. *Dilwale Dulhania Le Jayenge* is neither the first nor the last Hindi film to use songs intertextually as a metacommentary on the narrative, and it is certainly an effective device here. Moreover, as I point out later, *DDLJ* uses these melodic indexes to other films in precisely the same way that *DDLJ*'s music itself has been deployed by other filmmakers in later films. It is probable that this musical intertextuality, and the pleasures of recognition, is one of the core reasons for the popularity of this film.[10]

All of this intertextual music noted, I focus the rest of this chapter on the melodies that were composed for the film as songs, had their own song sequences, and were reused as background melodies in the film. While these melodies have any number of ways in which they might be used and reused outside this film, the particular filmic co-text imbues these melodies with relatively stable meanings that provide an additional layer of meaning within and between narrative moments, while also providing opportunities for these melodies to be mobilized in other filmic contexts. To this extent, these melodies are operating as lightly developed leitmotifs in ways that might be seen as operatic.

There are seven songs on the film's soundtrack, yet only four of these song melodies appear in the background score; the other three are largely absent from the film beyond their foregrounded moments as song sequences. Each of these four themes is attached to particular people, places, and ideas in the film in ways that amplify the affective narrative. In each case, I argue, these melodies are an index of desire, even though the modalities of desire are different (nostalgic desire, romantic/erotic desire, etc.). I discuss these themes in order of appearance in the film.

I also provide transcriptions of the melodies I discuss below, albeit with several caveats. First, these are textual representations of aural phenomena, which highlights certain attributes of musical experience even as it conceals others. Western music notation has well-known limitations in representing the nuances of vocal melody, particularly in non-Western contexts. At most the reader should view these transcriptions as an interpretive schematic of the melodies. Second, I have provided lyrics of the songs along with melody transcriptions not because the lyrics appear in the background score but because the lyrics will have a phantasmagoric presence for many listeners and will inform the way they experience these scenes. Finally, I have chosen to represent the melodies without accompanying information (e.g., instrumentation, orchestration, rhythmic background, or chord changes) because the melodies remain consistent and identifiable across their uses, even as other elements of the background scores change.

The melody of the first song of the film, "Ghar Aaja Pardesi" (Come home, Wanderer, GAP), is used consistently as a theme in the film. Tied to the character Baldev (Simran's father), the song melody is an index of both the Punjab and the family's dislocation from the homeland. In short, GAP is the sound of Baldev's nostalgia for the Punjab, and it comes to dominate the second half of the film as he is able to regulate his daughter's desires and pressure her to marry Kuljit, the son of a childhood friend. Unusually for a song sequence in a Hindi film, each of the verses is threaded throughout the film as it operates as a way to suture together the elements of Baldev's Punjabi nostalgia. The recording is long, and the verses are spread throughout the film, from the opening scene [verses 1, 2] to the arrival in Punjab, as Simran is unable to conceal her sadness over her family's return [verse 3] (1:32:42), then during the Karwa Chaut scene [verse 4] (2:35:35) and the Simran-Raj "telepathy" scene [verse 5] (2:52:03). This has the effect of propagating the nostalgia to the entire film, infecting many of the most important moments within it (up to and including the hero himself).[11] The fact that it is sung by female singers and a female chorus (including Pamela Chopra as noted earlier), the song calling Baldev home is noteworthy, as it is literally the voice of the motherland, the soil of her body and her body of traditions. Significantly, this is the only song sequence in the film in which the actors do not lip-sync. It is also appears in the background as Baldev discovers a photograph of Raj and Simrin at the end of the film and as he realizes that his nostalgic dream of familial union with his childhood friend is in danger. Variations and underscoring derived from the GAP interlude appear frequently in the postinterval moment of the film as the families prepare for Simran and Kuljit's wedding. While not precisely background scoring, it nevertheless provides an opening for a

Fig. 1. Transcription of "Ghar Aaja Pardesi." (Musical Transcription by the author)

nostalgic montage that draws from the memories of Baldev (in the first and second verses) and Simran (in the fifth verse) of an ostensibly simpler time in their lives.

Simran's song "Mere kwaabon mein jo aayi" (The One I Dream About, MKM) is also performed near the beginning of the film as characters are established. A poem that is depicted as having been written in the heroine's diary, MKM is composed as an upbeat and cheerful song sequence at a moderate tempo of 117 bpm. The music, choreography, and picturization provide insights into Simran's character as an independent and nubile young woman, albeit within the constraints of a conservative conception of "Indian tradition" as conceptualized by the filmmaker and amplified by the massive popularity of the film in India and abroad. The song was sung by the venerable Lata Mangeshkar, who was sixty-six at the time of recording, and the disjuncture between Lata's singing voice and actress Kajol's speaking voice is quite pronounced for the song sequence

Fig. 2. Musical transcription of "Mere Khwabon Mein." (Transcription by the author)

in this particular context. After the initial song sequence, the melody returns at a number of key moments in the film as an index of Simran's romantic desires, particularly when these desires are being thwarted by her familial obligations. These scenes most often, and most poignantly, feature Simran's conversations with her mother.[12] Simran is asked to sacrifice her romantic desires to suit patriarchal social-structural norms, just like her mother before her, and the melody of MKM is an affective cocontributor to a number of emotionally moving moments in which the heroine's desire is being overruled by filial expectations. Later appearances of the MKM theme in the background score also use Lata's voice, albeit at a much slower tempo of 78 bpm. As a theme of melancholy and frustration, Lata's vocables (nonlexical syllables) are given expansive reverb and accompanied by a guitar slowly arpeggiating the chords. The reverb on the voice creates a sense of space but also a sense of distance, as though Simran is already experiencing this pain as a distant memory. And, because all the scenes using the MKM theme include Simran and her mother, there is an underlying possibility that the melody mediates the transfer of thwarted desire and pain from mother to daughter. In these cases, Lata's voice seems much more appropriate to the context.

It is worth taking a closer look at some of these narrative moments in which MKM is present. In the moment early in the film, for example, the letter arriving from the Punjab reminds the family of Simran's childhood betrothal to Baldev's friend (17:16 to 19:22). Simran rushes out of the room, but Baldev misinterprets her action as traditional *sharm* (modesty) that exemplifies his success in raising traditional Hindustani daughters in London. The subsequent scene depicts Simran ripping the MKM poem from her diary as she says, "I had forgotten that I don't even have the right to dream." The melancholy version of MKM is present in the background score. In a similar interaction between Simran and her mother midway through the film (1:37:27 to 1:41:29), Simran's mother acknowledges persistent gender inequality yet nevertheless pressures her daughter to accede to patriarchal norms. The MKM melody appears again as Simran suppresses her own desires to conform to the desires of her father as mediated by her mother. In a later scene, in which Simran's mother encourages Raj and Simran to elope (2:40:40 to 2:44:43), the melody appears again, but this time in a faster tempo and played on an electric piano. The brighter timbre of the electric piano here has the consequence of transforming much of the melancholy affect of the scene, releasing much of the tension. Yet in this case the use of this theme moves into a moment of classical sitar and flute, which amplifies the pathos of the scene and the consequences for the institution of the Indian family. Raj famously refuses to elope, and he assures Simran's mother that he will find a way to convince Baldev of the correctness of their action. Once again, Simrin's desire is being circumvented by a man in her life but with a palpable difference, which is present in the background score. In each case, the MKM theme is used consistently and deliberately, but also covertly, to heighten the import of these scenes in the film.

If the sound of MKM in the background score embodies Simrin's sacrifice, and perhaps the sacrifices of many women before her, then "Ho gaya hai tujhko to pyar sajna" (Darling, You Have Fallen in Love, HGH) signals the recognition that the characters have, perhaps unintentionally, fallen in love. Like other songs on this soundtrack, the melody is based on a minor scale that adjusts to the harmonic needs of the chord progression (i.e., the F-sharp in measures 4–6) and thus generates a certain amount of melodic tension. The song from which this melody is derived has its foregrounded moment just before the interval of the film and opens with a rubato (free rhythm) that transitions into a moderate walking tempo. As such, both the first part, "na jaane mere" (I don't know what happened to my heart) and the second part, "ho gaya hai" (you've fallen in love), of the *mukhda* are featured at different moments within the background score, and the underlying grooves have a number

Fig. 3. Musical transcription of "Ho Gaya Hai Tujhko." (Transcription by the author)

of variations that are used in the underscoring consistently in the preinterval portion of the film.

The song sequence is set in London as they part in King's Cross Station after Simran's invitation to Raj to come her wedding in the Punjab, an invitation that Raj initially refuses. In the sequence, each of them comes to understand that the European experience they have shared has blossomed into something much greater. The song sequence bridges memories of each other while on the trip, some memories that the audience experienced along with the characters and others that the audience did not. Interestingly, the variations on the melody for HGH appear at least ten times in the background score before the song sequences, which, like the melody of "Tujhe Dekha To" (see below), foreshadows the future love affair but also creates a certain nostalgia in the moment, as the characters later have flashbacks of their European experiences, many of which are also accompanied by the HGH melody. Like the GAP tune, Jatin-Lalit not only used the melody of the *mukhda* in the score but also prominently featured the melody of the first musical interlude and variations on the HGH groove in the underscoring of several scenes. Finally, because the melody is most explicitly tied to Raj and Simrin's coming into realization of their memories and mutual desire, melodies of "Tujhe

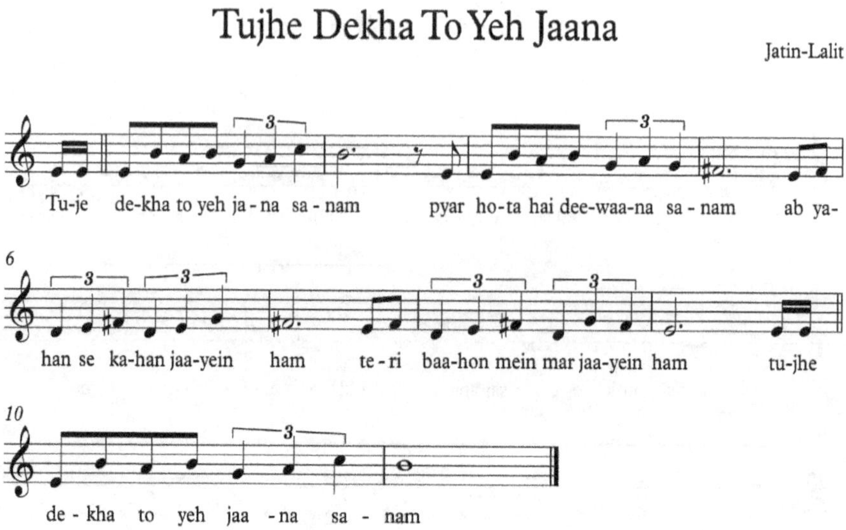

Fig. 4. Musical transcription of "Tujhe Dekha To Yeh Jaana." (Transcription by the author)

dekha" and HGH frequently appear together at the end of the film, one following the other.

By far the most important melody in the film is "Tujhe dekha to yeh jaana sanam" (I Saw You and I Knew It Was Love, Darling, TDT). It is not only the most repeated theme in the film, but it is the one most directly tied to Simrin and Raj's love affair, even as it is used as the dominant index of and for the film vis-à-vis the larger history of Indian filmmaking. This melody is used consistently throughout the film, appears in the opening credits, foreshadows the lovers' union, and eventually becomes the full-fledged song TDT when the Raj and Simrin are reunited in the iconic yellow mustard fields of a Punjabi village.

More than forty references to the *mukhda* of TDT are played by a variety of instruments in the film. The tune conforms to a melodic minor scale (or *asavari thaat*),[13] and, like many Hindi film songs, the *mukhda* stays within an octave. The melody seems to have been composed with a chord progression in mind, as the melody in bars 4–7 suggest. In the soundtrack, the melody sometimes appears without accompaniment, particularly when Raj is depicted as playing the instrument diegetically in the film or when Simran is remembering Raj playing the instrument as she confronts her impending wedding (see below). It is worth emphasizing that this is the only tune in the background score that has a diegetic presence in the film, and in several prominent moments Raj is depicted as playing or whistling it. However, very frequently the melody appears in preinterval portion of the film voiced by guitar or trumpet, with accompanying bongos, playing a common mediated samba (Latin American) rhythmic figure that had been used in Hindi films by R. D. Burman from the 1970s onward. After the interval, the theme most frequently appears with mandolin and dholak playing a North Indian folk rhythmic figure. The timbres of bongos and dholak, like the timbres of guitar and mandolin, are quite similar and sometimes stand in for each other. Yet the consistent transition from one set of instruments to the other as the location shifts from Europe to India is also a distinct, albeit subtle, shift in the narrative soundscape from the foreign to the familiar from the perspective of Indian audiences.

One of the things that makes *DDLJ* a bit unusual among Hindi films is the consistent physical presence of the mandolin in the film and various diegetic moments of the hero playing the instrument. In terms of its extramusical contexts, the mandolin has a long history in Hindi cinema. The instrument, along with other Middle Eastern lutes and zithers, was introduced to Hindi film orchestras by Jewish communities living in Bombay, namely, the musicians Faizulla Taghioff and Isaac-David Dandekar.[14] The music director, Naushad, is generally credited with introducing the sound of the instrument in the 1940s, but the mandolin is most strongly associated with the sound of classic Shankar-Jaikishan soundtracks for Raj Kapoor films of the 1950s (e.g., *Awara* and *Shree 420*). In essence, the mandolin is a bridge between the present and the past of filmic conventions, which makes it an ideal instrument with which to explore the norms of the Indian family of the 1990s. Why the mandolin and not another instrument? In a roundtable conversation between actors Shah Rukh Khan and Kajol sponsored by Bollywood Hungama celebrating one thousand weeks of *DDLJ*, Shah Rukh directly addressed this question. After confessing that he had confused the mandolin with the violin and did not even know the sound that the mandolin makes, Shah Rukh asked Aditya Chopra why he had chosen this ostensibly obscure instrument for the film. Chopra responded that it was his favorite instrument primarily because the sound of the mandolin was the mainstay of several classic Raj Kapoor soundtracks.[15] Beyond Chopra's explanation, one might add that the mandolin has a set of cultural associations that are distinct from those of the guitar, which in a *filmi* context is perceived as much more of a Western instrument with a more ambivalent set of associations despite the similar origins and histories of the two.[16] In the context of this family film, the image and sound of the mandolin have a different, more neutral set of associations, even as the sound of both guitar and mandolin are prominently featured in the background score. As such, the image and sound of the mandolin is indelibly associated with the actor Shah Rukh Khan in this film in ways that can be referenced in other films.

Within the narrative context of the film, TDT is strongly associated with the copresence of Raj and Simran on the screen. I will not discuss all forty-plus scenes in the film in which this melody appears, but the film and music directors used it for a number of purposes. This melody played by mandolin is the very first sound the audience hears as the title credits flash on the screen. In another important moment, the melody foreshadows the connection between the future lovers when Raj helps Simrin onto the train as they embark on their European tour (26:29). Several times in the film, Raj is depicted whistling the tune with instrument in hand (53:34) or he is playing the instrument as they journey through Europe (55:03). At other times, the sound of the mandolin is brought by the wind, defying the logic of space, boundary walls, railcar windows, and so on. (1:14:27). This aural trope, I would speculate, is drawn from Sanskrit and other poetic traditions, in particular the "messenger poems," like those inspired by Kalidasa's *Meghdut,* in which clouds, wind, and so forth are given instructions for delivering a message to a beloved from the one from whom he or she is physically separated. This messenger trope is also familiar in other family films of this period and include, among other things, pigeons in *Maine Pyar Kiya* and Tuffy the Dog in *Hum Aapke Hain Koun . . . !* In this case, it is the mischievous wind that blows the photograph of Raj and Simran to Baldev and otherwise reveals their love. The melody also operates as a mnemonic of Raj when Simrin is remembering him, as the sound of the melody intrudes on her immediate experience of the world, standing in for Raj as Simrin confronts her own desires in the context of her arranged marriage to Kuljit (1:42:31). After the intermission, the sound of the mandolin is delivered to the sleeping Simran by the wind as diegetic sound (1:44:15) and the melody becomes a full-blown (pun intended) film song (1:45:15). Finally, it operates as an index of their love in a moment of adversity and when that adversity is overcome. The final scene of the film (3:07:23) employs one of the most iconic musical themes in all of Hindi cinema, and the mandolin melody helps generate the poignancy of the moment. In essence, through a significant amount of repetition, this theme operates as an aural index of Raj and Simran that has become a portable and well-known aural reference with a relatively stable set of associations.

Concluding Thoughts

It is conceivable that a subset of people who have seen this film, upon later hearing these melodies on the soundtrack, might experience again a particular moment of the film narrative, thus fixing the cultural and filmic associations of these tunes in their minds. Indeed, some musical themes are so embedded in a particular cinematic context that their re-use seemingly automatically and involuntarily brings to mind particular associations (in a Proustian sense). Most listeners of a particular generation in the United States need only to hear John Williams's two pitches in low strings in a minor second interval to hear the theme to *Jaws* and to make the association with the film, regardless of the context in which it appears. Moreover, any approximation of these tones in particular contexts might provide a nonlexical (meta)commentary on, for example, some impending interactional event that interlocutors find humorous, foreboding, or otherwise dangerous. The powerful, screeching violins of Bernard Herrmann's score to *Psycho* are part of the cultural soundscape of American cinema that is indexed in many media and cultural contexts. So, too, the variations on Henry Mancini's *Pink Panther* theme, the variations of the *James Bond* and *Mission Impossible* themes, and many more. While the examples that I provide here are from Hollywood films, they have transnational significance, resonances that are so powerful that they transcend their respective films, thus operating as sound bridges of their own that are unmoored from their original contexts and deployed for creative effect. Consider, for example, the moment in *DDLJ* in which Raj ensnares Kuljit, pulls out a pistol, and shoots the rope holding Kuljit, even as he whistles Ennio Morricone's theme to *The Good, the Bad, and the Ugly*. I have never seen that film, nor do I imagine have most of *DDLJ*'s audience; nevertheless, we all got the message. By extension, the use of the TDT melody in the film *Chennai Express*, coupled with Shah Rukh Khan's presence on a departing train as he pulls the heroine onboard (10:43), carries a similar humorous payload that is only amplified with the delivery of his line "No, its ok. I've done this before."

Indian film directors and score composers desire precisely the same kinds of resonating cultural associations for the music of their films, although these musical-filmic resonances, like those I have described, most often emerge from song sequences rather than background scores. Yet, as I have illustrated here, the melodic material in the background score stands in for affective and ideological stances and is frequently repeated as a way of generating a covert musical narrative. I would suggest that these melodies are more than simply indexes; they are also operating at a lexical level (i.e., having a relatively fixed set of associations) within the field of Indian cinema. To that extent, I anticipate that this analysis will exemplify what uses of melodic materials one might encounter in many Hindi films.

In any multimedia analysis, there is no way to entirely account for the patterns of meaning that audiences bring and take with them in the experience of multimedia. Taken from a different theoretical perspective, the interconnections, histories, and affective relationships between an individual and any kind of text, or "stance" (Berger 2010), provide a ground out of which people make meaning in the world around them. It is worth asking how the moment by moment stances of a musician, a producer, or an audience member effect the way they interpret a sound in any given moment. Taken from a slightly different perspective, beyond their almost lexical uses, the sounds of melodramatic violin sections, fragments of melodies that index their *filmi*ness first and their particular films and rich sets of portable meanings second, are very much a component of the Indian soundscape. Film sounds penetrate this soundscape through public-facing speakers, in scraps of sound overheard in adjoining flats as one passes through neighborhoods, and so forth. These are *filmi* sounds that generate some of the many textures of the quotidian Indian experience.[17]

Finally, the film music scholar Caryl Flinn has pointed out that the Freudian "trace," or residue of memory in consuming a film or piece of music, is never fully digested; it remains with us to color our perceptions of other things we consume (1992, 104). As such, it interacts with memories on the level not only of the individual but of the language, art form, or other sign systems themselves. To this extent, the viscous quality of musical sound in film scores in general and Indian film scores in particular deserves a long, close listen.

Notes

1. See Dwyer 2000; Ganti 2012.
2. I am borrowing the term *co-text* from linguistics. Its typically used to refer to the surrounding text within an utterance. Here I would like to repurpose the term to refer to the musical themes in the context of all of the musical sound in a film.
3. For example, see Dwyer 2016.
4. See Smith (1998) for a discussion of the distinction between orchestral soundtrack and song-oriented soundtracks.

5. There are some exceptions to this dearth of discussion on film music. See Morcom (2007), Booth (2008), and Beaster-Jones (2015).

6. See also Gorbman (1987) on the modularity of certain musical tropes, such as the use of pentatonic melodies to create the sound of the savage Other.

7. See Uberoi (1997) for more discussion of this point.

8. Jatin-Lalit were given ten days to complete the score, according to Anupama Chopra (2002).

9. It is possible that these moments are meant to evoke a specific raga or rasa as a way to create another layer of emotional meaning for a scene. This will require more investigation in another context.

10. See also Peter Kvetko's discussion (2016) of the *antakshari* song sequence in *Maine Pyar Kiya.*

11. See Svetlana Boym's discussion (2002) of the notion of nostalgia as a pathological condition.

12. Patricia Uberoi (1997) has provided important details on the scenes that I describe here, although she does not discuss the role of the music in generating the affect of these scenes.

13. This melody is closest to Rag Asavari, which is associated with sacrifice and renunciation but does not strictly conform to the *arohi/avrohi* (rising/descending) patterns.

14. I am indebted to Naresh Fernandes for drawing my attention to this history.

15. For a video of this 2014 discussion on YouTube, see https://www.youtube.com/watch?v=18Ake3S49hM

16. See Sarrazin (2017) for a discussion of the cultural associations of the guitar in Hindi cinema.

17. I am borrowing this notion of aural texturing from Jo Tacchi (1998).

Works Cited

Beaster-Jones, Jayson. 2015. *Bollywood Sounds: The Cosmopolitan Mediations of Hindi Film Song.* Oxford: Oxford University Press.

Berger, Harris. 2010. *Stance: Ideas about Emotion, Style, and Meaning for the Study of Expressive Culture.* Middletown, CT: Wesleyan University Press.

Booth, Gregory. 2008. *Behind the Curtain: Making Music in Mumbai's Film Studios.* New York: Oxford University Press.

Boym, Svetlana. 2002. *The Future of Nostalgia.* New York: Basic Books.

Chion, Michel. 1994. *Audio-Vision: Sound on Screen.* New York: Columbia University Press.

Chopra, Anupama. 2002. *Dilwale Dulhania Le Jayenge: A Modern Classic.* London: BFI.

Dwyer, Rachel. 2000. *All You Want Is Money, All You Need Is Love: Sex and Romance in Modern India.* London: Cassell.

Dwyer, Rachel. 2016. "Mumbai Middlebrow: Ways of Thinking about the Middle Ground in Hindi Cinema." In *Middlebrow Cinema,* edited by Sally Faulkner, 65–82. New York: Routledge.

Flinn, Caryl. 1992. *Strains of Utopia: Gender, Nostalgia, and Hollywood Film Music.* Princeton, NJ: Princeton University Press.

Ganti, Tejaswini. 2012. *Producing Bollywood: Inside the Contemporary Hindi Film Industry.* Durham, NC: Duke University Press.

Ganti, Tejaswini. 2013. *Bollywood: A Guidebook to Popular Hindi Cinema.* 2nd ed. New York: Routledge.

Gorbman, Claudia. 1987. *Unheard Melodies: Narrative Film Music.* Bloomington: Indiana University Press.

Kalinak, Kathryn. 2010. *Film Music: A Very Short Introduction.* New York: Oxford University Press.

Kvetko, Peter. 2016. "Antakshari in Maine Pyar Kiya." In *Music in Contemporary Indian Film: Memory, Voice, Identity,* edited by Jayson Beaster-Jones and Natalie Sarrazin, 35–42. New York: Routledge.

Morcom, Anna. 2007. *Hindi Film Songs and the Cinema.* London: Ashgate.

Rajadhyaksha, Ashish. 2003. "The 'Bollywoodization' of the Indian Cinema: Cultural Nationalism in a Global Arena." *Inter-Asia Cultural Studies* 4, no. 1: 25–39.

Sarrazin, Natalie. 2017. "Magic, Destruction, and Redemption in the Soundtracks of *Aashiqui 2, RockStar,* and *Rock On!!*" In *Music in Contemporary Indian Film: Memory, Voice, Identity,* edited by Jayson Beaster-Jones and Natalie Sarrazin, 103–16. New York: Routledge.

Silverstein, Michael. 2003. "Indexical Order and the Dialectics of Sociolinguistic Life." *Language and Communication* 23, no. 3: 193–229.

Smith, Jeffrey. 1998. *The Sounds of Commerce: Marketing Popular Film Music.* New York: Columbia University Press.

Tagg, Philip, and Bob Clarida. 2003. *Ten Little Title Tunes: Towards a Musicology of the Mass Media.* Montreal, Mass Media Musicologists' Press.

Tacchi, Jo. 1998. "Radio Texture: Between Self and Others." In *Material Cultures: Why Some Things Matter,* edited by Daniel Miller, 25–45. Chicago: University of Chicago Press.

Terdiman, Richard. 1993. *Present Past: Modernity and the Memory Crisis.* Ithaca, NY: Cornell University Press.

Uberoi, Patricia. 1997. "The Diaspora Comes Home: Disciplining Desire in *DDLJ.*" *Contributions to Indian Sociology* 32, no. 2: 305–36.

Vernallis, Carol. 2013. *Unruly Media: YouTube, Music Video, and the New Digital Cinema.* New York: Oxford University Press.

Filmography

Awara. 1951. Directed by Raj Kapoor, music by Shankar-Jaikishan. R. K. Films.

Bobby. 1973. Directed by Raj Kapoor, music by Laxmikant-Pyarelal. R.K. Films,.

Chennai Express. 2010. Directed by Rohit Shetty, music by Vishal-Shekhar. Red Chillies Entertainment,.

C.I.D. 1956. Directed by Raj Khosla, music by O. P. Nayyar. Guru Dutt Films.

Deewar. 1975. Directed by Yash Chopra, music by R.D. Burman. Trimurti Films.

Dil To Pagal Hai. 1997. Directed by Yash Chopra, music by Uttam Singh. Yash Raj Films.

Dilwale Dulhania Le Jayenge. 1995. Directed by Aditya Chopra, music by Jatin-Lalit. Yashraj Films.

The Good, the Bad, and the Ugly. 1966. Directed by Sergio Leone, music by Ennio Morricone. Produzioni Europee Associati.

Hum Aapke Hain Koun . . . ! 1994. Directed by Sooraj R. Barjatya, music by Raam Laxman. Rajshri Productions.

Jaws. 1975. Directed by Steven Spielberg, music by John Williams. Universal Pictures.

Jo Jeeta Wohi Sikandar. 1992. Directed by Mansoor Khan, music by Jatin-Lalit. Nasir Hussain Films.

Kabhi Khushi Kabhie Gham. 2001. Directed by Karan Johar, music by Jatin-Lalit. Dharma Productions.

Kuch Kuch Hota Hai. 1998. Directed by Karan Johar, music by Jatin-Lalit, Dharma Productions,.

Maine Pyar Kiya. 1989. Directed by Sooraj R. Barjatya, music by Raam Laxman. Rajshri Productions.

Mohabbatein. 2000. Directed by Aditya Chopra, music by Jatin-Lalit. Yash Raj Films.

Mughal-e-Azam. 1960. Directed by K. Asif, music by Naushad Ali. Aarooyatmak Starlight International Corporation.

The Pink Panther. 1963. Directed by Blake Edwards, music by Henry Mancini. Mirisch G-E Productions.

Psycho. 1960. Directed by Alfred Hitchcock, music by Bernard Herrmann. Shamley Productions.

Sholay. 1975. Directed by Ramesh Sippy, music by R. D. Burman, Sippy Films.

Shor Machaye Shor. 1975. Directed by Ashok Roy. N. N. Sippy Productions.

Shree 420. 1955. Directed by Raj Kapoor, music by Shankar-Jaikishan. R. K. Films.

Teesri Manzil. 1966. Directed by Vijay Anand, music by R. D. Burman. Nasir Hussain Films.

Waqt. 1965. Directed by Yash Chopra, music by Ravi. B. R. Films.

ELEVEN | To Speak or Not to Speak

Publicity, Public Opinion, and Transition to Talkies (Calcutta, Bengal, 1931–35)

MADHUJA MUKHERJEE

This chapter addresses the dilemma and difficulties of the transition into sync sound technology in India (in Calcutta/Kolkata precisely) during early 1930s, alongside the rapid circulation of sound equipment across the Indian territories.[1] Deploying a close reading of the print material and some of the films that have survived the chapter shows how the eventual conversion to sync sound was connected to the political, cultural, and economic shifts and considers the concerns of the makers and the varied modes of application of sound technology despite a range of initial drawbacks. By evoking Rick Altman's proposition on "crisis historiography," the chapter considers a variety of advertisements of "talkie" machines and films and the debates published in contemporary journals and anthologies, as well as narratives of failed experiments, in an attempt to analyze the dramatic moment of the shift; the continuities, breaks, and overlaps; and the ways in which talking films became a norm in due course.

This chapter, hence, has two broad concerns. First, it specifically revisits the local innovation(s), for instance, the case of the Csystophone Sono-system, a local invention within the frame of nationalist fervour (discussed later), set against a backdrop of shifting industrial circumstances. With regard to this, it reexamines the moment of arrival of sync-sound in India by exploring the print publicity of new sound equipment and that of early talking films, published in Calcutta-based magazines such as *Filmland, Varieties Weekly, Chitrapanji* (Bengali), and so on, during the early 1930s. Moreover, it reconsiders the large body of articles and retraces the primary concerns of the producers and the public vis-à-vis the advent of sync sound, as well as the availability of a range of brands, along with a variety of talking films. Furthermore, with reference to the debates and discussions, the chapter tackles the writings of the American sound engineer, W. E. Deming Jr., published in *Varieties Weekly*, and examines the ways in which the uncertainties of the industry in relation to the coming of sound was transpiring, despite the massive and growing popularity of "All Talking, All Singing, All Dancing" films.[2] While research on the soundscapes of Indian cinema have—by and large—emphasized music and songs,[3] in the second part, the chapter focuses on the soundtrack and the application of sound in early talkies. It proposes that the eventual acceptance of the sound films—and certain prototypes—was made possible through a series of trialing, just as such narrative forms became an expressive tool. It particularly discusses the soundtrack and deployment of sound and music in films such as *Chandidas* (Debaki Bose, 1932) and *Devdas* (P. C. Barua, 1935) and rereads the varying characteristics and explorations of background score and effect sounds and thereby underlines the multiplanar movements of the period of transformation.

Contexts and Crisis

The "speed" of the transformation of Hollywood during the late 1920s, narratives of "invention," the wide acceptance of sync sound and the talkies have been studied with a certain degree of meticulousness. Douglas Gomery's seminal work, for instance, draws attention to the economics of this transformation vis-à-vis the studios (especially Warner Bros. and Fox). Other than debunking Donald Crafton's and others' propositions, Gomery insists in the introduction that it "was not chaos or disorder" (2005, xviii) but a rational transition occurring in the "market place" (2005,xix). Gomery's readings of cinema, radio, and vaudeville and their correlations became crucial for me in my earlier study on early practices and the "architecture of songs and music" in popular cinema. Crafton's analogy that the industry was like a "noisy bazaar" (1999, 6) nonetheless is a pointed argument, which becomes meaningful in the contexts of arrival of sound in India.[4] Crafton (8) suggests, "Metaphorically speaking, sound didn't arrive in town all at once like an express train. It came gradually "in little crates, over a period of more than ten years." Indeed, the scene in India was similar; furthermore, it was "complicated and messy," especially because, while the "invention" took place in the United States, the industrial setups in India scuttled to implement and innovate, and only partially succeeded, sometimes.[5]

Within this framework of the arrival of a "new" medium, Rick Altman's persuasive argument regarding "crisis historiography" is imperative. Altman's view that there are overlaps and conflicts as one mode of cinema evolves and merges into another, just as it obliterates and renews older media, has been influential.[6] In the Indian context, the case of Madans Theatres Ltd.'s (or Madans, Calcutta) may be described as exemplary. For example, as the Madans embarked on film production at the turn of the twentieth century following their successes in (Parsi) theater,[7] J. F. Madan, the proprietor, emerged as one of the pioneering figures of Indian cinema by building a forceful network of exhibition and distribution across British India.[8] The testimonies published in the *Indian Cinematograph Committee Report* (1927–28) also highlight Madans' monopolistic functioning and its influence over the market. Yet with the "coming of sound" Madans hurriedly attempted to restructure itself. Earlier, in the late 1920s, J. J. Madan, son of J. F. Madan, had traveled to New York and seen *The Jazz Singer* (Alan Crossland, 1927).[9] He apparently experienced the frenzy around the singing stars and, somewhat like the ambitious producer in *Singing in the Rain* (Gene Kelley and Stanley Donen, 1952), got an immediate indication of the changing production relations and up-and-coming genres. While the Madans continued to adapt nineteenth-century (Bengali) classics, they also swiftly imported RCA sound machines, constructed sound-compatible studios, and recorded certain scenes from popular theater.[10] Moreover, they conducted voice tests in their endeavor to reinvent themselves in the sound era and shot a few songs with the aid of American technicians.[11] And yet, while during 1932 Madans did good business, and the era of silent films and its popular stars continued until 1934, by 1933 its production had drastically declined to two per year, considering that new production companies had entered the scene via the new sonic channel, which ushered in unprecedented industrial and generic changes.

Rick Altman's *Silent Film Sound* (2007) hence becomes an effective methodological locus in this effort to read the intermittent history of "coming of sound" in India.[12] Confronting the subject of method, Altman enquires about "sound" films and "sound studies" and underscores the question of practice with regard to technological transformations. Thus, he proposes a "new historiography of American cinema" which may be "reconfigured through sound." Altman explains how silent film sound was neither homogeneous nor universally the same. More important, for my current project, are his deliberations on the records, which, by and large, remain "incomplete," "ambiguous," and sometimes misleading, and/or the perceptions of the concerned authorities. Altman's proposition of "crisis historiography," by means of which he addresses the "complex cultural signs," is central to such readings. According to him, "Crisis historiography assumes . . . that the definition of a representational technology is *both historically and sociological contingent*. . . . They also depend on the way users develop and understand them" (16). Besides, Altman is critical about the methods of history writing, which ignore contemporary concerns. It is in this setting of momentous debates on material and method that I raise a few pertinent questions with regard to the arrival of sync sound in India. Certainly, there wasn't any such "coming" of sound in India. Rather it "arrived" a little late and via a few detours.

While records of imports of equipment and actual investments, papers concerning the building of sound-compatible studios, and so on in India are virtually absent or remain illusive to date, one of the modes by means of which one may attempt to produce a narrative history of the times is through a close reading of the existing magazines—comprising advertisements for both equipment and films, as well as news, reports, articles, images, and cartoons—which lay out the gaping problem of the "advent of sound" in India. Consider, for instance, the "invention/innovation" of the Csystophone Sono-system by a Calcutta-based science graduate and its application in a 1932 film, as well, the excitement around its release.[13] Furthermore, the nationalist undercurrents provoking such "inventions" and applications may be emphasized considering that the Nobel Laureate and cultural figurehead Rabindranath Tagore and the maverick actor-director and politician Pramathesh Chandra Barua (P. C. Barua) were associated with the project and instrumental in its launch. One of Barua's projects—following his successful introduction of artificial lights with the film *Aparadhi* (Devaki Bose, 1931)—was a film curiously titled *Bengal 1983* (1932), which used the Csystophone Sono-system. Barua's first talkie venture and his experiments with the Csystophone Sono-system, however, were a miserable failure, and it left Barua virtually bankrupt.[14] The narratives and risks involved with such projects and projections, nevertheless, help us to make connections among nationalist concerns, political movements, and cultural strife in Bengal and India and with the industrial pursuits and technological expansions, which show that such vicissitudes are what Altman described as "*historically and sociological contingent.*"

One may reiterate James Lastra's (2000, 4) germinal and persuasive contestation.

> Regardless of its myriad other causes, the experience we describe as "modernity" . . . has been shaped decisively by the technological media. The cinema above all has come to stand for "modernity" itself, seeming to emblematize in the most compelling and even visceral way, the frequently violent shifts in social and cultural life, especially the newly possible (if not inevitable) forms of spatial, temporal, and sensual restructuring.

However, the manner in which the cinema/modernity dynamics and the "violent shifts in social and cultural life" were played out in disparate geopolitical contexts may be stressed. Furthermore, one may restate Miriam Hansen's (1999, 68) concerns by asking:

> How were the films programmed in the context of local film cultures, in particular conventions of exhibition and reception? . . . And how did American imports [of equipment, for example] figure within the public horizon of reception that might have included both indigenous products and films from other foreign countries?

Truly, the story of inauguration of Rupbani cinema, Calcutta, and the involvement of Tagore in the program, along with the (disastrous and delayed) screening of Barua's film during the occasion, is significant within such deliberations.[15] For instance, the inaugural brochure of Rupbani showcased Rabindranath Tagore as the "chief organizer." In a longish poem published in the brochure, Tagore celebrated the arrival of the "talkies" (and the "union" of *Rup*/Image and *Bani*/Voice) and wrote, "One hears *Akashvani* [voice from the skies] / . . . The disembodied image unites with disembodied speech / It floats on waves, across the yards of the body [of the film?]." Tagore, however, had argued contrarily in 1929. In a letter written to a friend, he enquired:[16]

> The main component of moving image is the scenic progression. The beauty and charm of scenic progression should be such that it is able to captivate the audience without speech. . . . The flow of music in songs reaches its greatness and words seem unnecessary. Similarly,

> why should the progression of scenes not be able to incite a *rasa* independently?

The arrival of the talkies thus seemed to have initiated a different register of aural and visual possibilities, which motivated erudite authors like Tagore and others to rethink their erstwhile recommendations. Truly, Rupbani's inauguration becomes a cue to many such paradoxes. On one hand, as mentioned earlier, the inaugural film was Barua's futuristic comedy *Bengal 1983* (1932), which utilized the up-to-date and locally manufactured sound equipment "Csystophone"—"invented" by the unusual science college scholar Bamapada Chatterjee. On the other, Tagore's active involvement with the theater, which was showcasing Bengali-language films for Bengali Bhadralok audiences (English-educated, urbane, Bengali middle classes and elites) indicate a broader nationalist paradigm.

As a matter of fact, the Csystophone Sono-system appears to have captured both the popular imagination and a certain sector of the market. An advertisement for Csystophone equipment published in 1932 urged exhibitors to "convert" their "Silent Cinema to a Permanent Talkie House" by retaining their existing projectors.[17] In fact, "Csystophone" sound systems could be attached to existing silent projectors and were installed across multiple cities of undivided Bengal. Advertised as "Made in India" products, the "Chatterjee-Sono-System" was distributed by Sarkar, Dutt, & Co., Calcutta. Moreover, following the initial failure of its recording system, a later newspaper advertisement (dated January 5, 1935) for the Csystophone Sono-system, published in a local newspaper, declared that it was capable of "crystal clear" recording and had executed such recordings during a "Science Congress."[18] Besides, yet another advertisement printed in the Bengali magazine fueled nationalist ardor.[19] It declared, "Don't use foreign equipment and spend on repair and eventually go bankrupt," further adding that if one deployed the "Made in India" Csystophone Sono-system he or she should be aware that it's far more "hardy," "skillful," and "durable" than foreign products. By 1937 the Csystophone Sono-system had been reinvented as the Csystophone "Talkie Machine" and was claiming to have renewed itself through up-to-date "scientific innovations" just as the company was accepting orders via the mail.[20]

Nonetheless, while Rupbani eventually replaced the Csystophone Sono-system with RCA machines following the misadventures during the show, *Filmland* was critical of such decisions and reported that Rupbani

13th August 1932. FILMLAND 23

success, speaking eloquently of the abilities of the producer.

Unlike the Madan productions in which either the story is a sorry mixture of romance and classicism, or the actors move about in a stiff and stagy manner and last of all the settings are only an altered view of the Corinthian stage, the Imperial Film has proved what can be done even from a most commonplace story by actions, photography and other technicalities. The characters of the play have shown a full realisation of the characteristic significance of the story, and have done justice to their roles.

Judged from an Indian stand point, this is what one can ordinarily expect. The sound technician who recorded the voices claims the unqualified praise of the audience. The photographer can also claim a place of honour—especially for the coloured picture of the marriage ceremony which has infused life into the film. I can not forget the scene of smoke going distinctly into the mouth of the king's daughter and afterwards inside the bottle. And the ghost inside it was a marvellous piece of photography. This is all that one can say about the brighter aspect of the picture.

The director would have done better if he had given a bit more care to the study of the Indian domestic etiquettes. For, all along his story he had betrayed a poor knowledge of it, and though there are minor points of criticism, in a good film like this, they should not be overlooked. When Susil came back to his sister's house with his wives and friend he was seen

Break Your Silence
INSTALL
CSYSTOPHONE
Made in India
SOUND FILM EQUIPMENT
BASED ON
CHATTERJEE-SONO-SYSTEM
Convert your Silent C nema to a Permanent Talkie House with your Existing Projectors
Best Material—Finest Service
Cheapest Price
For Particulars Write to—
SARKAR, DUTT & CO.
STEPHEN HOUSE Phone : Cal. 1919
5, DALHOUSIE SQUARE, CALCUTTA

Good News
TO ALL SHOWMEN
In India, Burma and Ceylon
LOOK OUT FOR
Sensational Talkies
RECORDED ON
RCA Photophone
To be Released by
The East India Film Company
2-1, Central Avenue South
CALCUTTA

FOR SALE
RCA
Portables &
Fixed Type
SOUND REPRODUCING
EQUIPMENTS
APPLY IMMEDIATE
FOR
Special Terms and
Particulars to
The East India Film Company
2-1, Central Avenue South
CALCUTTA

Fig. 1 "Made in India" Csystophone sound film equipment sold alongside RCA Photophone equipment. (*Filmland* 3, no. 122 [August 13, 1932]: 23)

was succumbing to the "whims" of "foreign distributors." Truly, there were many passages in the arrival of sync sound in India that traversed multiple failures and experimentations. Additionally, the case of the Csystophone Sono-system, despite its initial faulty functioning and its "quick-fix" solutions, may be read in the light of larger nationalist projects, considering that Barua himself was a member of the Congress Party and the Legislative Assembly (MLA), and since by then Tagore was a highly revered figure in political and cultural spheres. More important, subjects of technological and industrial augmentation were at the center of popular nationalist discourses, and thus one may argue that the arrival of sync sound activated such objectives.

In the context of nationalist imaginings and technological innovations, one may underline the complexity of the field by elaborating on how cinema was part of the larger production-consumption culture and the "Bazaar." By the mid-1930s, for instance, a range of consumer products, including soaps, teas, cosmetics, medicine, household items, and clothes, were circulating in the market along with newspapers, journals, novels, gramophone records, radio sets, and films.[21] Harminder Kaur (257) in an essay that connects the axes of small-scale industries and nationalist projects, analyzes in what ways the Bengali scientist Prafulla Chandra Ray

> saw the establishment of his Bengal Chemicals and Pharmaceutical Works [established in 1901] as his contribution to putting India on a global map. Manufacturing indigenous drugs as well as grooming products using modern scientific technology, Ray's plant was an effort to "restage the nation as a form of recovery."

Indeed, if Ray was a "scientist entrepreneur," so was Bamapada Chatterjee. Suvobrata Sarkar (2013, 460) in his article "Bengali Entrepreneurs and Western Technology," emphasizes:

> When we speak of Swadeshi [the nationalist movement], we generally think of the period which was directly linked with the [first] partition of Bengal (1905). In a broader sense, however, it embraces a larger period, started in the 1870s and continued till 1947. During that period, Swadeshi ideas of different strands took shape, handicraft industries showed signs of revival, modern industries were set up, and technical education was disseminated through the newly constructed technical institutions.

While I tackle the fervid debates, the types of sound equipment circulating in the market along with the films, and the ways in which several film journals and studio personnel strove to educate the technical work force later in this chapter, the "triad"— entrepreneurship, technological innovation and nationalism—may be delved into further.

Sarkar, for instance, also mentions the case of Hemendramohan Bose, popularly known as H. Bose, who manufactured perfumes, hair oil, fruit syrups, and hair wash products, during late nineteenth century. Bose was also a pioneering figure in the field of commercial voice recordings and launched a phonographic company in 1905. In 1906, when the nationalist momentum was at high tide, Bose released his first batch of phonographic—or cylinder—records. Labeled as H. Bose's Records, these comprised patriotic songs sung by Rabindranath Tagore and others. Moreover, with the advent of the disc record, Bose got into a partnership with Pathé, and released discs under the label of Pathé–H. Bose Records. While I have discussed elsewhere the intense connectivity among cinema, gramophone, and radio,[22] a point I wish to emphasize here is that Bose foreshadowed a crucial condition and was in fact the father of another significant figure in Indian cinema, Nitin Bose, the outstanding cinematographer and filmmaker who introduced the system of playback in India in 1934. In the absence of playback technology, Nitin Bose had "invented" a synchronizing gadget attachable to the editing system and thereafter was able to play back the songs and synchronize the same with the action and performance of the blind singer K. C. Dey during the shooting of *Dhoop Chhaon* (1934).

Nationalist influences, the zeal of innovation in the field of technology, and the tussle over local industrial products merged with the intensities produced by the arrival of sync sound and the sensorial experience of listening to sound and voices. To borrow from Lastra (2000, 4):

> The new modes of mass production, distribution, and consumption . . . institutional deployment and industrial exploitation of cinematic technology ramifies [or ramified] throughout the culture we call modern, shaping our experience of others, of history, of ourselves.

Likewise, if Hollywood's responses to new technology had been guided by the history of the nineteenth century, in the case of Indian film practice in Calcutta, it was far more decisive considering that a range of issues ignited and tackled during the nineteenth century was yet to be resolved.[23] Additionally, by 1930s, the independence movement was at its peak, and the involvement of a figure like Tagore with cinema—in addition to his pioneering role in literature, music, theater, and art, as well as his engagement with direct political action after 1905 and the founding of the Visva-Bharati school (now university)—must be stressed. Furthermore, during 1932 Tagore was credited as director and associated with the making of *Natir Puja*. Nevertheless, despite being publicized immensely through posters and handbills, and in spite of high expectations, when it was released in March 1932 *Natir Puja* was a commercial failure. *Filmland* reviewed it as an "amateurish production throughout."[24] Especially, its recording and photography were deemed the "worst," and it "was howled down everywhere it was shown." Clearly, during this transitory phase, even a stalwart like Tagore was both directly and obliquely connected to at least two failed projects. Thus, it is within such settings of many failed attempts, trial, errors, and some chance achievements, one proposes that one of the ways of doing "crisis historiography" is to explore the industrial conditions through an in-depth study of the articles published in "vernacular" languages (along with biographies, memoirs, letters, and so on) and consider the routes through which sound film—sometimes disrupted, sometimes like a reverberation—arrived in India.

Transition to Talkies

A range of advertisements for talkie films and novel equipment were regularly published in popular film magazines such as *Filmland* and *Variety Weekly*, which functioned both as trade journals and as popular fanzines. For example, a close reading of the advertisement for India's first "100 per cent" talking film, *Alam Ara* (A. Irani, 1931), illustrates the way the field was opening up because of multiple and varied components.[25] The advertisement, for instance, issued by the Dossani Film Corporation of Bombay (now Mumbai) mentions that it was the distributor of a number of Bombay-based productions across "Bengal, Bihar, Orissa, Assam and Burma" (the eastern territories of British India). Moreover, in the same advertisement the company announced the launch of the Imperial Film Company's "2nd 100 per cent TALKING, SINGING, DANCING" film—*Daulat-Ka-Nasha* (The Money). Another advertisement for *Daulat-Ka-Nasha,* which declared that the film was being released at Pearl Cinema, Calcutta, also indicated that it would "shortly" be followed by another talkie, namely, *Farebi* (Trapped).[26] Indeed, by 1931, the scene was exploding with manifold industrial forms and the arrival of a vast number of recording and exhibition equipment.

The October 1931 special issue of *Filmland* is a case in point.[27] The said issue contained a number of advertisements of a particular distributor, namely, the Mansata Film Hiring Service, Calcutta. Addressing primarily the exhibitors, the advertisements provide lists of films that were "Available for Ready Booking." Such lists include films produced predominantly by Bombay-based companies such as Ranjit Movietone and Sagar Talkies, which were widely held to employ remarkable stars, namely, Gohar, Madhuri, Sulochana, Zubeda, Pulti, and D. Billimoria. The lists also incorporate Bengal's productions, though, as is apparent in the number of advertisements in the issue—Masanta Film Hiring Service placed much emphasis on the Bombay stars, especially on "Glorious Gohar," who was one of the most popular actors of the period. Nevertheless, it must be noted that the catalog provided by the company was, as a matter of fact, that of silent films. In effect, the magazines of the period were teeming with multiple forces, and the simultaneous presence of both silent films and talkies was one of those. A full-page advertisement for the "ALL TALKING! SINGING!! DANCING!!!" film *Devi Devyani* (starring Gohar), for example, was placed opposite P. C. Barua's silent production *Aparadhi* (Debaki Bose, 1931), in which the influential filmmaker-actor introduced artificial light to the Indian scene.[28] In addition, the same October issue included an advertisement for the Indo American Film Distributing Company, which publicized (silent) films with "English, Bengali, Hindi and Urdu" intertitles.[29] Likewise, this was placed alongside an advertisement for the Victor Carreiro Photo Service (Hollywood, California, U.S.A), which offered "Autographed Photographs" of Hollywood stars for a certain price.

While the advertisers/distributors were targeting exhibitors due to the growing production of talking films they were also tackling the problems pertaining to the technicalities of sound films. An advertisement for Audio-Camex, for instance, addressing the producers, declared it a system that "speaks" and "not squeaks" (even though the issue included a range of full-page colored advertisements for silent Bengali films).[30] Moreover, advertisements for sound equipment became a common feature, particularly by 1932. An advertisement for Motiograph De Luxe, published in a special October issue of *Filmland* in 1932, was clearly summoning the producers.[31] It asserted that Motiograph De Luxe was "The Latest and Best Talkie Equipment Yet Invented" and aimed at reproducing the "Clearest Picture" and most "Faithful Sound." Operating from

Benaras/Varanasi, United Provinces (now Uttar Pradesh, North India), the distribution company, S. D. Sah and Company also promised to deliver "spare parts," a practice that in time became one of the key aspects of contemporary industrial conditions. More important, such advertisements (and articles discussed later) also show that, while the problem of projection was confronted first due to the quick availability of the talkies, the question of sync sound recording became pertinent soon after.

During 1932 the East India Film Company Sound Studio thus claimed to have set up a "New Up-to-Date Latest" sound studio in Calcutta.[32] It offered the "best arrangements" for sound recording since it had imported the RCA Photophone ("latest model") and Mitchell Sound Camera ("latest model" and the "costliest") along with the "Latest Laboratory Equipment" (an automatic developing machine). While recording and developing "sound" films speedily became fervent topics of discussion, the East India Film Company went on to produce quite a few celebrated Bengali films, just as, in time, RCA became one of the most accepted brands in India. The Simplex-Acme Sound Projector, which came along with RCA sound, was distributed by the Movie Camera Company, Bombay, and had branches in Calcutta, Delhi, and Bangalore (South India).[33] In effect, a well-organized distribution network, trained personnel, easily operable equipment, compatibility with older machines, and accessibility were some of the key factors of the eventual success of RCA machines in India.[34] However, the market for portable talkie equipment, like "Syncrofilm," distributed (for INR 3, 950 only) by the Chicago Telephone and Radio Company, Fort area, Bombay, brings to light the continued popularity of traveling shows across Bengal.[35]

The variability of the addresses provided in such advertisements speaks to the technical standards of sound films in Bengal, and in India, which was a matter of huge discomfort, even when a number of producers in Calcutta and Bombay were exploring the newest forms and embryonic business prospects just as such projects were becoming intricately linked to nationalist fervor. Thus, several articles (especially those on technology, technicalities, and techniques) suggested disparate methods of enhancement. The new technology of sync sound, its modus operandi, and its applications were indeed a concern of many of the articles published in the magazines. Consequently, an advertisement for Blue Seal Sound Devices declared, "Talkies are making roaring profits everywhere"; "Producing poor pictures spoils your name"; and "Produce worthy pictures with Blue Seal Sound Recorder and earn good money and good name."[36] It also added that Martin Johnson's *Congorilla* (1932) was

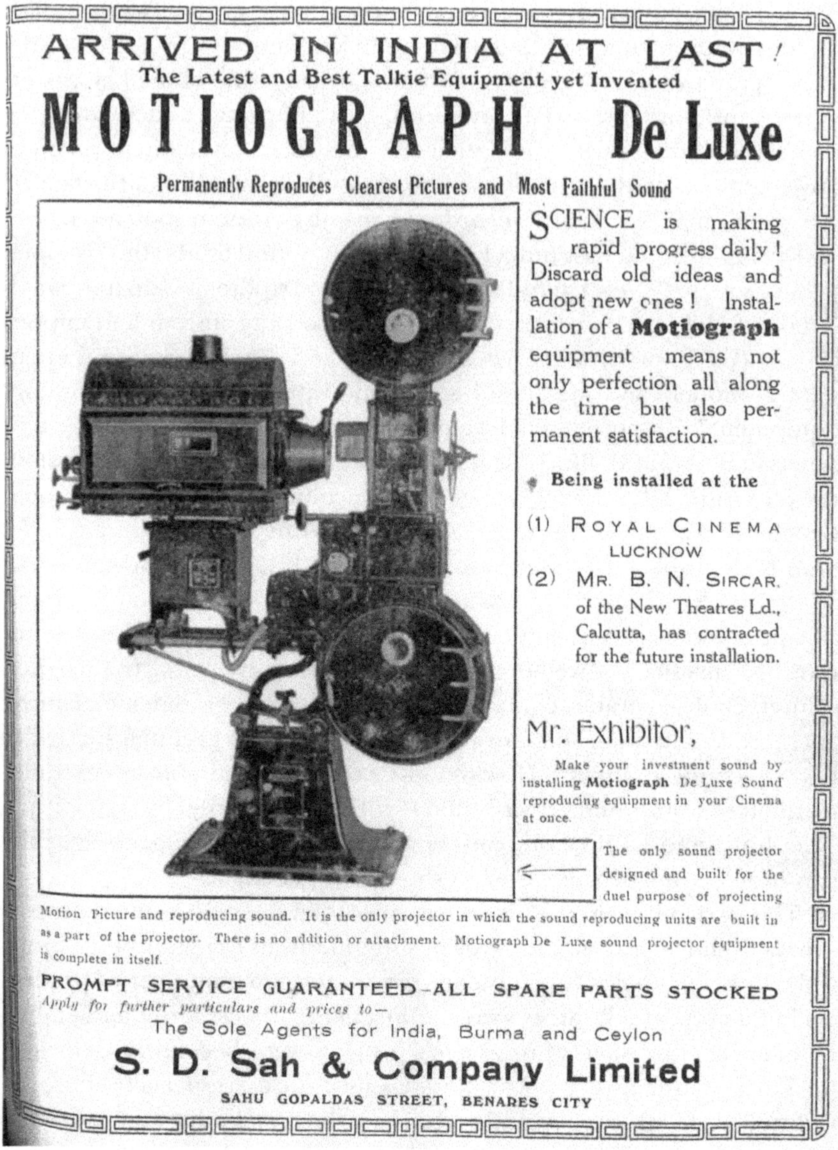

Fig. 2. Advertisement for the Motiograph recording and projection device, which was sold in India, Burma, and Ceylon. (*Filmland* 3, no. 127 [1932])

recorded using Blue Seal Sound Devices. The Chicago Telephone and Radio Company, Fort area, Bombay, was the agent for Blue Seal sound machines. The advertisement for "Rico" De Luxe promised to produce "Perfect Sound Pictures" and continued by stating, "TO COMPARE WITH FOREIGN PICTURES / IN SOUND TECHNIQUE / YOU MUST HAVE THE NEW / 'Rico' De Luxe" (capitals in original).[37] Rama Brothers, of Camp area, Karachi (now in Pakistan), were the distributors of "Rico" De Luxe.

An advertisement for the film *Jamuna Puliney*, produced by the East India Film Company, for instance, proclaimed that the film was being released at Rupbani, Calcutta, and was supported by the RCA sound system.[38] In point of fact, it became common for the talkies to highlight its sound recording system at the onset or specify it in the opening titles. Similarly, reviewers often mentioned the name of the sound-recording system and analyzed its merits. Furthermore, the uses of newly acquired machines were connected to the idea of the technical finesse of the film and the skill of the technicians. An advertisement for the film *Mirabai* (1932), for example, declared that Sagar's (of Bombay) list of "Super Talkies" involved "Clear Recording," "Scientific Singing," and "Good Photography"—in short, "Perfection."[39]An advertisement for *Grihalaxmi* (The Wife) announced that it was in the "Simplest Hindustani" language accompanied by "Mahatma Gandhi's Talkie Message."[40] An advertisement for *Pakdaman Raqasa* (Innocent Dancing Girls) announced that it involved "Well Known Singers," "Chaste and Simple Dialogues," and "Perfect and Clear Recording."[41]

Indeed, a Bengali magazine, *Chitrapanji*, printed an inventory of a hundred names—*satanaam*—of the new "deity," the "Beautiful Talkie" (*Sundari Talkie*).[42] The log, in alphabetical order, borrowed the names of various sound equipment products circulating across British India over the past couple of years. It included names such as Actorgraph, Audicine, Audima, Audio play, Audio picture, Cina sound, Cinelog, Cinemaphone, Dicodrama, Filmotalk, Phonofilm, Phonoplay, Photophone, Phonie, Pictalk, Movietalk, Motiotone, Movieplay, Oral films, Ora tone, Seephonie, Screen show, Sono film, Sound movies, Spekie, Talk art, Talkie, Vocam, View tone, View Voice, Vitaphone, Visatone, Vocal film, Zono tone, and so on. On one hand, this extensive list illustrates the wide variations in machinery and brands found in India, and, on the other, it shows the extraordinary leeway of the talkie. It also provokes us to study the way the word *talkie* came to represent a technology, a business proposition, and a mode of sociopolitical enunciation.

W. E. Deming Jr., whose writings I discuss below, was primarily a sales manager for RICO who had arrived in Calcutta via Bombay. In addition, he was assigned to produce newsreels, or "topicals," on India for the American market. By the early 1930s, however, Deming was regularly recording for a host of Bengali films, and his name featured in popular magazines (and in the reviews) along with P. Paul Juraschck, who worked for the RCA (Photophone) system and recorded the sound for films produced by Madans Theatres, Calcutta (India's pioneering production-distribution-exhibition company in the silent film era). The articles by Deming (published in *Varieties Weekly*) not only described, with certain amount of resentment, the pitiful working conditions in India (except at New Theatres, Calcutta, to which Deming was later attached) but also prescribed, with much enthusiasm, the possible remedies and appropriate methods of operating sound equipment and developing film. However, Deming was not alone since quite a few Bengali magazines also published articles on technical know-how. Nonetheless, a thorough reading of these writings demonstrates that there was a reciprocal connection between Deming's prescriptive articles (discussed below), attempts to educate technicians and the advertisements for sound equipment (like those of RICO) discussed so far.

Talking about films

I have discussed in length in my edited volume *Aural Films, Oral Cultures,* the ways in which articles published in *Filmland, Varieties Weekly,* and so on stressed upon and imagined Indian films, which would be—in the future—comparable to international productions. Indeed, the question of "fidelity," as emphasized by Lastra, was crucial within this framework.[43] For instance, an anonymous article published in the Bengali magazine *Chitralekha* (in 1930) suggested that the narrative techniques of literature, theater, and cinema are different.[44] The article ends with an invocation of sorts and insists that futurist films like *Metropolis* (Fritz Lang, 1926) should be produced in India since "All of us think of an *imagined nation* (*kalpanar rajya*)" and thus, "Why not write a scenario based on this imagination." The large pool of writings encompassed know-how in cinema, the problem of sync sound, uses of language in the talkies (Bengali/Hindi/Urdu/English), the (problematic) deployment of (classical) music in such films, the massive difficulties of operating the new equipment (recording, projection, etc.), the techniques of locally produced films, questions of cinema as art, comparisons between cinema and literature, etc. Debates on the advent of sound and the ways in which sync sound was becoming an integral part of film production were a pivotal aspect of such film discourses. More important, a number of these articles hint at the manner in which cinema was perceived as a project advancing Indian "modernity" and thereby defined *modernity* in terms of technology, technique, and industrial growth.[45] Furthermore, some of the articles contained comparative readings of Indian, American, and European films (e.g., articles by the influential journalist-writer-filmmaker K. A. Abbas on Soviet and German cinema). Clearly, cinema was envisioned as a medium onto which subjects of technology, industry, and cultural practice fused and also as a form that could be situated within a broader international framework, especially in an era of war and nationalism.

For instance, during early 1930s, the eminent Bengali author and reformer Naren Dev had written hundreds of short articles on the history, technology, and aesthetics of cinema. His large oeuvre was anthologized as *Chhaya ye Maya ye Bichitra Rahashya* (Manifold Mysteries of Shadow and Illusion) as early as 1934. His writings are divided into sections such as "Introduction" (which includes the history of the "firsts"), "Early History," "America and Europe in Film Business," "Scientific and Technical Aspects of Cinema," "Aesthetics of Cinema," "Visualization in Cinema," "Screenplay," "Narrative and Screenplay of Sound Films," "Studio," "Coloured Film," "Censor," "Shooting," Continuity," "Editing," and so on. In the essay "Arrival of Sound in Cinema," Dev presents a historical overview of the ways in which Leon Scott experimented with the Phonautograph in France in the nineteenth century. This was followed by T. A. Edison's Phonograph (in 1877), although his multiple attempts to produce the sound film failed eventually. Dev recounts the various experiments executed in England, Germany, Norway, and elsewhere and makes meaningful connections between the telephone, radio, and the making of the "sound" film. He also details how in 1926 the "Amazing" (*abak*) films became "Speaking" (*sabak*) films. He adds (1934, 62–63):[46]

> Gradually sound films have become extremely popular in America, Europe and everywhere. Sound waves have hit our [Indian] shores too, and talking films are being made in Bengali, Hindi, Tamil, Urdu! In our case, before Silent cinema could attain any maturity it started speaking at a vulnerable stage. Therefore, like an unfortunate twelve-year-old [underaged] mother it has not been successful. Sound films require skillful workers and engineers.[47]

The remainder of this chapter presents a detailed study of the technical aspects of producing sound films, including methods of recording, re-recording, and developing. Truly, even the popular journals of the period were teeming with critical writings regarding the technical quality and idiom of talking films, which sometimes included detailed notes on the processes of shooting and methods of developing a "sound" film.

I discussed earlier, through the case of Csystophone Sono-system, how the project of Bhadralok (modernity) became entwined with issues of technology in cinema and industrial growth. In point of fact, many of the articles in the popular magazines were anxious about the chastity of language (see the advertisements cited earlier) and the elaboration of music in talking films. Similarly, another article expressed concern over sound in films and emphasized,[48] "Charlie Chaplin who had total command over the world of cinema has been rejected from sound film." It is not unknown that this dilemma—to speak or not to speak—was evident in Chaplin's films and that he negotiated it in manifold ways, from the muffled voice of the boss in *Modern Times* (1936) to the gibberish song of the *City Lights* (1931). Nonetheless, the Little Tramp eventually delivered a speech in *The Great Dictator* (1940), which effectively became the last "Tramp" film. Clearly, despite telling shortages (elaborated later), many critics and filmmakers in India, and Bengal, shared a wider apprehension regarding the arrival of sync sound, the withering of a visual sensibility, and the growing popularity of talking films.[49] It was, however, not merely a matter of rejecting the unknown and the new, considering most of the articles published in English, Bengali, and other languages stressed the need to locate a suitable audiovisual language; rather it was about seeking methods by means of which sync sound could be recorded and projected appropriately.

There were in reality several writings like the above, which struggled over idea of talkies and their technical issues. As well, even the short reviews of films tackled the problem of the advent of sync sound. W. E. Deming Jr.'s imperious writings (even when his own work was criticized) thus add to the complications of the moment and help us gauge the working conditions in the studios. A close reading of his writings presents the densities of the industry, the ways in which it was still functioning within an artisanal mode, and the dire working conditions; moreover, these provoke us inquire about the need (Deming's personal zeal) to guide a large group of self-taught technicians. In his article "Recording Technique," for example, Deming explains at length the various modalities of recording and developing a sound film.[50] He discusses where and how to "place the microphone" in relation to the speakers and the camera. Moreover, with regard to the production of "illusion" (of realism) in cinema, Deming continues,

> Hollywood's first mistake, and one seemingly almost impossible to eliminate for years, consisted of forgetting the art of the "Motion Picture" and attempting to simply photograph stage plays. . . . This should be seriously avoided by the Indian Director.[51]

Such concerns regarding the uplifting of Indian artists and technicians were, in fact, not newfangled. The *Indian Cinematograph Committee Report* (1927–28), for example, had infamously expressed apprehensions about the budding industrial networks and had attempted to regulate the multifarious industrial settings.[52] However, Deming's qualms were more those of a paid technician, as the was the "White-Man's Burden." In an article titled "Hollywood Looks at India," Deming penned his opinion regarding "laboratory" conditions in India.[53] He observed that, while directors were " energetic and careful" and cinematography was "fairly modern," after the negatives were developed they were "full of flickers." In describing the state of "an average Indian studio laboratory" and the difficulties of developing a sound film, he writes:

> The developing solution is made up in a flat tank, and, temperature being of importance, an amount of ice is placed in the solution for cooling. In this tank the film is developed, in another similar one, washed and fixed . . .
>
> BUT, what of the ice? As it melts, additional ice is added. . . . And what is the result? . . . We begin to wonder where the fine quality and standard sound level have disappeared to.

The trouble with developing, or sheer disregard for technical standards, according to Deming, involved some of the basic hitches. In "Talking Picture in India," he describes how he had joined the Indian industry during the "fall of 1930" and been appalled by the working environment in Bombay, where conditions in the sound laboratory were inadequate. He expresses concern over the fact that a loss of one or two frames appeared "normal" due to the lack of technical hands and the mishandling of negatives. Thus it was difficult to produce "constant densities over any appreciable length." He asserts, with a certain amount of repugnance, that marks and scratches appeared on negatives as they passed from one rack to another through "driving drums." "Bubbles in the emulsion" were "caused by the racks of film being splashed about in the flat tanks." He added that he had witnessed "the waxing machine and an automatic splice" both lying "in dusty corner, covered by rust." In addition,[54]

> Slicing went on through the means of six or eight men squatting in the midst of a floor full of film. . . . The utter disregard of fire danger was surprising. . . . With the tongue the emulsion end was wet, then scraped with the scissor's blade, cement applied, and the splice held together until dry. . . .
>
> Calcutta [however] provided a complete surprise. . . . Here I was presented with the nucleus of what has become a real production unit [New Theatres Ltd.].

Besides a few obvious inferences, such as the fact that (1) Deming was only a sales agent turned sound engineer in a colonized country and therefore (2) his descriptions, including those of New Theatres, are of his personal experiences and opinions, although (3) the milieu in the industry was—by and large—quite abysmal and sound was handled by unskilled people, the questions I wish raise for the most part are not merely about the technical standards of the early talkies. Rather, I wish to explore the shift from "silent" to "sound" films (which was both a technical matter and an aesthetic one) and the artistic endeavors and creative drive that, *despite* the inadequacies and fragmentary growth of the industry, were supported by exceptionally well-trained musical talents (like R. C. Boral), inventive technicians (like the Bose brothers, who introduced the playback system to India), imaginative directors and artists (like P. C. Barua, who was an apprentice with French productions). Producers and filmmakers scavenged, re-created, and borrowed from multiple practices of performance and narration such as theater, the courtesan culture of Calcutta, popular gramophone music, and literature. The primary point of inquiry, therefore, is the emergent and popular forms that stemmed from such multiplaner contexts, following the somewhat interrupted travels of sound waves across territories.

Fig. 3. RCA recorder used by Sree Bharat Lakshmi Pictures, Kolkata

Discreet Soundtracks

I have discussed elsewhere the "architecture of songs and music" in Indian films and analyzed how popular cinema shared its boundaries with widely held forms like *Parsi* theater, as well as various types of urban and folk cultures. I demonstrate that by the mid-1930s and early 1940s a set structure (for musical composition and narrative for that matter) was already in place. The music composers and directors, therefore, often deployed staccato and pizzicato music for comic scenes and high-pitched, fast-paced violins and cellos to evoke fear; in a similar vein, joy and affection were often expressed through the sitar (a plucked string instrument) and via certain ragas, while surprise or grief would be emphasized by means a loud sound, such as rapidly struck piano chords or the sharp notes of a cello. More important, there were multiple variations of such patterns.

However, in the year in which Barua's *Bengal 1983* and Tagore's *Natir Puja* were released, there was *Chandidas* (Debaki Bose, 1932), which was upheld for its songs, music, and background score.[55] The film had a record run in theaters and remains a momentous interjection due to both its content and its formal explorations. Indeed, at the time *Chandidas* was released, it had no precedent in terms of narrative, visualization, and technical experiments, especially with regard to its sound recording and the creation of the background score. The film was celebrated by the popular press for what was described as lyrical blending, artistic evolution, and the psychological portrayal of life. Moreover, in an analysis of the musical score of the film, Kumar Sachindra Dev Barman (then a would-be eminent composer) wrote the following.[56]

> Most of the songs sung by Mr. K.C. Dey (as reproduced on the screen) were devoid of their natural grace and delicate touches. Particularly all the high notes were rendered unduly hoarse. . . .
>
> The opening song by Rami [the female protagonist], a well known Kirtan from *Padavali* [a devotional song] was spoilt due to improper recording. . . .
>
> The introduction of Sanai [an Indian oboe] in the temple was very appropriate and suitable for the atmosphere.
>
> The background music though ably conducted was not of any exceptional character. . . .

With *Chandidas,* Bose transported an entire range of popular sentiments into a cinematic text. *Chandidas* became a cult film, celebrated for its cinematic explorations and handling of social subjects of caste, romantic love, landownership, widow remarriage, and women's desires, which merged to produce situations of mass identification.

Within this framework, the exposition of the film is notable. As the film opens with a shot of a lotus, the camera pans to show Rami (the female protagonist, played by Uma Sashi), who is singing a devotional song and washing a sari. Rami sings "Alapo boyeshe piriti kori" (I have loved at a young age), looks intently at Chandidas (the male protagonist), and also poses in various ways apparently to incite him, just as she looks back into the camera and smiles now and then. Shot primarily in midshots and middle long shots, the takes are long and allow Rami to complete the musical composition, following which some closer shots are inserted. However, this structure is often altered at the point when emblematic close shots of Chandidas listening to her are added. Besides the evocative song, a few other sonic elements fill the screen. For instance, while a faint sound of the camera cranking is audible, the distinct sound of birds chirping creates the ambience. The sequence, however, doesn't add any other ambient and Foley sounds, such as the sounds of movement, rustling clothes, footsteps, and so on.[57]

At this juncture, as Kankanmala (Rami's friend and sister-in-law) enters the scene, there is an aural and visual shift. For example, as Kankanmala walks past Rami, approaches a pond, and fills her pitcher with water, the sound of water and the pitcher being filled become a discreet moment in the scene, which is otherwise focused around voice, music, and performance. Following this, Kankanmala voices typical social anxieties regarding Rami's flirtatious glances and fear of an unacceptable affair between a lower-caste widow and an upper-caste priest. Kankanmala inquires, "Do you know that, you are widow?" and "Do you know that, you are beautiful? And, young?" Rami's responses to these questions, addressing existing social prejudices, reduce Kankanmala's return to a comic gesture, and the genre music, in sync with her movement, adds to the situation. I contend that such uses of generic sounds and songs underscore larger concerns of the text and contexts. In reality, such juxtapositioning of a devotional song and a genre soundtrack, as well as the heightened uses of birds chirping and sound of the pitcher being filled with water in the absence of other ambient sounds suggest a complex cinematic imagination that evokes mythical narratives of the Radha-Krishna love story.

Likewise, in a later sequence, as mentioned in a review by Burman, Rami and Chandidas's relationship is reestablished within temple premises. In this scene, Rami, who sweeps the temple grounds, resolves to offer her prayers to the Devi (Goddess). However, her entry is restricted because of her caste position, and hence she demands an explanation. She argues with the king and high priest, saying, "No one can sanction [or take away] one's right to worship or offer prayers in a temple." This enrages the king, who assaults her in public and tosses away her offerings. Thereafter, as the king grasps her arm forcefully, she responds by crying, "Leave me . . . [for] my hand has been vilified [by your touch]." Deeply insulted and physically abused, Rami cries before Chandidas and tells him that he should throw her offerings into the river. Shot primarily through long shots, Devaki Bose creates an interesting montage of faces of the common people—of children, men, and women—who shed tears silently as Rami leaves, engulfed in her agony. The application of the sound of *shenai/sanai* (used primarily during marriages) in this scene "legitimizes" their transgressive relationship in the public domain.

By the mid-1930s, however, other tropes had emerged. P. C. Barua's magnum opus, *Devdas* (1935), which has had several remakes and continues to trigger a range of academic discussions, is significant in this regard.[58] *Devdas* has been read as a decisive text about a collective journey through and into "modernity" and praised for its aural and visual style. Consider, for instance, the elaborate explorations of *shenai* that seam disparate sequences. The scenes of Parvati's (the female protagonist's) marriage to an elderly widower and Devdas's larger than life suffering, followed by Parvati's entry into her in-laws' house, are connected and commented on in a remarkable and memorable way as music flows through multiple sequences and continues in the next sequence in which Devdas, the enigmatic protagonist of the film, is in Chandramukhi's (courtesan's) room and is haunted by Parvati's memory. While the musical composition is primarily used as a background score, it is reestablished as an ambient sound at the point where Devdas becomes intently cognizant of the sound and music of *shenai* (associated with marriage but repeatedly used to evoke separation and suffering) and hence shuts the window, thereby cutting the sound off abruptly. Such doubling of the background score and location sound illustrates the extent to which industrial practice and aesthetics had been transformed by 1935.

An analysis of other well-known sequences from the film illustrates how Barua was perceptive about the application of sound and camera movement. For instance, one of early the sequences, in which Parvati arrives at Devdas's room to propose a marriage alliance, the scene is practically devoid of background music except for the opening shots in which Parvati walks around through the shadows of the night. Cut to Devdas sleeping in his room, and Parvati enters. The musical composition (cello) continues until Parvati calls to Devdas and wakes him up. Barua's use of voices—especially that of the enigmatic performer K. L. Saigal—as a sonic category is remarkable in this setting.[59] Barring the Foley sounds of action, movement, and their conversations, the scene is thus curiously bare given its melodramatic intent. As the conversations continue, at the point where a rejected and dejected Parvati expresses her utter disappointment, the clock's ticking become audible, and thereafter it strikes two. Indeed, such controlled uses of sound were quite a deviation within an industrial context that was becoming heavily dependent on songs and music as narrative devices.

Similarly, toward the end of the film, at the point where Devdas, following several aimless and painful trips, is dying and begins to spit blood, the situation is intensified through intercutting. The sequence opens with Parvati (in her house) carrying a tray of flowers (for prayer), suddenly tumbling to the ground, and cut to Devdas (in a train) falling as well. The two shots (suggesting two disparate locations) are bridged via the sound of the speeding train. The heightened sound of the fast-moving train is both diegetic and evocative. Later, as Devdas realizes his end is approaching, he decides to visit Parvati, and the sound of the train engulfs the scene. In the next scene, as Devdas spits blood, he calls out to "Paru" (Parvati) in fear, with his hands held in a prayerlike gesture. Cut to Parvati standing next to a window, which opens with a gust of wind, and she cries out, "Kaun? [who?]." The sound of the strong wind, sharp and piercing, overlapping the sound of the train (while the camera tracks toward Parvati), creates one of the most memorable scenes of popular Indian cinema, one that has been re-created in several other adaptations of the plot.[60] While the scene continues with close-ups of Devdas looking into the darkness, the sound the speeding train lingers until a loud whistle marks the end of the scene, and the sound of train approaching a station suggests the beginning of the next sequence. Such thoughtful applications of sound, in fact, belie the concerns and failures that have been conferred so far. As a matter of fact, the varying nature of approaches and appropriation and reinvention of existing technologies and techniques shows how "crisis historiography" as a method fuels us to comprehend the alterations, disruptions, interconnections, and intersections.

Speaking Change

In conclusion, therefore, one may stress the fact that, while by the mid-1930s and early 1940s songs had emerged as a powerful and discreet category and the scene was beaming with extraordinary singers like K. L. Saigal and Kanan Bala, the popularity of the songs was escalated by the gramophone recording companies.[61] Indeed, by this time, the industrial situation had changed drastically due to formation of the big studios, an inflow of capital, the construction of spectacular theaters, and the emergence of trained, self-taught, and experienced technicians, actors, writers, musicians, and performers. Additionally, with the progress of Bengali-language cinema, several Bengal film magazines, like *Chitrapanji* and *Chitrabani*, not only became popular but published articles (and photographs) on both Bengali and Hollywood films and popular stars, along with thorough and "scientifically" oriented articles by Bengali technicians. For instance, in 1936 *Chitrapanji* published articles by the sound recordist Madhu Sil, who wrote specifically about the functions of the "cathode-ray oscillograph tube," which could be used in television, radio, and film sound recording.[62] In point of fact, the Bengali magazine *Chitrapanji* published several articles in English on technical subjects. The Puja or festival issue of *Chitrapanji* in 1936, for example, printed an article on the procedure for printing photographic plates in a tropical country. Nonetheless, caricature and cartoons continued to be published and drew attention to the problematic situation, which was being reorganized not only through technologically equipped and economically sound studios but also via the emergence of several local and phony (sound and other) studios, which continued to advertise a range of homegrown machineries. "Napta Sound Studio," of Barrackpore in the Calcutta suburbs, for example, described itself simply as "Bengali and Bengali's Own," without explaining any of it technical facilities.

By the 1940s, popular films not only quoted but also lampooned the films of the 1930s, especially the quality of "sound" recordings and their applications. A film like *Grihalakshmi* (1944–45), for example, recalls *Chandidas* through certain plot elements, uses of music, and performance styles, particularly the erstwhile nasal tone produced by the modes of recording and performance. While the plot recounts a popular story (that of a "good wife repossessing her husband"), a range of extradiegetic elements thickens the plot as its highlights contemporary production procedures and studio structures during the wartime period. Consider, for instance, the film-within-a-film scene in which the character Rami (of *Chandidas* fame) romances Romeo (of Shakespeare's *Romeo and Juliet*). As she and Romeo flirt with each other and plan to meet, Chandidas enters the scene. Rami promptly reminds him that his style of romance is "old-fashioned," and so she prefers Romeo. Thereafter a brawl takes place between Chandidas and Romeo, during which the actor playing Chandidas stumbles and the director shouts "Cut!" Following this, the director declares that they are wasting film "footage" this way and refers to the difficulty of rationing of acquiring film stock during the war.[63] The scene also showcases the types of equipment that were available during this period and therefore chronicles the industrial changes.[64] In time, Visatone and RCA became the two most acceptable pan-Indian sound recording systems. Thus, the films of the period not only underscored the equipment they used by way of citing it in the opening titles or through the narratives, but in the process they also produced a historical account of the "noise" of arrival of sound in India, which seems to be inscribed on the image itself. By and large, the state of affairs, so to speak, was as much cinematically charged as it was politically volatile and thus, to borrow a phrase from the political historian Sumit Sarkar, one may propose that "it was a historical magic hour" bursting with contradictions and possibilities. Briefly, while summing up, one may affirm that there were multiple comings and goings of sync sound in the Indian context and that the magazines of the period present a glimpse of this quilted history and inform us about the shifting terrain of sync sound technologies and the dissolving techniques of their application.

Notes

Acknowledgment: I thank Sree Bharat Lakshmi Pictures for allowing us to photograph their equipment.

1. The Indian territories at this point included present-day Pakistan, Sri Lanka, and Myanmar.

2. For a detailed reading of film and sound discourses during 1930s, see Mukherjee 2012b.

3. See Majumdar (2009),"Sound in Indian Cinema: Beyond the Song Sequence . . .".

4. See also Kaushik Bhaumik's PhD thesis (2001) on the formation of Bombay industry networks, the establishment of genres like "social," and his argument regarding "bazaar" cinema and the processes of its marginalization.

5. For a thorough study of the industry at this time, see Mukherjee 2019.

6. Note that Jacob Smith's (2011) proposition regarding the "continuing dynamics between continuity and change" becomes significant within this framework.

7. On Parsi theater, see Gupt 2005.

8. On Madans' massive distribution networks, see Govil and Hoyt 2014.

9. For further details, see Barnouw and Krishnaswamy 1980.

10. Note that it was a common practice in Calcutta to record scenes from theatrical performances and release them as "films."

11. See also Mukherjee 2008..

12. Also see Abel and Altman 2001.

13. Note that the story of "Csystophone" was found during the research conducted at the Media Lab, Department of Film Studies, Jadavpur University. I was the project coordinator of the Sound Cultures project. See also George 2011.

14. The writings in Bengali particularly emphasize on this point.

15. For a more elaborate study of Kolkata cinemas and Rupbani see Mukherjee 2017.

16. Mukherjee 2012b, 86.

17. *Filmland* 3, no. 122 (1932): 2

18. *Amrita Bazar Patrika,* January 5, 1935, 10.

19. *Deepali*, Saradiya Sankhya 1936, 132.
20. *Chitrapanji*, nos. 6–7 (1937).
21. See Deshpande 1993.
22. Mukherjee 2012a.
23. See Chatterjee 1993b.
24. Mukherjee 2012b, 121.
25. *Filmland* 2, no. 66 (1931): 15.
26. *Filmland* 2, no. 69 (1931): 15.
27. Puja issue of *Filmland* 2, no. 83 (1931): 14–15. Note that "Puja," meaning Durga Puja, marks a Hindu annual festival, which takes place around the month of October.
28. Ibid., 16–17.
29. Ibid., 22.
30. Ibid., 7.
31. Puja issue of *Filmland* 3, no. 127 (1932).
32. *Filmland* 3, no. 116 (1932): 12.
33. *Filmland* 4, no. 139 (1933): 22.
34. On RCA's functioning see Gomery 2005.
35. *Filmland* 4 , no. 154 (1933): 18.
36. *Filmland* 4, no. 139 (1933): 5.
37. *Filmland* 4, no. 162 (1933): 28.
38. *Varieties Weekly* 3, no. 16 (1933): back cover.
39. *The Cinema* 5, no. 8 (1932): 8.
40. *Filmland* 2, no. 66 (1931): 14.
41. *The Cinema* 5, no. 12 (1932): 6.
42. *Chitrapanji* 4, no. 1 (1934): 55.
43. See Lastra 2000, especially the chapter "Standards and Practice."
44. Mukherjee 2012b, 141.
45. To borrow from Miriam Bratu Hansen:

> [C]inema was not only part and symptom of modernity's experience and perception of crisis and upheaval; it was also, most importantly, the single most inclusive cultural horizon in which the traumatic effects of modernity were reflected, rejected or disavowed, transmuted or negotiated. (1999, 62, my emphasis)

See also Mukherjee (2009) and especially Lastra (2000).

46. Translation by the author.
47. This implicit reference to women's condition is directly connected to the nationalist discourses within which the enlightenment of women was pivotal. See Chatterjee 1993a, especially "The Nation and Its Women" and "Women and the Nation."
48. Mukherjee 2012b, 152.
49. On Chaplin, see Gomery 2005.
50. *Varieties Weekly* 1, no. 10 (1931): 14, 16.
51. Ibid., xx. On Hollywood's practices, see also Lastra 2000.
52. See also Dass 2009.

53. *Varieties Weekly* 1, no, 4 (1931): 6–8; *Varieties Weekly* 1, no. 5 (1931): 5–6.
54. *The Cinema,* June 1932, 20, 25–26.
55. For further elaboration see Mukherjee 2012c.
56. Quoted in Mukherjee 2012b, 195–96.
57. See Lastra 2000, especially the discussion in "Sound Space and Classical Narrative."
58. Also see Pooja Rangan 2007.
59. On Saigal's voice and performance, see Mukherjee 2007.
60. On the re-creation of Barua's last sequence in later adaptations, see Mukherjee 2011.
61. See also Gopal 2011.
62. *Chitrapanji,* year 6, no. 7 (1936): 386–88. The article continued in *Chitrapanji,* year 6, no. 11 (1936): 579–80.
63. For further elaboration, see Mukherjee 2009.
64. The production house Sree Bharat Lakshmi Pictures, for instance, had a locally manufactured crane that it used for shooting.

References

Abel, Richard, and Rick Altman. 2001. *The Sounds of Early Cinema.* Bloomington: Indiana University Press.

Altman, Rick. 2007. *Silent Film Sound.* New York: Columbia University Press.

Anon. *Indian Cinematograph Committee Report 1927–1928.* 1928. Calcutta: Government of India publication.

Barnouw, Eric, and S. Krishnaswamy. 1980. *Indian Film.* 2nd ed. New Delhi: Oxford University Press.

Bhaumik, Kaushik. 2001. "The Emergence of the Bombay Film Industry, 1913–1936." PhD thesis, University of Oxford.

Chatterjee, Partha. 1993a. *The Nation and Its Fragments, Colonial and Postcolonial Histories.* Princeton, NJ: Princeton University Press.

Chatterjee, Partha. 1993b. *Nationalist Thought and the Colonial World: A Derivative Discourse.* Minneapolis: University of Minnesota Press.

Crafton, Donald. 1999. *The Talkies: American Cinema veTransition to Sound, 1926–1931.* Berkeley/Los Angees/London: University of California Press.

Dass, Manishita. 2009. "The Crowd Outside the Lettered City: Imagining the Mass Audience in 1920s India." *Cinema Journal* 48, no. 4:77–98.

Deshpande, Satish. 1993. "Imagined Economies, Styles of Nation-Building in Twentieth-Century India." *Journal of Arts and Ideas,* nos. 25–26: 5–35.

George, Joppan. 2011. "The Many Passages of Sound: Indian Talkies in the 1930s." *Bioscope: South Asian Screen Studies* 2, no. 1: 83–98.

Gomery, Douglas. 2005. *The Coming of Sound: A History.* New York: Routledge.

Gopal, Sangita. 2011. *Conjugations: Marriage and Form in New Bollywood Cinema.* Chicago: University of Chicago Press.

Govil, Nitin, and E. Hoyt. 2014. "Thieves of Bombay: United Artists, Colonial Copyright, and Film Piracy in the 1920s." *BioScope: South Asian Screen Studies* 5, no. 1: 5–27.

Gupt, Somnath. 2005. *The Parsi Theatre: Its Origin and Development.* Translated and edited by Kathryn Hansen. Calcutta: Seagull Books.

Hansen, Miriam Bratu. 1999. "The Mass Production of the Senses: Classical Cinema as Vernacular Modernism." *Modernism/Modernity* 6, no. 2: 59–77.

Kaur, Harminder.2006. "Of Soaps and Scents: Corporeal Cleanliness in Urban Colonial India." In *Towards a History of Consumption in South Asia,* ed. Douglas E. Haynes, 246–67. New Delhi: Oxford University Press.

Lastra, James. 2000. *Sound Technology and the American Cinema.* New York: Columbia University Press.

Majumdar, Neepa. 2009. "Sound in Indian Cinema: Beyond the Song Sequence". In *Sound and Music in Film and Visual Media.* Edited by Graeme Harper, Ruth Doughty and Jochen Eisentraut, 303-24. New York: Continuum.

Mukherjee, Madhuja. 2007. "Early Indian Talkies: Voice, Performance, and Aura." *Journal of the Moving Image,* no. 6: 39–61.

Mukherjee, Madhuja. 2008. "The New Theatres Ltd.: 'The Cathedral of Culture' and the House of the Popular." PhD thesis, Jadavpur University.

Mukherjee, Madhuja. 2009. *New Theatres Ltd.: The Emblem of Art, the Picture of Success.* Pune: National Film Archive of India.

Mukherjee, Madhuja. 2011. "Remembering Devdas: Travels, Transformations, and the Persistence of Images, Bollywood-Style." *Topia: Canadian Journal of Cultural Studies* 26 (Fall): 69–84.

Mukherjee, Madhuja. 2012a. "The Architecture of Songs and Music: Soundmarks of Bollywood, a Popular Form and Its Emergent Texts." *Screen Sound Journal* 3: 9–34.

Mukherjee, Madhuja, ed. 2012b. *Aural Films, Oral Cultures: Essays on Cinema from the Early Sound Era.* Kolkata: Jadavpur University Press.

Mukherjee, Madhuja. 2012c. "Early Melodramatic Forms and the Subject of Bhakti: Gender, Sexuality, and Modes of Subversion." In *Religion and Popular Culture in the Indian Subcontinent,* edited by Gopa Gupta, Seema Kundu, and Shuchismita Mitra, 35–64. Kolkata: Bethune College.

Mukherjee, Madhuja. 2017. "Inside a Dark Hall: Space, Place, and Accounts of Some Single-Theatres in Kolkata." *South Asian History and Culture* 8, no. 2: 269–83.

Mukherjee, Madhuja. 2019. "When Was the 'Studio Era' in Bengal: Transition, Transformations, and Configurations during the 1930s." *Wide Screen* 8, no. 1. http://widescreenjournal.org//index.php/journal/article/view/128/165

Rangan, Pooja. 2007. "Transitions,Transactions: Bollywood As a Signifying Practice." *Sarai Reader* 7: 273–85.

Sarkar, Sumit. 1984. *Modern India, 1885–1947.* Delhi: Macmillan India.

Sarkar, Suvobrata. 2013. "Bengali Entrepreneurs and Western Technology in the Nineteenth Century: A Social Perspective." *Indian Journal of History of Science* 48, no. 3: 447–75.

Smith, Jacob. 2011. *Spoken Word: Postwar American Phonograph Cultures.* Berkeley: University of California Press.

TWELVE | "Listen My Heart"

Sound Art, Cinema, and the Possibilities of Surround Sound

ALEXIS BHAGAT AND LAUREN ROSATI

In 2006 we formed ((audience)), a New York–based nonprofit organization, to explore the multichannel sound environment of the cinema as a new presentation context for works by emerging and established sound artists, musicians, composers, and filmmakers. While the movie theater had not yet been explored as a venue for contemporary sound art, its origins as a site for listening date to the beginnings of cinema itself.[1] From late-nineteenth-century nickelodeons to early-twentieth-century movie palaces to the Dolby-equipped theaters of today, cinemas are more than a place to *watch* movies; they are exquisite places in which to *listen*. They have become the perfect concert halls for this century of electronic instrumentation and modular synthesis, digital sound recording, and telepresence.

((audience)) was conceived in response to an invitation from Khoj International Artists' Association in Delhi, India, to present a group show of sound art in that city. For acoustic reasons, it was decided that this exhibition would take place in a movie theater, as we explain. But the path to open up the cinema as a venue for sound art, for both artists and audiences, was marked by a series of obstacles—financial, technological, and institutional. It would take seven years for ((audience)) to present a program of sound art in India in a program we eventually titled *Listen My Heart* after a line from Rabindranath Tagore's poem *Stray Birds*.[2] While *Listen My Heart* succeeded at last in creating an opportunity for artists to present work in the cinema, a standard technical platform with a built-in audience, the challenge of presenting sound art in movie theaters, which ((audience)) continues to explore, highlights the numerous barriers erected by the cinema industry.

The term *sound art* was coined in 1983, but the forms it describes have a longer history, with roots that blossomed in fits and starts throughout the twentieth century in text-sound and sound poetry, in sound sculpture and *klangkunst*, in German experimental *neue hörspiel* (new radio plays), and in the public artworks of Max Neuhaus.[3] From the intermedia revolution of the 1960s to the new media revolution of the 1990s, these traditions developed as separate branches with distinct histories and concerns. When inexpensive digital recorders, made for recording sounds outside the studio, appeared on the market in the 1990s, thousands of enthusiastic phonographers set out into the world with an instrument much smaller and lighter than previous devices, capturing sounds free of tape hiss and the noise of the recording apparatus. During this explosion of new sonic material it became convenient to speak of any work that was not strictly musical in its concern as sound art.

We framed ((audience)) as a solution to four problems with sound art.

The Formal Problem. Sound art is an imprecise term that refers to a variety of creative practices focused on sound, hearing, and listening. It describes artworks that take a number of distinct forms and use sound as a material with which to engage with various concerns, such as acoustics, psychoacoustics, spatialization, sculpture, language, poetry, narrative, communication, and transmission. This ontological ambiguity and disciplinary porousness leads to . . .

The Institutional Problem. With the development in the early twenty-first century of curricula and degree programs in Music and Technology, Sound Art, Audio Art, and the like, some institutions have made progress in parsing the field. While organizations like Phonurgia Nova in France and Wave Farm in the United States have pushed forward models for supporting new sound and radio work, museums and art centers most often make forays into the intermedia of sound art through concert presentations.[4] The simplicity of this solution acts like a kind of gravitational force, pulling sound artists to the safe surface of a table at the head of a room full of people where they plug in their laptops and perform, as in a pianist's recital, whether or not that mode makes sense for their work or their concerns. This is related to . . .

The Technical Problem. Every work of sound art depends on a container in which to store or otherwise house a sonic artifact. This container could be a sculpture, a score, a computer, a recording medium, or an arrangement of microphones and filters, to name only several possibilities. Works also require a platform for transmission, such as an ensemble of machines and/or performers. With works that are directly acoustic—which either produce an "original sound" by striking or otherwise causing their container to resonate or work as an acoustic filter for the found sound of their site—the container doubles as platform. Typically, however, the platform exists as a playback setup—a public address system, a mixer-amp-speaker assemblage—that the artist can plug into. The need to plug a container into a platform presents the technical problem, which leads to . . .

The Situational Problem: One concert after another. Because institutions understand the concert format and because there is no standard acoustic platform for artists to "plug into," sound artists are often required to travel to an art center to set up a platform themselves and "perform" their works, interpreting and modulating the playback of their compositions while accounting for technical and acoustic variations in different sites. Artists who compose with recordings are thus asked to "perform" because it is impossible for someone to just "press play."

And yet, around the world, there exists an entire network of standardized auditoriums with built-in, multichannel sound. And they even serve popcorn.

Founded in 1997 as an annual workshop, and growing into a year-round residency center based in Delhi, Khoj has played a central role in the development of experimental and interdisciplinary art practices in India. In the mid-2000s, Khoj became focused on sound art, following a persistent interest in it among Khoj's artists-in-residence and an explosion of sound-themed art exhibitions in Europe and Asia around the turn of the millennium, including *Sound as Media* at the NTT InterCommunication

Center in Tokyo (2000), *Sonic Boom* at the Hayward Gallery in London (2000), *Sonic Process* at the Museu d'Art Contemporani de Barcelona and the Musée national d'art moderne in Paris (2002), and others. Wishing to provide a broad introduction to this art form to audiences in South Asia, Pooja Sood, the director of Khoj, invited Alexis Bhagat in 2006 to curate a sound art group show at the Apeejay Media Gallery in New Delhi, where Sood was also the curator at the time.

Apeejay is a two-thousand-square-foot modern gallery, described on its website as "an abstract glass box," designed primarily for projections and light-based works. Its open, transparent floor plan encourages focused, unobstructed *looking* at the art on view. But its sleek glass walls are extremely reverberant: far from ideal for engaged *listening*. Pooja and Alexis considered other spaces, including small visual arts galleries and the National Gallery of Modern Art, New Delhi, but the same architectural conditions existed everywhere: hard surfaces, glass, marble, concrete. Interior resonance seemed integral to the soundscape of India.

A few weeks later, at the movies, Alexis had a flash of realization: there was, in fact, a space in India that was acoustically dry and designed to play back recorded sound in high fidelity. And it was not a single, unique location but rather a network of ubiquitous theaters. Within the cinema, there were no open windows, no marble floors, no reverberant glass walls. Cinemas were the secular temples of modern India. And they were everywhere.

With the mandate from Khoj to produce a sound art group show at a movie theater in Delhi, ((audience)) was formed in New York as an organization devoted to exploring the cinema as a new presentation venue for sound art. By the fall of 2007, we had issued a call for multichannel works formatted to 5.1 surround sound and rented a Manhattan movie theater in which to listen to the pieces (which had been printed to DVD) and make final selections. There, in the theater's sweet spot, we experienced the first of many roadblocks: the DVD player did not connect to the cinema's surround system and thus could only play works in stereo. The lone connection to the surround amplifier was via the film projector, which decodes Dolby optical soundtracks imprinted on the margins of 35 mm filmstrips. This was our first exposure to the wall of proprietary technology separating the cinema system from the Wild West of "new media."

In 2007 the transition to digital cinema was not yet complete. Digital Cinema Initiatives, a creation of the seven major Hollywood studios that would standardize the distribution of digital cinema, was still finalizing its Digital Cinema Package (DCP) protocol. Digital cinema hardware had not yet replaced film projectors in most major theaters. To play sounds in a cinema, it seemed, we had to make a film.

At that time, there were two options for surround sound playback in a cinema: via a *box* or on a *film*. In both cases, the sound art works would be encoded as a Dolby soundtrack and then decoded in the movie theater. A "box" meant a tour kit containing a digital source, such as a computer or Blu-Ray player, connected to a Dolby DMA 8+ Digital Media Adapter, which could output decoded mono audio channels to a theater's sound system. A "film" meant 35 mm film stock with a black picture track and a Dolby Digital soundtrack imprinted on its edges. Enchanted by the physicality of the black screen film, we began to explore the latter option. We located a firm that would print the film for free as long as we purchased the film stock and a Dolby Digital license agreement, both of which were shockingly, prohibitively expensive. Proprietary technology struck again.

The former option proved to be more feasible for a possibly one-time-only screening of sound art, since playback through the DMA 8+ did not require Dolby licensing. We put together the box, made our final selections, and notified the artists. It was January 2008, and the show was planned for November of that year, just in time to hit a bigger roadblock: the global financial collapse that occurred later that year, which caused arts and culture funding in India to dry up. The exhibition was indefinitely postponed.

We managed to present the program in a scaled-down version in Syracuse, New York, in 2009 and continued to explore the cinema as a platform for sound art with screenings in New York at Lincoln Center (2011)—a "horror"-themed program that was part of the music festival Unsound New York—and at Tribeca Cinemas (2012), where we presented composer J. G. Thirlwell's surround-sound album *Dinoflagellate Blooms* (2011). At last, in 2012, funding came through for a show in conjunction with Khoj's fifteenth anniversary. Instead of an attempt to stage a sound art survey, as we had planned five years earlier, Pooja suggested that we present soundscapes of India from phonographers and composers. We issued a call for 5.1 surround sound or stereo sound art works that directly represented the unique soundscapes—urban, rural and media based—of the Indian subcontinent and established two submission themes: "Soundscapes" and "Bollywood in the Dark." Works in the "Soundscapes" category could have any subject or organizing conceit but had to incorporate field recordings from the Indian subcontinent

(India, Pakistan, Bangladesh, Nepal, Sri Lanka, etc.) as their source material. Works in the "Bollywood in the Dark" category were to be narrative sound films, reflections on Bollywood tropes and clichés, critical experiments with Bollywood musical content, or new musical compositions built from samples of popular films.

We received sixteen submissions from artists based in Canada, Chile, Denmark, Germany, India, Italy, Pakistan, the United Arab Emirates, the United Kingdom, and the United States, all in the "Soundscapes" category. Seven of these were selected (by Iain Armstrong, Budhaditya Chattopadhyay, diFfuSed beats, Michael Northam, the Raqs Media Collective, Ujjwal Utkarsh, and Hildegard Westerkamp) and formed the basis of *Listen My Heart.*

Since no artists responded to the "Bollywood in the Dark" theme, we decided to play one Bollywood film with exceptional sound design in a movie theater without the picture. (The idea for this grew out of a previous ((audience)) project, a 2009 Walter Murch radio retrospective for which we played the audio of *Apocalypse Now, The Conversation,* and other films by the eminent sound editor over the radio).[5] At first, we looked for films with unconventional synthesizer sounds in their soundtracks. There was a flowering of criticism at the time about the legacy of film score composer R. D. Burman and the influence of the Moog synthesizer in Bollywood. Alexander Keefe, a young critic and Khoj visiting scholar, had also recently presented new research on the Buchla synthesizer in India and interactions between Indian musicians and the American avant-garde.[6] We asked filmmakers in Mumbai and New York to suggest Indian films that used the Buchla, a nonkeyboard analog synthesizer known for its "otherworldy" sounds, in their soundtracks. While no one offered suggestions, artist-filmmaker Shaina Anand and others recommended instead Kamal Swaroop's *Om-Dar-b-Dar* (1988), a postmodernist film and cult favorite that had never been commercially released in India. After viewing the opening scene, which showed a wedding band rehearsing in the background, fading into a group of Rajasthani ladies with jangling jewelry, followed by a montage of historical scenes of Partition and the scripting of a natal chart, fading into a slow scene of a loving elderly father drawing a sheet over his children's feet while a *pungi* drones hypnotically, we were convinced. We reached out to Paddy, the sound designer of *Om-Dar-b-Dar,* who declared categorically, "before *Om-Dar-b-Dar,* there was no concept of sound design in Indian cinema. There was only music and dialogue."[7] The perfect film for "Bollywood in the Dark" had been found.[8]

The exhibition venue for *Listen My Heart,* DT Cinemas in the Select City Walk shopping mall, had six auditoriums. The surround and stereo submissions were spread across five theaters, and the sixth played a sound-only version of *Om-Dar-b-Dar.* Weird Bollywood, in the dark.

Listen My Heart is a collection of soundscapes that integrates two important trajectories of sound art: *acoustic ecology* and *cinema pour l'oreille* (cinema for the ear). The subject and compositional form of *acoustic ecology* comprise the "soundscape," a double term, like *landscape,* which means both the world of sound around us and a composition that represents that audible world.[9] Acoustic ecology emerged in Canada through the work of R. Murray Schafer and his collaborators at the World Soundscape Project. Both a scientific discipline and a foundation for new compositional practices, acoustic ecology studies the relationship between living beings and their environment as mediated through sound.

The idea of the soundscape emerged, perhaps, in 1930, when the German filmmaker Walter Ruttmann produced *Weekend,* a collage of recorded words, musical fragments, and ambient recordings that told the story of a weekend trip to the country. This "movie without images" produced a "narrative based on the mental images projected by the sounds alone"; it was, in other words, the first cinema for the ear.[10] The Soviet filmmaker Dziga Vertov followed the next year with *Enthusiasm,* the most ambitious field-recording work of its time. In the 1990s, *cinema pour l'oreille* emerged as a Francophone tradition rooted in the work of Pierre Schaeffer and the Groupe de recherches musicales, the pioneering tape compositions of Luc Ferrari, the acousmatic music of Francis Dhomont and Robert Normandeau, and the audio work of Michel Chion. Prioritizing multichannel audio diffusion and Schaeffer's concept of reduced listening, *cinema pour l'oreille* has (with the notable exception of Ferrari) avoided or rejected sonic representation. It explores sound as an object in itself independent of source and meaning.[11] As Brandon LaBelle has suggested in *Background Noise,* the soundscapes of Hildegard Westerkamp (whose work was included in *Listen My Heart*) bridge the "Schafer-Schaeffer Divide" between representation and abstraction, "harnessing the real while getting closer to its submerged sonority."[12]

Listen My Heart draws together these traditions of acoustic ecology and *cinema pour l'oreille* into a phonographic journey that begins high in the Himalayas, at the sacred shrine of Muktinath, with its one hundred springs of water.[13] From the Himalayan peaks, the water of the

Yamuna flows to the plains. Listeners can slowly follow the waters in Iain Armstrong's *Annapurna Pastoral—One Hundred Springs* (2012) or hop on a train in Ujjwal Utkarsh's *Yatra* (2012), jumping off at the Raqs Media Collective's *N Dl Jn (New Delhi Junction)* (2002). If they are stuck in Delhi traffic, Michael Northam's *AGGREGATES* (2012) will transform the noise. Budhaditya Chattopadhyay's *The Well-Tempered City: Book I* (2012) transports listeners to an abstracted city of sound, while Hildegard Westerkamp's *Into the Labyrinth* (2000, 2012) leads them through it. And diFfuSed beats's *Sonic City* (2011–12) folds the sounds of Delhi into the streets of Zurich over a rhythmic beat in search of the ur-sound of an ur-city without border guards or police. Finally, Kamal Swaroop invites listeners to experience the dreams of a boy named Om.

These were the seven works presented in 2013 by Khoj in Delhi. As part of Northwestern University's Sounds of South Asia symposium, from which this volume emerged, three of these works, by Iain Armstrong, Michael Northam, and Hildegard Westerkamp, were presented at the Block Museum in 2016 and another, the digitally restored version of *Om-Dar-b-Dar*, was screened at Annie May Swift Hall in 2017.

Iain Armstrong describes his *Annapurna Pastoral—One Hundred Springs* (2012) as a meditation on the soundscapes of Annapurna, a protected high peaks region of the Himalayas in central Nepal: "A loose narrative of a pilgrimage to Muktinath (also known as Chumig Gyatsa, the site of "One Hundred Springs"), the work aims to capture the peaceful, pastoral nature of these remote locations while referencing the deep-rooted spiritualism that the Himalayas inspire. Subverted references to the musical pastorale can be heard in the sound of the bansuri, sarangi, and the use of drones."[14]

The fifteen-minute recording begins and ends with a Tibetan singing bowl acting as a sort of transporter, or landing site, into a world of bells. The principal sound sources were recorded by the artist during a trek of the Annapurna circuit in Nepal in 2007 and include passing mule trains with bells; ambient sounds of birds, insects, and water; the Mani Wall prayer wheels in Chame, Manang; and the bells and springs of the Muktinath temple complex. Composed primarily with straight field recordings modified by delays, its rhythms are based on walking, in the measure of footsteps. It is a human-sized composition and an experience of telepresence.

According to Michael Northam, his composition *Mnemonic Debris: AGGREGATES* (2012) "attempts to demonstrate how abrasive urban sound can be transformed through attentive listening, accepting *what is there* in the noise of daily life as opposed to what we would like it to be. *AGGREGATES* plays with clusters of events and situations. This accumulation of sonic material opens up the opportunity to hear new relations and patterns of association."[15]

This eleven-minute recording reflects on ways in which memories produce mood, using sound spatialization to open up the metaphor of "piles of memories" into a three-dimensional space of overgrown, overloaded impressions. A noise composition that plays with the "cocktail-party effect," wherein listeners can focus their attention on a particular stimulus while filtering out others, *AGGREGATES* invites them to enter into noise and find meaning in a particular sound—a broom or car horns—or to immerse themselves in the totality as in a sonic bath. Northam composed and arranged the work in 2012 at the Villa Waldberta, Feldafing, Germany, using field recordings from India captured between 2006 and 2008. The dominant recordings are of a single, everyday Delhi traffic jam and a sweeper moving a broom across a veranda.

Hildegard Westerkamp describes *Into the Labyrinth* (2000, 2012) as "a sonic journey between dream and reality into Indian culture and the Indian soundscape."[16] Originally commissioned by New Adventures in Sound, Toronto, the work premiered as an eight-channel composition at the Gibraltar Point Arts Centre, Toronto Island, in 2000. In 2012 Westerkamp created a 5.1 surround sound version specifically for *Listen My Heart.* Sources for the work were recorded between 1992 and 1998 in Delhi, Rajasthan, Goa, and Rishikesh and include voices, musicians, and ambient sounds, including traffic, animals, and films and recorded music played through loudspeakers.

The fifteen-minute recording was the most "musical" of all the works presented in the program, with expert field recordings of musical performances. Westerkamp's beautiful capturing of temple bells and train horns, used as "sonic archetypes" of India, also marked it (at least to some listeners in Delhi) as the most "orientalist" work in the show. The response to the piece was also divided along generational lines. For many older listeners, it provoked nostalgia for a lost India, one before automobiles and cell phones. Younger listeners in twenty-first-century Delhi were incredulous that the recordings were made in their modern capital. Given the rapid social and technological changes in India since 1995, Westerkamp's source recordings offer an important sound archive deserving of preservation and deeper listening.

Kamal Swaroop's *Om-Dar-b-Dar* (101 minutes, 1988) is a nonlinear film, the narrative of which has been described thusly.

> Horoscope, dead frog, cloudy sky, the moon, radio program, caste reservation, bicycle, Mount Everest, women's liberation, communism, sleeveless blouse, Yuri Gagarin, miniature book, Nitrogen fixation, man on moon, terrorist tadpoles, computer, biology class, turtles, Hema Malini, typewriter, sleazy magazines, hibernation, text inside nose, googly, James Bond, severed tongue, fish rain, shoes in a temple, World War, assassin creed, Gandhi, illicit trade, the lake, goggles, hopping currency, helium breath, counterfeit coins, underwater treasure, diamonds inside frogs, fireworks, the zoo, explosives, town at night, dead man, visit of God, the Panchsheel Pact, foreign tourists, Promise toothpaste, holy men, Fish keychain, Ram Rajya, food chain disruption, anti-cooperation movement, birth control, bagpipes, gecko, Jawaharlal Nehru, Aviation centers, Potassium Cyanide.[17]

That list offers an accurate description of the disparate scenes that unfold for a viewer of the film. For the listener, *Om-Dar-b-Dar* offers a mad collage of the sounds of a Rajasthani village, inside homes, in nature, and on the streets, with absurdist dialogue shouted throughout, a surreal radio playing parody songs like "Babur from Babylon," an Indian wedding band, and long drones made by all manner of instruments, including *shehnai*, *tambura*, and *pungi*, as well as synthesizers, insects, and children.

While ((audience)) remains the only organization dedicated to exploring the cinema as a venue for sound art, larger institutions have adopted the movie theater as a way to reach new audiences for other art forms, including opera, stage drama, and music concerts. For example, since 2006 New York's Metropolitan Opera has transmitted performances live, via satellite, to cinemas around the world, an initiative that has expanded in recent years. *The Met Opera: Live in HD* broadcasts illustrate the numerous gates and back doors that digital cinema—which decouples the picture and sound from the physical medium of film—has punched into the walls of proprietary cinema technology in recent years, enabling ((audience)) to present unconventional programming in movie theaters. Before the crossover to digital cinema, a project like *The Met Opera: Live in HD*, or newer broadcasts of theatrical productions and concert tours, would have been impossible to present in a Dolby-equipped theater and on an ongoing basis, as cinemas were not constructed to receive transmissions and Dolby sound processors were connected directly to film projectors and decoded only the optical soundtrack running on the film. In the digital cinema age, transmission via the internet or live satellite broadcast has replaced shipments of film reels, engendering a new industry of "event cinema."

Cinema sound platforms have also undergone seismic shifts since the complete transition to digital cinema. Several months before the premiere of *Listen My Heart,* in June 2012, Dolby released Atmos, which brought a third atmospheric dimension to immersive sound experiences and forecast the potential demise of what is now called "channel-based mixing." With up to 128 discrete audio tracks sent to an array of speakers around and over the audience, Atmos enables a greater specificity of sound design since engineers can assign sounds to any particular point in space rather than to a finite number of speaker channels.

Yet "object-based" audio technologies—such as Atmos and other newly developed spatial audio techniques, like Auro 3D and Iosono Wave Field Synthesis—have remained somewhat inaccessible to audiences in the United States and India. While the technology was swiftly embraced by the Indian film community, only a small number of theaters in major cities have installed Atmos, and atmospheric sound mixing remains unaffordable for most film productions. Since 2012 only about 275 movies have been mixed in Atmos, most of which are big-budget blockbusters.[18] (Two Indian films were released in Atmos in the first year of its launch: one a Tamil film, *Shivaji 3D* [2012]; and the other a Hindi film, *Race 2* [2013]). Although it is still at a nascent stage, three-dimensional sound offers sound artists and composers exciting new ways to compose in space.

Listen My Heart emerged from Khoj's intention to introduce Indian audiences to sound art, and the field now flourishes in India. In Chennai, electronic artist Yashas Shetty hosts international sound artists for residencies at the Indian Sonic Research Organization (ISRO), where they work with a collective of instrument builders and with students at the Shrishti Institute of Art, Design, and Technology. Art critics at major Indian newspapers are familiar with sound art and regularly review sound installations. Artist Shilpa Gupta won the 2019 India Today New Media Artist of the Year award for a sound installation—*For, in your tongue, I cannot hide*—which premiered in Edinburgh and traveled to India for the 2018 Kochi-Murzis Biennale. Curated by Khoj founding member Anita Dube, the biennale mobilized film sound, installation, and performance as a way of rejecting "a world mediated primarily through images—a society of the spectacle."[19] And the Sound Reasons Festival, founded in

Khirkee Gaon, just up the street from Khoj, has produced six international sound art and experimental music festivals since 2012. In short, India has emerged as a key site for global discourse on sound art thanks in no small part to Khoj's concerted efforts and indirect influence.

Listen My Heart attempted to open up the field of sound studies beyond a Eurocentric model by focusing on the soundscapes of India and its surrounding regions. In establishing the cinema as a unique venue for the dissemination and circulation of sound art, we sought to open up an accessible site in which artists could present their work beyond the rarefied spaces of contemporary art galleries and concert halls. While artists continue to explore emerging digital sound technologies and the cinema as a standard acoustic presentation site, new opportunities for exhibition and performance point to a wide-open field for sound artists on the Indian subcontinent.

Notes

1. This text contains excerpts from "Curatorial Note," published by the Khoj International Artists' Association in February 2013 on the occasion of the exhibition *Listen My Heart* at DT Cinemas.

2. Rabindranath Tagore, *Stray Birds* (New York: Macmillan, 1916). Part 13 reads, "LISTEN, my heart, to the whispers of the world with which it makes love to you."

3. The term *sound art* was first used in the catalog for the exhibition *Sound/Art* at the Sculpture Center, New York. See *Sound/Art* (New York: The Foundation, 1983).

4. Established in 1986, Phonurgia Nova celebrates international radio and sound art, bestowing the annual Phonurgia Nova prizes. Wave Farm is a research and residency center in upstate New York, which also operates a radio station, WGXC. Founded by Galen Joseph-Hunter and Tom Roe, Wave Farm pioneered the concept of "Transmission Arts."

5. *Movies on the Radio*, as the program was called, played every evening at midnight for two weeks on Red House Radio, based at the Red House Arts Center in Syracuse, New York. We would only later learn about the artist Louise Lawler's work, *A MOVIE WILL BE SHOWN WITHOUT THE PICTURE* (1979 to the present), for which she screens a film without its image, authoring the result as a work of her own.

6. Alexander Keefe, "Lord of the Drone: Pandit Pran Nath and the American Underground," *Bidoun* 20 (Spring 2010). http://bidoun.org/articles/lord-of-the-drone, accessed January 27, 2019.

7. Paddy does not use a last name, as is customary in Bollywood for those who have dropped their family or caste names for personal reasons. Paddy, phone conversation with the authors, November 2012.

8. It was also the perfect time for *Om-Dar-b-Dar*. We first attempted to ob-

tain the film from the Satyajit Ray Film and Television Institute (SRFTI) in West Bengal. After a few weeks, we were told that the film was unavailable, with no explanation or response to further enquiries. A year after *Listen My Heart* played in Delhi, *Om Dar-b-Dar* was released for the first time in Indian theaters; we would later learn that the SRFTI copy had been loaned to create the new digitally restored print.

9. See also the Emily Thompson quote in the "Introduction" in this volume.

10. Eduardo Kac, "Aspects of the Aesthetics of Telecommunications," in *SIGGRAPH Visual Proceedings*, ed. John Grimes and Gray Lorig (New York: Association of Computing Machinery, 1992), p. 7.

11. As Chion has described Schaeffer's concept, "Pierre Schaeffer gave the name *reduced listening* to the listening mode that focuses on the traits of the sound itself, independent of its cause and of its meaning. Reduced listening takes the sound—verbal, played on an instrument, noises, or whatever—as itself the object to be observed instead of as a vehicle for something else." Michel Chion, "The Three Listening Modes," in *The Sound Studies Reader*, ed. Jonathan Sterne (London: Routledge, 2012), 50.

12. Brandon LaBelle, *Background Noise: Perspectives on Sonic Art* (New York: Continuum, 2006), 204–5.

13. As Schafer has written, the first sound heard is "the caress of the waters." R. Murray Schafer, *The Soundscape: Our Sonic Environment and the Tuning of the World* (Rochester, VT: Destiny Books, 1993), 15.

14. Iain Armstrong - "Annapurna Pastoral - One Hundred Springs," https://soundcloud.com/naisa/iain-armstrong-annapurna?in=naisa%2Fsets%2Fdeep-wireless-9, accessed January 27, 2019.

15. Bhagat, Alexis and Lauren Rosati, Listen My Heart to the Whispers of the World. (Khoj International Artists' Association: Delhi, 2013), 22.

16. Westerkamp, Hildegard. *Into India*, earsay productions, es02002, 2002 compact disc. Liner notes.

17. *The Seventh Art* (blog), July 11, 2009, https://theseventhart.info/2009/07/11/flashback-63/, accessed January 27, 2019.

18. See "Theatrical Releases in Dolby Vision and Dolby Atmos," https://www.dolby.com/us/en/cinema/theatrical-releases.html, accessed January 27, 2019

19. Anita Dube, "Possibilities for a Non-Alienated Life," curatorial concept, 2018 Kochi-Murzis Biennale, https://universes.art/en/kochi-muziris-biennale/2019/curatorial-text, accessed January 27, 2019.

Contributors

Jayson Beaster-Jones is Associate Professor of Music in the Global Arts Studies Program at the University of California, Merced. He is an ethnomusicologist whose work focuses on the music industry of India. His first book, *Bollywood Sounds: The Cosmopolitan Mediations of Hindi Film Song* (Oxford University Press, 2014) explores seventy years of Bollywood film songs and their musical and social meanings. His current research project, "Music as Merchandise: Music Commodities, Markets, and Values in India," examines music retail stores as sites of cultural production in contemporary India, focusing in particular on the kinds of economic and social values that are produced as music is sold, as well as the meanings that accompany music commodities in retail contexts. The project also addresses the cultural and media histories of the Indian music industry, the discourses of piracy and intellectual property, and the social changes that have accompanied India's economic liberalization reforms.

Alexis Bhagat and **Lauren Rosati** are cofounders of ((audience)), an organization dedicated to the advancement of aural arts by providing new contexts for sound art.

Laura Brueck is Associate Professor of South Asian Literature and Culture at Northwestern University. She is the author of *Writing Resistance: The Rhetorical Imagination of Hindi Dalit Literature* (Columbia University Press, 2014) which analyzes the vernacular discursive sphere of contemporary Hindi Dalit literature. A collection of her translations of Hindi short stories, *Unclaimed Terrain: Stories by Ajay Navaria* (Navayana Press, 2013), was named a Best Book of 2013 by Pankaj Mishra in *The Guardian.* Her current book project considers Indian "pulp" fiction, particularly the genre of detective fiction and crime narratives in Hindi, Urdu, and English.

Praseeda Gopinath is Associate Professor of English, General Literature, and Rhetoric at Binghamton University (State University of New York) and the author of *Scarecrows of Chivalry: English Masculinities after Empire* (University of Virginia Press, 2013). Building on current theories of alternative cosmopolitanism, Gopinath's new book project examines the articulation of elite Indian masculinities and the "liberal" institutions that produced them. Taking as its object of study literary texts, the cultural/national reception of authors, and institutional archives—including recordings of the political oratory of Indian prime ministers from Nehru to Modi—this project examines how and why urbane and urban Indian men and the liberal, postcolonial educational institutions that made them came to embody the changing ideals of secular Indianness, both within and without the nation-state.

Kathryn C. Hardy is an anthropologist who focuses broadly on questions of language and belonging in South Asia. She has performed extensive fieldwork on the production, circulation, and reception of Bhojpuri cinema in India with particular attention to its sonic geographies. Centered in Mumbai, home to many Bhojpuri-speaking migrant laborers originally hailing from rural Uttar Pradesh and Bihar, Hardy's research focuses on locally specific shifts in filmmaking practices, regional language categories, and the built environment across urban and rural India. In addition to her work on Bhojpuri cinema, Hardy is also working on a book project, currently titled "Dirt and Noise: Sonic Geographies of Belonging and Exclusion in 'Regional' Mumbai," which explores the links between homeland and metropolis that emerge when cheaply recorded, amplified Bhojpuri devotional songs create noisy irruptions of "the regional" in Mumbai.

Roanne L. Kantor is Assistant Professor of English at Stanford University. Her primary field is global anglophone literature and its relationship with other literary traditions of the Global South. She also works on the conditions for interdisciplinary research in the humanities, especially literature's interface with medicine and the humanistic social sciences. Kantor is also a translator and winner of the Susan Sontag Prize for Translation. Before coming to Stanford, she taught at Harvard, Boston, and Brandeis Universities and the University of Texas at Austin, where she earned her masters and doctoral degrees.

Peter Kvetko is Associate Professor of Ethnomusicology at Salem State University. He publishes on popular North Indian music beyond the confines of the Bollywood cinema industry. His publications include "Private Music: Individualism, Authenticity and Genre Boundaries in the Bombay Music Industry" (in *Popular Culture in a Globalised India*, Routledge 2009) and "Mimesis and Authenticity: The Case of 'Thanda Thanda Pani' and Questions of Versioning in North Indian Popular Music" (in *More Than Bollywood: Studies in Indian Popular Music*, Oxford University Press 2013).

Neepa Majumdar is Associate Professor of English and Film Studies at the University of Pittsburgh. Her research interests include star studies, film sound, South Asian early cinema, documentary film, and questions of film history and historiography. Her *Wanted Cultured Ladies Only: Female Stardom and Cinema in India, 1930s to 1950s* (University of Illinois Press, 2009) won an Honorable Mention in the 2010 Best First Book Awards of the Society for Cinema and Media Studies. Her essays have appeared in the *Canadian Journal of Film Studies*, *South Asian Popular Culture*, and *Post Script*, as well as in collections such as *The Continuum Companion to Sound in Film and Visual Media* (ed. Graeme Harper, Continuum 2009), *Film Analysis: A Norton Reader* (ed. R. L. Rutsky and Jeffrey Gieger, Norton and Co. 2005), and *Soundtrack Available: Essays on Film and Popular Music* (ed. Arthur Knight and Pamela Wojcik, Duke University Press 2001).

Sriram Mohan is a PhD candidate in the Department of Communication Studies at the University of Michigan, Ann Arbor. His research revolves around digital media, cultural politics, and technology use in South Asian contexts. His work has appeared in the journals *Television & New Media* and the *International Journal of Communication*. He is also a coeditor of *Global Digital Cultures: Perspectives from South Asia* (University of Michigan Press 2019).

Madhuja Mukherjee teaches in the Department of Film Studies, Jadavpur University, Kolkata. She has published on the film industry, studio history, gender, work, and sound cultures. She edited the volume *Voices and Verses of the Talking Stars: The Women of Indian Cinema and Beyond* (Sage, 2016) and is also a filmmaker and graphic artist. *Qissa* (2013) written by her (and the director) won an Inalco Jury award at the Twentieth Vesoul International Film Festival of Asian Cinema, held in France. She is completing a graphic narrative on the subject of Ruby Myers.

Aswin Punathambekar is Associate Professor in the Department of Media Studies at the University of Virginia. His research and teaching revolve around globalization, media industries and production cultures, media convergence, media history, and public culture with a focus on South Asia and the South Asian diaspora. He is the author of *From Bombay to Bollywood: The Making of a Global Media Industry* (New York University Press, 2013) and coeditor of *Global Bollywood* (New York University Press, 2008) and *Television at Large in South Asia* (Routledge, 2013). His current book project, provisionally titled "Mobile Publics: Cultural Politics of Participation in Digital India," examines the ways in which convergence between television and mobile media technologies (the internet and the mobile phone) is reconfiguring the meanings and performance of citizenship. He is also part of a Social Science Research Council project, "Media, Activism, and the New Political," which brings together a group of scholars analyzing mediated activism across India, China, and the Middle East–North Africa region. His research for this project addresses the formation of "networked publics" over a three-decade span in India.

Jacob Smith is Professor in the Department of Radio-Television-Film and Director of the masters program in Sound Arts and Industries at Northwestern University. He has written several books, including *Vocal Tracks: Performance and Sound Media* (University of California Press, 2008), *Spoken Word: Postwar American Phonograph Cultures* (University of California Press, 2011), and *Eco-Sonic Media* (University of California Press, 2015) and has published articles on media history, sound, and performance. His latest project, ESC: Sonic Adventure in the Anthropocene (University of Michigan Press, 2019), is an experimental audiobook that can be heard here: https://doi.org/10.3998/mpub.10120795.

Pavitra Sundar is Assistant Professor of Literature at Hamilton College. Her research and teaching interests span the fields of cinema studies, sound studies, postcolonial literary and cultural studies, and gender-sexuality studies. In her current book project, she analyzes the politics and pleasures of Bollywood film sound and music. She has published articles in several journals, including *Meridians*, *Jump Cut*, and, most recently *Communication, Culture, and Critique.* She has also contributed essays to anthologies on South Asian and other global cinematic traditions. Sundar earned her doctorate in women's studies and English at the University of Michigan and held a Mellon Postdoctoral Fellowship in Film and Media Studies at Dartmouth College.

Samhita Sunya is Assistant Professor of Cinema in the Department of Middle Eastern and South Asian Languages and Cultures, at the University of Virginia. Her research and teaching interests include world film history, intersections of (old and new) audiovisual media and literature, sound studies, and postcolonial literature. Current and planned publications include essays that build on her dissertation research, exploring transnational circuits of romantic Hindi film/songs in relation to questions of cinematic translation, authorship, and institutions of "world cinema" in the postwar/post-Independence decades.

Sejal Sutaria is a Visiting Assistant Professor of Postcolonial Literature at Grinnell College and recently completed a Marie Curie Fellowship at King's College, London. Her current book manuscript, "The Making of Multipolar Modernity: Britain, India, and the Sounding of Postcolonial Resistance" examines how sound archives amplify our understanding of the role that globally circulating ideas, capital, and migrants played in shaping anticolonial resistance in the colony and the metropole. She has published essays in The *Global Literature Review, The Encyclopedia of Pop Culture in Asia and Oceania,* and has forthcoming work in *Modernism/Modernity* Print Plus. She has also contributed a piece about Venu Chitale to the *100 Voices that Made the BBC* and posted on the English Department blog for King's College London.

Neil Verma is Assistant Professor in the Department of Radio-Television-Film at Northwestern University. He is the author of *Theater of the Mind: Imagination, Aesthetics, and American Radio Drama* (University of Chicago Press, 2012), the winner of the Best First Book award from the Society for Cinema and Media Studies. He is coeditor of *Anatomy of Sound: Norman Corwin and Media Authorship* (University of California Press, 2016), winner of the Best Moving Image Book award from the Kraszna-Krausz Foundation. He was corecipient of a 2017 Digital Humanities Advancement grant from the National Endowment for the Humanities to develop digital tools for vocal analysis. He is the founder of the Great Lakes Association for Sound Studies (GLASS).

Index

Page locators from figures are indicated with italics.